The Heart of a Duke

Victoria Morgan

BERKLEY SENSATION, NEW YORK

THE BERKLEY PUBLISHING GROUP
Published by the Penguin Group
Penguin Group (USA) LLC
375 Hudson Street, New York, New York 10014

USA • Canada • UK • Ireland • Australia • New Zealand • India • South Africa • China

penguin.com

A Penguin Random House Company

THE HEART OF A DUKE

A Berkley Sensation Book / published by arrangement with the author

Berkley Sensation Books are published by The Berkley Publishing Group.
BERKLEY SENSATION® is a registered trademark of Penguin Group (USA) LLC.
The "B" design is a trademark of Penguin Group (USA) LLC.

For information, address: The Berkley Publishing Group,
a division of Penguin Group (USA) LLC,
375 Hudson Street, New York, New York 10014.

ISBN: 978-0-425-26483-6

PUBLISHING HISTORY
Berkley Sensation mass-market edition / December 2013

PRINTED IN THE UNITED STATES OF AMERICA

10   9   8   7   6   5   4   3   2   1

Cover art by Aleta Rafton.
Cover design by George Long.
Interior text design by Kristin del Rosario.

To my family,
for their love and never-ending patience.

ACKNOWLEDGMENTS

As always, love and thanks to my family (immediate and extended) for being my biggest fans. Special thanks to my Junior Mint critique partners, Penny Watson and Samantha Wayland, who had the courage to tell me when my book wasn't working—even when I didn't want to hear it—and the patience to help me kick it back into shape with Black Belt Revisions 101. Thanks for believing in me (there really was a point to that fishing scene). I would also like to thank my fabulous agent, Laura Bradford (bradfordlit.com), and my lovely editor, Leis Pederson, at Berkley Publishing Group, who helped to polish my book so that it shines.

Chapter One

≫◆≪

SHE knew what they said about her.
    Dumped by a duke. Bedford's forgotten fiancée. The hushed murmurs circulated in a widening pool of ripples. The betrothal contract was still good, just yet to be honored. If the man hadn't wedded and bedded her yet, he never would—or so pledged some of the wagers filling White's infamous betting book. Others proved more generous, wagering on the year—or decade—of the pending nuptials.

Long after the news should no longer have been grist for the gossip mill, it still managed to turn the wheel. After all, she was Lady Julia Chandler, the daughter of an earl, an heiress and renowned beauty. But that was yesterday. Today, she was a fading flower, waiting and wilting at the ancient age of three-and-twenty.

She knew what they asked about her. The question circulated in the same hushed stage whispers. *What is wrong with her*?

Of course, the fault had to lie with *her*. After all, Bedford was a duke, practically royalty, perched at the pinnacle of the revered aristocratic pyramid. Toss in young, handsome, and rich, and who dared to question such sterling credentials? No one.

Except Julia.

And she knew the answers to the questions—or at least to most of them.

Today she vowed to get the rest.

Julia tightened her hands on the reins and dug her heel into Constance's flank, leaning low over her sidesaddle and streaking across the field. She relished the bite of the wind against her cheeks, the whip of it through her riding habit. The feel of freedom. The sense of purpose.

Edmund was in Bedfordshire. Spotted in town. Her Damn Duke—for that was her name for him these days. Still evoked with affection, but lacking the reverence she'd used when he had been her Beautiful Bedford or her Earnest Edmund. After all, there was a price to pay for his paucity of visits, letters, and, of course, those nasty rumors he never deigned to squelch. "Damn Duke," she muttered. But he was still *her* Damn Duke, and today, she vowed to remind him of it.

She did not know what made her choose the shortcut through Lakeview Manor, which abutted her father's estate. Despite the scenic views overlooking the lake, the skeletal remains of the burned-out manor haunted. Charred timbers rose like a plaintive plea to the heavens to rebuild. A riotous mass of untamed weeds, ferns, and brambles snaked, weaved, and climbed into the sandstone foundation and over the crumbling brick walls like wild decorations breathing life into the desolate landscape.

She wondered why Edmund hadn't cleared out the remaining debris. His brother had inherited it by way of his maternal *grand-mère*, but he had left England years ago. Edmund had said he had never cared for it, so why let it sit and rot over the past decade, a morose symbol of loss? Why not tear it down and rebuild?

She reined in Constance, coming to a halt on a bluff overlooking the remains. The site held a macabre fascination for her. How could it not, tangled up in so many childhood memo-

ries? Those were the days when Edmund had been beautiful.
And she had been happy.

She shook her head, bemused. *Had been happy?* One would
think she heeded the rumors about her . . . and Edmund. Well,
she was not quite ready for a silver-tipped walking cane, and
she *was* happy. Planned to be happier if her courage did not
desert her. But still, her gaze drifted back to those stark,
ghostly timbers, and she frowned.

"Bleak but still beautiful."

Julia started at the words, her sudden movement irritating
Constance, who grunted, tossed her head, and danced back a
step. Julia lay a calming hand on the mare's neck as she turned
to confront the intruder. Her heart thudded and her mouth went
bone dry.

Edmund.

Tall and lean, he stood in the shadows of a copse of trees.
As she straightened, he moved forward and into the sunlight.
Months had passed since she had last seen him, and she drank
in the changes to his appearance.

He looked thinner, his hair unfashionably longer and lighter
than she remembered. Thick, wavy, and golden brown, it curled
over the collar of his crisp white shirt. His black riding jacket
hugged his lean frame, the tight fit of his buff-colored trousers
accentuating his muscular thighs and long legs as he strode
toward her with an easy grace.

A gust of wind lifted a stray lock of hair from his forehead,
and her gaze roved over his handsome features; the strong
jawline, the sharp cheekbones, and the intriguing cleft denting
his chin. But it was his eyes that were so arresting, a rich, deep
moss green. Edmund was vain and clever enough to appreciate
the asset, spearing many a maiden heart with a well-aimed
look.

He stopped a few feet away, and Julia found her own heart
endangered when those eyes locked on her. Her breath caught
at his expression. Never before had he studied her with such
intensity, looking at her as if she were some ghostly apparition
or as if he were seeing her for the first time. She squelched the

urge to shift in her saddle, like so many giggling, twittering maids did under his regard. There were advantages to being older. She rarely giggled and had never twittered.

"Julia." His lips curved into a slow, devastating smile.

She swallowed. What game was he playing now? Edmund liked his games. More so, he liked to win. Well, today she refused to play—at least by his rules.

"You are beautiful. I knew you would be," he said.

She stared at him, bemused at his words, wondering if he was seeking to undermine her with that dangerous charm of his. When he chose to wield it, it was lethal. She cursed the heat climbing her neck and the traitorous leap to her pulse. "We need to talk."

He paused and raised a brow at her words, but then nodded. "That we do." He strode forward, "May I?" He lifted his hands, but waited for her to acquiesce before assisting her to dismount.

She nearly gasped at the touch of his hands on her waist, the cotton fabric of her riding jacket but a thin barrier between them. Her gloved fingers curled over his sturdy shoulders as he easily set her on her feet before him. Rather than step back as a gentleman should, he stood too close, staring down at her with a rather odd and un-Edmund-like smile curving those sensuous lips.

Her body temperature, already elevated, soared higher. She had forgotten how tall he was. She had to tip her head back to meet his mesmerizing smile. When she did, her heart took another leap.

Good lord, he was beautiful.

He stood so close she could smell sandalwood soap and a hint of some musky, masculine cologne. She blinked.

This would not do. Betrothed or not, they were not married and they were unchaperoned, for she had refused a companion for this private affair. She preferred no one witness her vulnerability—or worse, her humiliation should she fail. Tamping down her flutter of nerves, she retreated a few steps, putting distance between her and Edmund. "I will start."

He looked surprised and then smiled. "You always did like to go first."

The comment, delivered with warm amusement, further disconcerted her. He really was not behaving like himself. "Yes, well, they do say ladies first."

He grinned. "So they do."

She paused at his manner. Edmund had always alternated between charming and impatient in his dealings with her, confounding traits, as they either compelled or repelled her, depending on which mood she confronted at the time. She was not familiar with this Edmund and hoped this would not complicate matters. Things needed to be said, and her Damn Duke had the uncanny habit of disappearing for long periods of time.

"You do know that my father is no longer grieving the loss of my mother, Jonathan has turned a robust five, and Emily is doing much, much better, so I think—"

"I am glad."

Surprised at his interruption, she paused.

"I am glad to hear about your father and Emily. Grieving over the loss of a loved one is always a difficult journey."

She frowned. *Difficult?* The word was too tame a description for her sister's bedridden despair after Jason's death in India. However, that *was* so like Edmund. He had never liked to discuss Emily's "illness," as he referred to it. Back on familiar footing, she continued. "Yes, well, now that my family's concerns and my obligations have lightened, I think we are finally . . ." She paused to swallow, her words caught in her throat. "What I mean to say is . . ." She trailed off, and heat climbed her neck.

She might have acted impetuously upon hearing Edmund was in town. She should have taken time to collect her thoughts and prepare a proper speech. She was at a loss as to how to proceed. And her Damn Duke appeared to have no intention of rescuing her.

He watched her with a slightly amused expression, looking as if he enjoyed her discomfiture. Maybe she should have left this meeting to her father. She gritted her teeth. No, because by the time he got around to addressing the matter, she would need that silver-tipped cane to assist her to hobble down the aisle.

She began to pace as she groped for a proper lead-in, well aware of Edmund's eyes trailing her, not making matters easy. "I just thought it is only reasonable that after so many years of waiting, we now—"

"Waiting? I am not sure I—"

She stopped and frowned at his furrowed brow. Edmund was not obtuse, so she could not fathom what he gained in pretending to be so. "For goodness' sake, it has been five years. Bets are being wagered at White's as we speak. I think it is time."

"Time?" he echoed. Suddenly his eyes widened and he retreated a step. "I am beginning to understand." He lifted his hand to rub his neck, a tinge of color spotting his cheeks.

Julia's lips parted at the un-Edmund-like reaction.

What was wrong with the man?

A rueful smile curved his lips. "However, there is something I need to clarify before you continue." He held up his hands. "You see, I am not who—"

"No, it's not necessary," she broke in, cursing her earlier outburst and seeking to avoid the tired explanations over what the two of them had long understood. "I have always appreciated and been grateful for your patience and discretion while my family worked through these travails. But it is our time now. I want to honor the betrothal contract. I could not before, but now I can. I—"

"Julia, wait, stop! I do need to explain—"

"You don't need to explain anything to me." Before her flagging courage abandoned her, she stepped closer to him, lifted her chin, and taking a deep breath, gazed straight into his eyes. "All I need you to do is kiss me and tell me that everything is going to be all right. That *we* will be all right."

"You don't understand. I am . . . excuse me?" His hands dropped, and he cleared his throat before he could continue. "Ah, what was that about kissing?"

Feminine satisfaction filled her, helping her to regain her

lost footing. Emboldened, she decided that if Edmund could behave un-Edmund-like, then for once, she could abandon the calm, prim, and proper Julia. Tired of being trapped by her responsibilities, she wanted to feel young and reckless. She wanted to relish the beat of her heart in her chest and the heat spiraling through her body as Edmund fastened his beautiful eyes on her. More so, she wanted to fill the emptiness deep inside her. To feel wanted and desired.

Shoring up her courage, she lifted her arms and slid her hands up his chest, marveling at the feel of warm, hard strength through his jacket and wondering why she had never dared do this before. Why had she waited so long, particularly as she felt his heart thud against her palms? It felt good. *He* felt good.

His fingers curled over her forearms. "Julia—"

"Edmund." She cocked her head to the side. "Aren't betrothals sealed with a kiss? We never did do so, and I think it's long past time we do." Freeing her arms, she curled her hands around his neck, threading her fingers into the soft curls teasing his cravat and smiling at the flare of light in his eyes. "I am not a girl anymore, but all grown up now and tired of waiting for you."

She watched him swallow, felt his hands on her waist, but frowned when he held her away from him.

"You certainly are no longer a girl," he grinned. "That I noticed straight away. You have grown into a beautiful woman. But you see—"

"I do see. I see that you are wasting time. I also see that you are stammering when you could be kissing me. Don't you want to kiss me?" Before she lost her nerve, she moistened her lips as Emily had once showed her to do to make them more alluring.

He expelled a choked laugh. "Of course I want to kiss you. A man would have to be lacking a pulse to reject such an offer. But Jules—"

She paused at the old childhood nickname. He hadn't used it in years. But his hands had drawn her back to him. "You do have a pulse, don't you?" she whispered. She was standing so close that she could see his long eyelashes, the black rim circling the lovely green of his irises, and how his eyes warmed at her question.

"For the moment," he returned dryly. "And I would prefer to retain it. Should we proceed further with this, that could be dangerous for both of us."

He had a point, and the old Julia would have heeded it, considering the warmth of his gaze sent her pulse skipping into a treacherous rhythm. However, his look and the grip of his hands on her waist made the new Julia feel young, beautiful, and desired, something Edmund had not made her feel in years. "Really, Edmund, it is one kiss. How dangerous could it be?" She raised a brow, knowing Edmund never could refuse a challenge.

He sucked in a sharp breath and stared at her. After a beat, he exhaled and swore softly. "Hell, I have been living danger-ously my whole life." His eyes dipped to her parted lips. "Why stop now?" He yanked her to him, his arms vising around her waist and crushing her tight.

She gasped at the explosive heat of his body against hers. Her eyes widened when his head lowered and, inches away, the warmth of his breath whispered onto her parted lips. "For-give me."

His mouth closed over hers and he kissed her as she had never before been kissed. Kissed her as if he had waited as long as she had and was desperate to catch up.

His lips were warm and velvet soft. She clung to him, her arms circling his neck, and was dimly aware of his grip tight-ening when her legs turned to liquid jelly and were unable to support her. And still he kissed her. Deeply, erotically, and expertly.

Better yet, she kissed him back.

She savored the taste of him as her mouth surrendered to his. He was a mixture of ale and cider. The sensual assault of taste, touch, and scent overwhelmed her. She loved the feel of his body, hard, warm, and muscular crushed against her, and when he broke away to draw breath, she inhaled the rich mas-culine scent of him. A wave of molten heat cascaded through her limbs.

When his tongue ran along her lips, she gasped and drew back. She needed to breathe, to pause and gather her thoughts, which had scattered like leaves to the winds. "We should stop. We cannot—"

"You are so right." She shuddered at the smoldering look he gave her. "But Julia, I did warn you about this being dangerous. Now, it is too late."

His mouth swooped down and plundered, devouring and demanding more and still more. Ripples of pleasure coursed through her body. He aroused yearnings in her that she hadn't known she possessed. Had recently begun to wonder if Edmund could evoke such feeling in her.

He drew back and Julia blinked up at him, struggling to clear the sensual haze engulfing her. When clarity returned, she realized she was still pressed intimately against his body. His arms around her waist fully supported her, and through her riding habit, she could feel his heart pounding against hers.

Flushing, she tugged free of his embrace and straightened, grateful her legs managed to support her weight when she stepped away.

"Well, then." Her voice was breathless and sounded strange to her ears. Lifting an unsteady hand, she tucked an errant curl under her bonnet.

"Well, then indeed." He smiled. "I had doubts about returning, but no more."

Her breath caught at the sultry look he swept over her. She wished she could say she was glad, too. The new Julia would have done so, but she was feeling more and more her old responsible self and a bit appalled at her brazen behavior. She tugged down her riding jacket, but refused the urge to run her fingers over her swollen lips. "So we are agreed. It is long past time we set a date and stop the run of wagers at White's."

She frowned when the smile curving his lips froze and then disappeared.

He rubbed his hand along his neck in that strange, new adopted mannerism of his. "Ah, about that date. There is one minor complication in regard to that."

"Oh?" Her hand stilled. "And what is that?"

"As much as I wish it otherwise, I cannot set any future dates with you."

"What are you talking about?" she demanded, a cold chill suffusing her, dousing the simmering embers of their shared passion. "You are not backing out of the betrothal agreement. You cannot. My father would ruin you."

"Particularly after that kiss," he agreed quite amicably, leaning close to her as his eyes flashed with a spark of defiance. "But it was worth it."

She stepped back and fisted her hands at her sides, a hard ball of suspicion curdling deep in her gut. She should have listened to his earlier stammers—or warnings. Hoped it was not too late to do so.

"Your father's desire to murder me would be for different reasons than you think. I cannot set a date because I am not in a position to do so, which is what I tried to explain earlier."

She simply stared at him, waiting him out. She was done talking. Done with being young and foolish and reckless. Feared she was about to pay the price for allowing herself to be so for one lovely moment.

"You see, I am not Edmund."

Chapter Two

❧❦

JULIA blinked, not fully comprehending his words.

He lifted his hands and spread them in a mute apology, a rueful smile curving his lips. "I have never regretted it—until now."

What was he talking about?

She rubbed her temple, tamping down her rising hysteria. "What game are you playing now? How can that be . . . ?" Her words trailed off and her eyes narrowed.

No, it couldn't be.

He had disappeared a decade ago. Long lost and forgotten. Edmund had refused to allow even his name to be uttered.

"Daniel," she breathed, unconsciously echoing his tone when he had first voiced her name. Edmund's twin.

Lord Bryant, but she had known him as a boy, and he was Daniel to her then.

"At your service." He dipped into a mock bow and, lifting his head, beamed that potent smile at her.

While they had been identical twins, dark haired and fine featured, their size had always differentiated them. Edmund was tall and dashing and, well, beautiful. Daniel had been a head shorter and of a slighter build. It was as if Edmund had sucked up all the nutrients in the womb and left nothing for Daniel. *The runt.* That was what Edmund had called him. Incredulity filled her.

As if reading her thoughts, he broke the tense silence with an explanation of sorts. "It is not unusual for a boy to grow. Edmund simply had a head start on me, always did." His eyes darkened, and his gaze lifted to stare out over the ruins behind her, the whistling rustle of the wind filling the silence. "But I have had ten years to catch up." His jaw clenched. His gaze snapped to hers. She stumbled back from the hard gleam of them. "And you can be sure that I will not be following in Edmund's footsteps ever again."

Too late she saw the differences. Should have seen them earlier. Would have if her single-minded purpose had not distracted her.

Their features were identical, so it was easy to mistake them for each other, but if one took a second look, Daniel was leaner, his features more chiseled. Harder. Edmund lived the rich, coddled life of a duke. The carousing lifestyle of the Season's social obligations was catching up with him. Edmund was thicker about the neck, his build not heavy, but softer. And while his smile could equally disarm, Edmund carried his ducal authority like a second skin and rarely lowered his guard to tease. He believed . . . Her thoughts trailed off and her back went poker straight. *Good lord.*

She had kissed her fiancé's brother.

She had asked Daniel how dangerous one kiss could be. Well, she had her answer.

This was far worse than when he had left her locked in the root cellar, abandoning a thirteen-year-old girl to shiver and shake in the cold, damp darkness for hours. She had been frightened then, but now . . . now she was terrified. *Of him. Of her. Of them.*

"I tried to tell you, but you wouldn't listen. You—"

"Too late." She held up her hand to stop him. "You are too damn late." She stripped off her leather glove as she closed the distance separating them, and the air cracked with the slap of her hand striking his face. She spun away and stormed over to Constance. Collecting the mare's reins, she hurried over to the dilapidated remnants of the stone wall, climbed onto it, and mounted Constance without assistance.

"Julia! Julia, wait!"

She ignored his cry and dug her heel into Constance's flank, leaning low and letting the mare run. She blinked back the tears blurring her vision. She would not cry.

Not over Daniel. Not over Edmund.

Neither man deserved her tears.

≫≪

"THAT WENT WELL," Daniel muttered as Julia disappeared over the hillside.

He blew out a frustrated breath and tamped down the impulse to rub his burning cheek. As a girl, Lady Julia Chandler had been a fierce whirlwind of energy. It was little surprise she had grown into a passionate woman with a strong arm and a face that should be immortalized on canvas.

She did not possess the classic looks of the delicate, porcelain-skinned, golden-haired English rose—thank God. Hers was a more vibrant beauty that struck a man right between the eyes.

Her hair was a rich, lustrous brown that burst from her bonnet, her eyes a deep blue that stared you down rather than demurely lowered or fluttered. No girlish simpering for Julia, her stare direct and bordered on challenging. She had full, sensual lips that when not pressed in a contemplative line, could kiss a man senseless. Add to that a figure carved with curves in all the right places.

Like a regal warrior, she had dared him, and he cursed himself for not being able to resist her.

He remembered her body cradled in his arms, her full breasts crushed against his chest. He never should have touched her, let alone kissed her, but no warm-blooded man could resist Julia. Unless he was a eunuch, and the throbbing in his loins squelched any doubts about that. He could not deny her plea. Or himself. But her parting words resonated.

You are too late. Too damn late.

The cursed words appeared to be the theme of his life and would no doubt be the epitaph for his gravestone. *Too little, too late* had been one of Edmund's favorite taunts. Daniel had arrived five minutes after his twin, thus Edmund had inherited the dukedom.

Sickly and tipping the scale at barely over a quarter stone, he had been destined to die like a full dozen of his siblings before him—except for Edmund. For those first few weeks when he had lingered between life and death, he went name-less. They had called him *the runt*. Edmund had adopted the nickname after he had heard the story and understood the word's meaning. More so, its use as a weapon to inflict pain. Edmund had liked to collect weapons, both those he could wield verbally and those that drew blood.

He shook off the dark thoughts. He was a runt no longer, and over the years, he had polished his own methods of defense.

He lifted his gaze to the path Julia had taken. He had never coveted anything belonging to Edmund . . . until now.

He never should have returned. He cursed the enigmatic missive that had lured him back after ten years away.

It is time. Come home and claim your destiny.

Addressed to his Boston residence, the letter had been from his late father's solicitor and included a plea to see him as soon as he arrived in England. Away on business, Daniel had received the letter months after its delivery. Scoffing at the note's melodrama, he had tossed it aside. There was nothing left for him in England.

His gaze roamed over the charred remains of Lakeview Manor. A stab of pain pierced his heart. The beloved estate and sanctuary was now a bleak symbol of his lost inheritance and a stark reminder that he had no home here, let alone any destiny to claim.

Months after the mysterious letter had arrived, he had stum-bled across it again while riffling through papers on his desk. He had set it aside a second time, but like a splinter wedged under his skin, the words stuck. They reminded him of questions that ten years later still begged to be answered.

It is time.

It was time. After all, a man deserved to know if someone had tried to murder him.

He clenched his jaw, the pain in his cheek reminding him of another pressing matter. He needed to determine how to save Lady Julia Chandler from marriage to his brother.

Her parting words forced him to rephrase his thought.

Would the lady *let him* save her?

It did not matter. He had made up his mind the minute his lips had touched hers.

She deserved better than Edmund. He just needed to convince her of it.

∞

THE BLACK STALLION was a stunning example of equine beauty, all undulating muscle and whipcord strength as he circled the paddock, avoiding the large man with the coiled rope held loosely at his side. Daniel leaned over the paddock fence, resting his arms on the top rail. He grinned when the stallion rose on his hind legs and pawed the air, nostrils flaring, eyes wild.

"I think you have met your match in this one, Tanner. Why don't you let a real horseman have a go at him?"

The man whirled, his impatient scowl transforming into surprise. His prominent Adam's apple bobbed like a buoy as he swallowed. "Your Grace, I didn't know you were here. I—"

Daniel snorted. "Please. As if my brother would risk being tossed on his precious aristocratic arse. If he survived the fall, the indignity of it would scar him for life."

Robbie Tanner's brown eyes homed in on Daniel's features. Soon a broad smile split his face, and he planted his hands on his hips. "I'll be. The prodigal son returns, and here I am fresh out of fatted calves."

"You never did leave any extras," he rejoined, eyeing a frame that carried well over eighteen stone and peaked above six feet.

Robbie grunted. "Good thing you no longer need any. America must agree with you. You've added a few stone, but could carry a bit more." He cut the distance separating them and tossed his rope over the fence. With an agility that belied his size, he vaulted over it. "It's been too damn long." He beamed a smile.

Daniel ignored the beefy hand thrust at him and pulled his friend into a hug. As Robbie pounded his back, he feared a bruising if he did not extricate himself soon. Disentangling himself, he smiled at his friend. Not all his childhood memories were bad. Some were good, and Robbie Tanner often played a role in the happier ones.

The Tanner family was the local landed gentry. They owned well over a hundred acres, and for generations, they had prospered in the breeding and trade of prime bloodstock. If one sought quality horseflesh at a fair price, they found their way to the Tanner Stables. Having an affinity for horses and coveting an escape from the echoing silence in Bedford Hall, Daniel had often gravitated to the Tanners' household.

Robbie nodded toward High Street. "Did you come through the village proper?"

"No, I rode the back way. I was forewarned that the fall festival was in full swing."

Taunton Village was known for it its abundance of wildlife and the bountiful fish populating its rivers, but come September, those assets fell secondary to the fall festival. Striped booths sprung up to host vendors peddling their wares, magicians weaving their magic, and fortune-tellers spinning prophesies. Aromas of fresh-baked goods and mouthwatering pastries competed with the succulent smells of roasted pig, duck, and beef.

Games and contests were organized, as well as exhibitions demonstrating daring feats of horsemanship, fine marksmanship, or athletic prowess. It was a plethora of activities to entice the patrons into emptying their pockets of coveted coins. He recalled losing a few quid on various ventures.

Today he had given the village a wide berth, not wanting word of his return to reach Edmund until he was ready. His brother had a canny ability of knocking one's plans awry. Daniel had no intention of tipping his hand until he was prepared to deflect his brother's interference.

"Good. It's a madhouse out there, and your arrival would have been like tossing a stick into a beehive. Best stay clear of it until you are ready to weather the response. Now then, absent a fatted calf, we will have to settle for breaking out my good whiskey. Shall we retire to my office?"

"After you," he said. "Ah, is it still in the loft above the stables?"

Robbie looked affronted. "I'll have you know that like you, my prospects have improved over the past decade. As the heir apparent, I have a real office now."

Daniel fell into step beside Robbie as they strolled down the lane abutting the paddock. They passed through a gate and along a slate path leading to the limestone manor. The afternoon sun glinted off the mullioned bay windows, and ropes of ivy plastered the façade in a dark green web. The garden beds abutting the walkway and lining the perimeter of the house were wild and unkempt, similar to the Tanner brood.

"Of course, with six brothers biting at my heels, I do have to share some of the space. But no worries, I keep the good whiskey locked up tight, and I am the only one with the key." He winked at Daniel and patted his jacket pocket. "Besides, the lot of them will be at the fair now. You chose a good time to return."

"I thought you wrote that some of your brothers had married." He followed Robbie inside and down the front hall. Kitchen odors of cinnamon and apples mingled with the smells of lemon polish and laundry soap. His stomach rumbled as he recalled rhubarb custard pie and mouthwatering apple tarts. He hoped Robbie might serve something of sustenance with that whiskey.

"Alas, a few were not as fleet of foot as I, and the fillies corralled them into matrimony. You'd be hard pressed to recognize the poor blokes with their moon-eyed looks and besotted grins. 'Tis a sorry sight, and you are fortunate to be spared the spectacle."

"Good thing you have fast feet." He dubiously eyed Robbie's tree trunk thighs and thick calves, but recalling his dexterity with the fence, withheld comment.

"Too true." Robbie agreed affably as he entered his office. "And yourself? Your letters contained a glaring paucity of kiss-and-tell, so I take it you are still in the bachelor state?"

"Most definitely," Daniel responded quickly, even as his thoughts drifted to Lady Julia Chandler. Their kiss was another detail best kept to himself.

Robbie's office appeared part business and part makeshift storage room. Bridles, reins, and sundry other equestrian detritus littered the room. The equipment competed with stacks of papers and ledgers shoved haphazardly onto shelves lining one wall. Two desks filled the space and Robbie cleared one of a stack of leather-bound ledgers. "Bit of clutter here, wasn't expecting company. Just dig out a seat."

Daniel removed a pair of stirrups from a chair and brushed it clean before lifting his jacket and daring to sit.

Circling his desk, Robbie leaned over and fiddled with the lock on a drawer. Rummaging inside, he withdrew a bottle of whiskey and two tumblers.

He quirked a brow as Robbie generously filled the glasses.

He handed Daniel his, raising his own in a toast. "To the return of a long lost friend. May he be forever found."

Daniel paused in lifting his drink, staring at Robbie, who drained his glass in one fluid swallow.

Wiping his mouth with his hand, Robbie grunted. "Can't understand why neither of my brothers allowed me to toast them at their wedding."

"I haven't the foggiest idea." He commented dryly, struggling to keep his expression blank as he savored his whiskey at a slower pace.

"Now then," Robbie said, dropping into his desk chair, leaning back, and studying him. "While I am delighted to be toasting your return, I have to ask, were you so busy running your company that you couldn't let me know you were returning for a visit? You might think mills, timber, and transatlantic shipping routes make for edifying reading, but if you were planning a trip home, you might have saved my eyes from glazing over. You could have caught me up in person."

His lips twitched at Robbie's cavalier dismissal of his now-prosperous company, Curtis Shipping. He had launched the enterprise with an American friend, Brett Curtis, well over eight years ago. However, news of the company filled the

London financial pages as the firm recently expanded its ports from London into Bristol and Liverpool. Brett had accompanied Daniel on this voyage to visit their London office and oversee the expansion. "My apologies that the last ten years of my life made for such dull reading. Next time I'll add salacious details."

"Now those letters I would have finished!" Robbie grinned, unrepentant.

He laughed. "Truth be told, I was a bit buried in work, so your reading material would have been slim to none."

"My favorite kind. Listen to you. You sound like a tradesman or an American. Don't know what your aristocratic peers will make of you now."

Daniel stiffened. "I don't give a damn for their opinions."

"Now you're sounding like yourself." Robbie beamed, delighted. "So what brings you home? When you left England, you vowed never to return."

He slipped his hand into his jacket pocket, withdrew the enigmatic missive from the solicitor, and tossed it onto Robbie's desk. "This planted the seed."

Robbie eyed the note curiously before reading.

Daniel sprang to his feet, too restless to sit. He sipped his whiskey and paced the confines of the office, careful to avoid the debris littering the floor.

"Why wasn't this addressed to Bedford? Shouldn't your father's solicitor be contacting him?" Robbie furrowed his brow.

"He probably wrote to both of us." He shrugged.

"What destiny are you to claim?" Robbie held up the letter to the ribbon of light streaming through the window. He scrunched up his features and examined the paper as if the light would magically illuminate the answers he sought.

"That's not relevant. It is the first line that brought me back."

Robbie looked at the note, then at him, frowning. "It is time?"

"Exactly." He stopped before Robbie's desk and brandished his glass at him, excitement lacing his words. "It *is* time. Ten years ago, I left with nothing but the clothes on my back and a paltry savings. I lost everything when Lakeview Manor burned to the ground. Well, it *is* time. Time to get it all back. Time I rebuild what's mine. What I lost." His voice lowered. "What we both know was stolen from me."

"You are going to rebuild Lakeview Manor?"

"I am." He nodded. "A decade ago, I did not have the resolve or the capital to succeed. To rebuild as I wanted or needed to. But today I can, thanks to Curtis Shipping."

Robbie set the letter down and quietly assessed him. "You do remember why you left?"

He paused, the silence echoing between them as the years fell away. Orange flames and a thick, suffocating wall of gray smoke flashed before him. Escaping the fire, Daniel had sought refuge at the Tanners', where he had been given the care he never would have received at Bedford Hall. After the reading of his father's will a fortnight before, Edmund had kicked Daniel out of the house and was busy drowning himself in drink. Sober, Edmund would have lamented Daniel's survival rather than his burned flesh.

As Daniel healed, stories had circulated that the curtains had caught fire, and thanks had been given that the house had stood empty. Daniel hadn't bothered to correct the misinformation. Having lost all he had ever cared about, he hadn't given a damn, and had eventually sailed to America with Brett, never looking back. Until now.

He shook off the old nightmare and lifted his chin. "I do."

"For God's sake, Daniel." Robbie leaned forward, his tone heated, his eyes hard. "Someone tried to kill you. They burned your house to the ground with you in it. You barely made it out alive."

"I am well aware of that." He kept his voice level, despite his strained patience. "I am the one carrying the scars, so you can be sure I will not ever forget."

"What makes you think that whoever wanted you dead isn't around to finish the job today?"

"It's another reason I have returned. It is time to catch the bastard. To get justice."

"And how do you propose to do that ten years later?" Robbie scoffed. "You didn't know who set the fire back then, have you learned something new?"

"No, but I intend to." He frowned, irked at his mulish tone.

Grabbing the bottle of whiskey, Robbie refilled his glass and topped off Daniel's. "To a man with a death wish. Can your partner manage the firm without you?"

"He can, but I am not planning on his needing to. My thanks for your support." He lifted his drink and took a sip, seeking to wash away his friend's cynicism.

The distant whine of a horse and clatter of dishes drifted to them. Robbie blew out a breath. "All right. I will bite. How the hell are we going to catch the bastard?"

"I heard them that night," he confided. He perched on Robbie's desk, his words passionate. "It's what saved my life, because it woke me up. Their voices carried across the lake. If I heard them, someone else may have as well. Someone might have seen something."

"Are you planning to ask around? Post a notice asking anyone with information to come forward?"

He bristled at the skepticism lacing Robbie's words. "There will be no posting of any notices. This has to be done quietly. I intend to speak to a select few who might know something. I will inform them that information is sought about the fire and ask them to spread the word that there is money to be had for any intelligence provided. Nothing might come of it, but I need to do this, Robbie. I don't want vengeance, but I deserve justice. Help me to get it." His finger tapped the discarded letter as he pressed his point home. "It *is* time. Past time."

Robbie scowled, and then swiped his hands down his face and muttered a few ripe curses beneath his breath. "Fine, fine. But God knows if you want it done quietly, we can't have the long lost lord waltzing home and asking suspicious questions. No lid will keep that cover on for long. It will simmer and boil over right quick. *I* will do the asking. Hell, after ten years away, you wouldn't know whom to ask anyway."

The lost lord? And he never waltzed. "Thank you, Robbie. I knew I could count on you."

Robbie's sharp brown eyes narrowed suspiciously. "If you planned this from the start, keep that to yourself. I do not care to know you talked me into another one of your bloody schemes. To know you still can. One of these days I'm going to stop listening. And then where will you be?"

Daniel smiled, the knot of tension within him unfurling. "I would be lost without you." He lifted his glass in a toast.

"Very true, and don't you forget it." Robbie sipped his whiskey and eyed Daniel over its rim. "So you are here to rebuild Lakeview Manor and catch a murderer. You will be busy."

He paused and rubbed his neck. "Ah, there is one other item."

"Finding a murderer before he finds you is not enough to keep you busy?"

He sighed. "I am aware of the dangers posed in my opening this investigation. I will watch my back, Robbie, but I doubt whoever tried to kill me is waiting in the wings to strike again after all this time."

"You may be right, but we don't know why they tried the first time. They might still harbor motive," Robbie pointed out. "What is the other item?"

"It is about my brother's betrothal to Lady Julia Chandler. Why hasn't Edmund set a wedding date yet?" The question had been on his mind ever since his lips had touched Julia's. She was a temptress incarnate. If she were his, he would have wedded and . . . He did not let himself finish the thought.

She was not his. Could never be.

Lady Julia Chandler was marriage material, and as Daniel had assured Robbie, he was an emphatic bachelor. A wife and family were ties that bound, and he preferred his life unfettered. Always had.

Surprise crossed Robbie's face at the change in topic. "Well, I'm not in His Grace's confidences, for he doesn't condescend to speak to me as a peer. But it was my understanding that Lady Julia postponed the nuptials first when her mother died, and then after her sister lost her fiancé. I mentioned those events in my letters."

So it was Julia, not Edmund. It was understandable she

would not abandon her father or Emily while they grieved. Apparently, he had fate and family loyalty to thank for saving her from Edmund thus far.

He jerked as Robbie's fist pounded his desk, snapping him from his thoughts.

"Damn it, man! That is what you need to accomplish while you are here. Forget the murder mystery. Stop Lady Julia from marrying that stuffed-up, no-good, bloody bastard!"

His eyes locked with Robbie's and his lips curved. "My thoughts exactly."

Robbie's fierce expression eased, and he grinned. "So then. We'll add that to your agenda. What do we have so far? Rebuild Lakeview Manor, find out who tried to murder you, keep them from killing you, and break up Lady Julia and your brother's engagement. That is, without ruining her, which could be complicated . . ." Robbie's words trailed off, and he furrowed his brow as if mulling over a difficult equation.

Daniel grunted at Robbie's colossal understatement. One did not sever a betrothal contract to a duke with impunity, but it couldn't be helped. It had to be done. Julia deserved better. He just had to figure out how the devil to do it. These things had to be done delicately.

"Did I leave anything out?" Robbie interrupted his thoughts.

"That ought to cover it." He smiled at the teasing glint in Robbie's eyes. "Too much?"

"Nah, nothing to it. Just don't catch the first boat home." Robbie winked before his mien turned serious. "Actually, there is another matter. You need to go to Bedford Hall and see your father's estate before Edmund runs it into the ground."

His humor fled. "Is it still bad?"

Robbie nodded. "It is. I know you don't give a damn about your brother, but Bedford Hall was once your home, too, and the tenants were your father's people. You might want to have a look. See if there is anything you can do."

Conflicting emotions warred within him. His childhood years had been cold, lonely, and abusive under Edmund's fists. But splashes of light had sporadically illuminated the darkness.

He recalled his father seeking him out to ride over the estate, meet with tenants, and discuss his plans for the land. Like water given to a desert traveler, he had lapped up every moment, desperate to fill the cavernous hole of his loneliness. It served to remind him that his father hadn't entirely forgotten him.

So how could he forget his father or neglect his legacy?

He could not. But Bedford Hall was Edmund's domain, and Daniel's options were limited. His brother had made it clear when he inherited the title that he did not want, nor appreciate, Daniel's input or advice in regard to estate matters. All he desired from Daniel was the view of his backside kicked out the front door and his promise to never return.

An image of Julia's flushed features flashed before him. Hell, the damage had been done. He had already trespassed on forbidden ground, and he'd be damned if he regretted doing so.

In for a penny, in for a pound.

He would visit his father's estates and see the changes Edmund's management had wrought. Resolved, he glanced up at Robbie. "And where is my evil twin these days? In London? Or rusticating here in the country?"

Robbie smiled. "A buyer of mine mentioned he was joining Bedford at a hunting party in Kent, so that should give you some time.

"While the cat's away . . ." He let his words trail off.

"Exactly. The wee mice can strategize . . ." Robbie agreed.

Edmund had not only left his lands open to trespassers, but had left his lovely fiancée alone as well.

Daniel surmised Julia would make an appearance at the fall festival. Attending the fair had moved to the top of his agenda.

He anticipated their paths crossing again. She would still be spitting mad, but he could not summon regret for kissing her. Would make no apologies for doing so. Damned if he did not want to do it again.

Privately he added that to his growing agenda.

Chapter Three

✄

JULIA had spent a restless night tossing and turning, feeling hot and sweaty one moment and in the next, yearning for something just beyond her grasp . . .

As she traversed the fairgrounds the next morning, she worried her lower lip, oblivious to the crowds jostling her as she pondered her reaction. Should a kiss affect one so? Considering it had been her first, she had no idea. Something tightened in her chest, pain at having to concede that Daniel's kiss had been her first, for she was long past the age when a woman should have a few illicit pecks to boast about.

More to the point, her first kiss should have been with Edmund. It should have been special, memorable. Not to say that Daniel did not kiss very well, or as well as she could judge, having no comparisons in regard to such matters. She furrowed her brow, finding it hard to believe another kiss could be more thorough than theirs had been, or be done more expertly, or be more . . .

"Julia?"

The amused voice penetrated her runaway thoughts and Julia jumped, turning to blink at her sister. "What . . . where?"

"I believe those are my questions." Emily laughed. "What in the world are you thinking about? Your cheeks are bright pink." Emily studied her more closely. "In fact, you look a bit feverish, are you all right? Really, Julia, you have not been yourself since you rushed into the house yesterday, looking as if the Hounds of Hell were on your heels. What *is* the matter with you?"

It was an incredibly long speech for Emily, for her sister had become a woman of few words since Jason's death two years ago. It put Julia in a quandary, for while delighted to see Emily find her voice, it was an inopportune moment for her to do so—or to be so astute.

"Julia?"

"Well, I . . ." She felt as if she had been caught doing something forbidden. And she was not, or she was not anymore. Feeling her cheeks flame, she met Emily's amused regard, struggling to form a response when none came to mind.

The surrounding crowds rescued her from her reticence. Snatches of conversations rose above the din.

"He's right crazy!"

"Don't care. I got me two bob ridin' on Black Devil tossing the toff on his arse. I aim to get me a new trowel with me winnings."

"He must have lost his wits in America. It's right dangerous for a bloke to be witless round Black Devil."

"Well, here's hoping he don't find 'em. I need me a new trowel."

"He's got the looks of His Grace, and His Grace has a right fine seat on a horse. Might want to be rethin' your wager."

Julia heard no more. The comparison to His Grace identified the witless toff. As much as she'd like to see Robbie Tanner's new, unbroken stallion toss Lord Daniel Bryant on his hindquarters, she could not face the man just yet. Not when tongue-tied and under Emily's suspicious regard.

Unfortunately, the decision was not hers to make. Julia looped her arm securely through Emily's as they found themselves carried along with the throngs of villagers, moved like flotsam in a river of people. Excitement rippled through the crowds. They appeared to be heading toward the paddocks next to Tanner Stables, which abutted the village square.

"Oh dear, Robbie must be taking bets on that poor horse unseating all challengers. It is not right, Julia." Emily said, worry edging her voice.

She squeezed Emily's forearm. "He will find a buyer for him soon. The horse is too valuable for him to stable for long. Robbie deals in the sale of prime bloodstock, not losing pounds over the board and keep of them."

"But if the horse is mad . . ."

"He is not mad. Just spirited." She slid her arm around her sister's waist, disturbed at her choice of words.

Madness was not something Julia wished to contemplate, not after the past year. An image of Emily standing with a pair of shears clutched in her hand flashed before her. Covering her sister's bare feet were the golden strands of her once beautiful long hair. Emily's eyes had pooled with tears. *Jason loved my hair,* she had said.

She tightened her grip on Emily and buried the image. After all, Emily was much, much better now. Taking her away to the Lake District for a few months had been restorative. No one need ever know of how dark that period had been, for no one knew the true extent of her sister's despair but Edmund and the family. He had kept their family's confidence, his future linked with theirs through his betrothal to Julia. Julia frowned at her train of thought. Of course, Edmund would have been discreet had they not been betrothed.

The proximity of the crowds drew her attention. They had thinned around her as they became aware of whom they carried in their midst. Her father, the earl, was highly esteemed in Taunton, generous and benevolent to the village. She smiled at familiar faces, nodding to those who bobbed a brief curtsy despite the ruckus surrounding them. "My ladies." The murmurs reached her as a path was cleared for them to move forward.

They joined the audience standing before the paddock

fence. Men propped their elbows on the top rails and hooted encouragement at the scene unfolding before them. Young boys perched on the fence rail to gain a better vantage point. The whisper of a breeze swept the audience, the sky a vast canvas of cerulean blue. The afternoon sun dazzled, a bright beacon to grace the day.

She scanned the crowds for her younger brother's towhead. Her father had succumbed to his pleading and escorted him to the festival earlier in the day. She caught sight of Jonathan's shining face from his perch atop one of the rails, one arm slung around a nearby post. Her heart lifted at the sight of her father's tall figure hovering protectively beside him, the intimate tableau another reminder that all was well with her family.

Lifting her arm to wave, her gesture froze in midair as the man standing a short distance away from her brother's perch distracted her.

One couldn't miss him, for he towered half a head taller than most of the men, his fine clothes marking him as aristocracy. From his pristine dark blue riding jacket, custom fit over his broad shoulders, to the tips of his Hessian riding boots, the man exuded an aura of wealth and power. A ten-year absence did not eradicate blood ties, and Lord Daniel Bryant was aristocratic to the bone, the brother of a duke and his heir apparent. Her eyes scanned the crowd, and she saw the ripple effect his presence had caused.

Eyes narrowed in speculation, the men elbowing each other and nodding toward Daniel. Coins exchanging hands clinked as wages were laid. Women neatened their skirts and tucked stray strands of hair under their mobcaps while their eyes lapped up Daniel's tall figure like a succulent treat they'd like to sample. Julia noted the brazen looks, a few just short of ogling.

"So that's Bryant. I had heard that he had returned," Emily murmured, wonder in her voice. "Hasn't he grown up well."

"One would think one had never seen a handsome man before." She shrugged. "The years have been kind to him. He is taller."

Emily stared at her, and then burst out laughing.

Two conflicting emotions battled within her, joy at the rare sound of her sister's laughter and annoyance at the cause of it. The latter overrode her pleasure. "What is it? I do not see what all the fuss is about it. The man is good looking, but—"

"He is a mirror image of his brother. What do you call him, *Beautiful Bedford*?"

It had been a weak moment when she had confided in her sister.

"I wonder why he has finally returned home after all these years away?"

Emily's question echoed her own during her restless night. She frowned at Daniel, who stood with his head bowed listening to Robbie, who gestured to the closed doors of the stables behind them.

Why did you come back?

His exodus had been as abrupt as his return. He had disappeared but a month after his father's funeral, and a fortnight after Lakeview Manor had burned to the ground. Edmund claimed that in his haste to depart, he had left behind most of his belongings.

She was five years younger than the twins, who had been eighteen at the time. She recalled her parents' surprise at his leaving Edmund to step into his title and shoulder the responsibility for the estates alone. Rumors circulated that Daniel's grief over the combined loss of his father and Lakeview Manor had propelled his flight.

Grief might explain his departure, but it did not explain the ensuing silence. It had been as if Daniel was swallowed up by the night, his disappearance complete when Edmund forbade even the mention of his name.

And why, after a decade's absence, had he returned?

It couldn't be just to torment her. As if he had heard the accusation, Daniel's head lifted and his gaze locked on her. His eyes traveled from the blue velvet ribbons topping her bonnet, down the buttons lining her bodice, to the bottom of her blue skirts and back up. Goose bumps rose on her arms, her high-waisted spencer jacket and layered petticoats poor protection against his slow scrutiny.

When his eyes fastened on her mouth, a slow, intimate smile curved those familiar lips. The heated perusal combined with the memory of his mouth, warm and insistent on hers, caused her to catch her breath and retreat a step.

His smile broadened and he tipped his head in an imperceptible greeting before he returned his attention to Robbie. She exhaled.

"I do believe he remembers you." Emily arched a delicate brow at Julia, amused.

Avoiding Emily's eyes, she shrugged. "Perhaps."

"I wonder if he's staying with his brother."

Unsettled, she spoke without thinking. "I wouldn't know. He did not say."

"Pardon?" Emily stared at her. "You have spoken to him? When? Why did you not mention it?"

Cursing her slip, she waved her hand airily, unable to meet her sister's eyes. "We happened to cross paths yesterday. It was very brief. We did not get a chance to catch up." He had been too busy posing as Edmund and kissing her senseless.

"Why didn't you tell me? Is that what had you so flustered yesterday—?"

"Look." She interrupted Emily, desperate to redirect her attention. She needed time for her cheeks to cool and to form a plausible denial. She moved closer to the fence, aware that her sister's speculative look followed her.

Robbie slid one of the stable doors open, his imposing size blocking the entrance, leaving a gap wide enough for Daniel to slip through. The sounds of the crowd had dropped to expectant rumbles, all eyes riveted to Robbie's broad back. He peered over his shoulder and beamed a smile at the crowd, his brown eyes brimming with anticipation. A bit of a showman, Robbie savored exhibitions of his horses, and having a long lost lord participate could only double his delight.

Bracing his shoulder against the door, he swung it fully open, then dove quickly to the side to avoid over nine hundred stone of pulsating, wild black stallion plowing into him as the animal half leapt, half galloped outside.

The crowd responded in a collective gasp as Black Devil

gathered speed and cantered around the paddock with Daniel astride, riding bareback on the beast. His back straight, the reins grasped loosely as he circled the paddock. There was none of the stallion's usual antics, the frenzied bucking or wild rearing to dislodge his rider. Absent was the feral gleam igniting his coal black eyes, the savage snarl that bared his teeth, or the hooves pawing the air and reaching for the nearest head to decapitate.

"Glory be! Will ye look at that!"

"That be Black Devil? *Robbie's* Black Devil?"

"More like a little lamb."

"What did the toff do to him?"

"Bollocks! I needed me a new trowel."

Julia stared as the horse reared back, the thick cords in his neck bulging as he tossed his mane, his snow-white forelegs pawing the air.

An incredible specimen of horse, all quivering muscle and sinew, the sun burnished his coat to a fine, black sheen. She curled her fingers over the fence rail in a white-knuckled grip. Blood drained from her head as she feared witnessing Daniel cracking his skull open, but one look at his expression had her catching her breath.

The idiot was laughing! His handsome features were alight, his white teeth flashing, and his dark hair wind-combed and wild. The grip of his muscular thighs pressing into the stallion's sides braced him on the horse. Her heart gave a traitorous leap at the pure, masculine beauty of man and beast in full accord as the animal settled back on all fours. At a gentle urging from Daniel, Black Devil circled the paddock for an encore performance while the crowd roared its approval, hats tossed in the air.

Daniel rode with athletic grace, ease, and unabashed joy. This stunt settled one matter for her—she would never mistake this man for his brother again.

They were like opposing faces on a coin. While they looked alike, Bedford was self-contained, aloof, and, well . . . aristocratic. Daniel's years abroad had clearly stamped their imprint on him. Like his adopted country, from the little she had viewed of him, Daniel was bold, unconventional, and daring . . . if not a bit wild. All marked him as dangerous. She vowed to keep her distance from the man even as she leaned forward to get an unobstructed view of horse and rider.

After coming full circle, Daniel bent over the stallion's neck and suddenly the pair were trotting straight toward her.

Stunned, she stood rooted in place, watching Daniel dismount before her.

He jumped clear of the horse, tossed the reins to Robbie as he landed, dark hair tousled, eyes alight, and a rakish smile splitting his face. He strode over to where she stood. From the buttonhole of his jacket, he withdrew a perfect bloodred rose.

Bowing low, he presented his offering. "My lady, this humble English rose is but a pale tribute to your dazzling beauty."

The pounding in her heart matched the thunderous applause, while Daniel's gallant action confirmed her worst fear.

He *had* returned to torment her.

Worse, he was succeeding.

Chapter Four

⋙⋘

DANIEL watched the play of emotions cross Julia's expressive features. She looked as if she yearned to toss his tribute back in his face, but with an audience of so many, she refrained. The bold, reckless, kiss-me-if-you-dare Julia of yesterday would have, but not this poised and collected lady. Dressed in a tidy sapphire blue jacket and light blue day gown, she was miss prim and proper.

He preferred the Julia of yesterday. He would like to strip away the layers she wore like a protective shield and find the unconventional Julia, particularly if it involved more kisses.

Julia snatched the rose from his hand. She hadn't doused all of yesterday's fire. Some of it still simmered. Good, he liked a woman with spirit.

"Well said," someone hooted.

Daniel lifted an arm to acknowledge their audience, who brandished their hats in approval. When he turned back to Julia, he caught sight of Emily, and his smile broadened. "I see I have need of a second gift." He bowed again. "My apologies."

"You remember my younger sister, Lady Emily." Julia edged closer to her sister.

He noted the protective move. His gaze shifted between them, marveling at the differences. Both had the deep blue Chandler eyes, but while Julia had a riotous mass of curling hair, Emily was fair, her hair a tidy, sun-kissed yellow. Julia's countenance was coolly assessing, Emily's open and warm. Emily was reed thin, a strong gust of wind capable of toppling her. Daniel usually preferred his women willow slim, but as of yesterday, his preference had changed. Curves on a fuller figure were definitely an asset he had overlooked. He would not do so again.

"Charm *and* a splendid seat, my lord," Emily said. "Pray tell, what spells have you woven to turn Robbie's horse from devil to angel?"

"No magic. I simply had a chat with him, and we came to an understanding. Angel?" He tested the name out on his tongue, looking over to study Black Devil, whom Robbie was leading in an encore circle of the paddock. "Black Angel." Yes, it would do beautifully. He smiled at Emily. "I was wondering what to rename him. I could not have chosen better myself. Forget the single rose, I owe you a dozen."

"And what does Robbie have to say about your renaming his prized stallion?" Julia said, regarding him with suspicion.

"Robbie has no say in the matter. The horse is mine. Black Angel will do."

"You bought Black Devil?" She looked surprised.

"I did, along with another stallion trained to saddle, a handsome chestnut named Chase. I have need of a horse during my visit."

"And how long will you be staying?" Emily asked.

"I do not intend on leaving too soon. I have a lot of catching up to do. Ten years' worth." His eyes locked with Julia's, and when a high-pitched bellow of Emily's name distracted her, he could not resist leaning toward Julia. Lowering his voice, his eyes dipped to her mouth. "And I am enjoying catching up very much."

Spots of pink colored her cheeks, and the rose she held took a precarious dive as her fist strangled around its stem.

"If you will excuse me, that bellow is for me," Emily said dryly. "Welcome home, Lord Bryant. I do hope you enjoy your visit and Black Angel."

"Oh, I already am." He smiled, holding Julia's gaze.

Once Emily had departed, Julia arched a delicate brow. "Have you had a chance to catch up with your brother yet? Or have you quite forgotten about him?"

Like her slap of yesterday, her words found their mark, and he straightened. "No, I have not forgotten Edmund. I will deal with him. But I will do so in my own time."

"What do you mean? Deal with him?" Confusion crossed her features. "How exactly do you intend to *deal with* Edmund?"

He shrugged. "As I always have, very carefully." Unable to resist, he let his eyes again lower to her mouth. "Particularly after yesterday."

She drew in a sharp breath and cast a furtive glance around. The crowds were beginning to disperse, so she edged closer to the fence separating them and dropped her voice to a desperate hiss. "You must understand that was a mistake. I thought you were Edmund!"

He braced his arms over the top rail, grinning when she stumbled back. "There was no mistake on my part. I knew who you were at all times."

"You took advantage of the situation. You—"

"My dear Julia, it would have taken a far stronger man than I to deny your plea. I am willing to concede to being weak, but not stupid, for I gave you fair warning that what you requested of me was dangerous."

"Dangerous? By God, you could have been killed!"

Daniel spun at the comment, stepping back from the fence upon recognizing Julia's father, Lord Taunton. A decade older, the earl's dark hair was peppered with streaks of silver and gray, but his eyes—Julia's eyes—were a lively blue. Robbie had opened the nearest paddock gate and released Black Devil into another enclosure, so Lord Taunton advanced without threat.

"Lord Bryant, I must say, you do know how to make an entrance." He grasped Daniel's hand in his, pumping it up and down. "That was quite a show. I had bets laid that Robbie would have to put the horse down. Pray tell, how did you tame the beast? And when did you return? You must come and dine with us this very evening. I will not take no for an answer. You have some long overdue explanations to make, young man."

Daniel shook his head with a laugh. Another voice piped up to forestall his reply.

"Cor blimey, it were brilliant! Smashing good."

A young boy, no more than five, scrambled through the fence rails and dashed to his side, craning his head back to beam a smile up at him.

"My son, Lord Jonathan." Pride laced Lord Taunton's words.

The introduction was superfluous, for the boy's vibrant blue eyes mirrored his father's and sisters'. Daniel dipped into a bow. "It is a pleasure."

Emily joined their group, looking apologetic. "I held him back as long as I could."

"Are you a horseman?" he addressed the boy.

"I ride Mindy, my pony, but I want to ride Black Devil. Can I? Please?"

"Absolutely," he said. He was quick to add, "As soon as you pile on a bit more height and weight, we will have you on his back in no time."

Jonathan looked crestfallen. "I know," he declared, brightening, "I'll eat that green stuff that Cook says will make me grow. I'll stop stuffing it in my napkin, and I'll be big in no time."

"Sounds like a good plan." Daniel nodded solemnly, his lips twitching.

"Speaking of plans, we must be keeping you from yours," Julia said, circling around the fence rail and through the open gate to rest her hand on her brother's shoulder.

"We have taken up enough of your time," Julia continued. "We—"

He did not let her finish. "On the contrary." She was seeking an escape, and he had no intention of providing her with one.

"My time is yours, for I have no plans but to enjoy the pleasure of your company."

Julia made no comment, but he noted her hand tightened on Jonathan's shoulder, who with a grunt of protest, dodged free.

"And, my lord, I accept your kind offer to dine."

"Wonderful, we look forward to it." Her father beamed.

Daniel's eyes met Julia's, unable to hide his triumph. He swallowed his laugh when she looked discomfited and quickly dropped her gaze to her brother, speaking to him.

"Jonathan, you mentioned wanting to see Punch and Judy? I spied their red and white tent over by the blacksmith shop, and that distant squawk is unmistakably Punch."

"Why don't we head over there?" Emily looped her arm through her father's.

Jonathan frowned. "I can't see them."

"You need a better vantage point. How is this?" Daniel bent, scooped up the little boy, and settled him on his shoulders. "Now, Captain, steer me to their tent." He walked to the open gate, Jonathan's squeal of delight ringing out.

"Well done." Emily laughed.

He thought so, but from Julia's expression, he surmised she was of a different opinion. He wondered if she wished Black Angel had flipped him onto his arse.

❦

The Chandlers were a close family. As the afternoon wore on, Daniel witnessed firsthand the tight-knit bond they shared and had a better understanding of why Julia would postpone her wedding to care for her family. After leaving the antics of Punch and Judy, they perused various games, savored a vendor's mouthwatering pastries, and lightened their pockets on various trinkets.

Julia tilted her head back to laugh at a comment from Emily, affectionately looping her arm through her sister's. Earlier, Jonathan's triumphant shout during a game of ring toss had elicited Taunton's praise, and his hand had brushed over his son's hair in a casual caress. Interactions had flowed between them in a smooth, calm current. No darkness simmered beneath the surface, no undercurrent disrupted their relations.

No Edmund.

Daniel scowled. There was freedom in not being shackled with family ties, and he coveted his freedom. After all, independence was all that his family had ever given him.

His father's time had been divided between his estate responsibilities and grooming Edmund for the title, carving out those sporadic bites of time for the spare heir. As for his brother, well, their fraternal bond was but a tenuous thread Edmund had severed early. Unfettered by family ties, Daniel came and went as he pleased. He answered to no one, and he liked it that way. Shrugging off the recollection, he returned his attention to Julia.

She bent over, her expression a picture of grave concern as a village girl prattled on about her bandaged finger, which she thrust in Julia's face for closer inspection.

He had observed Julia mingle with the villagers, engage with vendors, and skillfully evade zealous peddlers seeking her patronage. She was kind and personal, yet not overly familiar. She had inquired after the welfare of someone's prized pig and award-winning roses and had listened with the same attention she paid to this tyke's account of her tussle with Robbie's tomcat.

The knee-scraped animal rescuer he recollected from his childhood was long gone. As was the vulnerable young girl he had once comforted in his arms when Edmund had tricked her into hiding in a root cellar, not bothering to tell Daniel he was to search for her. She was like a familiar childhood book but with new, unexplored chapters. He wanted to revisit her story and devour every word.

Julia touched her lips to the girl's wound, kissing it better and earning a smile from the apple-cheeked child. Daniel frowned. He blamed another kiss, the one that never should have happened, for his fascination. It created an inexorable pull toward Julia.

With no other woman had he felt this relentless tug, like an anchor tied to her prow. Over the years, he had discovered there were benefits to the fairer sex that he had overlooked, having his nose buried in business ledgers as he struggled to launch a company. Like most lusty young men, he had found that he liked those benefits . . . very much.

Julia straightened and joined her family at an adjacent tent. A gust of wind molded her skirts to her slim hips, and he bit back a curse. In the midst of a crowded thoroughfare, beside his brother's beautiful fiancée, was not the time nor place to recall those benefits. She was not his and never could be.

"You don't enjoy the performance?"

Daniel jerked at the amused voice and found Emily beside him, regarding him with a *caught you* look. Heat itched up his neck as he studied the exhibit he had been neglecting. Jugglers threw spinning balls into the air, adding wooden stakes into the spiraling mix. Gasps rose from the audience when knives were tossed into the frantically whirling objects.

"If I appear too interested, they might ask for volunteers. I have need of my limbs, find I prefer them attached to my body."

"I don't know if staring at my sister is any safer. You do recall that she is betrothed to Edmund? Your *twin* brother? Has been for years?"

Definitely caught. His smile faded. "So you both keep reminding me."

"Mmh. I saw Julia when she returned home yesterday." He stilled, but Emily's attention remained on the performance. "She looked flustered and incredibly distracted, which is not like my sister at all."

"Really?" He kept his tone neutral.

"Really," she confirmed. "I could not figure out what had her so bothered." Emily looked at him then. "Until I saw you." Her gaze strayed to Julia. If he was not watching her, he might have missed her next words, so quiet were they. "I do not know why you decided to return home or how long you intend to stay, but your arrival is opportune, for my sister could use a distraction. And"—her eyes lifted to his, a teasing spark in them—"it would not hurt for her to be pink-cheeked and flustered as well."

Surprised, he raised a brow. Soon thereafter, he was too busy thanking his change in fortunes to ponder Emily's enigmatic comment. Jonathan and Lord Taunton had departed to observe an archery competition, and Emily's commitment to judge a flower show had her making her excuses as well. In a desperate ploy to escape him, Julia was quick to offer her assistance with the judging.

"I wouldn't hear of it." Emily looked rueful. "Mistress Turner has declared your gardening talents both dangerous and deadly—her words, not mine—so I fear she wouldn't hear of it either. Really, Julia, Father would be most upset if you left Lord Bryant here bereft of an escort so soon after his return home." Emily's pitiful look in Daniel's direction had him biting his tongue to suppress his smile. She cleverly played to her sister's weaknesses. He would have to remember to guard his.

"Well, I—" Julia stammered.

He needed no further encouragement than Emily's *what are you waiting for?* look. "Yes, I would be quite lost without Lady Julia's company. So now that that is settled, I think we should be off before the day is lost." Or Julia escaped. He caught her arm and, ignoring her tug of resistance, looped it securely through his, clasping his hand over hers and trapping her by his side.

He bowed to Emily, swung Julia around, and ventured forward. As if he had won a coveted prize and he had no intention of losing her.

"What are you doing?" Julia asked, looking pink-cheeked and flustered as she removed her arm from his.

He admired the color on her fair features. "Enjoying the fair, the day, and the company of a beautiful woman." He tossed a coin to a village girl who braced a basket brimming with floral bouquets against her broad hip. He extracted one and offered it to Julia, inclining his head. "For a fair damsel."

She hesitated, then grabbed the flowers, frowning when the girl scurried away, her trill of laughter floating behind her. "I cannot fathom why after ten years away, without word or warning, you have decided to return home. But—"

"I wrote. I wrote to Robbie. I would have visited sooner had I known I was missed. Emily said—"

"That is enough." Seeing curious stares turn their way, she closed her mouth and caught his arm. "Please, come with me. There are matters that need to be settled."

Surprised, he found himself towed in her wake.

She drew him down an alley separating the jugglers' tent from one showcasing a fortune-teller. She must be a bit of a bluestocking, for a young lady did not touch, let alone drag, a gentleman anywhere. Another admirable character trait; for after his years in America, he was finding England a bit straightlaced, like a stiff-backed old woman, set in her ways and resistant to change.

She released his arm and faced him. "Please, you have to stop giving me flowers. I am betrothed to your brother. More importantly, I do not know what you and Emily were whispering about earlier, but you need to promise me that you will stay away from her. Emily's been through too much already, and—"

"You cannot be serious," he cut her off, a choked laugh escaping him. "I have no designs on Emily."

Instead of his response placating her, she reeled back as if stricken. "And why not? What is wrong with my sister? She is perfect, gentle and kind. Everyone loves Emily."

"Just like a woman." He shook his head. "Condemned both ways. What makes you think I have any designs on your sister? After all, it was you that I kissed. It is you whom I—"

"Please," she cut him off, casting a furtive glance around the empty alley. Rumbles of laughter carried to them, and an occasional shout rose from a satisfied patron. "Please, let us not bring that up again. I told you, it was a mistake, a minor indiscretion that a gentleman would not keep—"

"I am beginning to think you have never been kissed before." He crossed his arms, amused.

"Excuse me?" she breathed, the color draining from her face.

"To classify that kiss as minor reveals your ignorance of the matter." He shrugged. "A peck on the cheek or lips pressed to a gloved hand is minor, but what we did was explosive. Smoldering. It lit—"

"Stop! It may not . . . ah, did you say explosive? Really?" She paused, her annoyance forgotten, replaced by wide-eyed intrigue.

Delighted, he inclined his head toward her and lowered his voice to a husky timbre. "And smoldering. I have never—"

"Enough," she cried. She had been leaning toward him as well, his soft words reeling her in, but sudden awareness of her actions caused her to straighten like a poker. "If I agree with you that it was . . . well, it was done rather well, you must agree with me that it was dangerous *and* more important, a mistake." She pressed a hand against her temple. "I cannot believe I am having this conversation with you. It is ridiculous. I do not do ridiculous, am far too old for it."

Amused and fascinated, he watched her struggle to compose herself.

He preferred her pink-cheeked and flustered.

She drew in a ragged breath. "We cannot discuss this again. Please. It may have been lovely for one moment and done rather well, but . . ." She stopped and started again as if she had lost the thread of her thought. "The point of the matter is, it was a mistake, and one we both need to forget."

The finality of her words irked him. He did not like being dismissed like the forgotten boy he had once been. "You are absolutely right." He unfolded his arms and stepped closer, crowding her. She regarded him warily, but held her ground. He caught her upper arms and drew her to him, ignoring the alarm swimming in those luminous blue depths. "We are done talking. I think a demonstration is in order. You see, you keep saying our kiss was a mistake."

"Yes, it was—"

"My dear Julia." His eyes roved over her features, admiring the perfect symmetry and soft, flushed skin. "There is something you should know about me." He cradled her cheek, lowered his head, his mouth inches from hers. "I am a man who likes to correct his mistakes." When her lips parted in surprise, he captured them in a deep kiss. He kissed her as he had dreamed of doing again since yesterday afternoon.

She tasted better than he remembered, his memory a pale comparison to the reality of holding her warm, supple body flush to his. His arms circled her, one hand sliding up the curve of her back and pressing her closer and still closer, the flowers she held crushed between them.

Desire roared through him as he kissed her deeply, thoroughly. Her lips were full and soft. He tasted honey, apple, and cinnamon, the remnants from a tart she had eaten earlier. The taste was bold and sweet, capturing the essence of her. He delved deeper, his tongue dancing with hers as he drank her in. She was fire and passion, and for one fleeting moment, he could pretend she was his.

He lifted his head and stared into her heavy-lidded, glazed eyes. "You might have been right about yesterday being a mistake. I am glad we corrected it, for this was much better."

"Excuse me?" Julia moistened her swollen lips and blinked up at him, her expression dazed.

"If you do not agree, we could always try again." He dropped his eyes to her lips.

"No!" She came alive, shoving him away and swatting at him with the squashed bouquet. Sweeping her gaze around the secluded pathway, she tugged down the waist of her jacket, and held out a hand to hold him at bay. "Don't! Please Lord Bryant, this has to stop. You are not allowed to kiss me, it is—"

"I know, exciting—"

"And wrong," she gasped, stumbling back.

He frowned. "I thought we got it right that time. You still disagree? Perhaps we should try again."

"No!" She planted her hands on his chest, the flowers slapping his chin. "We cannot—" Suddenly she quieted and paled. Breaking away, she glanced around the area. "I . . . I thought I saw someone."

Too late, the familiar prickle climbed his neck. Immediately alert, he searched the area, but found no one. "Let us continue this in a more public venue." Catching her arm, he cast another glance around as he escorted her from the secluded path and onto the festival's busy thoroughfare.

The bustle and cries of vendors and patrons would cover their conversation, but it could not drown out his unease. He cursed his lapse in a vigilance he usually wore like a second skin when in Edmund's territory. He blamed Julia for distracting him. He had known she was dangerous, now he knew just how much.

"We will not be continuing anything." She tugged free, her blue eyes flashing, her lips swollen, and her color high.

She looked magnificent.

"This is over." She drew herself up, and with an unsteady hand, she swiped back the stray curls tumbling over her forehead. "Should you kiss me again, you will have Edmund to deal with. Then you will truly understand the meaning of the word *dangerous*." She spun on her heel, momentarily stumbled, but righted herself before he could assist her.

She looked just as magnificent from the back.

But she was wrong. He was well versed in danger. When Lakeview Manor had been set ablaze and he nearly lost his life, he had learned the true meaning of it. His brother had also introduced him to dark shades of it years earlier. Daniel would be damned if he let his brother teach it to Julia. He tipped his face to the sky, and blew out a frustrated breath.

He did not think it possible to hate his brother more than he already did.

Kissing Julia a second time taught him otherwise.

Chapter Five

❧

Two kisses. Two mistakes. Julia paced a well-worn path in the Aubusson carpet of her room. She did not know what had come over her. Actually, she did, and it was not a *what* but rather a *who*.

The man was bold and reckless. He was as dangerous as the kiss they had shared, or rather *kisses*. But there would be no more. One couldn't continue kissing one's fiancé's twin brother. It just was not done.

She rubbed a hand against her throbbing temple. *Of course*, kissing a man who was not your intended was not done. It was scandalous. Should word of it reach Edmund, she dared not contemplate what other foreboding adjectives could be added to that list. When *disastrous* sprang to mind, she dropped into the chair before her vanity, propped her elbows on its glass surface, and cradled her head in her hands.

She used to be a responsible woman. She was never ridiculous, nor did she drag gentlemen into alleys to take them to task. And she certainly did not exchange kisses with *any* men—her fiancé included.

And why was that?

At the betraying thought, she lifted her head and met her startled reflection in the mirror. Guilt pricked at her, but she refused to back down, for they were fair questions. Why wasn't Edmund trying to kiss her senseless in empty alleys? Or on secluded paths? Or anywhere? Why wasn't *he* buying her flowers at the fair? His brother was having no trouble doing so—and doing a very fine job of it, too. She bit her lip, but she was not so cowardly as to deny it in the privacy of her own bedroom.

Daniel had only spoken the truth. Their kiss had been powerful. But what he did not know, could never know, was how deeply it had touched her. It had dug into yearnings she had buried in the deepest corner of her heart. Uncovered tugging aches to feel wanted . . . desired . . . beautiful. To be seen as more than the dutiful daughter, the doting sister, or the mortar that kept her family from crumbling in their grief.

Since her eighteenth birthday, when these stirrings had simmered, she had hoped Edmund would satisfy them once they became betrothed. When Edmund had failed to do so, and Daniel had answered her needs with one scorching kiss, she had responded.

How could she not when he gave her all she had craved for so very long?

She could never forgive him. Not for kissing her, but for not being his brother.

Her vision blurred and she sprang to her feet, renewing her pacing. Her loyalty belonged to Edmund. She was duty bound, and being the daughter of an earl, she was raised to honor her duty. As a duke, so was Edmund. And as such, Edmund was preoccupied with far more lofty matters than dallying with his fiancée, alleviating her doubts, or kissing her senseless. He had numerous estates, thousands of acres, and hundreds of tenants dependent upon him.

More importantly, Edmund needed her. Daniel had not been there to support Edmund when he had gained his title and the weight of its responsibilities, but she would be. She knew about holding a family together *and* running an estate.

Daniel might have stoked long-buried feelings, but there was no reason to believe she wouldn't respond similarly to overtures from Edmund.

Her heart lightened, and she tapped her brush against her palm as she pondered how to proceed.

There could be no more transgressions with Daniel. She was not too concerned over the matter, for he would soon return to America, and the vast breadth of the Atlantic Ocean created a formidable barrier between them. Until then, she would erect her own defenses, and do so quickly, for at her father's invitation, Lord Bryant was due to join them for supper that evening.

Daniel trespassed on *her* grounds now, and he wouldn't dare behave with impropriety before her father.

Or would he?

For goodness' sake, Lord Bryant was to be her future brother-in-law. As such, she would treat him with courtesy and respect. In return, she expected him to treat her with equal civility.

To bolster her confidence, she would wear her high-waisted Empire gown, the sapphire blue one that highlighted her eyes. Belgian lace circled the puffed sleeves and the daring décolletage, while an embroidery of scattered leaves lined its hem. Emily had said it set off her figure beautifully. She usually dismissed her sister's compliments, but tonight she hoped she spoke true. She needed to be firm in her resolution and not falter when Lord Bryant's eyes dipped to her mouth . . . or hers to his.

❧

FOR THE TEMPERATE September evening, the French doors to the upstairs drawing room had been thrown open to allow a breeze to whistle inside. Distant cries lured Julia onto the balcony. She crossed to the balustrade, her gaze drifting over the stretch of pristine back lawns, her brother's squeals piercing the air.

Her lips parted at the sight meeting her. Jonathan dangled precariously over Daniel's shoulders, his legs kicking, his fists pounding Daniel's back. His protests were interspersed with high-pitched yelps of delight as Daniel dipped and twirled the wildcat he carried like a sack of seed over his shoulder.

Daniel's state of dress—or rather undress—kept Julia frozen in place, as riveted to the sight before her as she had been to the foreign exhibits at the fair.

He had discarded his hat and jacket, and his dark waistcoat stretched taut over his lean torso. The sleeves of his white linen shirt had been rolled back, leaving his muscular forearms brazenly bare. Beguiled, Julia's gaze was glued to the teasing display of naked skin, and she swallowed.

"Jonathan could use a big brother, being coddled and cosseted by the two of us."

Julia snapped her mouth closed as Emily joined her. Her sister's comment gave her pause. Edmund would be Jonathan's brother, *not* Daniel. But she could not fathom her haughty duke with one gleaming button undone, let alone wildly frolicking with her brother. Or perching him on his shoulders as Daniel had done earlier at the fair.

Truth be told, Edmund bowed politely in Jonathan's direction and gave him a proper how-do-you-do. He then sought out Jonathan's nurse, as if greeting her brother was another duty to be dispensed with and the boy summarily dismissed.

"Few men interact well with children, Julia," Emily said softly. "I am sure it's different when it comes to their own."

Disconcerted at her sister's astute reading of her thoughts, Julia summoned a brave face and forced conviction into her tone. "Of course. I am sure Edmund will make a wonderful father."

"Mmh," Emily said.

Julia worried over her sister's noncommittal response, but another cry from Jonathan returned her attention to the scene below. A breeze combed through Daniel's dark hair, and as if it carried her scent, his head lifted and those compelling green eyes caught hers. As their gazes locked, he flashed her a white-toothed smile.

His gaze roamed over the blue ribbon securing her recalcitrant curls into a tight chignon, her bare shoulders, and the décolletage of her bodice. Like a ray of sun, his bold, admiring perusal warmed where it touched.

His smile abruptly vanished and he grunted, doubling over. With his guard down, Jonathan's foot had managed to connect with Daniel's gut. Recovering, Daniel caught Jonathan in time to slow his snakelike slither down Daniel's lean body and smooth the boy's landing on the ground.

The spell broken, Julia stepped back and savored the breeze that cooled her body.

Emily's laughter trilled, and she curled her arm through Julia's. "Shall we rescue our guest before Jonathan inflicts serious damage?"

She allowed Emily to draw her inside as a voice piped up in the back recesses of her mind.

And who would protect them from their guest?

❧

"He is an American sailor," Jonathan explained over a mouthful of succulent duck as he bounced up and down in his seat. "My ship captured him to help us fight Napoleon. He is my prisoner now."

"I see. While I am impressed by your exploits, I cannot say the same in regard to your display of table manners, or lack thereof," the Earl of Taunton said dryly, addressing his son. "Manners dictate one finishes chewing their food before speaking *and* refrains from fidgeting at the table."

Chastised, Jonathan slumped in his seat and regarded his father balefully. He dropped his fork with a clatter onto the fine Limoges china, the earl's crest gracing the top rim of the plate. "Done! Can I take my prisoner to walk the plank now?"

Her father eyed Jonathan's discarded fork and sighed. "It appears we have more work to do before you are ready to join the adult table. Your prisoner is our guest for the remainder of the meal, so plank walking will have to commence at a later date. You are excused, but next time *ask*." He waved his hand dismissively. "See to your ship in the kitchen."

"But you're eating with the enemy!" Jonathan protested.

Julia had to agree with her brother as she observed Daniel

glower at him in a mock threat, which Jonathan met with a ferocious scowl of his own.

They had settled in the family rooms, their intimate party too small for the cavernous formal dining area. Julia was stationed at the head of the table opposite her father, Daniel to her right, and Emily across from him. Jacket securely in place, snow-white cravat neatly tied, tousled hair tamed, Daniel was the portrait of a proper English gentleman. But like her brother, Julia knew what dangers simmered beneath his handsome, well-groomed façade.

"I think we can brave his company for the remainder of the evening. That will be all, Jonathan."

Jonathan sighed dramatically as he slid from his seat, snatched his napkin from his neck and stomped from the room, muttering under his breath. "As the captain, I should be giving the orders."

"Yes, well, if our Navy had refrained from conscripting, or rather, impressing American sailors in the first place, it might have saved us the expenses of what our foreign minister called that *millstone of an American war*," her father grumbled. "Waste of men and money with nary a thing to show for it."

"Actually, the Navy's poor compensation to their sailors planted the real seeds of the war," Daniel corrected. "Bad business practices."

"Bad business?" Her father furrowed his brow.

"The Navy first began seizing American merchant ships to recapture their own sailors who had fled by the thousands to the American vessels because they paid twice the amount in wages as the Royal Navy. You cannot blame the poor blokes for deserting in droves. The Royal Navy should have increased the sailors' pay, but with resources stretched to cover two wars, they were unable to do so." Daniel shrugged. "Inadequate wages breeds disgruntled workers, which leads to mutiny, or in this case, desertion."

"Hmph, good point," her father conceded.

"Is the war the reason you were unable to return home, Lord Bryant?" Emily asked, and Julia's interest perked at the question. She noted Daniel's slight hesitation before he responded.

"Partially. I left in 1810, and as the Royal Navy had blockaded all of America's eastern ports by 1814, a return trip would have proved difficult. That being said, the blockade proved a fortuitous boon for my company, so I am grateful to it despite its inconvenience." Giving a rueful smile, he lifted his glass and took a sip of his claret.

"How, pray tell, does a blockade benefit a transatlantic shipping company?" She could not hide her bafflement in response to his curious words.

Daniel faced Julia, a spark of interest lighting his eyes, and his smile broadened. "You are aware of my company? Curtis Shipping?"

She shifted in her seat, not willing to admit to having avidly scoured the morning papers for news on Curtis Shipping.

Her father rescued her from a reply. "Don't let her skirts fool you. Julia's head for business is more keen than mine. She and my bailiff ran Taunton Court the year following my wife's death. I . . . Well, I was not as focused on matters as I ought to have been."

Pleased at his praise, Julia smiled at her father. When her eyes met Daniel's, she was surprised to see a shadow darkening his features as he twirled his wine glass in his hand, staring into the liquid depths.

"Grief does take its toll. I am sorry for your loss, sir, but you are fortunate that Lady Julia was able to step in and manage matters. Not many would be able to do so. Not because of your gender, but rather your age." He smiled at her, quick to allay her protest as he continued. "Five years ago, you had barely turned eighteen. That is very young to have shouldered such responsibility. I am impressed." He dipped his head and lifted his glass in a toast. "As to your earlier question, you are very perceptive. Curtis Shipping did not benefit from the blockade, but rather the end of it."

"How so?" her father asked, leaning forward.

"While it was in place, Britain was starved of American

goods such as timber, cotton, and tobacco. During the war, my partner, Brett Curtis, and I cultivated relationships with the New England mill owners as well as the tobacco and cotton farmers riddling the south. We invested in a fleet of ships so when the blockade ended, we were poised to take advantage of the renewal of trade between the countries." Daniel grinned. "We exported the coveted goods, and the relationship benefited both parties, unlike the war."

"Brilliant, absolutely brilliant," her father said, admiration lighting his eyes. "Someone should have profited from that quagmire of a war." Mirroring Daniel's earlier gesture, he raised his glass in a toast. "Considering our poor harvest last year, your arrival home is fortuitous."

Daniel looked bemused. "Is there a correlation between exports and agriculture?"

"No. But there is a need for someone with a keen eye for accessing successful business ventures as well as reading those that are less profitable. You appear to possess an aptitude for both."

Puzzled, Daniel turned to Julia for further explanation, but her father's words equally baffled her. "I thought Lady Julia has managed—"

"It is not for me. I do not need assistance, but I am concerned that your brother does."

Out of the corner of her eye, Julia saw Daniel's smile falter, and she hastened to smooth over the impact of her father's words. "Daniel has no experience in running estates. I am not sure—"

"Running a company is not so different from running an estate," her father said, cutting her off. "There are men to manage, finances to be addressed, products to be obtained whether they are acquired through mills or farming." He paused and his eyes narrowed on Daniel. "Have you visited Bedford Hall yet?"

"No," Daniel replied after a slight hesitation. "To be honest, I was just discussing with Robbie Tanner my plans for the duration of my visit. Bedford Hall came up, but Robbie informed me that my brother is away hunting in Kent."

"Yes," the earl conceded. "However, that might be to your advantage, as Bedford is proprietary about his estate and has a right to be. That being said, you are family and Julia is his fiancée. As such, I doubt your visiting the property should arouse his ire. If you combined your keen head for business with Julia's talent for estate management, the two of you can assess matters, or at least determine the root of the tenants' concerns that have come to my attention. Together you can present your findings to Bedford and get the man to listen, as he refuses to do with me. Of course, Emily will join you as well."

Julia stared at her father, but when she glanced at Daniel, he appeared as stunned as she.

Daniel recovered more quickly, for a dazzling smile split his handsome features. "That's a brilliant idea, I'd be delighted to assess matters with Lady Julia and help in any capacity that I can. That is, if she is willing to accept my assistance and my company." He lifted a brow, awaiting her response.

He appeared thoroughly amused at her quandary.

She also recognized a challenging gleam in his eyes, as if he were tossing a gauntlet at her feet. She met his gaze straight on, for she was no coward. While wary of any joint venture with Daniel, Bedford Hall was to be her home—that is if her Damn Duke ever set a wedding date. Taunton had shared with her the grievances of Edmund's tenants. When she had questioned Edmund about the matter, he had assured her that the estate was turning a profit, and he had dismissed the matter with a haughty wave of his hand.

While she had not been successful, she balked at the idea of Daniel waltzing back, and like Homer's *Odyssey*, setting everything to rights after a decade away. As if he was the only one who could.

She had managed Taunton Court for nearly two years. She could take care of Bedford Hall once she was married. If working with Daniel gave her a rare opportunity to assess what she would be facing, she would not squander it. She lifted her chin and snatched up the gauntlet. "Maybe Lord Bryant and I can talk to a few tenants and get a better understanding of their needs. They might speak more freely without Edmund's presence, and once we have gathered some information, we can share it with Edmund." Anticipation filled her at the prospect of doing something active. Finally.

"Good, then it is settled." Her father appeared pleased. "Now then, I believe it is time for port. If you ladies will excuse us, I promise to keep an eye on the prisoner until your return," he grinned.

"You might want to curtail Lord Bryant's walk down the plank if you need his assistance for the foreseeable future," Emily added as she stood with Julia.

"You are right. After a lesson on table manners, I will teach Jonathan the meaning of clemency."

"I am indebted to you for your mercy," Daniel said, his eyes on Julia. His gaze swept over her bare collarbones and dipped to linger briefly upon the round curves of her breasts.

His look left her breathless, as if she had run up a flight of stairs, and her resolve momentarily wavered. Had she been too hasty in agreeing to this idea? No, she had not. Together they could accomplish so much, and her growing anticipation reaffirmed her decision. It was the right one.

In the future, she would simply dress more appropriately.

Chapter Six

❧

DANIEL did not know how the stars had aligned so that the next morning he found himself riding with the Chandler siblings to Bedford Hall. It was like Christmas morning had arrived early, and he had been given a precious gift.

Julia's straight-backed figure rode sidesaddle ahead, Jonathan beside her on his pony. She wore a sky blue riding habit and a bonnet set at a jaunty angle on her head with a scattering of flowers adorning its rim.

As he admired her competent handling of Constance, he mulled over how to get into her good graces. He needed to do so in order to decipher her true feelings for his brother. He could then determine the best way to tell Julia her fiancé was a coldhearted, good-for-nothing bastard. She'd be better off ruined through the scandal of a broken engagement than through marriage to him.

Such news had to be delivered delicately.

He shrugged off his misgivings. Julia was a strong woman. She would weather the news. Her management of her father's estates demonstrated her courage and strength.

An image of her blazing blue eyes and stinging slap had him shifting in his saddle and flexing his jaw, his confidence wavering.

So much for Christmas morning. Truth be told, his Christmases had never been all that grand, because they were spent with his father and Edmund. Why the devil should this be any better if he were given a present that he could never touch, let alone ever unwrap?

"You are scowling. Are you having doubts already?"

He jumped to find Julia beside him. "I am not allowed second thoughts, because I have been threatened with the dungeon should I fail. Worse, I am to be deprived of iced pudding and apple tarts."

"I see. Dire repercussions indeed." The twitch to her lips belied her somber tone. "'Tis a pity that we are finally at peace, and yet you remain a prisoner of a war that ended nigh on five years ago."

"Perhaps my timing was not as fortuitous as your father believes." He grinned. "Speaking of wars, peace, and my arrival, I am afraid we got off to a poor start with each other. I would like to make amends for that, as I am sorry for it."

A flicker of surprise crossed her features, and her gaze shot to Emily, who was pointing something out to Jonathan, oblivious to their exchange.

Daniel lowered his voice and pressed on. "I'd like it if we could begin again. This venture is important to both of us. You are protecting what will be your future, and I suppose I am safeguarding my past, or more specifically, my father's legacy. For our venture to succeed, we need to work together. If I promise to behave and try not to—"

"I understand. So a new beginning for the sake of what we find at Bedford Hall?" She appeared to ponder his words. "It might be wise to consider one for the sake of our future relations as well. After all, we will be brother and sister."

His hand shot up to cover his sudden spasm of coughs. *Over his dead body.* But he held his tongue. No point in negotiating an issue that might be rendered moot.

She looked at him strangely, clarifying her meaning. "Well,

one does not . . ." Her words tapered off and a pink flame
streaked the slim column of her neck. "That is, sisters and
brothers do not . . ."

"I understand." Unfortunately, he did. All too well. "So
shall we begin again?"

"I can agree to that," Julia replied, looking relieved at his
steering them back on topic. "Yes, I would like that. That is if
you stop behaving like a—"

"And I agree to that." He did not let her finish. Her words
might include *arrogant*, *brazen*, or *arse*. None of which were
diplomatic *or* flattering.

"Well, then. Welcome home, Daniel. It's been too long."

"Thank you."

She smiled, and when he returned her smile, something
hummed between them. An awareness of each other that hovered in the air like a warm breeze. For a few moments, he
savored the connection, which was severed when Julia tore
her gaze from his.

"Is it strange to be traveling over familiar ground after so
many years away?"

Distracted over thoughts of Julia and Edmund, Daniel had
paid little heed to the countryside they traversed. He stared
out over the lush, verdant rolling hills where splashes of sunlight created pools of yellow and gold on the lush green carpet.
His family seat was situated north of the Earl of Taunton's
property in Bedford, with Lakeview Manor dividing the neigh-
boring estates.

The familiar scents of sun-warmed grass, hay, and crisp
fresh air brought back a rush of memories. His father's love
of the land had been a tangible thing, a coat he wore like a
second skin and bequeathed to his sons. Years later, the rich
timbre of his father's voice resonated in Daniel's memories,
his pride palpable as he recounted their family's centuries-old
connection to it.

The Duke of Bedford's title had been created and rendered extinct several times. Throughout the centuries, their
fortunes had risen and fallen depending on the whims of the
monarch wielding power. It was not until the seventeenth

century, after the Glorious Revolution and its overthrow of the Catholic King James II, that their title was secured. Their support of the protestant William III on the throne had solidified their hold to the title, securing it for successive generations. Securing it for Edmund.

For Edmund to squander.

Or mishandle or whatever the hell he had done to it. "It is strange to be back, but pleasant, too. Being the spare heir, my connection to the land was different from my father and Edmund's, but I always felt it was strong. My father deeply ingrained his love and respect for the land and our heritage into both of us." He had neglected to ensure they cared for one another, but he had looked out for the land. "So what has happened over the years with Edmund and his estate? Has he lost that?"

Julia's blue eyes darkened. "I don't know too much about the past five years, other than to say that the tenants' discontent has been vocal enough to reach my father. The first few years, difficulties arose from neglect. After Edmund inherited the title and you sailed for America, Edmund left for London and rarely returned. It was as if he were avoiding home." Her voice softened. "As you said last night, grief takes its toll. I have witnessed that with both my father and Emily."

He clenched his jaw so tight, he feared it might crack. Edmund's mourning of their father had involved a fortnight of drunken revelry. He doubted his own departure had warranted a backward glance.

"A bailiff oversaw the estate, so things weren't perfect, but they weren't totally neglected."

"So he was mourning in London?" He struggled to keep his voice neutral, realized he had failed when Julia shot him a look.

"For the first few years, yes. I think . . . well, I believe that like my father, he was afraid to accept his responsibilities. It is not uncommon—"

"Your father?"

"My mother said my father also escaped to town when he inherited his title. He was a bit of a rake when she first met him, sowing his wild oats before donning the heavy mantle of an earl, so to speak. My mother eventually quite reformed him of his wicked ways." Pride laced her words.

"I have no doubt she turned him into a veritable saint," he murmured distractedly, her comment stirring up a wave of old memories. One after another tumbled over each other.

He saw Julia as a young girl, her hair a mop of wild and windblown curls and her cheeks dirt smudged. She was saving a collie, the runt of the litter, from a drowning. In another, she was pleading with him to help her make a nest for a wounded thrush. Later she had wheedled him into freeing a rabbit ensnared in a trap belonging to Weasel, Bedfordshire's notorious poacher. And Daniel had. How odd. Even as a girl, when she turned those beseeching blue eyes on him, he hadn't been able to resist her.

Some things never changed.

He studied her profile, noting the wistful smile that curved her lips as if she were lost in nostalgic memories of her parents.

He stilled and it was as if someone had sucked the air from his lungs.

Good God, is Julia planning to save Edmund as her mother had reformed her father?

He drew back on his reins, bringing Chase, the chestnut stallion he had procured from Robbie, to a stop.

Surprised, Julia glanced back at him and slowed her own mount, her expression one of concern. "Daniel?"

They both ignored Emily and Jonathan, who continued on. "Is that what you are hoping to do?"

"Excuse me?" Julia looked at him as if he had spoken in a foreign tongue.

"Do you hope to reform a rake?" He cocked a brow at her, daring her to refute his claim.

Her lips parted and she leaned away. They stared at each other in a silence that lengthened uncomfortably between them. Finally, her chin jutted in a familiar stubborn thrust. "People can and do change." Her eyes narrowed. "You are an example of that. Are you the same man that left home a decade ago?"

He stifled the urge to press a hand to his chest, for her point had struck its mark. It was painful, for the answer was no. No, he most certainly was not. He was a far cry from the runt who had fled for his life. He did not like to concede that, for it begged the question that if he was a different man from the one who had left, his brother might be, too. Or to acknowledge that with Julia's help, his brother could change.

For if anyone could save someone, Julia could. She had saved her father, his estate, and Emily, just as she had rescued the wounded animals in her childhood. It took a strong and loyal woman to do that.

Could her strength change Edmund? Her loyalty save him?

No. Every bone in his body, once bruised and battered from years under Edmund's fists, screamed a denial. Cruelty was not an item like clothing that one outgrew, or a trait easily shed like a second skin, but rather an attribute inherent to a person and which grew and matured with them. Or so Daniel believed.

Ten years was a long time, and Daniel could not in good conscience malign his brother until he had determined for himself if Edmund *had* changed. He had to judge his brother on the man he was today, not the man he had left behind. He did not like it, but for Julia's sake, he would try to do so.

"Yes. People do change." He spoke in a curt, clipped tone, as if each word was wrenched from him under torture. "So then, who is there for you?"

"I beg your pardon?" Her smile wavered.

"I was just wondering. Over the years, you have cared for your father, your brother, your father's estates, and your sister. Postponing your own marriage and life to do so. Now you are going to save Edmund and help him salvage his estates. I was just wondering, who is looking out for you?"

His question appeared to disarm her, for her eyes dropped to her lap, and she tightened her hands on her reins. In protest, Constance irritably tossed her head and whinnied until Julia loosened her grip. She regrouped quickly, straightening in her saddle and responding with a calm that belied her agitation. "As you can see, I am all grown up now, and quite capable of taking care of myself, thank you very much. Now I think we best catch up to Emily and Jonathan." She nudged Constance into a gentle trot.

He had caught the sheen of moisture blurring her vision before she turned away. Like Achilles, even the strongest warriors had their weak points, and he cursed himself for piercing hers.

Seeking to make amends, he urged Chase abreast of Constance. "I believe your father is right, and my arrival is fortuitous. As your future brother-in-law," he said, not choking over the words despite their bitter taste, "I will keep an eye out for you."

"Really, that is not necessary."

"Nevertheless, it is my pleasure to do so. As you say, we will be family, and that is what brothers do." He could not resist tossing her own words back at her, particularly when they served his purposes so well. "Look out for their sisters— even if they can save the world on their own. Don Quixote did not conquer his windmills alone. He had his faithful squire what's-his-name assisting him."

Julia's lips curved. "Sancho Panza, who was a simple farmer. Don Quixote was going off to fight *ferocious giants*, but which were windmills in reality." She looked dubious. "That's the best analogy you could come up with?"

"It serves my point." He waved his hand airily. "Which is, they did it *together*."

She looked pensive, as if giving serious consideration to his words, and then nodded. "Fine. You can be the short, squat Sancho Panza if you insist." She tossed him an arch look, pressed her heels into Constance's sides, and urged the mare to catch up with Emily and Jonathan, her laughter trailing behind her.

The lyrical cadence of it washed over Daniel in a warm wave, so beguiling him that it took him a few minutes before he realized he sat grinning like an idiot. He nudged Chase into a canter.

Her clever wit delighted him, but she was wrong about his analogy being poor. It was right.

Julia was the idealistic Don Quixote, mistaking a blackguard for a rake. Once again, Daniel was the cynical runt. So much for ten years of change. But like Don Quixote, the brave knight, he would look after his lady. Her momentary falter had told him, as Julia never would, that no one else had thought to do so.

His brave, beautiful warrior had been on her own far too long. It was time someone looked after her, for like poor Cervantes's illustrious knight, she was in for a painful awakening once her illusions were shattered.

Chapter Seven

Since its founding, Bedfordshire had been predominately a county of agriculture. The Dukes of Bedford and their tenant farmers had planted the age-old staple products of wheat, barley, and oats. Sheep and cattle grazed the grounds until the sheep were sheered in May. Drovers then herded the sheep and cattle to sell them off at the market before winter. Being mid-September, the farmers had finished harvesting most of the fields, and those that they had ridden past were in the process of being plowed.

Ploughboys dotted the carpet of brown fields, laboring to drive the plough in straight lines and break up the ground in preparation to be harrowed. Straw hats protected their heads from the sun, but its blinding rays stretched like long talons, plastering their shirts to their bent frames. Streaks of sweat drenched their backs and transformed white cotton shirts to a brownish-gray.

Daniel's father had directed servants to the fields with water and treats to alleviate the monotony of the tedious task. Daniel squinted down the dirt road curving like a beige ribbon between the fields and up the hill toward Bedford Hall. He frowned at the emptiness meeting the eye all the way to the horizon line.

"It's awfully warm, and I do not see any water barrels," Julia said. "I packed some parcels that include bread and cheese, but I believe thirst would be their priority." Julia echoed his thoughts.

"Let us continue on. See if we can determine if anyone is bringing something out, or if they are due to take a break soon."

"Are you sure we shouldn't speak to Edmund's bailiff? Shouldn't he view the grounds with us?"

There was a good reason Edmund's bailiff was not accompanying them. Depending on his size, or more important, his awareness of Daniel and Edmund's relationship, Daniel could not risk being tossed off the estate. His departure might not be feetfirst or in one piece. Riding would be difficult with broken bones.

He decided against sharing his dilemma with Julia. "The bailiff, like Edmund, might hinder the tenants from speaking freely, particularly if the aim of our visit is to encourage them to voice their concerns without fear of repercussion."

Julia considered his words and nodded. "They might not be willing to speak to us either, which is why I packed some of Cook's treats." She grinned. "Bribery does wonders to loosen one's tongue, as do Cook's sugar biscuits."

Seeing the mischievous glint in her eyes, he smiled. He was not the only one who understood the need for subterfuge and guile to gain the tenants' trust. Combining their talents might be more successful than he had anticipated. "I remember those biscuits. One bite should dissolve any misgivings about our visit. Nothing says 'we come in peace' better than sugar biscuits."

"Let us hope they are as easily bribed as you. You always had a sweet tooth as a boy. Last night, I learned that has not changed."

"Some things aren't worth changing." He smiled, unrepentant.

"Eating four slices of Cook's cheesecake for example?" Julia looked dubious.

"Most definitely," Daniel agreed, pleased she had noticed his overindulgence. That she had noticed him, period. Which wasn't right. He had no need of her noticing anything about him. That was not the future of their friendship. He would be wise to remember that.

They rode on, bypassing the fields. Eventually they turned onto the lane of small, rustic houses leased to Bedford's tenants.

The color had been bleached out of the area, leaving the somber earth tones of beige, sandy wheat, and brown umber. The ubiquitous wildflowers, spilling over the grounds of most English homes, were absent. The houses sat in a row like square-box sentries, bleak, weather-beaten, and enshrouded in a stillness and silence so complete it deafened.

He frowned, recalling from his childhood the cries of children, laundry flapping on clotheslines, dogs barking, and chickens squawking as they dodged the horses' powerful hooves. It was as if another scene had been painted over the one he remembered, the transformation so complete.

On medieval English maps, mapmakers marked those areas that reach beyond the perimeters of their known world, "here be dragons." He had an urge to peer around for those dragons, but he wouldn't find them here. The beast was hunting in Kent.

Disturbed, he drew back on the reins and eased Chase to a stop. "Let us continue on foot."

Dismounting, he led Chase over to a split rail fence, tying him securely. He assisted the others to dismount, careful not to linger with his hands around Julia's waist.

Despite his intentions, he could not resist inhaling her fresh and clean scent before forcing himself to step back. He directed her to tie her horse with Emily's and Jonathan's to a birch tree away from Chase and downwind from his scent.

They had finished securing the horses, when Jonathan's cry rang out. "Something hit me!" He clutched his back.

Daniel whirled, his body tense, his senses alert. Catching sight of an apple rolling along the ground, he relaxed. He searched for the source of the apple's launch, and caught a flash of movement in a nearby tree.

"This means war." Jonathan bellowed and dashed toward the offender.

Cursing under his breath, Daniel bolted after the boy. Catching up to him, he hooked his arm around Jonathan's waist and hoisted him onto his hip. "Hold up there, Captain. We are trespassing on someone else's property, and they have a right to protect it."

"They fired without warning." Like an entrapped snake, Jonathan protested and wiggled in Daniel's grip.

Daniel cursed the legacy of a war-weary country. Despite being at peace for over five years, fighting a war on two fronts had left its brand on past generations and clearly had made inroads into future ones as well.

"Go away! We don't want no more bloomin' foreigners stealing our jobs. And we ain't payin' no more higher rents."

"We come in peace." Daniel called out, keeping his tone conciliatory. "And we bear gifts." He arched his hand over his eyes to protect it from the sun's glare as he peered up into the dark web of branches.

"You sound American, for isn't that how the Pilgrims greeted the Indians?" Julia murmured.

"If so, they were soon feasting together." He spoke as quietly as she. "That tree is laden with apples, so there's hope for us. Unless our loose cannon gets free," he hissed under his breath, shifting Jonathan onto his shoulders. "See anyone from that vantage point?"

"No sign of the enemy yet," Jonathan yelled back.

Julia covered her mouth to stifle her laughter. Daniel was about to ask her if she planned to enjoy the show or assist in diffusing the war, when a pair of spindly legs in beat-up boots dangled from the tree and dropped to the ground.

A young girl sprawled in the dirt. Springing to her feet, she tugged down her skirts and her dust-covered apron. She straightened her mobcap, two black braids swinging beneath it. She appeared to be around seven or eight years old. "You sure you ain't no good for nothin', grotty Irish eejits here to nick our jobs and the food out of our bellies?" Her eyes blazed in dark fury, her small fists raised.

"Cor, she needs a tongue washing," Jonathan giggled.

"Shh." He squeezed Jonathan's calf. The girl's anger had been stoked by a parent's bitter ire, voiced without censure.

Something was rotten in the state of Denmark. If the girl's words were to be believed, it involved raised rents and the hiring of Irish laborers. Before he had left America, there were signs of Irish immigrants moving into the mills populating New England. Undoubtedly, they sought a warmer welcome across the Atlantic, for the roots of the animosity between the Irish and English were planted centuries ago and dug deep.

Julia stepped forward. "I assure you we are as English as you, and as Lord Bryant says, we come bearing food. I am Lady Julia Chandler, and you are?"

The girl gaped at Julia, her eyes midnight black and enormous. They roamed over them, until they pinned Jonathan in an accusatory glare.

"He is harmless. But should he get out of hand, I will tie him up with the horses," Daniel promised, his expression solemn.

"Will not," Jonathan squealed, kicking out.

"Will, too," Daniel shot back, trapping his legs with a gloved hand and winking at the girl.

A giggle escaped. "Blimey, you don't sound like no Irish eejits. You be a lord, like yonder damn duke?"

Jonathan hooted. "Now she's done it! She'll be swallowing soapsuds for sure."

"Beatrice. Beatrice Alice Mabry!" a voice thundered, causing the girl to freeze and hunch her shoulders.

The deep baritone belonged to a large man with lined, weatherworn features, who hastened over. His hair and eyes were as black as his daughter's and just as cold as they leveled on their group. He carried a large spade and wore dirt-stained overalls. He planted a protective hand over the girl's shoulders.

"Your Grace." A tic vibrated in his cheek, a telltale sign he struggled to cap the anger the young girl could not. "I apologize for my daughter. Beatrice can be outspoken." He cleared his throat, but forged on. "Can I assist you with anything? Your bailiff was down here last week and spoke to us about the vacant houses." He jerked his head down the street.

While curious to hear what the man had to say, Daniel had learned from Julia that people did not like to be deceived. "I am sorry, I am His Grace's twin, Lord Bryant, and I have recently returned after years abroad."

The man scrutinized Daniel's features, and his grip on his daughter's shoulder relaxed. Something flared in his eyes, a recognition. The tension gripping him eased, and his smile was tentative. "Lord Bryant, welcome home."

Daniel caught the hint of warmth coloring his tone. He had always been on friendlier terms with the tenants, Edmund keeping his ducal distance. From their polar opposite welcomes, it was clear that some things had not changed.

"Lady Julia, my brother's lovely fiancée; her sister, Lady Emily; along with their younger brother, Lord Jonathan, have graciously accompanied me on this visit, because Bedford is in Kent on a hunting trip." He tried to look apologetic. "I am afraid, my impatience got the better of me, and I could not wait for his return. Is your offer of assistance still open?"

"Of course." Worry darkened his eyes. "But my wife be sick. I can't leave her for long. She—"

"Please, Mr. . . . ?" Julia interceded, stepping forward, her expression concerned.

"Mabry, Tim Mabry, and this here is my Beatrice."

"I'm just Bea," his daughter corrected. "'Cause I can sting like a bee," she proclaimed.

Having weathered her sting, Daniel's lips twitched at the apt name.

"I'm Jonathan 'cause . . . 'cause that's what my father named me. Can I get down?" He bounced excitedly on Daniel's shoulders. "I want to climb Just Bea's tree, scout for Irish eejits, and fire apples at them."

Daniel ducked his head to hide his snicker as he lifted Jonathan and set him onto his feet.

"There will be absolutely no firing apples at anyone," Julia spoke firmly, not as amused as he. "Not one, Jonathan. But if you stay on the lowest branches, and Bea keeps an eye on you, you may climb the tree," Julia relented.

"Fine. Fine," he muttered, tossing her a mulish look.

Bea looked to her father, who nodded his permission, and she scampered to the apple tree, Jonathan in close pursuit.

"Is there still an orchard on the southwest corner of the estate?" Daniel asked.

Mabry looked surprised. "Yes, sir, there is."

"I remember climbing those trees as a boy," he marveled. The memory lightened his mood. Some things don't change.

"Mr. Mabry, you mentioned your wife was ill?" Julia said, her brow furrowed.

"Yes, my Izzy. She was laid low with a mean sickness. Fever broke, and she is recoverin' her strength, but it's been slow goin'."

Julia stepped forward. "I am relieved to hear that. Mr. Mabry, one of the reasons we are here is to check up on the tenants in the duke's absence. Determine if they have any needs with which we can assist. Why don't you let Emily and me see to your wife? In that manner, you can take some time to catch Lord Bryant up on the years he has missed."

"That's a good idea." Emily smiled at Julia.

Daniel agreed. Mabry might hesitate to voice his concerns to Edmund's fiancée, let alone discuss working conditions with a woman, despite Julia's accomplishments. Divide and conquer. Deftly done. His admiration for Julia grew.

Mabry scratched his head, a picture of indecision.

"Please, let us do this for your wife. It would mean so much to Lord Bryant to travel the grounds with someone who has knowledge of the land."

"Well, I don't know. With my Izzy sick, the house is upside down. I'm not too good a hand at—" A flush darkened his worn features.

"I understand." Julia employed a soothing cadence. "I am sure you have done the best you can, but for now let us assist you. That is why we are here."

Before Mabry could voice another protest, Julia and Emily

smiled reassuringly. Julia gave Daniel a pointed look before they headed to Mabry's front gate.

Mr. Mabry stared blankly at the women as they walked up the path to his closed door.

"She has a way about her once her mind is made up," Daniel said ruefully.

Mr. Mabry rubbed a hand over his crown of dark hair, looking a bit lost. "Well, I . . . Well, then." His wariness had returned. "Did you want to speak to His Grace's bailiff, I'm sure he could—"

"I am sure he could, but as I am here now, why don't I begin with you? I can speak with the bailiff in due course." It was a half-truth. "Please, will you walk the immediate grounds with me?"

Mabry appeared torn but after a brief struggle, he gave a curt nod. "I can."

"Good. Why don't you lead the way. I understand my brother is bringing in Irish laborers?" He refrained from explaining where he had received his information, omitting its colorful delivery. "Are there not enough tenants to do the work? You mentioned vacant houses?"

As they walked, broken panes of glass, loose shutters, and other signs of disrepair on a few houses answered his question. What he did not understand was why they were left in such a state, not to mention vacant, rather than turned over to new tenants. Why hadn't Edmund overseen their upkeep?

Mabry thrust his hands into his pockets. He studied the unoccupied houses, and then his focus settled on Daniel, his eyes narrowing. "Are you returned for good, sir? Or just visiting?"

He understood the underlying question. Did he hold a position of authority in regard to matters of the estate? The short and definitive answer was no. Daniel hadn't inherited the estates, but he had inherited his father's love of the land and a sense of responsibility to honor his family's legacy. He refused to sit by and see Edmund squander it.

"I am not leaving for a while, and I do plan to speak to my brother about any concerns I have in regard to the estate. Any information you can share provides me with a better under-standing of where things stand today and helps me to make a more informed decision." He spoke the truth.

Perhaps Julia was right, and Edmund had changed, and he would listen to Daniel. Right. And soon Daniel would be joust-ing with windmills. He met Mabry's hard look. "More impor-tantly, I give you my word that anything you share with me will be kept in strict confidence between us. No names will be mentioned. I promise you, you can speak freely."

Mabry gave Daniel the same keen scrutiny that he had earlier, and finally replied with a curt nod. He continued walk-ing. "My family has been tenants on this land for nigh on five generations. I grew up here and remember you and your brother ridin' with the late duke." He glanced at Daniel and fell quiet for a few strides.

"Your father liked to visit the tenants, to ride over the land, to speak with the farmers. Sometimes with his bailiff and some-times without." They stopped when they came to the edge of one of the fields. He gazed out over the ploughboys, thrusting his hands into his overall pockets. "Your father was a different type of landholder than your brother."

"Bedford doesn't visit too much?"

"He does not." He echoed Julia's account of Bedford's early years in London, filling in the later years that she could not account for. "Bedford returned about six years ago. First thing he did was to get a new bailiff, firin' your father's man. Rents were doubled and household repairs were to come out of our own pockets." Mabry rubbed his neck. "Tenants left." He nod-ded to the empty houses.

"We got by. A year passed, and Napoleon was defeated. The war with America also ended, and then the soldiers started comin' home in droves. Millions of discharged veterans seekin' work. Many willin' to take lower wages to get it." Mabry shrugged. "Your brother hired 'em. Cut our wages to match theirs. Then the Irish started comin'." He nodded to the ploughboys, his expression grim. "An even cheaper labor. Get-tin' by got a bit harder, as many of us were forced off the fields. Not enough work for everyone. More tenants left." Mabry kicked at a stone in the dirt, sending it skittering across the road. "The end of the wars also meant foreign grain could enter Britain, so our grain prices fell. In response, our wages were further lowered, while the price of bread rose.

"Last year was a bad harvest. We could have muddled through with what we reaped the year before, but many of the workers being immigrants and veterans, some have never farmed or worked the land before. They didn't know to get the corn ricks thatched and covered before the first rain, and we lost half a crop. Rations down, people go hungry." He faced Daniel. "Hungry people lead to poachin' and crime. Lost a few cattle and some sheep last winter.

"Your brother soon started runnin' through bailiffs. If one listened to our complaints, he was replaced." He nodded in the direction of Bedford Hall. "Two more families gave notice 'cause ain't no guarantee of work no more. Pretty soon all the work will go to seasonal laborers. If we resort to doing just seasonal work, we can't claim relief from the poor rate because you have to work at least a year to be able to make a claim."

Mabry spat on the ground and lifted his gaze to Daniel's, bitterness contorting his features. "Sir, I suggest you have that talk with your brother. I suggest you do so before their ain't no more of us left. I expect that's not what you wanted to hear for your homecomin', but somebody needs to hear it, fore it's too late." He clamped his jaw shut, and his brooding gaze moved back to the fields.

Mabry had said more than enough. Daniel looked out over the lines of ploughed earth, seeing nothing, his thoughts churning.

Robbie had written of the grumbles over Bedford's management, and Taunton had warned of the same. Daniel had expected problems, but along the lines of neglected repairs, tenants' feuds, bad crops, and the fallout of a poor harvest. Not this. A tale of stringent, penny-pinching, parsimonious management.

The six ducal properties, covering two hundred thousand acres, should bring in an annual income of eighty thousand pounds. It was a small fortune. Thus, it begged the question, why the bloody hell did Edmund need more money? Was he in debt? And what long-term price was he willing to pay to extract it?

The estate's profits were reaped through the land. Without reliable, stable, and loyal men to work it, the whole system collapsed. It didn't take an astute businessman to understand the age-old cycle, or that Edmund's cost-cutting measures were like shoving a wedge into the spokes of a spinning wheel. If he continued unabated, everything would grind to a stop. Daniel's words to Taunton echoed. *Inadequate wages breeds disgruntled workers, which leads to mutiny or desertion.* Not to mention, poaching and crime.

He scrubbed his hands down his face. Damn Edmund. Damn him for apparently not changing a whit in ten years. For being a cruel, selfish bastard.

He dropped his arms. Changes had to be made. He didn't know what or how, but he had to intercede. Things could not continue on as they were. He recalled the letter that had lured him back to England. *Claim your destiny.* His eyes squinted out over the fields. This was his destiny. He might not be able to claim it, but he could bloody well save it. He'd have Robbie add it to his agenda.

At least Mabry's words removed one item from his growing list. He no longer needed to speak to Julia about Edmund. If she was as bright a businesswoman as her father touted her to be, everything that needed to be said was right here.

If Julia was still bent on marrying Edmund, well, then, she was not the woman Daniel believed her to be. Like Don Quixote, his beautiful warrior would be seeing illusions instead of windmills.

But Daniel believed otherwise. He had come to know Julia over the past couple of days. She may be idealistic, but she was strong and brave. She would see the truth. And he would be there to help her pick up the pieces once she did.

That was what faithful squires did.

Chapter Eight

J ULIA spread a blanket on the ground near the apple tree where Jonathan and Bea scrambled like monkeys. Neatening her skirts, she leaned back against the chipped and peeling picket fence and closed her eyes. She needed to sit for a minute.

Bea and Jonathan's bellows drifted to her. She had banned Jonathan's use of the word *eejits*, but dared not contemplate what choice language would replace it. She doubted her father would find his son's expanded lexicon as amusing as Daniel had.

Thinking of Daniel, she opened her eyes to peer along the stretch of road leading to the fields. He had disappeared well over an hour ago, which was fine, for it had taken her and Emily that long to deal with the disarray in Mabry's cottage.

At least Mrs. Mabry was recovering. She had even regained enough strength to deliver a stinging diatribe against Edmund's bailiff. While Emily shared a small repast with Mrs. Mabry, Julia had escaped outside, having lost her appetite over all she had heard. She had also wanted to check on Jonathan, ensure he hadn't killed anyone.

She squinted into the apple tree, locating her brother. He straddled a low branch, a wide-eyed, owlish look crossing his features as he listened to Bea, who no doubt was prattling on about the ills of the Irish. Julia's lips twitched, for truth be told, she shared Daniel's amusement toward Bea. She admired her audacity. It reminded her of herself as a girl before she had to pin her hair up.

Her attention returned to Jonathan. The ton would not approve of the heir to an earldom romping about with Just Bea and her saucy tongue. But nor would they approve of an earl's daughter shoving up her sleeves and plunging her arms elbow deep into soapsuds and dirty dishwater. But she had done so, and if need be, would do so again. The need to do something to help out that poor, bedridden woman had erased all Julia's doubts.

That was why she had never belonged in London. She belonged here, listening to the rewarding sound of Mrs. Mabry's laughter when Julia had teased her about Bea's colorful vocabulary. Mrs. Mabry's pride in her daughter had matched her derision for Edmund's bailiff.

Julia's mood plummeted. She shaded her eyes and squinted down the road, looking for signs of Daniel.

Where was he? And what had he learned?

Some squire he was. She gnawed on her lower lip as she recalled his vow to look out for her. It had caught her off guard, for she could not remember the last time someone had offered to help her. Then again, she had never asked for help. However, Daniel's vow didn't concern her too much, for where was he now? Nowhere to be found.

"Now who is looking doubtful?"

As if he had heard her rebuke, there he was. He stood in a halo of sunlight, like an archangel grinning at her. More like a fallen angel. At the sight of his devilish grin, something fluttered in her chest. He had discarded his jacket, gloves, and hat, and once again rolled up his sleeves to his elbows. The sight of his naked forearms so boldly displayed had her struggling to stand.

Daniel offered his hand, and after a slight hesitation, she

accepted it. Slipping her fingers into his, the heat of his skin seeped through her leather glove. His forearm was hard muscle and strong, and he pulled her up with ease. Her traitorous heart emitted another flutter.

He was so close, she could smell his masculine scent, sweat mixed with a lingering hint of sandalwood soap. A lock of hair fell over his forehead, and his eyes were as green as the meadows they had ridden past. He was her Beautiful Bedford . . . only he was not.

A clamp constricted her chest, stifling its flutters. She withdrew her hand and stepped back. "Where have you been? Where is Mr. Mabry?"

"He stayed at the fields. Did you miss me?"

Was he serious? Or teasing?

When she simply looked at him, he laughed. He nodded to Mabry's house. "What are you doing out here? Have you been sitting here all this time? Where's Emily?"

"Sitting out here?" she echoed. "Yes, I have just been whiling away the hour, watching the apples grow and the wind blow because I daren't get my hands dirty or my riding habit dusty."

She had his attention now. His eyes snapped back to her, his gaze roving over her hair, which she imagined looked like a bird's nest with loose strands and tendrils sticking out in every which way. When she had confronted the disarray comprising Mabry's house, she had removed her bonnet and riding jacket and rolled up her sleeves. She was well aware that her pristine riding habit was streaked with dust, dirt, and God knew what else she had collected as she and Emily had swept the place clean.

His smile vanished. "My apologies. Was it terrible? Will she be all right?"

His apology stole the wind from the sails of her irritation. "Well, Mrs. Mabry is regaining her strength. She should be on her feet in a week or two. However, with her bedridden so long, the house was in as sorry a state. It needed a thorough cleaning. Mabry had stoked the fire, so we were able to warm a kettle of water and dispense with the dishes. They don't own

many, but of the few they do, I believe Mabry used them all."
She grinned.

"You did the dishes?"

She wondered if she had dirt on her face, for he stared at
her so strangely. "Well, yes, short of a maid, who else was
there?"

"Who else indeed," he murmured.

"We sorted out the clothes strewn everywhere, did a bit of
dusting and sweeping. I cleaned one of the windows to get
some light into the rooms, and Emily filled their cupboard
with some of the loaves of bread and wedges of cheese I
brought."

"Is that all?"

"Well, I will send a maid down to collect the wicker basket
of dirty clothes to have them laundered at Taunton Court.
There is no other way. I intend to speak to the vicar, make
arrangements for someone to check in on them regularly. We
will have to assess the situation of the other tenants. I will
advise the parish to put together more food supplies for others
in need. But on the whole, it was nothing we could not
handle."

"Except for the laundry."

Surprised, she looked at him, but his tone was teasing, and
she relaxed. "Yes, but I have taken care of that."

"Of course you have."

She froze when, light as a feather, his fingers swept something from her hair.

"Just a cobweb." He shook his hand, sending the gossamer
threads sailing in the wind.

"If you find anything else in there, don't tell me, particularly if it lives." She shuddered.

Laughing, he leaned close to peer into her hair. He tucked
a loose strand behind her ear, a warmth in his eyes. "Nothing
else. You are quite safe, except for some dirt just here." His
finger brushed her cheek.

Her face flamed, and her hand shot up to scrub the dirt-
streaked area.

"Now you've done it," he laughed. "Look at your gloves."

Following his gaze, she gasped. Her gloves were beyond filthy.

He crossed to the fence over which he had draped his jacket, withdrawing a handkerchief from its inside pocket. Returning, he presented it to her. "Try this."

"Thank you." She accepted it and stepped back as she wiped her cheek. He was too big and too close, and his teasing smile disturbed her pulse. Besides, she had an urge to brush back that errant lock of hair and press her finger to the intriguing dent in his chin. "All gone? How do I look?"

His gaze roved over her features so carefully that she squirmed. His smile was slow and easy. "Beautiful, as always."

Her lips parted. *Beautiful*. No one had ever called her so. Emily was the classic English beauty with her fair looks, while Julia had fine eyes. She closed her mouth and tucked the compliment away to savor later. It was a weak vanity, but betrothed to Bedford, men were circumspect in their attentions to her. Few praised her outright, and none complimented her. *Until Daniel.*

"I don't suppose it ever occurred to you that you could have collected some servants to assist you with cleaning up? That you did not have to do it all yourself?"

She returned his handkerchief. "Actually, Emily did suggest that. But contrary to my social status exempting me from doing so, I am quite capable of washing a dish and pushing a broom." She shrugged. "That family needed our help, and they will be my tenants soon, too. That makes their welfare my responsibility. I could not very well turn my back on them."

"Of course you couldn't. Nor would you seek assistance. What was I thinking?"

She wondered at the strange glow in his eyes and its odd effect on her. After a moment, she recovered her voice. "And the grounds? How bad is the situation?"

The glow faded and his expression darkened. He gestured to the blanket on the ground. "Why don't we sit and I will update you." Jonathan and Bea's giggles carried to them, and they observed the two dangling from a low branch. "I see Bea and Jonathan have joined forces. The Irish don't stand a chance."

She smiled. "I fear you are right."

"Excuse me for one second." He winked and strode over to the tree. He spoke to Bea, and tossed something to her, which she snagged. She then scrambled up the tree and dropped two apples into Daniel's waiting grasp. He bowed graciously, flashed his potent smile, and returned to her side.

"What was that all about?"

"A business transaction. One bob for two apples." He grinned. "I believe she got the better of the deal. Apple?"

She stripped off her dirty gloves and lifted her hands to catch his offering.

He hesitated, a teasing gleam entering his eyes. "Maybe I should reconsider. Remember what happened to Eve when she ate the apple? She got exiled."

"But she gained wisdom, which made her smart enough to put some clothes on."

"And therein lies the true biblical tragedy." Daniel sighed as he lobbed the apple to her. "If she hadn't been tempted by Satan, we would all be naked, happy, and still frolicking in the Garden of Eden."

"What happens when winter comes? It could get chilly."

"That is the best part." He sat on the blanket, then caught her bare hand and pulled her down. He leaned against the fence, and when she had settled her skirts around her and leaned back beside him, he tapped his shoulder to hers. "We would have to combine our body heat to stay warm."

Smiling, she shifted away from him and shook her head. "I fear that would fail. Without knowledge, they would be too slow to do so, and would freeze to death. It would be the end of all mankind. Eve was wise to eat that apple." She bit into her own.

He laughed. "Clever. I see why you were so competent managing Taunton's estates. Nothing escapes you and you are willing to get your hands dirty. You have a keen mind for resolving problems you cannot manage on your own, as shown in your arranging the laundry to be cleaned at Taunton Court. Will you work for my company?"

More compliments to tuck away with the other. As much as they pleased her, his words reminded her why they had come, and her smile faded. "I am needed here. More than I realized." She set her apple down. She had lost her appetite again.

Daniel appeared to sober as well. "Did Mrs. Mabry say anything to you?"

She recounted the woman's harangue. "What did you learn from Mabry?" He filled her in on Mabry's account of the last few years. The two accounts differed in one manner. "She blamed Edmund's bailiffs. Refused to believe Bedford was sanctioning their stringent measures. Contrary to her husband, she believes Bedford is not as informed on matters as the late duke had been. He doesn't . . . Edmund doesn't visit the tenants or ride over the grounds."

"What are your thoughts?" He had finished his apple and tossed the core onto the blanket beside them.

She gnawed on her lower lip, her emotions in conflict. She wanted to defend Edmund. But she could not. *The estate turns a profit.* Edmund's cold and dismissive words haunted her. "I . . . I honestly do not know. But it appears that things have been neglected."

"Yes, they have. But as you said, that is why you are needed here." He gave her a reassuring smile.

"Yes, it is. I'll . . . I will speak to Edmund. See what he has to say."

He nodded. "That is a start."

The doubt in his voice gave her pause. "Do you think he will listen?" The question escaped her before she could bite it back, but she was desperate to know his opinion.

He pursed his lips as if contemplating the matter, and then grinned as if an amusing thought had struck him. "If anyone can get Edmund to listen, it would be you. After all, you possess another talent. You are very persuasive about getting people to do your bidding." His eyes dipped to her lips.

She blinked, but refused to rise to his bait. "Not everyone is as easily persuaded as you."

He laughed. "I had a keen interest in what you offered." He winked at her, and ignoring her quelling glance, he continued. "It is all about dangling the right rewards to get someone to do your bidding. So what does Edmund want?"

He still stared at her mouth, and she found her gaze dropping to his. She noticed his bottom lip was fuller than his top. She swallowed. What was his question? Her mind had gone utterly blank, like an unwritten page expectantly waiting to be filled. She dared not voice with what.

"I have a bellyache."

She jerked back. Good lord, had she been leaning toward Daniel? Admiring his lips? She lifted an unsteady hand to comb it through her hair, struggling to focus on Jonathan, who had crumpled onto the blanket and lay curled in a ball, groaning.

"Poor boy, someone has overindulged in too many apples," she crooned. "Lie down, love. Hopefully it will settle in a little while."

Daniel came to his feet. Grabbing his jacket from the fence, he laid it over Jonathan. He folded it around his small figure, scooping up a lone apple that had rolled free of Jonathan's clutch.

The now-familiar flutter kicked beneath her breast. She pressed her hand to her chest as Daniel leaned against the fence, tossed the apple into the air and deftly caught it. He never could sit still. She had noticed that earlier. He was always fidgeting, like a coiled ball of energy. Almost like a five-year-old boy. Her eyes strayed to Jonathan, who was flat out.

"Edmund wants a profit. You need to present him with a business proposal that helps the tenants and profits Edmund. The real problem is the surplus labor that is taking jobs and cutting into the tenants' wages. Some of these men are foreigners, but many are returning veterans who need and deserve the work." He frowned.

"So we need more work?" she asked.

"Right," he answered distractedly, his eyes on Bea, who was shuffling slowly toward them, holding her apron out in front of her. In it, she cradled half a dozen apples.

She spoke to Daniel. "Six bob for the lot."

Daniel eyed the number of apples and cocked a brow. "In twenty minutes, your price has doubled?"

Bea glowered. "I done picked 'em. That makes the price for the apples *and* labor."

He rubbed his chin, appearing in deep contemplation. "Four bob and you have a deal. Three for the apples and one for your bold business style."

Bea huffed out her breath. "Fine, fine." She knelt and unfurled her apron onto the blanket. Daniel handed over the coins, and she held them in her fist, her smile radiant.

"I'm going to show me mum," Bea cried. She bobbed a curtsy and dashed off.

Julia smiled. "I see why you are a successful businessman. Very clever negotiation."

"I am good at negotiating. Had to be to cut a deal with New England mill owners. A bunch of tight-fisted, reticent, intractable . . ." His words trailed off. His eyes studied the apple he held, turning it over in his hand. When his eyes lifted to hers, wonder crossed his features. "I know how we can get more work."

"How?"

"A cider mill!" His smile was blinding. "The cider mills in New England are a booming industry. In addition to the cider, the apples and edible waste from the mills provide feed for the pigs and other livestock. Mabry mentioned there are still orchards on the southeast acreage, and a few trees are clearly scattered around some of the tenants' property." He strode over to the apple tree, plucked one down and brandished it at Julia.

"That will cost you a half bob," she warned with a grin. She stood, drawn to his infectious excitement.

"Worth it." He winked. "Edmund gets his profit by leasing the land to a mill owner, the veterans can get work in building and operating it, the tenants get their jobs back, and can also sell their apples to the mill. A lot of owners like a variety of apples to blend and make cider of variable juice types, in addition to making the hard cider. They could also custom press the tenants' apples, if the tenants desire. They would charge a nominal crushing fee for that."

"And if the venture is successful, Edmund could reinvest the money he charged for leasing the property back into the mill and glean a share of the profits," Julia added.

"That is if your duke is smart enough to soil his hands in trade." He caught her hand, plunked the apple into it, and curled her fingers around it. "You win the prize of the day. You are incredible. Do not let anyone tell you otherwise."

Warmth suffused her. Another compliment. *Incredible*. She might like this one best of all, but *beautiful* was a close second. "It was your idea. I now understand why Curtis Shipping is such a success."

"You have read about my firm," Daniel accused.

"I have," she conceded, laughing at his look of surprised delight. "You have done well. You should be proud."

Looking pleased, he inclined his head. "Thank you. But I had help. As I have said, I have an American partner, Brett Curtis, who is an old friend of mine. I met him while at Dunbar Academy. To my everlasting gratitude, his mother was from here and demanded her only son be educated in England."

"It appears that combining forces to work together rather than separately is smart business sense. Good thing I have my faithful squire."

He grinned. "Let us just hope that Edmund is of like mind."

Her smile wavered, and it took her a minute before she could recover. "Yes, well, we should head back now. We have already lost one member of our party." She nodded to Jonathan. "I should collect Emily."

"Apples and scouting for the Irish eejits take their toll," Daniel quipped. "He can ride with me. We will tie his pony to Constance."

"That is kind of you."

"It is my pleasure."

His words were soft and warm and curled around her. She

stood transfixed before she forced herself to move away. Her steps were heavy as she made her way to the Mabrys' house, her thoughts straying to Edmund.

Surely he would listen to her. Like his brother, he would understand. They could not be that different, could they? But if she were honest, she had absolutely no idea of what Edmund would do, and that frightened her most of all. She should know the man's thoughts. After all, she was going to marry him. To spend her life with him.

She firmed her lips and lifted her chin. She would speak to Edmund, and soon she would know everything. She had gotten one side of the story here. It was time to get the other. Edmund's side.

Chapter Nine

❧❧

THEY visited more tenants over the next few weeks. Julia and Emily wheedled their way into their good graces with food baskets and queries about needs the parish might be able to address. While Julia dispersed their bounty, Daniel met with some of the veterans working in the fields, culling those out who had building, engineering, or experience working in a mill. He spoke to Taunton about potential mill owners or men in trade who might be interested in leasing the land.

As he gained Mabry's trust, Daniel casually asked if the tenants recalled the fire at Lakeview Manor and any discussion of it afterward. Mabry's reply had been strangely enigmatic, and they were the only words he had ever recounted as having come directly from Edmund.

Fire was of grave concern to anyone living in the vicinity, so his brother had made a rare appearance after the manor's blaze to assure the tenants of it being an isolated incident. He had told them that now that Lord Bryant had left the country, they were not to worry over it. Mabry repeated Edmund's words with a dismissive shrug while Daniel had snorted at the strange, Shakespearian edict. All was well, so sayeth His Grace, the arrogant prig of a duke.

But what the devil did he mean?

Had he held Daniel responsible for the fire? And therefore with his absence, they were safe? It had been all he could do to hold his tongue before Mabry. He forced himself to shelve his questions, but they simmered.

Like his and Julia's project, he had reached another impasse. Until Robbie turned up something in regard to the fire, he had no leads to pursue. And until Edmund returned and sanctioned their business proposals, they could not implement their plans. It was like waiting for the blockade to end all over again. The forced inertia rankled, and he noticed Julia's impatience was palpable as well. Both shared a restless spirit, biting at the bit to put into action all they had discussed. To act.

Each day his admiration for her increased. Like peeling back the layer of a succulent fruit, he had been delighted to uncover the woman beneath. She was sweet and magnificent. Her striking beauty had first arrested him, then her dare that had culminated in their kiss, but there was so much more to her. She fascinated him.

Why in God's name is she marrying my bastard of a brother?

Like a knife plunged in his gut, it damn near killed him. When he was not fighting his urge to yank Julia into his arms and kiss her again, he wanted to reach out and shake her. To make a blind woman see.

His mood souring, he brooded as he returned to his room at the inn. The Regal Swan was located on the outskirts of town, a first welcome before travelers reached the village proper. He had chosen it for its location away from the raucous festival near the common.

He stormed inside, startling the stooped innkeeper, who stood behind the front desk. He quickly regrouped, but his expression was apologetic. "My apologies, my lord, I didn't see you leave again. I take it you have your key this time? Haven't forgotten it?"

Daniel stopped short, staring at the man as if he had lost

his sense. *His key*? The hairs on the back of his neck stood up, and a sixth sense born during years under Edmund's fists kicked in. The blockade had ended.

Edmund had arrived.

Worse, the bastard had taken advantage of being his twin to gain entrance into Daniel's room. He cleared his throat. "No, thank you. I am quite set."

"Good, good. And as requested, I sent up a decanter of my best vintage cognac. I take it you received it? Did it meet with your approval?"

"Ah, I have yet to have a chance to partake." He had to give Edmund points for the order, for it was cleverly done. It should set Daniel back a pound note or two.

Nodding to the innkeeper, he hurried upstairs, taking the steps two at a time. He strode down the foyer and shoved open the door to his room, appreciating the resounding crash of the heavy oak against the wall and his brother's startled expression. "Edmund. Do come in and make yourself comfortable. Oh, my apologies, you have already done so. Some things never change."

His brother's unguarded flicker of surprise passed, and a look of detached impassivity veiled his features. Time hung suspended as they took each other's measure, assessing the similarities and differences the years had wrought.

Edmund had settled into the room's leather armchair, one long leg crossed over the other, his leather gloves on the nearby table and a snifter of the amber cognac in his hand. Daniel found it disconcerting to see his own features mirrored back at him, but their resemblance ended there, for his brother was no longer the whipcord-thin, angled young man that Daniel remembered. Like himself, a decade had etched its changes into Edmund.

The man before him wore his dark hair short, his starched white neck cloth as stiff as his posture, his raven-black custom-tailored clothes like a second skin. He had the pale skin of a life spent indoors, the telltale sign of a pampered aristocrat. In contrast, his eyes were hard and locked on Daniel with a cold and calculating look that Daniel knew well.

Disdain dripped from his brother. "So it is true. Lazarus has risen from the dead. I did not think you would ever return. And yet here you are."

"And all these years I did not think you had ever given me a thought. And yet you did." Daniel shrugged. "Guess we were both proved wrong. If I believed you truly cared, I would be touched, but I know otherwise." He let the door swing shut behind him.

"I see you have adopted the insolence that is common in the American colonials."

"And the pleasantries are dispensed with. Give me my bloody room key back."

"You always were proprietary about your possessions. Then, so am I." He gave Daniel a hard look. "But we will get to that momentarily. A drink might take the edge off your impatience. That has not changed either. You are still like a skittish colt, never could stand still." He leaned forward and poured Daniel a snifter.

Daniel's restlessness was a legacy left over from years of being poised for flight. At the mention of possessions, his gaze circled his room, his jaw clenching at the signs of his books and papers having been shuffled around and thumbed through. Edmund always had trespassing fingers. Irritated, Daniel snatched the snifter Edmund offered, careful to avoid touching him. He noted the bottle was already two-thirds drained. Edmund had been here awhile. "What do you want?"

Edmund cocked an imperious brow and sipped his cognac, the ducal seal flashing on his middle finger. "I think the question to be asked is, what do you want? What brings you home after years of avoiding our sceptered isle? There is nothing for you here. Lakeview Manor is gone. You do not hold the title, which you have apparently forgotten since your return." He took another drink when Daniel remained silent.

"Have you returned for my nuptials? I understand you have learned I am to marry our neighbor, Lady Julia Chandler. You remember Julia? The homely swallow has transformed into an elegant swan. But you know that, too. Who would have thought it? She was such a wild thing, always tromping in the woods saving some pathetic wounded creature." He snorted before continuing.

"She is quite tamed now, and seeing how lovely the years have been to her, I could not let her fly away. Not when I have a need of a wife, preferably a country bird who will nest at home, while I roost in the city. The arrangement suited me, being neighbors and all. Her family and eventually our own should keep her occupied, and more important, out of my business."

Daniel sneered. "Why bother with a wife? You should acquire a dog. It sounds like you are training your wife to be a tamed breeder." Disgust laced his words. "You don't know Julia if you honestly believe you can plant her in the background of your life like some decorative lawn statue."

Edmund's nostrils flared, the only sign Daniel's barb had hit its mark, for Edmund continued in that deceptively calm manner of his. "Yes, news of her recent activities have been brought to my attention, and it appears she still possesses a wild streak. I attribute it to the bad company she has been keeping of late. Nothing I cannot remedy, and I look forward to reining her in." He lifted his glass in a toast, a picture of ruthless nobility.

It took Daniel some time to find his voice, for Edmund had always known where to land his punches. This one went straight to his sternum, temporarily winding Daniel. "You bastard. You goddamn bastard." He stormed to the door and whipped it open. "Get out. We are finished. For Julia's sake, I had hoped to talk to you. About the estate. About the tenants. I had hopes that you might have changed. Had matured and learned to listen. But you are still the same. Not worth my time."

Edmund stood and straightened to his full height. Surprise lit his eyes when they met Daniel's straight on. He could almost see his brother absorbing the shock of their being of equal height and build. It was as if he were seeing Daniel for the first time, and he did not approve of the changes the years had etched, for he could no longer employ his size to dominate. Or to bully.

Nevertheless, he stood in an upright soldier's stance, his shoulders back, his chin elevated as if that could add the needed height. He raked Daniel with unconcealed contempt. "Nor have you changed. You never understood the estates are mine, not yours. You used to ride over them with father as if you owned them, as if they were yours as much as mine. And by God, you are still doing it. What the devil were you thinking? Going to Bedford Hall behind my back. Using my fiancée to wheedle your way in. Speaking to my tenants and—"

"Somebody needs to do it, because you have not deigned to do so," Daniel rejoined. He released the door to let it slam shut again, the noise reverberating in the room. He stepped close to Edmund, crowding him. "The title may be yours, but the legacy of the Bedford peerage goes back hundreds of years and will continue for a hundred more unless you grind it into dust with your tightfisted, blind incompetence."

"That is enough! Good lord, you have resided among the commoners far too long. I will not be spoken to in such an uncivilized manner."

Daniel bit back a madcap desire to laugh. "My apologies if my delivery offends your sensibilities, but while you may not want to hear this, you would be wise to listen. If not to me, then to Julia. She has proposals that will alleviate matters. It is not too late to save things, to turn them around, but if you do not make any changes, I promise you, you will lose everything. Including the respect of the peerage, which appears to be the only thing, besides profits, that you do give a damn about."

Edmund sucked in his breath, his face pale. Then a strange, icy calm descended over him and the room chilled. He finished his drink, set it on the cherrywood table, collected his tall hat and gloves, and stepped toward the door.

"You are right. We are finished." He yanked on his gloves and put on his hat. "I do not know why you returned, nor do I care. Just remember this—stay out of my business and off my property. The title, the estate, the lovely Julia Chandler, are all mine. Not yours. *Mine.* Anyone who dares to trespass on my property does so at his own peril. In the future, you would be wise to remember that. I will not warn you again. My thanks for the cognac."

He neatened his cuffs, straightened his jacket, and gave Daniel a dismissive nod. "*Runt,*" he sneered the word like a dirty expletive.

As he passed Daniel, he slammed his shoulder into him, knocking him so hard Daniel's drink splattered over his jacket. The childish aspersion combined with the shove lifted the lid on years of percolating anger.

Slamming his drink onto the table, Daniel caught Edmund, whipped him around, and heaved him back against the door. "No, Edmund. I am a grown man now, and from where I am standing, your equal, if not your better in every way. Next time, *you* would be wise to remember that, for touch me again and you do so at *your* peril." Daniel dropped his hands and stepped back, unable to bear the touch of his brother a second longer.

Edmund regarded Daniel with white lips, his hatred emanating like a raging storm. After a tense moment, he tugged his jacket into place and brushed off the imprint of Daniel's hand, as if flicking off something foul that had soiled the fabric. "Well, then, we'd best stay out of each other's way," he said, a quiet menace in his tone. With that, he was gone.

The silence following in his wake was deafening.

Daniel stood motionless for a long time. Eventually, he lifted his hands and stared at them as if Edmund's arms had replaced his own, for brutality was not him, had never been. That was Edmund, and it frightened Daniel to know that he harbored that inside of him. It was another thing to hold against his brother. That he could dredge up the very worst in Daniel.

He snatched up his drink, drained it, then whipped the snifter into the stone hearth, shattering the glass as easily as Edmund had destroyed all his plans. And all of Julia's delusions.

The only salvation in his brother's visit was the cognac. He snatched up the bottle, sank into the chair Edmund had vacated, and lifted it to his lips. Waste of damn fine cognac. It would not alleviate matters or assuage the throbbing in his head, but it might wash down the bile choking him and help him to drown out Edmund's plans for Julia. To forget that she was marrying the bastard.

No! Absolutely not.

There would be no marriage. There would be no marriage because it would have to take place over Daniel's dead body. And no one had killed him—yet. From now on, he would guard his back much more carefully, because he needed to survive. To live long enough to save Julia. And his father's estates.

He had an agenda, and as a successful businessman and expert negotiator, he would not fail. To borrow his brother's pompous edict, Edmund would be wise to learn that or suffer the consequences at his peril. The arrogant, tightfisted, sick bastard.

And on that, Daniel drank.

❧

"DAMN IT ALL. You look bloody foxed."

The resounding crash of the door had Daniel shooting to a sitting position and blinking at the bellowing voice. Robbie stood framed in the doorway, the candlelight from the hallway sconces flickering over him. Daniel pressed his hand to his throbbing temple and groaned. He needed to speak to the innkeeper about getting springs on the door. Better yet, he should have locked it.

Robbie strolled into the room, eyeing Daniel's cognac-splattered jacket discarded on the bed. "Smell like it, too." He scooped up Daniel's neck cloth from the floor and tossed it next to the coat. "What the hell is wrong with you? You were to meet me at the pub over an hour ago. And you've started drinking without me. Bastard." He lifted the bottle, and scrunched up his features. "Ah, good thing you have, this is not in my price range. Christ, who gets soused on Barker's best cognac?"

"Barker?" Baffled, Daniel cleared his throat, for it was full of cotton. His head felt no better. An orchestra had taken up residence and was pounding out an off-key tune.

"The innkeeper," Robbie supplied. He strode to the commode in the corner, lifted the pitcher, and poured a generous tumbler of water. Circling back to Daniel's side, he shoved it at him. "Sober up and talk to dear old Robbie. Tell me all about the goddess Lady Julia and how beautiful and perfect and clever and splendid and . . . Oh wait, you already did that. All bloody week. This has to stop. You are—"

"Jesus, Robbie, stop yammering at me." He snatched the proffered glass from Robbie, gulped half of it and slammed it on the table, wiping his mouth. "If you don't have a guillotine on hand, go away. I already went a round with Edmund, not you, too." His last words had Robbie snapping his mouth closed and straightening.

Savoring the silence, Daniel lurched to his feet and strode over to the commode. He leaned over its cavernous china bowl, lifted the pitcher, and poured the rest of the water over his head. Like a baptism, he needed to be cleansed. He sucked in a sharp breath and staggered back. "Blimey! That's ice cold. Why the devil didn't you warn me?" He shook his head, sending water droplets splattering, and snatched the towel off the nearby rack to dry his hair.

Robbie grunted. "Didn't think you'd dump your thick head into it." He walked over to the hearth and draped an elbow over the mantel. "Edmund came here?" he asked quietly, concerned.

Daniel jerked his head toward the empty bottle of cognac. "Do you really believe I would drop a fortune on Barker's best?" He scowled. "Edmund impersonated me, and doubled my bill while making himself comfortable rifling through my possessions. Just like old bloody times." He dragged a hand through his wet hair, shoving it off his forehead. With the towel draped around his neck, he returned to the leather chair and dropped into it.

"What did he want?" Robbie asked.

"What do you think? He wanted to plant his fist in my face. As I said, just like old times. Cain and Abel, that is us."

"Are you . . . did he . . . ?"

Daniel's eyes shot to Robbie's and he frowned. Over the

years, he had landed on Robbie's doorstep bruised and battered too many times for Robbie's family not to glean more than he'd wanted them to. "Verbal punches, Robbie. He cannot hurt me now. I am a runt no longer." His voice was harsh, and he shifted in his seat, aggrieved the childhood taunt still drew blood a decade later. "It would be a fair fight. And we both know Edmund does not fight fair. Never did."

"I take that to mean he would not listen to any of your plans for the estate?"

Daniel snorted. Lifting the tumbler of water, he sipped. "I never really believed he would. I just . . . well, for Julia's sake, I felt I had . . . well . . ."

"I understand." Robbie nodded. "So now what should we do?"

Irritation gripped Daniel. "What do you mean 'what should we do'? I am going to stop Julia from marrying that bastard and save the estate, that is what I intend to do. Nothing has changed."

"And how do you propose to do that? Edmund holds the title, and Julia is betrothed to him. That is a legally binding contract. Breaking it would be a serious breach and create a huge scandal. You have been in America too long. You forget, here titles are like the Holy Grail; they come with power and prestige. Bedford may be your brother, but he is a duke. Unless you are wearing a crown, it does not get more powerful than that."

"Bloody hell, Robbie," he groused. "Whose side are you on?"

Robbie held up his hands in a placating gesture. "I am on yours, but as you are a bit under the weather, I thought I would clarify some minor details. Point out the obstacles you need to consider, so you don't trip over them."

"Since when have you been one for details? You barely remember to store your riding equipment in the stables. Half of it litters your office."

"Those items need to be fixed, or more orders placed for them," Robbie protested.

"And jotting it down on a piece of paper will not suffice?"

Robbie narrowed his eyes. "Well, yes, I suppose it would.

But when I am busy dodging nine hundred stone of enraged stallion bearing down on me, and I see he needs a new bridle, an inkwell and pen can be hard to find at that moment."

"I understand your point," Daniel conceded. Then he grinned. "But your office is still a mess."

Robbie grunted. "No more so than this room. Look at this place."

Puzzled, Daniel straightened and peered around. In addition to the disarray of his books and papers, the desk drawers as well as those in his bureau jutted out. His closet door stood ajar, and his valise lay on its side.

He abruptly shot to his feet and snatched his jacket from the bed. Shoving his hand in its pocket, he relaxed when his fingers closed over the letter from his father's solicitor. He did not know what the devil Edmund was looking for, didn't give a damn, but his finding the letter would toss a match onto an already smoldering confrontation. "The mess is compliments of Edmund."

"Why?" Robbie looked baffled.

Daniel shrugged. "Who knows what goes on in his mind? I do not waste time bothering to decipher it." He moved to his desk, shoved the letter into a book, and slammed it closed. "Probably thought I stole some tenant's crockery," he muttered.

"Do you have any idea of how you are going to accomplish these things? Saving the estate and Julia?" Robbie asked.

"As you said, there are obstacles. It has to be done delicately." He shrugged, grinning at the understatement.

Robbie rolled his eyes. "Please tell me that's the brandy talking."

Ignoring him, Daniel leaned back against his desk and folded his arms across his chest. "An idea came to me in regard to the fire. Mabry again mentioned problems with poachers, and it struck a chord with me. Do you remember Weasel?"

Weasel's given name was Nate Corkery. He was a village boy whose nimble fingers and clever guile had earned him his nickname as the prince of poaching. Like the weasel, he trespassed at will and pinched coveted game. At Robbie's curt nod, Daniel continued. "Mabry mentioned he disappeared immediately after the fire. Said he was spouting crazy talk about it. Any chance you can locate him?"

Robbie frowned. "I can try. But it has been a while. Might be hard."

"Try. I have a feeling about this."

"Your sixth sense working up?" Amusement laced Robbie's words.

"Well, if Weasel did witness anything, it would be in someone's best interest to brand him mad."

"True," Robbie nodded. "So what else is on your agenda that is obstacle free? Rebuilding Lakeview Manor?"

Daniel stilled at Robbie's words. *Rebuilding Lakeview Manor.* He abruptly straightened. "That's brilliant! Just brilliant."

Robbie looked baffled. "Come again?"

"Let's get that drink at the pub, for we are celebrating. You have just given me a splendid idea."

"Fine, but you're buying."

Daniel warily eyed Robbie's considerable size. "I will stick to cider to keep the bill down. And do you have a spare room at your place? This place is contaminated."

"You can have my old office above the stables. As you know, the gear has been moved into the house."

At Daniel's expression, Robbie laughed. "I was jesting."

"It was a poor one." Daniel shook his head as he crossed to his closet for a change of clothes. He could not wait to share his plans with Julia . . . *Julia*. His smile faded and his arms felt heavy, as weighed down as his mood as he unbuttoned his waistcoat and shrugged it off.

One thing was certain. Julia was used to being in charge, or if not in charge, at least consulted. She would take umbrage at Edmund's plans to abandon her in the country. She was used to being needed, not dismissed or forgotten.

Edmund's pompous words had only confirmed that Julia deserved better than him. It was time she had a glimpse of what better looked like. Daniel intended to show her.

His mood improved, and he dressed quickly. If all went

well, he was confident his Julia would choose ruination over Edmund. He would bet a crate of Barker's vintage cognac on it.

"I recognize that look. You are thinking about her again," Robbie complained. "I don't want to hear it. Not one word. It is no surprise someone wanted to kill you, because I am having a devil of a time restraining myself." He stomped to the door.

Daniel laughed as he collected his jacket. He paused and cursed, for damned if his brother had never returned Daniel's room key.

Chapter Ten

≈≈

JULIA loosely gripped Constance's reins as she wended her way through the wooded path leading to Lakeview Manor. She had received a note from Daniel asking her to meet him on the grounds. His message had coincided with another delivery. Recognizing the Bedford crest, she had eagerly slid open the elegant, cream-colored envelope. It contained an invitation to a dinner party Edmund was hosting the following evening at Bedford Hall.

She wondered if Edmund was squeezing her into his schedule in response to her spending time with Daniel. Guilt stabbed her at the uncharitable thought. It was not a competition. She was betrothed to Edmund, and he could not possibly be jealous of his own brother. After all, he had no idea of the two kisses they had shared.

In any case, that was a thing of the past. Over and forgotten. Well, not entirely forgotten. She was still working on that.

The point of the matter was that Edmund was home now. This could be the new beginning she had hoped to initiate that day when she had accosted Daniel, believing him to be

Edmund. This is what she had yearned for. A chance to discuss their future. To discuss Bedford Hall.

She worried her lower lip, doubts assailing her, which was unsettling in itself for she rarely suffered uncertainty. She was a strong, competent woman. She blamed Edmund for making her feel otherwise, and she didn't like it. Thus, Daniel's enigmatic invitation was opportune. She needed a distraction, and his was timely.

> *Plans have changed.*
> *If you have the time, please honor me with your company at Lakeview Manor at noon tomorrow.*
>
> *Daniel.*

Daniel had disappeared over the last few days, this invite the first she had heard from him. At least it was a request. Edmund's tone was more a directive. Another difference between the brothers, and those were adding up. Directive or not, Daniel had her thoroughly intrigued, so she had no other recourse but to respond.

She rode without a chaperone. Julia chafed at the idea of a companion. This was the country, not London. Besides, Daniel was nearly family, and he had treated her with the utmost courtesy for weeks. She frowned, wondering why that should nettle her. It was what she had wanted, wasn't it?

Her question hung unanswered, for she had emerged through a path of trees to see Lakeview Manor's sweeping vista unfurl before her. She drew Constance to a stop and paused to wonder at the beehive of activity before her.

Men in overalls and work gloves swarmed over the grounds like a colony of ants. The scraping, clattering, and clunking noises produced by hoes, rakes, and shovels filled the air. In tandem, they worked to roll back the blanket of nature that carpeted the skeletal remains of the manor and grounds. They tugged, cropped, and swatted at tangled ferns, brambles, sticks, and other debris that had breathed life into the desolate scene, giving it its natural beauty.

More men, a few women, and clusters of children scampered along the banks of the lake. A fishing line carved a white streak into the sky blue backdrop as it arched over the windbrushed water.

"You came. I was hoping you would."

She turned to see Daniel stride forward with that easy, athletic gait. He wore a navy blue riding coat, brown breeches, and a pair of scuffed Hessian boots. His hair, minus his tall hat, was wind tousled, his linen cravat loosely tied, his cheeks flushed from the cool breeze. He looked more country squire than nobleman.

It often disarmed her to see this Edmund look-alike melding into the pastoral setting as if he belonged, while Edmund never had. Edmund rarely looked less than a duke, neat, polished, and poised to greet royalty.

"What do you think?"

"Impressive. Are we to be neighbors again?" she teased, but hope caught in her throat as she awaited his reply.

"We are." He slid his hands around her waist, lifting her down. "I promised to keep an eye on you, didn't I?" His finger flicked one of the flowers lining her bonnet.

"So you did." She stepped back, putting distance between herself and his potent smile. "But as I said, I am quite capable of taking care of myself. Besides, Edmund is home now. And . . ." She paused as Daniel's smile vanished. "You knew that, didn't you?"

He gave a curt nod. "I did."

She waited for him to continue, but he remained annoyingly reticent, forcing her to fill the void. "I will miss the wild, rustic beauty of the place." It reminded her of its owner. She blinked, the words almost escaping her.

"It is for a worthy sacrifice, for while I cannot sanction the apple mill or influence Edmund's management, I can rebuild here. Doing so adds more work and alleviates some of the problem of the surplus laborers."

"And hopefully separates the farmers from those whose talents are better served wielding hammer and ax," she added.

"Hopefully," Daniel agreed. "Pity I cannot rehire grand-mère's cook. Her nougat almond cake and Bakewell Tarts could make royalty beg. I could always follow the mouthwatering smells home. It trumped Hamelin's musical pipe. Those kids were never seen again. I, on the other hand, returned to feast on dessert biscuits and trifle."

She smiled. "I do hope her magic seeped into the rest of the meal as well."

"Haven't a clue."

She shook her head at the teasing light in his eyes. "You called this home. Was this more home to you than Bedford Hall?"

"Yes. Bedford Hall was Edmund's. Lakeview Manor was mine." Possessive pride laced his words.

"Is that why you left? Because you lost your home?"

He did not answer her at first, but when he did, his response was cryptic and he avoided her gaze. "I left because of the fire. After all, there wasn't anything left for me here."

It was as if he had closed a door, leaving her stranded on the opposite side. She believed he spoke the truth, just not the whole of it. Despite the sting of that, she kept her tone light. "Maybe next time when you leave, you will not stay away as long, because now you will have something to return home to."

Immediately his expression transformed, his features softening, his gaze warm as it met hers. "Yes. It is always good to have something or someone to lure one home."

She paused, quite sure he no longer referred to the house. Disconcerted, she waved a hand toward the lake. "Was this your idea as well? Opening the lake up to fishing?"

He nodded. "I don't have apple trees, but I have a lake brimming with trout, perch, and whatever other fish swim in it. Due to last year's poor harvest, they need the provisions. I had Mabry spread the word that the men can eat, sell, mount or fatten the cat with whatever they catch. I also provided them with supplies to do so. What do you think?"

"I think you have been busy."

"I have. Shall we join them?"

"Fishing?"

He looked amused. "Well, it is too chilly to swim and you are not dressed appropriately. So yes, fishing."

"Please tell me we are not at the mercy of your expertise for dinner, because I remember that you never caught a thing. Have you refined your technique in America?"

Daniel took umbrage at that. "I filled your bucket with all those minnows or shiners or whatever those things were. That is not nothing."

"You netted those." She nearly smiled. "And we could not eat them."

"I beg to disagree. Your cat dined on them with nary a word of complaint. Besides, you always released the larger fish. Hated the idea of them being killed, so if we had been dependent on your talents for dinner, we would have fared no better." He winked, turned, and strolled down to the lake.

He had her there. They made a pair. She fell into step beside him.

The manor was aptly named for the view of the lake, a two-hundred-acre expanse of shimmering glass mirroring the brilliant blue sky. Children scampered past, a few men tipped their hats in greeting, while the women gave shy smiles.

Two fishing rods were propped against a birch tree, a trowel on the ground beside them. Daniel knelt, used the trowel to scrape an area free of debris, and dug into the cleared patch of soil. His breeches tightened over his strong thighs, and his jacket stretched across his shoulders. A gust of wind blew a lock of hair over his forehead, and Julia swallowed. He rivaled the beauty of the vista before her. Rattled at the thought, she faced the lake. "Is this the change of plans you referred to in your note? Fishing?"

"No, this is a pleasurable side benefit." After a few more minutes of digging, he stood. "Follow me." He entered a path that cut through a thicket of bushes bordering the banks of the lake.

"Where are we going?" Curious, she fell into step behind him, but as they drifted farther away from the others, she wondered if this was a good idea.

He stopped at a private clearing and nodded to an overturned tree trunk edging the lake. "I had the men drag a seat over for us." Withdrawing his linen handkerchief, he swept the rough-hewn bark clean. "After you, my lady." He bowed and gestured for her to be seated.

Grinning at his gallantry, she stepped forward and gingerly lowered herself onto the trunk. She tucked the skirts of her riding habit around her, while Daniel flipped his coat tails out of the way and took his seat beside her. He then proceeded to efficiently bait both rods, handing her one.

The heat of his body seeped into hers, his muscular thigh mere inches from her own. She needed another distraction. "If this is simply an enjoyable diversion, what is the change of plans?"

He nodded to her fishing rod. "I did not bait these for nothing, did I?"

She lifted her rod, the grip of the ash wood well worn and smooth in her hand. With a flick of her wrist, she cast over the lake.

"I spoke to Edmund, Julia. He visited me a few days ago."

Her arm fell, fishing forgotten as her eyes eagerly sought his. "And?"

"Let us hope you have more success than I." His expression was apologetic, but she noted his eyes had darkened and he avoided her gaze.

Something dropped inside of her. She feared it was her hopes. "He would not listen?"

"To *me*, Julia. He would not listen to *me*," he clarified. "That just means we need a change of plans."

"But . . . why? I do not understand. You are his brother. It was your home, too." It was like a support beam had been stripped from beneath her, and she was caught off balance. It was another unfamiliar feeling, for she had never leaned on anyone before. Not that she was doing so with Daniel, but she did feel as if they had embarked on this venture together.

Don Quixote and his faithful squire.

"Most families are not like yours, Julia, and with nothing binding them but blood ties, well, they do not often hold.

Unlike you and Emily, Edmund and I, we were never close. To be honest, I was the brother Edmund never wanted and would never care for. Edmund liked to remind me of it, which did not help foster brotherly devotion. For a while I tried, but then"—he shrugged—"I stopped. Edmund did not like me. *Does not* like me. I do not know why, but I stopped caring enough to discern his reasons." The rustle of the breeze, the distant sounds of children and the workers filled the silence that followed his answer.

Shaken by his confidence, she opened her mouth to protest that they were *twins,* as if that should be a sacred bond, but closed it as she recalled Edmund's disdain for Daniel. It was little wonder Daniel had kept his distance, that he had become the quiet shadow of a boy, a solitary figure who circled the lake or wandered the grounds at Lakeview Manor.

A stab of pain assailed her. She had believed Edmund had forbidden Daniel's name to be uttered because he was angry over his desertion after their father's death. Clearly his feelings ran much deeper. "I am sorry. That must have been lonely for you. I now understand why you left. You needed to begin again in America," she ventured softly.

Seeing her distress, Daniel tapped his shoulder to hers. "I was not always lonely. I was at Dunbar Academy most of the time, where I met Brett. Edmund was at Eton, so I got expelled by choice."

"Expelled by choice?"

"Yes. I had a choice to release the skunk into the head proctor's room or not. The school was not big enough for Edmund and me together, so I decided one of us had to go. As Edmund did not appear to be leaving, it was to be me."

Her hand covered her mouth. "No! You didn't. I never knew what the reason was. I just remember your father was scandalized."

Daniel shrugged. "He should have let me transfer schools when I requested it. In any case, I had Dunbar, Brett, and I spent my summers here, where a wild wood sprite often traipsed after me, getting me into trouble springing traps and rescuing drowned puppies." He gave her shoulder another affectionate nudge.

She lifted her chin. "I found homes for all six of those puppies."

"I have little doubt of that." Daniel smiled.

After a span of companionable silence, she surprised herself by sharing her own confession. "I suppose I got expelled by choice as well."

"You suppose?" he teased.

"I did not consider allowing a starving, mangy border collie to continue to run wild a choice. Not when I had a perfectly good room for him to lodge in and more than enough food to share. Or, I did once I pinched it from the dining hall."

"You did not."

"I did. I would have gotten away with it as I had for over a week, but Mary Reynolds took umbrage to her shoes being his second course. As if she did not have enough pairs, carrying on so over the loss of a few." She frowned, still irked at the memory.

Daniel threw back his head and laughed.

"I am glad you find it amusing. Mary and the headmistress did not see the humor in it," she continued in a more serious vein. "Truth be told, I was always horrifically homesick. I was better off with a governess. I belong here."

"Looks like we both managed to figure out a way to get where we wanted to be, despite our challenges." He paused. "I am sorry about your mother and Jason, Julia. Sorry I was not here for you during that difficult time. It must have been lonely, handling so much on your own."

His compassion caught her off guard. She dropped her gaze, blinking at the stinging behind her eyes. No one had ever dared to address those years, or thought to ask how she had fared.

She had been so scared, tired, and desperately lonely after she had lost her mother, watching despair steal first her father and then Emily from her. Her loneliness was compounded when all of her friends married and drifted away as they built their own families.

For the first time in years, she found herself wanting to confide in someone who would understand how deeply alone one can be while still surrounded by family.

"My father blamed Jonathan for my mother's death." It was a confidence she had shared with no one. She spoke softly, the pain of those years still raw. "He refused to see him. He would travel, visit other estates, or stay in London. Anything to keep him away from home. So I did what I had to. I took care of Jonathan and worked with the bailiff to keep things running."

He nodded. "I cannot imagine you would do anything less."

The compliment was like a warm wave suffusing her, moving her almost as much as seeing her family heal. His praise meant something, for he was the first to deliver it.

"Your father was devoted to your mother, so I can only imagine the depth of his loss. Few marriages have what your parents had. Mine certainly did not. What turned him around?"

That brought a smile to her lips. "One day, when Jonathan had turned two, he was outside with his nurse. She got distracted and he disappeared. My father thankfully was home then, and he orchestrated the search for him. We found him in an empty well. He had slipped in feet first and by God's grace, landed in the bucket, which held his weight." Daniel's hand closed over hers as she drew a ragged breath. She did not pull away from the quiet comfort he offered. "When he was hauled up and into my father's arms, it severed whatever held my father tethered to his grief. It took the near loss of his son for my father to find him."

"Sometimes it takes the threat of losing something precious for someone to realize its true value."

"Like Lakeview Manor?"

"Yes," he said, as if he'd been considering something else of which he had belatedly realized its value. "And Emily? How did you almost lose her, if you don't mind my asking?"

"She loved Jason in the same manner as my father loved my mother. And she did not have a child to pull her back. It was like a light had been snuffed out inside of her. She went to a very dark place, and . . . there were times, I feared she would never return. I thought if I took her away from everything that reminded her of Jason, it would help her to heal. I took her to Windermere, in the Lake District, and with time and distance, she began to find her way back to us, like my father."

"They were both fortunate to have you."

Surprised, she glanced at him. When his eyes smiled into hers, her voice dropped to a quiet murmur, for she feared if she spoke too loud she would sever this fragile thread binding them. "They would do the same for me."

"I do not doubt it. That is the difference between your family and mine. Edmund and I never had that. I was not close with my father either, but in his last years, he did make more of an effort to seek out my company." He shrugged. "I suspect he had spent so many years grooming Edmund for the title, that he was trying to catch up with me during those last few years."

She turned her hand palm up, threading her fingers through his. For just a few minutes. The silence that settled over them was comfortable, the bond tethering them together sweet. She did not want to let go of it just yet.

"I apologize, Julia. I should have been honest with you earlier about Edmund's and my relationship, but I wanted the chance to begin again with you. To set things right. I agreed to assist you with this venture for my father's sake and yours, not Edmund's. In truth, my brother never crossed my mind. I promised to assist you, and I will not renege on that."

Her faithful squire.

Her pulse skittered, and she withdrew her hand from his, needing to regain some distance. Needing to ignore the tumultuous feelings the simple touch of his hand evoked. Like a gentle caress, it stoked buried yearnings. Ones he could not answer.

She gripped her fishing rod with both hands. "I appreciate your helping me. If Edmund will not listen, you don't perchance have any other ideas of what we can do?"

He shifted his position on the hard bench. "Well, we still have the ace up our sleeve."

"What ace?"

"*You*. Edmund has a right to reject my interference, but you are his fiancée, who can be very persuasive when she wishes to be. You got me to kiss—"

"Yes, yes. Let us not revise that." She ignored his low rumble of laughter.

"Edmund must know of and admire your fine head for business. He has to be aware of how much of an asset you will be to him."

"Well, I am not sure . . . That is . . ." Her voice trailed off.

Daniel continued. "I can imagine that at the beginning of your courtship, Edmund, like most men, was dazzled by your beauty. That is understandable, but as he got to know you better, I am sure that, like myself, he saw how clever you are, so it is little surprise that he asked for your hand."

She did not think Daniel should be saying such things. He should not be discussing her dazzling beauty or her cleverness, but she could not summon up the will to stop him.

"Edmund clearly perceived you to be an intelligent woman who spoke her mind. One he would want to keep at his side at all times." He shrugged. "That is where I would keep you. If you were mine, I would never let you out of my sight. I would be afraid someone might steal you from me, for you would be my most valued asset. I would have to keep you under lock and key."

The sweet tenor of his voice was low and seductive, and like trailing a tantalizing aroma, she followed his words off topic and into dangerous territory. Riveted, she struggled to remember what they were discussing. Hadn't a clue. All she heard was *intelligent woman* and *most valued asset*. Cheeks burning, she needed to end things before she couldn't circle back to safety. "Please, you should not say such things."

"Why? It is the truth. Doesn't Edmund tell you the same? Tell you how lovely you are and incredibly talented, being able to manage estates, wash dishes, sweep floors, and if asked, you probably could rebuild Lakeview Manor." A huskiness entered his voice. "Or does he talk about the color of your eyes, how they shine like blue diamonds, or that your skin looks satin soft and how he must yearn—"

"No, no, he does not," she snapped, desperate to quiet him, for she could bear no more. "Please, what Edmund does or does not say is not relevant. What is important is that you cannot speak to me like that because I am marrying your brother, and—"

"So you keep reminding me, which makes it difficult to forget," Daniel grumbled. "And I really want to forget it."

She stared at him. When his eyes met hers, she froze, for she read in them things she shouldn't see. The smoldering intensity in his expression stirred feelings she didn't want to feel. Touched places that had never been touched. Forbidden feelings and dangerous places. Her breath hitched and her heart ached.

She looked away. This would not do. "You need to try," she whispered. "For me. For the sake of our friendship."

Silence fell and Daniel said no more. He reeled his line in, lifted it from the water, and recast into the lake.

She resisted the urge to press her hand to her chest, where a throbbing ache pulsed.

She sought to appreciate the beauty of the crisp day, the windswept lake, and the distant cry of a songbird. She used to steal away to Lakeview Manor, its tranquility settling her during those years when her life had been in turmoil. She prayed for it to settle her now.

But she couldn't focus. It was all a blur as Daniel's words wrapped around her like a warm blanket. *Eyes like blue diamonds. Satin-soft skin. Dazzling beauty.* They were more compliments she would add to the keepsake box deep in her heart, where she could take them out and savor later, when she had no others to fill it. When she sought to recapture this moment, the touch of his hand, the sound of his voice . . .

"I have a bite," Daniel cried, jarring her from her thoughts.

Daniel jostled her as he stood, severing the spell that had woven around her. She shook her head and stood on unsteady legs.

"He is strong." He struggled to reel in his catch.

"Hang on," she said, finding her voice. As she watched his line stretch taut, her nerves settled. The wind whipped her skirts around her and cooled her overheated body. She resisted the urge to reach out and grasp his fishing rod and tug with him as she would have with Jonathan. "Don't let it get away."

"What do you think I am doing? He is not budging." He grunted as he yanked harder, the wooden rod arching in a half moon. "It is caught on something. Rooted."

"Fish do not put down roots."

"Tell that to this one," he muttered, leaning back. "His friends are helping him, holding him back. Fish are smart, they swim in schools."

Her gaze was glued to the line, but at his banal jest, she glanced up in surprise. It was a mistake, for his eyes danced with laughter and she feared she diagnosed the throbbing pain in her chest. Feared it was her heart being wrenched in two.

His smile faded, his eyes shifting back to the rod. "Ah, why don't you give me a hand? Even things out?"

His words shattered her immobility, though she hesitated before placing her gloved hands over his, adding her strength.

"Now it is fair game," he said, grinning.

He retreated a few steps and she stayed with him, frowning as the line refused to break the surface. "What . . ." Her question ended in a screech, for suddenly the line broke free with an explosive splash of water.

The tension abruptly released like a popped cork and Daniel lost his balance, stumbling backward.

Involuntarily she sought to assist him as his arm circled her waist.

His knees backed into the overturned trunk, and the next thing she knew, she was tumbling over the makeshift bench.

She cried out, vaguely aware of Daniel catching her against his side as they landed with a thud that knocked the wind from her. Daniel's body cushioned her fall, as much as a rock-solid muscular chest could soften anything.

Daniel grunted as her elbow connected with his stomach and she ended up sprawled half on him, half beside him. Mortified at the feel of his body intimately aligned with hers, the heat of him seeping through her riding habit, she quickly rolled to the side, too winded to speak or sidle farther away. She hoped the fall had knocked some sense into her.

"Who's idea was this?" Daniel groaned.

"You never could catch anything."

Rather than take offense at her comments as Edmund might have, his laughter vibrated through her side in a delicious ripple.

He turned his head to face her, and his proximity stole what little breath she had managed to draw. Good lord, he was handsome. She wanted to reach out and press her finger into that enticing cleft in his chin.

"I caught you," he whispered, his breath warm against her cheek.

It was then she realized it was not a branch digging into her back but Daniel's arm, and he was slowly drawing her closer.

"What are you doing?" she gasped.

"Reeling you in."

His arms were like iron bands, her body now sprawled on top of his, one of her legs intimately tucked between his.

"Let go of me!" She squirmed, then stilled when his grip tightened at her movements. The shock of his body beneath hers, a sturdy muscular wall of strength, had her hesitating, for her hips were intimately pressed to his. Mortified, she shoved at his chest, but found it immovable.

Her eyes widened when he lifted his head to sniff at her neck, as if she were a puppy dog. "What are you doing?" She arched away.

"Rosemary and mint." He sounded pleased.

A calloused finger skimmed the curve of her cheek. She stared into his mesmerizing eyes. She was so close she could see the rim of black circling his irises, feel each breath he drew gently lifting her, savor his arms, strong and cradling her to him. Holding her. If only she could stay there for just a little while longer.

When Daniel's fingers moved from her cheek to her lips in a featherlight touch, it brought her back to her senses. Her voice shook as she spoke. "You must stop. This is not proper."

"And you are always proper?"

The husky cadence sent shivers down her spine and goose bumps rising on her arms. It took all her willpower to ignore them, for the answer was yes. Despite her desperately wishing it was no. She wished to be that girl who first met Daniel, reckless, daring, and so very improper. To lean low and press her lips to his as she had done that fateful day. To touch him as her heart yearned to do.

But it was not to be.

She was the dutiful daughter of an earl. She was proper, dependable, and responsible.

And she was marrying his brother.

She twisted away, the tear in her heart widening, her vision blurring. "I cannot. Please. I cannot," she cried, planting her hands on his chest and scrambling to her feet. She swiped at a blinding strand of her hair that had tumbled loose in her fall, securing it behind her ear. "I have to go. I have to go now." She cursed the breaking hitch in her voice.

"Julia, wait," he called, leaping to his feet. He held up his hands in a placating gesture. "I apologize. Please, if I promise to behave and keep my distance, please stay."

She could not. They had crossed over the boundary between them. If she stayed, she questioned her ability to redraw it, or Daniel's ability to remain on his side of it. "I cannot. I have to go. Good-bye, Daniel."

She left her fishing rod and hurried down the path and up the hill to where she had tethered Constance, not daring to look back to see if Daniel followed. Untying the horse, she guided her to a mounting perch on the stone wall.

"Julia."

Face flaming, she glanced over her shoulder from her seat on Constance. Daniel stood a few yards from her, his cravat askew and his thick hair attractively tousled. He looked so heart-wrenchingly handsome that her pulse gave a traitorous leap.

"We discussed why I had left, but the more important issue is why I returned." The intensity in his gaze had her bracing herself for his next words. "I think I was meant to return for you. To help you." He opened his mouth to say something more, but then closed it. "And I promise to do so."

Her lips parted, her heart hammering against her chest. The silence grew until she gave Constance a gentle nudge with her heel, urging her toward Taunton Court.

I think I was meant to come home for you.

A wave of anguish had her nearly crumbling, for she had waited forever to hear such words. But from Edmund. Edmund should have been there for her. But he had never been—or not as Daniel had managed to be over the last week. Daniel had made her feel beautiful, like the woman she wished she were. He made her feel intelligent and desired. He made her smile. He made her laugh. And she hadn't had much to laugh about in a long, long time.

The tears pooling in her eyes were nearly blinding. She cursed Daniel, for she had always been sure of herself, and he made her uncertain. She had always known what she wanted, and he was making her question that.

Worse, he had her wondering if perhaps . . . perhaps she wanted something different.

Something she could never have.

Chapter Eleven

❧❧

THE grand entrance of Bedford Hall, with its spacious fifty-foot-high ceiling, was a portrait in palatial splendor and opulence. A marble staircase climbed to the second-story balcony where the molding was of gilded bronze with decorative leaves and fruit, and elaborate fleur-de-lis punctuating the corners. A dazzling chandelier hung suspended beneath a Rubenesque oil painting of voluptuous angels, hovering over them as if poised to swoop down and bless all visitors.

Edmund had added the painting after his father's death to highlight the baroque architecture of the house that was built in the sixteenth century. When her father had seen Edmund's addition, he had quoted Shakespeare's *King John*, commenting for once that the misguided king had gotten it right. "To gild refined gold, to paint the lily, To throw perfume on the violet, . . . is wasteful and ridiculous excess." Julia had wisely withheld judgment, for it was to be her home. She hoped to rein in Edmund's excesses as her mother had done with her father. The estate might be making a profit, but it was too high a price to pay if used to cover such ostentatious displays.

Upon her arrival, the coaches lining the drive had surprised her, for she had believed it to be an intimate dinner party with her family and Edmund in attendance. She should have guessed that was not to be the case. Like his decorating, Edmund never did anything on a small scale. His idea of an intimate party would be limiting the guest list to a mere hundred.

She followed Emily into the formal drawing room. Three enormous chandeliers cast flickering highlights over the burgundy furnishings, crystal decanters, and Oriental rug. Six alabaster columns lined the room, and guests clustered in scattered groups. The women's pastel gowns created a mosaic of color, their jewels catching in the dancing light, while the gentlemen provided a sharp contrast in their formal black.

Many of the faces were familiar, and all appeared to be members of the peerage. Her gaze swept the room, searching for Edmund, while struggling to tamp down the unfamiliar nerves that flapped like large bats, rather than genteel butterflies, in her belly. She neatened the satin skirts of her rose-colored gown, pressing an unsteady hand to her stomach to settle her nerves.

"I thought it was to be just the family," Emily murmured.

She caught the dismay in her sister's voice and slipped her arm around Emily's waist, giving her a reassuring squeeze. Emily was improving with crowds, but made limited appearances at large gatherings of the ton. "As did I. I am sorry, Emily."

"Regrets already? We cannot have that. Please, forgive me for not greeting you immediately and allow me to make it up to you."

Julia whirled, her heart hammering at the sight of Edmund in all his formal attire standing before her. He looked a picture of refined elegance and so incredibly handsome, he stole her breath as he gave her a blinding smile, dipping into a low bow.

He caught her hand and raised it to his lips, his eyes shining into hers. "My lovely fiancée, it has been too long. I had forgotten how beautiful you are, and how fortunate I am." He pressed his lips to her gloved hand. "I am so glad you are here to remind me."

It was disconcerting to see this mirror image of Daniel, yet with subtle differences. Like looking through an altered reflection of him.

Edmund was heavier set and thicker in the neck. His hair was the same rich dark brown, but worn slightly shorter, and he stared at her with Daniel's beautiful, moss green eyes. His black jacket and waistcoat were pristine, no foppish pins marring his muslin cravat. He looked every inch the regal duke, and she found herself responding to the title, rather than the man. "Welcome home, Your Grace."

He arched a brow. "Your Grace, is it? I have clearly been remiss in my affections if we have returned to formalities. Please, it is Edmund, and now *you* have something to remember."

"Edmund." She smiled, feeling the familiar jump in her pulse rate, and was glad of it.

He greeted her sister. "Emily, it is an honor to have you joining us and looking as lovely as always."

"Thank you, Your Grace," Emily replied, dropping into a curtsy.

"And where is your father? Ah, here is the earl now. Taunton, welcome to my humble estate." Edmund dipped in another bow.

"Hmph," her father grunted. "Nothing humble about you, Edmund. Never has been. I was admiring the odd statue on your front portico. It has two heads."

Edmund looked pleased. "You had the honor of meeting Janus, the god of new beginnings. He usually stands sentry at doorways and gates. Two headed so he can look to the future and past. I carried him home from Rome in the hopes that he will keep an eye on mine." His eyes strayed to Julia, his voice like a soft caress. "Particularly my future, as I have bright hopes for it."

Her eyes widened. Wait until she told Daniel that.

She shook her head at the stray thought. Janus would have to look out for Daniel, for he was firmly in her past.

Her father looked wary. "I cannot boast to knowing much about Roman gods, but I cannot say I trust one with two heads.

I like to meet a man eye-to-eye, and how am I suppose to do that if he has four of them?"

"Fair point, sir. I had not considered that, but will do so." Edmund's response was solemn, but Julia caught the slight twitch to his lips.

"While you contemplate the matter, I see the Belhams over there," Emily intervened. "Why don't we say hello to them. Father? You enjoy Lord Belham, don't you?"

"I do, he has a fine stable. Should have one, considering he filled it with half of Tanner's prime stock. Bought a mare I had my eye on," he grumbled.

"All the more reason to speak to him. Perhaps you can persuade him to sell." Emily glanced at Julia, sharing a discreet eye roll with her. "Your Grace." She curtsied, looped her arm through their father's, and led him away.

"I apologize for any aspersions my father cast on your new acquisition," Julia said.

"No apologies needed. He gave me something to mull over when the vicar is droning on and I run out of daydreaming material." He grinned. "Now then, I have been remiss as a host. We must get you some punch and catch up where we left off the last time we were together. As I said, it has been too long."

And whose fault is that? Julia's smile wavered as the annoying voice piped up.

Edmund lifted his arm, and she curled hers through it. The thick, masculine strength of it reminded her of another, and she bit her lip. She forced her attention to Edmund, who was speaking.

"You look worried. Don't. I promise you, Janus will be fine. He is sculpted of granite, so his hide better withstand the elements as well as a few verbal slings, or I will have paid a fortune for a fake."

He was charming and witty, *her Beautiful Bedford.* "Now that will be a true misfortune, for it would be twofold, being an attack on both your pride and your purse."

Edmund laughed. "Too true."

At the sound of his laughter, heads turned their way. Like Janus, everyone had too many eyes and they all were locked on her. Since her engagement, a hum of voices followed her, like a tune the orchestra played upon her entrance. It was always the same melody, with the same snippets of gossip. Thus Julia was able to ignore their audience.

At the refreshment table, sterling silver trays were loaded with crystal goblets, and in the center of the table sat an enormous crystal bowl of ruby-colored punch. Sundry fruits bobbed like buoys over its surface.

Edmund filled a glass, handing it to her. "Alas there is no liquor in it, but I am sure we will have no need of it this evening." His eyes dipped to hers and lingered as he sipped.

Her hopes climbed as well, the bats in her stomach having settled and the annoying commentary silenced. She sipped her punch. "You were in Italy last spring, were you not?"

"I was. With the exception of Janus, this trip was more wine tasting than the pursuit of Roman antiquities. Tuscan vineyards have the finest wines in the world. I find them superior to the French, which is a grave insult to them. All the more reason to voice my opinion of this whenever I can." He grinned, unabashed, and swept a stray tendril of hair from her cheek, tucking it behind her ear. "I look forward to visiting some of the vineyards with you. We could go to Montepulciano." The Italian pronunciation of the town rolled effortlessly off his tongue.

The punch must have alcohol in it, for her head spun. *Italy.* She had always wanted to travel.

He looped her arm through his and escorted her deeper into the room. "Would you like to visit Italy? Amble through the vineyards, drinking wine, sitting at outdoor cafes and following in the footsteps of Caesar and Augustus."

She had to moisten her lips before she could respond, for she was salivating at the picture he painted. "It sounds lovely." And relaxing. She would like to relax, to have no responsibilities.

But who would oversee the estate?

The voice had returned, but she refused to heed it. She would enjoy this lovely Italian fantasy for one damn minute.

But there are so many issues that need to be addressed.
Again the voice. Well, she would be drinking in Italy, so someone else would have to address them. She could not be expected
to handle everything all the time.

She stopped and withdrew her arm to face Edmund. "You
are able to get away again so soon after your return?" She kept
her voice light.

Edmund winked at her. "That is the benefit of being a duke.
I can do what I want, when I want. My dear Julia, I am well
aware of how much you have had to handle over the past few
years. It is past time you joined me in doing what *you* want.
Don't you think you have earned a much-deserved trip abroad?
Or rather honeymoon?" He smiled into her eyes.

A honeymoon. Yes, she certainly deserved that. And he
was right; she had earned it after the past five years. She had
a lot of drinking in vineyards and ambling in Roman ruins to
do to make up for those lost years. "I do," she laughed. "I will
speak to Father, see when he can best handle matters without
my . . ." Edmund's laughter interrupted her. "What is so
amusing?"

He shook his head. "This will not do."

"What will not do?" She stared at him baffled.

"This." His finger drew a whisper-soft line along her forehead, laughing when her eyes rose as if she could follow his
touch. "Your brow is furrowed. It is my responsibility as your
future husband to erase these lines to ensure that your beautiful
skin is not so marred." His arm dropped. "The last few years
have given you cause to worry. Let me speak to your father. I
have never allowed for business to bother any beautiful
woman, so I assure you that I am not going to allow it to distress my own wife."

Was he being patronizing or kind? She was surprised at
how desperately she wanted to believe it was the latter.

"Perhaps you are right, and I have been used to handling
everything myself." Hadn't Daniel said she needed a faithful
squire? She took a sip of the punch and managed a smile. "A
honeymoon in Italy sounds wonderful."

"I am glad we agree. Let us hope this is the first time of many."

She opened her mouth to respond, but a gentleman begged their pardon, requesting a brief word with Edmund. She frowned as she noted the beads of sweat lining the man's brow, and the look of quiet desperation clouding his dark eyes.

"In a minute, Richards."

"Of course." Richards dipped his head and quickly retreated.

Edmund gave her an apologetic look. "Poor Richards. I won a trinket from him in a game of cards and he seeks to redeem it."

"Nothing too valuable I hope?"

"I found it a rather vulgar piece, but apparently it is a prized family heirloom that was to go to his fiancée," he explained.

"Oh dear. Perhaps he can offer you another item in fair exchange for it?"

"Oh, I think not," Edmund drawled, looking amused. "He is old enough to pay the price for his follies, and the ring should bring a pretty penny. Besides, I am doing him a favor. The girl's a horsey-mouthed thing and her father is in trade. Richards believes himself in love, but I know better." His eyes swept the room, oblivious to her sharp intake of breath. His smile faded. "I do not see your sister. Perhaps you should find out where she is?"

"Emily?" Something cold curdled in her stomach.

"Come now, Julia." His voice lowered with an edge of strained patience. "We do not want a repeat performance of the last time she was here. Her gliding about like mad Ophelia, collecting flowers from the centerpieces to place on dear Jason's grave. You must understand that could be damaging to both of us."

"No, we cannot have that," she murmured, the blood draining from her head. It might tarnish his esteemed stature to have his fiancée's family tainted with a strain of madness. The punch of pain stole her breath.

Not Emily. Skewering Richards's poor homely fiancée was in poor taste. But Emily, maligning Emily was . . . unforgivable.

"I am glad you understand." His smile returned, and with

a finger beneath her punch glass, he prodded it toward her. "Drink, it will relax you." And with a stiff bow, he was gone.

She took a fortifying sip of her punch, needing a minute to collect herself. Edmund had always greeted Emily and dismissed her in much the same manner as he did Jonathan. It had never occurred to Julia that he might harbor the superstition that Emily could contaminate him. As if her debilitating grief was a disease he could catch.

Julia's unease was twofold, for she knew without a shadow of a doubt that she could never presume to voice her concerns over his estate management. From their short exchange, His Grace had made it clear he did not want her worrying her pretty little head over business matters. She pressed an unsteady hand to her temple, feeling the beginnings of a headache.

"Lady Julia, it is lovely to see you. We missed you at Lord Collins's."

Julia turned to see Lady Miranda Matthews and her sister Lily. She had shared her first season with Miranda, who was married and a mother now. Julia believed Lily had come out two years ago.

After greeting them, she addressed Miranda. "Excuse me, Lord Collins's?"

She did not miss the look Miranda passed her sister before giving her reply. "The hunting party in Kent. Edmund said you were busy with family concerns and could not make the trip."

Mmh. How kind of Edmund to make her excuses despite her never having given any, not having been invited in the first place. He should have told them the truth, that she was busy assisting his disgruntled tenants. Her smile was brittle. "Yes, well, family does come first."

"I understand," Miranda said. "You did not miss a thing. Just the usual barking hounds, fast foxes, and red-coated riders. Lily?"

"If you forgot anything, it is captured in the ubiquitous hunting portraits that are mandatory in every Englishman's study or library."

Grateful for the reprieve from her conflicted thoughts, Julia grinned. "I do believe that is by royal decree. As my father has heeded that requirement, I have not missed much."

"What did you not miss?"

Lady Jessica Stevens had joined them. Julia was not on familiar terms with her.

"We were catching Lady Julia up on Collins's hunting party. She could not attend due to family obligations."

"Mmh, yes. Well, you need not worry over Bedford. I assure you, he was quite well taken care of. Isn't that right, ladies?"

Julia nearly gasped at the insinuation, but Miranda appeared as horrified as she and was quick to respond.

"As you well know, Jessica, being as you are so accomplished at it, many women can flirt, but Edmund made it clear tonight and at Collins's that he only has eyes for Lady Julia." She faced Julia, a teasing light warming her eyes. "And what were you discussing so intently? Do tell. He appeared as if he could not take his eyes off of you, which is no surprise, for you look lovely. Your gown is exquisite."

"Thank you," Julia said, grateful for Miranda's rescue. She still had some friends.

The gown had been another of Emily's recommendations. She had said the rose tint made her skin look peaches and cream soft. Naked is what came to Julia's mind when she saw its plunging décolletage. It was little wonder Edmund couldn't peel his eyes from her.

She paused at the brazen thought, but she was no longer an innocent debutante. Being older and wiser had its benefits. She smiled brightly at Jessica. "We were discussing our honeymoon. Edmund insists on Italy, and I quite agree with him. After all, they have long, lovely siestas with nothing to do but relax and rest all afternoon, which is what we intend to do when we are not engaged in other . . . activities." She gave Jessica a deliberate look, but hoped to escape before her burning cheeks betrayed her. "Now if you will excuse me, I must find my sister. I fear she has disappeared."

"I saw her heading onto the balcony with Lady Collins," Lily supplied.

"Thank you." Julia dipped into a curtsy, deposited her drink with a passing waiter, and with purposeful strides headed out the French doors before anyone could waylay her. She sought refuge in an empty alcove at the far end of the balcony. She would look for Emily in a minute. She needed to cool her rising ire at Jessica's comments.

It was early evening. The daylight was fading, the moon just climbing as the sun finished its languid descent. A gentle breeze brushed over her, and she curled her arms around her waist.

Was Miranda right and it had been innocent flirting? She did not know. She had never been good at deciphering the games women played to undermine one another. That was popular at London gatherings, and the complexities and subtle undercurrents had always eluded Julia.

If she married Edmund, would she be expected to engage in such skirmishes? Again, she did not know. What she did not know was adding up. She no longer knew what to expect from Edmund or, more important, what he expected of her as his wife, except to keep her mad sister hidden and to be beautiful. The throbbing in her temple increased.

She had never felt beautiful. Until Daniel. But he made her feel more than that. When she was with him, she was clever and smart. Someone who could run an estate *and* build a house. *Much better than beautiful.*

She blew out a frustrated breath, for she was in deep trouble.

And Daniel could not assist her, for he was the very man responsible.

Chapter Twelve

❧❧

"T HERE you are."

She jumped at the amused voice, whirling to see that Edmund had stolen upon her. Her heart thundered, for bathed in the glow of moonlight, he looked like one of the Roman statues he collected—tall, godlike, and regal. She couldn't blame women for flirting with him. He was heart-stopping handsome with those mesmerizing eyes and dashing smile.

Like his brother.

Except for his comment on Emily, and his dismissal of poor Richards's family heirloom and horsey fiancée, and his flirting . . .

"So where were we before we were so rudely interrupted?"

"You were taking me to Italy for our honeymoon." She valiantly plastered a bright smile on her face, desperate to salvage the evening.

"So I was." His teeth flashed white in the waning evening light. "And we were to visit vineyards and drink wine and enjoy the long, languid siestas."

His reply echoed hers to Jessica. Had he overheard her? "Yes, and not worry ourselves with any estate matters."

"You learn quickly. We should get along beautifully." He paused, a pensive look crossing his features. "Julia, it has come to my attention that a few of my tenants have voiced complaints to you, and you have spent time in my brother's company. While I do not approve of either, I need to advise you that contrary to whatever my brother has told you, he has never run an estate before, and I do not intend to let him start practicing with the running of mine."

"Of course not. He would never presume to do so." He did not use Daniel's name. She wondered if he found *runt* too undignified to repeat in mixed company.

Why did he hate Daniel so much, and if Daniel was to be believed, at so young an age?

"However, to allay concerns my brother stoked, you should know that times are changing. Disgruntled tenants will be a thing of the past, because I intend to replace them with seasonal laborers at lower wages. The estate profits from this—and thus, so do we." He softened his tone. "Bedfords have been on this land for generations and will continue on it for generations to come. So we are free to escape to Italy and concentrate on more important matters, like starting that next generation." He smiled at her. "Do you understand?"

"I am beginning to," she murmured, her heart pained as she thought of Mabry and Just Bea, and the fate of so many other families dependent upon the munificence of Bedford Hall.

Edmund smiled. "I am so glad. Now, the evening is still young. And there is another thing I understand. The most important matter, and one which you have forgotten."

"Oh, and what is that?"

He laughed. "That we are bathed in a soft glow of moonlight on a lovely, balmy evening. I am in the company of a beautiful woman, who is soon to be my wife, and there is a hint of something wonderfully seductive drifting in the air."

"What is it? I do not smell hints of anything drifting."

Puzzled, she struggled to focus. Edmund's callous dismissal of his tenants and all responsibility toward them still had her distracted.

So much for her powers of persuasion. Extracting a kiss was one thing, but getting a duke to dip his haughty chin low enough for him to see those beneath him was another matter altogether.

She now understood why the twins were never close. They were like parallel lines that would never, ever come together.

Edmund's laughter snapped her out of her thoughts. It was a deep rumble and combined with the look in his heavy-lidded eyes, she found herself backing away.

She recognized that sultry look. It was a mirror image of his brother's. He was going to kiss her. In place of a racing pulse, her skittish nerves returned. She had waited forever for this moment. It could not be happening *now*. Not when she was so upset and conflicted her stomach was balled in knots, and she was desperate for him to understand things that she feared he could not, or worse, would not.

He stepped forward and slipped his arms around her waist, oblivious to her turmoil. "Good lord, when you walked in here in that dress, looking so delectable, it's been all I could do to keep my hands off of you."

She swallowed as Edmund's head lowered. The hard press of his body against hers was discomfiting, like a poorly tailored frock. She resisted the urge to slip her arms between them when his eyes lowered to the swells of her breasts. She tamped her nerves down. He was her betrothed, even if he could be arrogant, obtuse, and so very charming. An aching pain pulsated in her chest.

She had no choice . . . even if she wished it otherwise.

She struggled to relax as she braced herself for the press of his mouth against hers. He had a right to the intimacy, but a voice deep in the chambers of her heart cried out in protest. Unwittingly, she found herself heeding the cry and tipping her head away from his as if she could avoid the inevitable. *As if she could avoid him.*

The touch never came.

A guttural throat clearing interrupted them.

Edmund straightened so abruptly that she staggered back a step, stunned at the relief that surged through her.

"My apologies, Your Grace."

She couldn't identify the dark-haired gentleman hastily stepping back, but she recognized the shimmering turquoise gown of the woman accompanying him. *Jessica*.

"I always am interrupting you at the most inopportune moments. While the alley at the fall festival was a more public venue, this one is not, so I have no excuse for my intrusion. Forgive me. Maybe it's my exits I should work on. At least at the fair, I slipped away unnoticed, but then you were in a far more compromising situation then."

"Lud, Brimston, you never know when to quit chattering on," Jessica hissed. "They are not interested in apologies or company. Forgive us and Brimston, in particular, for being a blind idiot." She dipped into a brief curtsy and dragged her companion away.

The silence that fell was heavy with recriminations. The blood drained from Julia's face. Her heart pounded, like an orchestra in full concert, blasting out an operatic tragedy of epic proportions.

"Again? The festival? Compromising situation?" Edmund repeated, his voice so frigid, it could freeze water.

"Edmund, let me explain . . ." She cursed the sound of her desperation, the tremors seizing her.

"Please do. I never deigned to make an appearance at the fair. Apparently you did and found it far more pleasurable than I ever could have imagined."

"No," she gasped at the insinuation, recoiling. "Please, you misunderstand."

"No? Then please do enlighten me, for I believe I missed much." His voice never rose, but held a quiet menace that was louder than a barking reprimand.

Feeling like a trapped rabbit, her heart thudded and she moistened her lips, her mouth dry. "Well, you see, Daniel was—"

"Daniel." He stiffened, and his nostrils flared. "My brother has a canny ability for turning up where I least expect him to be, or should I say, where he doesn't belong. That explains Brimston's mistake, but it doesn't explain yours. Please, continue."

He had finally voiced his brother's name, albeit hissed under his breath like a filthy expletive. "You must understand, I warned Daniel that—"

"It appears you did far more than warn him. You were seen in a compromising position. Brimston may be an idiot, but contrary to Jessica's words, blind he is not. Do you deny it?"

"No, but, I can explain—"

His hand shot up, his white glove an implacable barrier glowing in the fading light as he continued in an icy drawl. "Do not bother. You have said more than enough. I had heard my brother attended that village fete, and he had made a public spectacle of himself on some half-crazed stallion. What I did not know was how intimately your paths had crossed."

"It is not what you are thinking. It was a mistake and—"

"Enough," he snarled, looming over her. His hands vised around her upper arms, ignoring her sharp cry as his fingers dug deep. "If you think I want to hear one more word about it, you think wrong." He abruptly released her as if the touch of her burned or, worse, sickened him. "Spare me the sordid details."

Silenced, she stumbled back, more frightened by his sudden calm than she had been by the fleeting spark of temper. She curled her hands around her upper arms, where undoubtedly bruises would form.

"I can forgive many things, but an indiscretion with my own brother is not one of them. It is finished." He straightened his jacket and pulled his sleeves down. "Now then, let us not make a scene tonight, for that will unfold soon enough. Tomorrow, I will speak to your father and then be in contact with my solicitors."

He made to turn away, but paused to rake his eyes over her with an insolence that stripped her bare, his gaze lingering on her breasts. "Had you waited until after our marriage, I would have been receptive to your seeking your pleasure elsewhere, that is, with the exception of my brother." At her shocked gasp, he snorted. "Please, spare me the theatrics of a sheltered innocent, for we both know otherwise. You did not think I would settle for a provincial marriage? And disappoint my mistress? There would have been enough for you both, but she will be pleased to know she does not have to share."

Stunned, the fulcrum upon which her life had pivoted for the past five years had abruptly tipped and dumped her flat on her arse.

It took her a minute to pull herself together, to gather up the broken pieces of her childish hopes and dreams, and to regain a sliver of the dignity Edmund had stripped from her. Despite the tremors shaking her body and the scandal that was sure to erupt and drop her to her knees, she was the daughter of an earl, and she refused to let Edmund see her shatter.

She drew herself up to her full height, her voice quiet but steady. "Your brother was right. I have been chasing windmills after all. My condolences to your mistress." She dipped into a curtsy. "Your Grace." On unsteady legs, she dodged around him, gasping when his hand shot out and curled around her upper arm again. He drew her close, his face inches from hers.

"You forget, Julia, this is breach of contract. You are ruined. Finished. And do not expect my brother to rescue you. He has never been the loyal type, cannot be trusted worth a damn, and his life is in America. My condolences to *you*."

He released her and she dashed out of his reach. This time, when she lifted her skirts and hurried away, she did not look back.

Through her tear-blurred vision, she would only see a two-faced duplicitous Janus, one face oozing charm, the other cruelty.

Chapter Thirteen

DANIEL gave Chase free rein, for the stallion had a penchant for speed, and he needed to arrive in time to contain the damage from Edmund's incendiary confrontation with Taunton. Thank God Emily had the foresight to send for him. Her cryptic note warned him of the fallout from his and Julia's infamous "mistake." *Betrayed by a kiss.* It had a biblical ring to it. He just hoped to save Julia from further persecution.

He crested the ridge overlooking Taunton Court. Majestic elms, like royal guards, lined the drive to the sandstone Georgian house. With its perfect symmetry, classical pilaster columns, a sandstone staircase climbing to the front portico, the house sat like a jewel, the sky blue day the perfect setting to frame its grandeur.

Oblivious to the view, Daniel's gaze locked on the coach blocking the front entrance. The polished burgundy cab gleamed, an ink black silhouette of a stallion prancing across the Bedford crest. A coachman and footman wore Bedford's jade green livery and were stationed beside the coach.

The men turned at his approach, their reactions revealing

as they recognized the resemblance to his brother. Their posture became as rigid as the pillars propping up the front portico, their eyes cast forward, impersonal and professional. Edmund would not tolerate familiarity in his staff, and he had dismissed his father's servants within the month before Daniel left. According to Edmund, years of servitude to their father had made their loyalties suspect and their familiarity unacceptable.

He stopped Chase a few yards from the carriage. As he dismounted, Taunton's groom hurried forth to take the reins.

The cloudless sky provided an ironic backdrop for the day, for it belied the pending storm. He straightened his shoulders and started forward, but paused when the front door opened.

Edmund's gloves were fisted in one hand, slapping against his thigh. His stride was brisk as he descended the steps and made his way to his carriage. So intent on his destination, he didn't immediately see Daniel. When he did, he stopped short, his eyes flaring, and his expression thunderous. "Taunton is not receiving visitors. And your presence, in particular, is not welcome. I would think you'd understand."

"I doubt Taunton needs you to speak for him, Edmund, as I am sure you have said quite enough."

"I have said enough? What the devil do you think you have done?" he roared. "You have ruined his daughter. She is tarnished goods. But the real question is, did you intend this all along? Was ruining my fiancée your way of getting back at me for your childhood slights?"

"You are not serious," Daniel scoffed, incredulous.

"I am. If that was your plan, you have made a grave error. You see, I do not give a damn." He shrugged. "If I had, I would have wedded and bedded her years ago."

"What the devil are you talking about?"

"She is a pretty thing, of good lineage, and she came with a hefty dowry. I am in need of an heir to replace you, and she is of prime bloodstock. I would have honored my contract and married her. But now that you have given me a means of extricating myself while keeping her dowry, which I insisted on Taunton forfeiting in payment for breach of contract, I have concluded it is for the best. In lieu of all that has occurred over the past few years, it is clear to me that madness permeates the Chandler bloodline. Therefore, it is best that our families not merge and risk tainting the Bedford lineage."

Daniel's lips parted. He had expected Edmund to accuse Julia of many things, none of them good, but he had never fathomed this disturbing charge.

"I have to admit, I thought more of Julia. Thought she had refined taste, but her indiscretion with you proves otherwise. Pity." He made a disapproving face as he yanked on his gloves. "However, it matters not. It is finished, and I am glad of it." He nodded toward Daniel. "As my heir, you need to maintain your distance from her. You must understand. The families cannot merge." A tic vibrated in his cheek as he eyed Daniel, almost daring him to question him.

Daniel was rendered speechless. When he recovered his voice, bafflement laced his words. "How odd. We finally agree on something."

Edmund nodded. "I thought you would be difficult. But I am glad that we are of like minds in regard to this matter."

"You misunderstand," Daniel said. "I agree on your earlier point. I, too, am glad it is over and Julia is free of you. She deserves so much better. Or at the very least, a husband who thinks better of her."

Edmund drew himself up and peered at Daniel as if he were a dimwitted clod whom he deigned to educate. "You forget, I am a duke, and here in England, with the exception of a prince, there is none better. I don't accept tainted goods, least of all my brother's castoffs."

Daniel did not think, but lunged. Their bodies collided.

The force of the impact sent them flying to the ground, Daniel sprawled on top of Edmund. "You bloody bastard!"

Scrambling to his knees, he landed two solid punches to Edmund's gut before Edmund's men yanked him off.

Edmund staggered to his feet and leaning over, braced his hands on his thighs, gasping for breath.

Daniel fought against the men restraining him. However, chosen for size and height, to do the uniform of the Bedford livery justice, he could not break their hold.

When Edmund recovered, he dove at Daniel, his fist hurling into his face. The force of the blow snapped Daniel's head back. Preparing for another hit, Daniel lifted his feet, forcing the footmen to stagger and struggle to maintain their grip.

"Release him. He is not worth it," Edmund ordered, flexing his hand, his attention on a pair of Taunton's groomsmen running their way. Edmund had never liked an audience to witness his loss of temper.

One of the footmen handed Edmund his hat, which had flown off in his fall.

"Go back to America. I give you fair warning. Because if you don't, you will not survive our next encounter."

Daniel straightened, ignoring the throbbing pain in his cheek. "Rot in hell, *Your Grace.*"

Edmund stared at him, the glacial hatred in his eyes so frigid that Daniel almost recoiled. Then he simply smiled and turned away.

This fight was far from over, but Daniel was not going anywhere. Not yet. He had an agenda, and the item now topping the list was to ask for Julia's hand in marriage.

He had vowed to save her from his brother. He had never meant to do it through the bonds of marriage, but if that is what it took, so be it. He had told Julia on that fateful day at the fair that he was a man who corrected his mistakes, and he had meant it.

≫≪

DANIEL KEPT HIS attention on the imposing mahogany desk dominating the study. Two chairs sat before it, and it seemed like only yesterday that he had warmed one, while Edmund occupied the other as Taunton had spoken to them about keeping a protective eye on Julia, who appeared determined to romp after them. He and Edmund had been fourteen to Julia's precocious nine years and had little interest in her catching them.

His eyes strayed to the Queen Anne cherrywood tall-case clock, recalling Taunton admonishing Edmund for noting the time more than Taunton's words. Once again, Daniel was awaiting sanction from Taunton for the same transgression: not looking out for Julia. But he was here to prove him wrong.

Ceiling-high bookcases filled one side of the room, a stone hearth the other. Above the mantel hung an oil painting of the bucolic English countryside. The earl stood across the room before windows overlooking the back courtyard and lawns. Hands clasped behind his back, he appeared lost in the scenic vista outside.

The butler's introduction had rebounded off the walls and filled the room. Daniel had opened his mouth to speak, but found he had been at a loss for words, the etiquette for this situation having eluded him. He had never ruined anyone's daughter before.

Taunton rescued him from his indecision. He faced Daniel, his tone deceptively calm for a man bent on avenging his daughter. "I see you ran into Edmund, or rather his fist, as he was leaving. You will have to ice that cheek, it is blooming a mean black and blue. I hope you got a shot in for me." Taunton did not wait for a response. "Edmund ended the engagement. He cited breach of contract due to Julia's indiscretion with another party." He narrowed his eyes. "I believe you are aware of the particulars, being the other party identified."

He held Taunton's gaze, surprised to find no censure there and gave a curt nod. "I am, sir."

"So it is true?" Taunton pressed. "You kissed Julia, your *twin brother's* fiancée, in broad daylight, in a main thoroughfare at the fair?"

Edmund always had been a lying bastard. As if they had been a bloody exhibit at the fair. He clamped his mouth shut. The truth could not be buried in Edmund's lies. Julia deserved better.

He straightened to his full height, clasped his hands behind his back, and looked Taunton straight in the eyes. "Yes, sir, I did. And I am here to make things right and do the honorable thing. I would like your permission for Lady Julia's hand in marriage." He anticipated Edmund's bellow of rage. He hoped his brother choked on it.

Another silence stretched between them, this one drawn tight as a bowstring.

Taunton shook his head. "It is the damnedest thing. I cannot decide if I want to call you out or thank you. Therein lies the problem."

"Sir, I understand your desire for pistols at dawn," Daniel said as he shifted his stance, sweat pooling between his shoulder blades. "However, my obtaining a special license might alleviate matters. I do—"

Taunton held up his hand. "Pistols at dawn will not be necessary—yet." He strolled over to a tall glass cabinet and extracted a decanter of brandy and two snifters. He handed one to Daniel, generously filled them, lifted his glass in a toast, and then downed it. "You see, while I signed the betrothal contract, I had reservations." He poured himself another, gesturing to the chair in front of his desk, motioning Daniel to sit.

Daniel hesitated. The conversation was not going in the direction he had expected. His request for Julia's hand hung suspended between them. He warily took his seat, but found, unlike Taunton, he could not relax.

Taunton leaned back against his desk and twirled his glass in his hand, brooding into it. "I never thought Edmund the right man for my Julia, but she seemed quite decided on him. At the time, her mother was alive, and she thought Julia would be a good influence over Edmund. As my Meg had been on me." He shrugged. "Now it is a moot point, which brings us to our present predicament."

"Sir, I am quite prepared to—"

"So you say. But you are asking the wrong person. You need to speak to Julia. My apologies, but you might as well learn sooner rather than later, Julia is too old and too strong willed to be browbeaten by me or anyone else." He looked rueful, but then his eyes hardened. "But while I concede that she is old enough to make up her own mind, you need to make damn sure she makes it up in your favor."

"Yes, sir. I understand. But . . . ah . . . will she speak to me?" He cursed his hesitancy, but he needed to know.

"Julia is upset and confused. She is packing her bags as we speak, determined to go to London, to put as much distance as possible between herself and Bedford Hall." He shrugged. "London will be quiet. Being out of season, most families will be at their country houses. A change of scenery might help to settle her nerves, for I fear that right now Julia is leaning toward ruination over another engagement. It is your job to convince her otherwise."

"That could be difficult if she refuses to speak to me, and if she flees to London," he said, his tone bleak.

"If she was totally averse to you, we would not be sitting here in the first place, having this particular conversation, would we?" Taunton gave him a wry look.

Heat climbed Daniel's neck. Taunton had a point. He refused to believe Julia would have kissed him with so much passion if she had not felt something for him.

"Edmund has agreed to wait a fortnight before announcing the broken engagement. Those were my terms if he wanted me to forgive his debts to me and forfeit Julia's dowry. One more thing, Daniel. There is no money for another dowry. I am—"

"Julia's hand in marriage is payment enough."

"On the bright side, after last night and today, Edmund is no longer your problem. However, on the dark side, the obstacle you need to breach will be my lovely daughter's sheer stubbornness. Just remember that Julia is all about family." His voice lowered to a quiet murmur. "She deserves one of her own."

⇒≈

Julia paced the library, her heart so heavy it weighed down her steps. She searched for a book to occupy her during the journey to London. She needed an escape, preferably a wrenching saga of war and mayhem. A scene of carnage to rival her own. She bypassed the volumes of Shakespeare, for her life already embodied a Shakespearian tragedy, complete with mistaken identity, mixed twins, and star-crossed lovers. She paused, the latter notion discomfiting.

She did not love Edmund. She blinked back the moisture

in her eyes. Last night in Emily's arms, she had shed enough tears, but none over the loss of her Damn Duke. The tears were shed over her own youthful folly.

She shuddered at how close she had come to paying a price for being young and besotted. She had almost been tethered to a man she not only could not love, but could never respect. That would have been a far too grievous price to pay. People survived loveless marriages, the ton being full of them, and she would have survived hers. But not without respect.

She rested her head against a bookshelf, the cool cherry-wood soothing against her aching temple.

Had she ever loved Edmund?

She recalled their whirlwind courtship. Edmund had been a larger-than-life figure in her childhood. She had not been able to believe he deigned to smile at her, let alone single her out for his attentions and offer for her hand. Handsome, charming, and dashing, what woman could resist Beautiful Bedford? And then he was hers. Only he never really had been. After she had postponed their wedding twice for her family's sake, Edmund's visits had become as rare as rain during a drought, their relations becoming distant and cordial.

She never knew what Edmund had thought of her. He had never said. She feared neither of them had glanced beyond the surface, like settling for icing on a cake. After his father's death and Daniel's departure, she believed Edmund had needed her. She was wrong. He only had need of a wife to adorn his arm and bear him heirs, while she wanted someone to relieve her aching loneliness. To make her feel all those things she yearned to feel. But he was not a man she could love, and she had been a fool to think otherwise.

Now she was paying the price for her mistake. Would be paying for it forever.

One did not break a betrothal contract with a duke without suffering repercussions that would reverberate for years. She had a fortnight before the storm broke.

She lifted her head and pressed her hand to her forehead. "Julia."

She whirled, stunned to see Daniel standing inside the

library. So lost in her thoughts, she had not heard the door open and close behind him.

His expression was solemn, his eyes dark, and he had a mean swelling on his cheek. She wondered if it was compliments of her father or Edmund. The bruising only added to his rakish appeal, for he still looked unbearably handsome. Her traitorous heart leapt, but then it crashed down. She had made a grave mistake in accepting Edmund's suit all those years ago, but she had youthful folly to blame for her actions then. She had no such excuse for her reckless behavior with Daniel.

And all that it would cost her family.

"You need to leave. You have done quite enough." She stepped back from the bookcase and curled her arms around her waist, cursing her shaking voice.

"Julia, please listen to me," he implored. "I know about Edmund and your severed betrothal. I have spoken to your father—"

"Please," she cut him off, not wanting to hear more. "There is nothing you can say or do that can alter my situation." She had to pause as her voice hitched. She lifted her chin, blinking furiously. "It is not possible to avoid the scandal that is going to engulf my family. After all they have been through—"

"Julia, I have come to make it right. I have asked—"

"You cannot make it right," she cried. "There is nothing we can do to make it right. We cannot turn back time and erase our mistake. *My* mistake. It is impossible."

"We can marry," Daniel insisted. "You are not ruined if you marry. Marry me, Julia." He held his hand out toward her, his eyes entreating.

Stunned, Julia froze. His words touched something within her, lit a flickering hope that quickly spluttered and died. "No, I cannot." Her words were soft, and she shook her head, tears streaking her cheeks. "It is too late. I will not . . . I will not accept another proposal for the wrong reasons. I did that once, and I will be paying for that mistake forever. Please. You must go."

She hurried to the door and started to open it, needing to escape before she broke down completely. She didn't get far.

Daniel was behind her, slamming his palm against the door above her head, preventing her from opening it.

"It is the right reason, Julia. It is the right thing to do." He spoke to her bent head, for she refused to turn around.

She pressed her forehead against the door, aware of the heat of his large frame, crowding her, his breath warm on the nape of her neck. "I cannot," she whispered. "Your home is in America and mine is here. I cannot leave my family, not after the scandal I have brought them. I will not do it. Do not ask me to."

He dropped his hand and sighed. "Look, you do not have to accept my proposal now. But please, at least give me a chance to convince you otherwise." His voice was low and urgent. "I have wronged you, and I offer my most sincere apologies that my transgression has put your family in this difficult situation. I can only beg of you to let me make amends. To make it right."

She closed her eyes, her heart bleeding, her emotions warring within her. She wanted to say yes, and let him enfold her in his arms. To sail to America and never look back. Let the wagging tongues flap away over her brazen conduct. She knew from past experience that when word of her severed engagement spread, the rising speculation would be cruel. As it had been over the last five years, the questions would be innocent at first, then ever more demeaning.

What happened? Is it true that she was discovered in a compromising situation? With His Grace's twin brother? Oh dear. Dumped by a duke. And sailed off to America? With the brother?

Her disgrace would be an incriminating shadow trailing her family. It would scare away any of Emily's potential suitors.

Julia had just gotten her family back on their feet. She could not bear knowing that her behavior would bring them low again.

More importantly, she refused to accept a man for the wrong reasons again.

It was a proposal made out of pity, and her heart rebelled at the thought. Last night had given her wisdom beyond her years. She now knew what she needed in a marriage proposal, or from any man who wanted to share his life with her.

She wanted what her parents had had. What Emily had found with Jason. She wanted to be loved. The man who asked for her hand needed to do so not because he thought her beautiful, or deserved an heir, or he needed to save her from ruin. He needed to do so because he loved her. He loved her with such desperation that the loss of her would drop him to his knees.

She would settle for no less.

"It will not work, Daniel," she whispered above the pounding in her head and the anguished cry of her heart. She would go to London. To escape. To think. To unravel emotions tangled up like a knotted ball of yarn. "It is over. I am leaving for London, and you need to return to America."

"It is not over. We are not through," he insisted and spun her around. "We have something together. We have always had something, and you cannot deny it."

"It was two kisses," she cried. "Stop making it into something more."

Daniel's eyes narrowed. "I am not making it into anything more than what it is. Perhaps you need a reminder."

Before she could protest, his head lowered and he captured her mouth in a scalding kiss. He kissed her as she had forgotten he could kiss. Powerfully. Expertly. She gasped, and when her mouth opened, he deepened the kiss, his tongue parrying with hers. The heady combination of Daniel and brandy had her knees weakening. Her hands crept up to curl around his shoulders, holding on as her world tilted and still he kissed her. Desire coursed through her and she groaned. His arm slid around her waist, bracing her weight against his.

He lifted his head, and his eyes, heavy-lidded and smoldering, stared into hers.

Dazed, she gazed up at him.

"It *is* something more. Do not make it into less than it is." His words were soft and entreating. "You cannot escape it in London." He held her with one arm and brushed a tendril of hair from her forehead. "Because I will come after you, Julia. We are not finished. This is not finished. But I will give you some time."

He released her as she recovered her senses and found her footing. She stepped away and straightened her gown, her pulse skittering.

"Just not too much of it," he warned as he opened the door and closed it softly behind him.

Julia pressed an unsteady hand to her throbbing lips. She had more to think about in London then she originally surmised. How like Daniel to complicate matters. To muddy the water.

She could not marry a man like that. Who did not heed her wishes. Who kissed her without leave or permission. Who was a bit wild and . . . dangerous.

Then again, if he loved her, she did not know how she could not. After all, she deserved no less.

But he was leaving for America.

And she belonged here.

Chapter Fourteen

≫≪

Daniel dismounted on the lane leading to Tanner Stables. After leaving Taunton Court, he had spent the morning riding over the undulating hills of Bedfordshire. As a boy, this unfettered freedom had always been his release from all that pressed upon him. As he had galloped across the lush green landscape, the whip of the wind and exhilaration of the ride had provided a healing solace to his roiling emotions. It also served to remind him that Julia was wrong.

Yes, he had built up a life in America, but his home was here. This land spoke to him. And it always would. After listening to the tenants, wandering over well-worn grounds and revisiting the charred remains of Lakeview Manor, he could never escape it. It was in his soul.

America had given him time to heal after the fire, but he was better now. He did not know if or when he would leave, for he had a business in Boston. He only knew that no one could force him to flee again, not the person who had scared him away all those years ago, not Edmund with his threats or Julia with her pleas.

Julia.

With an irritable kick, he sent a stone skittering across the road. Taunton had said Julia was all about family and deserved one of her own. His family had never been close; he had no plans to marry and knew nothing about being a father. But by God, he would learn for Julia—even if it terrified him. It was the right thing to do. He just needed to convince her of that. Taunton knew his daughter well, for her stubbornness was a formidable barrier.

He understood she was struggling with the realization that she had made a mistake in accepting Edmund's hand, but she could not possibly compare him to Edmund and fear making another one? After all they had done together, he refused to believe she could still be confusing them. So why was his proposal a mistake? He did not see anything wrong with it. He thought it quite timely. Would it not save her from ruination? What did she want? Bended knee and flowers?

He thought he understood Julia. Feared he did not, which did not bode well for a future together. Her decision to flee to London rather than staying to resolve matters particularly irked him. How was a man to convince a woman to marry him if she was in a different city? Well, as he said, he would give her time, but not too much of it.

He led Chase into the Tanner Stables, greeting Robbie, who was storing up tack.

"Shouldn't those bridles go in your office?"

"Do not start nattering on about that again," Robbie warned. "You were up and out a mite early. A maid said the footman delivered you a note while you were breaking the fast, and you were off like a wild horse. Was there a fire you needed to put out?"

"There was," he said. Seeing as they were alone, he continued. "Bedford severed his betrothal with Julia. Cited breach of contract. Apparently, she was seen in a compromising situation with—"

"What? That's bollocks," Robbie thundered. "What kind of grotty, underhanded good-for-nothing son of a whore would ruin Lady Julia? Only a blackguard of the worst sort. A real son of a bitch . . . Ah, hell, you didn't, did you?"

Daniel cursed Robbie as heat burned his neck like a brand of guilt. "Keep your voice down," he snapped. "I do not need the whole village to hear. The announcement is not yet public." Robbie unhitched Chase's saddle, while Daniel removed his bridle.

"I intend to make it right." He leaned forward and practically hissed the words. "I may be a good-for-nothing blackguard, but I am not Edmund. For God's sake, Robbie, it would have been like giving a bird to a feral cat. It was not how I intended to severe their engagement, but I refuse to apologize for the demise of it."

With a grunt, Robbie hefted off Chase's saddle and set it down. Planting his hands on his hips, he blew out a breath. "Can't argue with you there. Is that where you disappeared to this morning? To make things right?" He nodded to Daniel's cheek. "Is that from Taunton?"

"Edmund," he muttered.

Robbie's eyes widened. "You met up with him? Or rather his fist?"

Daniel scowled at his echo of Taunton, his words defensive. "He did not leave unscathed. Turns out, unlike his daughter, Taunton is amiable to my suit. He had reservations about Edmund. Wise man."

"You are the only bloke I know who can ruin a man's daughter and have him thank you for saving her. You titled gents get all the good fortune." Robbie shook his head.

Taunton's support was an odd turn of events. Daniel was not used to being championed over Edmund. In the past, it had been his word against Edmund's. Edmund was the heir apparent. Once Daniel had realized no one was listening to his side, he had stopped talking.

"So Lady Julia hasn't accepted your offer?"

"She will," Daniel grumbled. "I am working on it."

He filled Robbie in on Edmund waiting a fortnight before making the news of the severed engagement public. "What I would like to know is why is Edmund borrowing money from

Taunton? How much are the loans Taunton paid out to him? Where the devil is he pouring the profit that he is leeching from his estate?"

Robbie leaned down and hefted the saddle into his arms, carrying it over to deposit it with the tack needing cleaning. "I am not privy to the man's finances." He tossed a brush to Daniel. "My stable hands are busy elsewhere, make yourself useful. Rub your own horse down."

Robbie collected a pitchfork and moved to a storage bin, proceeding to dig out straw and toss it into a wheelbarrow. "Bedford resides in London during the Season. He could have accumulated gambling debts or a mistress. I would not be in the know about that, but keeping a sweet bit of fluff would cost a good amount in lodging and trinkets."

A mistress would not put Edmund into debt, but it might explain Edmund's willingness to prolong his engagement, for he doubted Julia would tolerate sharing her husband. After she finished with the unfortunate woman, what was left of her would be sent packing. Thankfully, he found one woman trouble enough. The idea of juggling two had him loosening his cravat.

He sighed. His brother's strained finances, like his estate, were none of his business. However, as Taunton had ceded Julia's dowry to Edmund and planned to forgive other debts as well, Daniel had a vested interest and a burning curiosity to know what sponge was sucking up the Bedford fortune.

"While I can't account for Edmund's debt, I can assist you in another area. I located Weasel." Robbie straightened and his grim expression gave Daniel pause.

"Where is he?"

"He is in London. But there's something you should know. Bedford caught Weasel poaching on his land, laid a trap for him no doubt." Robbie's brown eyes darkened.

Daniel stilled, his mouth bone dry. Edmund had liked to set his traps, but he liked his punishments more.

"Bedford's the magistrate now, and he delivers a harsh justice. I didn't know how harsh, but I have learned. Apparently, he sanctioned slicing off two fingers on the poor sod's right hand in punishment for his poaching." Robbie spat in the newly laid straw as Daniel sucked in his breath. "Then Weasel disappeared. Rumors say he is sequestered in town and has been working at a gambling hell for the past two years."

Daniel strode to the open stable door, letting the fresh air cool his rising fury. Robbie's words stirred up buried memories. Idly he rubbed his thumb over a jagged line on his index finger. Edmund had cut it, curious to test the blade of his new knife. They had been at Eton, and after nearly losing his finger, Daniel had made his decision to leave the school.

These scars had served to remind him of who his brother was, but Weasel's fate reminded him of much more. Daniel had stained Julia's reputation, but he had not ruined her—that Edmund would have done. His freedom for Julia's was a sacrifice he would never regret.

Feeling a renewed purpose, he vowed to woo his beautiful, obstinate warrior and pry the necessary acceptance from her. Difficult, but not impossible, remembering their kiss. She felt something for him, and that gave him a flicker of hope. He just needed to fan the flames a bit higher and hotter—and he would.

He faced Robbie. "Well, then, it looks like a trip to London is in order."

"You are going to look for Weasel? You really think he knows something?"

He shrugged. "It is the only lead I have for now. If nothing comes of it, my partner came over with me and is in the city, so I can visit Curtis Shipping while there." *And Julia.* "However, before I leave, where can I get a special license to wed?"

Robbie grinned. "Now *that* we might have more success finding. We can—" Robbie began, but was cut short at the sound of a throat being cleared.

They turned to see Davie, Robbie's brother, who was half the size of Robbie but with the same dark eyes and shock of unruly hair. "You need to come inside," he said, addressing Daniel. "Something has come up." He did not wait for either of them to respond, but turned on his heels and headed back out.

Daniel exchanged a curious look with Robbie before following him outside.

They trailed Davie into the house, upstairs, down a long hallway, and toward the guest quarters and Daniel's room, where his bedroom door stood ajar. Davie gestured Daniel inside with a nod of his head.

Frowning, Daniel quickened his step, but stopped short at the sight greeting him. A young housemaid stood inside, wringing her hands before her. Daniel noted her anxious expression, but was too stunned at the disarray in his room to give her much heed.

It was as if a gust of wind had whipped through and tossed everything asunder. His books and papers were dispersed, some on the floor, some crumpled up. Drawers jutted out with items spilling from them, his wardrobe door gaped open, and clothing was strewn on the ground. The only broken item was the porcelain bowl that had sat on the commode. It looked as if it had been hurled in anger, for it was shattered into pieces before the hearth.

What in the world . . . ?

"In a bit of temper before you left, were you?" Davie said.

Incredulous, Daniel's eyes shot to him. "You believe I did this?"

"Well, if you didn't, who did? Are any of the other rooms ransacked like this?" Robbie asked the maid.

"No, sir. Thot's wot I was tellin' Master Davie here," she said. "I had done a proper cleanin' when my lord first left early this mornin'. I didn't plan to do another when ye returned, but I noticed the door was ajar after ye left again and I came to close it, I did, and thot's when—"

"When I returned? This morning?" Unease swept through Daniel.

"Yes, sir." She looked at him oddly.

"You saw me return? Did I speak to you or anyone?"

"No, my lord. But Lanie, said ye . . . well, she said ye smiled at her when ye climbed the stairs." She flushed, but sobered when Daniel simply stared. "But ye seemed in a hurry, otherwise she would have asked ye if ye wanted a proper cup of tea brought up."

Daniel faced Robbie. "This is the first time I have returned since my leave-taking early this morning. Whoever smiled at Lanie, it was not me."

Robbie addressed the maid. "Corrine, can you get Lanie for us? That might assist us with clarifying matters." The maid bobbed a quick curtsy and hurried from the room, looking relieved to escape.

"Only one other person could be mistaken for you," Robbie said. "I would ask why, but we both know he has cause for his anger."

"What cause? What do we know?" Davie said, his interest perked at Robbie's meaningful look.

Daniel waved a hand dismissively. "My brother and I had a bit of a row earlier."

Davie whistled. "Cor, me and Robbie go at it all the time, but I never thought the duke had it in him. Always so high in the instep. That explains your black and blue. Did you triumph?"

Robbie cuffed his brother on the head. "Can you focus here? We need to find out if Bedford took anything."

Davie rubbed his head. "You just said he did it 'cause he was in a fit of temper, so I doubt he pocketed anything. He lost the fight, then?" He gave Daniel a hopeful look, but Daniel simply shook his head. "Fine, don't share the interesting details."

"Davie," Robbie's patience snapped. "What makes you so bloody sure he didn't take anything?"

"'Cause I picked this off the floor," he said, striding over to the mantel and lifting a gold watch fob. "This is a pretty piece. Looks like it has the Bedford crest on it. Doubt he would leave it, if he was here to loot. Besides, he's a duke, he has to have everything a man could want or the funds to buy what he doesn't."

Daniel swiped his hands down his face. Did Edmund seriously visit his room simply to vent his rage? *Go home. I give you fair warning.* Edmund *had* threatened him. He frowned.

It seemed extreme even for his nefarious brother, but there was rage here. No denying that. His eyes strayed to the remnants of the shattered bowl.

"Sir? Corrine said you wanted to see me?" A petite maid hovered in the doorframe. Her wide blue eyes nearly swallowed up her gamin face.

"Yes, Lanie. Did you see Lord Bryant return to his lodgings mid morning?"

Her eyes strayed to Daniel, and a pretty blush suffused her face. "Well, yes I . . ." Her words trailed off and she stared at Daniel, looking puzzled.

"What is it, Lanie?" Robbie asked.

She lifted her hand to indicate her hair, and nodded toward Daniel's head. "It's . . . well, sir, your hair looked as if it was cropped a mite shorter this mornin'."

"Thank you, Lanie, that will be all." Robbie nodded to the maid, who was as happy to depart as Corrine.

"The bastard," Daniel snarled. "He waltzes in here without a by-your-leave and rifles through my stuff for a second time. I . . ." His words tapered off and he bolted to the desk, picking up each discarded book and flipping through its pages. *Gone. It was gone.* He looked at Robbie. "Something *was* taken. The letter from my father's solicitor."

Robbie frowned. "Well, it didn't say too much. Just a cryptic note about claiming your destiny, which you already did in America. And you believed Bedford had received a copy of the letter anyway."

"I did." Daniel furrowed his brow, and ignored Davie's curious look as he paced the room. "What if he did not write to Edmund?" His thoughts spiraled. "The note said I was to visit him as soon as I arrived. What if he wanted to tell me something that Edmund did not want me to hear? Or rather, give me something that Edmund did not want me to have? That would explain my tossed stuff. Edmund's looking for it."

"What? What is it?" Davie blurted, utterly fascinated.

Daniel shook his head. "I have no idea. Everything I owned burned in the fire." He nodded to Robbie. "Whatever money I had left from my inheritance, I poured into Curtis Shipping."

Davie warily eyed the mess of the room. "Whatever it is, you need to return it. He is a duke and all."

"Will you be quiet," Robbie snarled at his brother, causing him to jump. "Maybe it is time you did as the letter advised and spoke with this solicitor. Perhaps your father left you something in his will, and his solicitor learned that Edmund never gave it to you?"

Daniel nodded, picturing a rotund, jovial man, his features wrinkled like a walnut. "I agree. I need to speak to Abel Shaw. I remember him well because my father liked to make him wait for over an hour before seeing him. Believed it set the tone of a meeting by demonstrating who controlled matters from the onset. Abel thwarted my father's power game, though, for he came prepared, always carried a deck of cards and a cheroot. Taught me to play vingt-et-un."

"Do you believe he is still in London?" Robbie said.

"He should be." Daniel shrugged. "He posted the letter at the beginning of the year."

"Do you remember anything from when he read your father's will? Were you present when it was read?" Robbie pressed.

Daniel shook his head regretfully. "No, I was there for the beginning. Then it was just Edmund. Edmund's first act as Bedford was to let Shaw go and hire his own firm. Reading my father's will was the last legal service Shaw provided."

"No, writing to you was his last service to your family," Davie corrected.

Robbie whirled on his brother. "Don't you have a stall to muck or a woman to irritate?"

Davie muttered something under his breath, but fled the room when Robbie made a threatening advance.

When Davie had departed, Daniel sighed. "I had planned to visit Shaw, but I was not in any rush to do so. I had claimed my destiny, so his words read more melodramatic than impera-tive to me. And as you know, I had more pressing matters topping my agenda while home."

"I understand. But you need to visit him now, and I should go to London with you." Robbie eyed Daniel's bruised cheek.

"You might need someone to keep you out of trouble. And it is time my idiot brother learned some responsibility, I think." He tossed a wary look in the direction that Davie had disappeared.

"Fine," Daniel said. He could use another set of eyes and ears to keep a lookout.

Daniel would have his hands full, for he had another reward he valued far more.

He had a potential woman to woo and win.

Once again, his agenda was full.

Chapter Fifteen

As Daniel alighted from the hackney, he resisted the urge to cover his nose with his handkerchief. He had only been in London for a few days, but he had already concluded that if the stench did not kill him, the cacophony of noise would. The clatter of carriage wheels, horses' hooves, various bells, and vendor shouts composed the strident city orchestra.

They were meeting Brett at a tavern near the offices of Curtis Shipping, which were located in South London near the docks. Inside the tavern, more smells and noise assaulted Daniel. Ale, cheap gin, and other rank odors permeated the atmosphere. Men stood in groups, sat among the scattered tables, or congregated along the strip of the stained bar, their voices a buzzing hum. Daniel scanned the tavern for his friend, locating him at a table in the corner.

Brett Curtis unfurled his tall frame and rose to his feet, lifting his pint in greeting as Daniel and Robbie threaded their way over to him. Candlelight flickered over Brett's thick blond hair, and his grin flashed white as his gaze narrowed on Daniel's cheek. "What happened? Someone finally try to put a damper on your smart mouth and missed? Is this the reason for your guard?"

"I am still prettier than you," Daniel fired back. "You remember my good friend, Robbie Tanner. Be kind to him or I will let him hurt you." The two had met while Daniel was recovering at Robbie's after the fire at Lakeview Manor. Once Daniel was well enough to be moved, he had sailed with Brett to America.

Brett snorted. "He can try." Robbie simply puffed out his broad chest, cracking knuckles on ham-size fists. Brett retreated, his blue eyes dancing with laughter. "Good thing I am always kind. Had to be with three sisters. Charming is my middle name." Brett dropped into his chair and motioned for a waitress to bring them a round of pints and a pitcher.

Daniel shrugged out of his redingote and hung it on the brass hook beside the table, settling into a chair beside the two men.

"Other than the bruises, you appear none the worse for wear. Even better, no one has killed you yet. Maybe I will not need to stand as your pallbearer after all."

Robbie grinned. "Gallows humor. I like it."

"Ignore him. He is devoted to me," Daniel said.

"I cannot survive without him. Oh, my mistake, I have for the past two weeks while I have struggled to broker two new business contracts. And you were doing what? Trying to solve a decade-old mystery. Any success with that?"

"Brett did not approve of my return trip," Daniel explained to Robbie, his eyes on his friend. "Did not think it a good idea I tempt fate a second time, particularly when my life is in America, and there was nothing here for me to risk it for. Except a burned-out hull of a home, an evil twin, and bad memories. Have I covered all your points? I might have missed a few, for you did tend to drone on."

"You will not be laughing when you are six feet under." Brett slammed his pint down.

"You have made your point." Daniel lifted his hand, relenting. "I do understand your reservations, but let us not air them all over again. My decision has been made."

Brett tightened his lips, and eventually turned his attention to Robbie. "So, Tanner of the illustrious Tanner Stables. How have you passed the decade since I saw you last? Have you acquired a Mrs. Tanner?"

"Hmph. I prefer the females in my stables. They don't bite. Or most of them don't," Robbie said.

"Nothing like a high-spirited filly." Brett winked at the waitress, who colored a pretty pink as she served them.

"Will thot be all, gents?" She eyed Brett suggestively, practically preening.

His smile was apologetic. "Alas, for now, it will have to suffice."

Daniel coughed as the waitress gave a lingering glance and then sauntered off, her hips in full tilt. Brett drew women to him like flies to food. "So then, there are matters that need to be discussed."

Brett sobered. "So you received my letter? I wondered, as your note did not mention it."

"What letter?" Daniel set down his pint.

"The one I sent via courier last week."

Robbie snorted. "He might have missed it. He was busy responding to another note that had him scurrying to redress a transgression."

"Be quiet, Robbie." Daniel narrowed his eyes in warning.

Brett glanced between them. "What transgression? Another robbery?"

Daniel silenced Robbie with a hand and leaned forward. "What robbery are *you* talking about? Your note must have crossed paths with my trip to the city."

"I sent it last week to that inn where you were staying," Brett said.

"I moved lodgings, and did not provide a forwarding address." He had not wanted his location known. To Edmund. "I will explain later."

Brett gave him a questioning look, but continued. "It was at our offices. The place was thoroughly ransacked. But here is the interesting part. Nothing was taken. The Bow Street Runners whom I hired to investigate speculated that whoever did the damage wanted it to look like a robbery. Considering they left the only things of value, those nautical portraits you purchased, it was suspect."

Robbie swore. "What the devil does he want? That's three suspicious searches in just under a fortnight."

"He?" Brett stared at Daniel, who gruffly updated him on the others, as well as Edmund's involvement. "Do you have something of value that your brother wants? Something that belongs to him?"

"I have no idea. However, this morning, Robbie and I paid a visit to the offices of Messrs. Shaw, Dodges, and Fuller to speak to my father's solicitor, Abel Shaw, as his letter requested. It was not a productive visit. Abel Shaw is dead."

"Christ, that's untimely," Brett muttered.

It was as if some perverse hand of fate was tossing one obstacle after another into his path. "What was so important that he could not have written it in a letter?" Impatience laced Daniel's tone. "He died nigh on three months ago. He must have been on his deathbed as I was making arrangements to sail over here."

"Perhaps that was what precipitated his writing to you after all these years. A deathbed confession," Robbie suggested.

Daniel feared Robbie was right. But he would be damned if he'd give up. Abel Shaw might have confided in someone, and if so, Daniel vowed to find out whom.

Brett nodded, appearing to consider the matter before venturing to another point. "Do you think these searches and the fire are connected?"

Robbie lowered his voice. "Bedford can't find what he wants if he incinerates the place. More so, if Bedford was responsible for that . . . that's fratricide. Accusing a duke, a peer of the realm of . . . of murder, well, that might go over in America, but here . . . well, here it would be suicide."

"Unless he is guilty. Surely even your anointed peerage is not above justice?" Brett rejoined, cocking a brow at Robbie.

Daniel interceded, seeing Robbie's expression blacken. "Edmund despises me, but not enough to murder me. If so, he had ample opportunity throughout our childhood. And what would he gain from my death? He inherited the title and all that goes with it. It does not make any sense. I pose no threat to him, and he would jeopardize everything he values if he kills me."

They fell silent.

"We need to begin where it all started," Brett said. "With your father's solicitor's letter. He had the information that he wanted to impart to Daniel."

"On that we agree." Robbie took a sip of his ale and swiped his mouth.

"So we will begin with Shaw's partners, who were not in residence when we visited. One of their clerks met with us. We will have to return and speak to one of the partners. Learn where Shaw's papers reside now, what solicitors took over his work, and glean any other information they can provide. Shaw may be dead, but some seeds of information must be alive."

"And find his family. He might have spoken to them," Brett said. "Or his papers might have passed on to them."

"And Weasel, he might have information about the fire," Robbie added.

"We will be busy. Good thing I don't have an expanding company to oversee," Brett said wryly.

Robbie waved his hand. "That's child's play. Daniel here has a woman to woo. And she wants nothing to do with him, considering he is responsible for ruining her—"

"Quiet, Robbie," Daniel warned.

Brett smiled, studying Daniel with renewed interest. "Well, then *you* have been busy. However, had you told me you were looking for a wife, I would have given you one of my sisters. I have three, you know."

"As you keep reminding me," Daniel said dryly, well aware his friend knew his sisters regarded Daniel more as a brother than a suitor, having watched them grow from gangly young girls to dangerous young women.

Brett shoved Daniel's pint closer to him and leaned forward. "Drink up and tell me everything, particularly the salacious details. Those are the best part."

"That's what I told him," Robbie exclaimed and slapped Brett on his back.

Daniel lifted his drink and took a big sip. He would need it.

❧❧

HOURS LATER, THEY staggered out of the tavern. Daniel cursed the last pint that he hadn't needed. His head felt two sizes two big and his feet were having trouble navigating the dirt road. Robbie and Brett followed, Brett's arm slung around Robbie's broad shoulders. The two men had bonded over their comical—that is, comical to them—suggestions on how to get Julia to accept Daniel's hand. Bunch of idiots.

Brett had suggested he scale Juliet's balcony and spout Shakespeare. Daniel refrained from correcting Julia's name or pointing out that he doubted Taunton's London residence had a balcony, or if so, that Julia's room would be near it. Nor would there be any poetry spouting coming from him. Ever.

Lost in his thoughts, he did not give the three men walking toward them much heed. When they came abreast of their trio, the man directly in front of Daniel raised his arm. Daniel saw the streak of silver just in time to pivot to his side. There was no chance to fully dodge the knife's cut, but it sliced along his side, rather than directly into his gut.

And then the fists went flying.

A feral rage gripping him, Daniel ignored his wound as he sank his fist into a soft belly. The man released a grunt of gin-soaked breath. As Daniel drew back for another, the man clipped his cheek. It ripped open, the man's hand breaking the already damaged skin and causing Daniel to see stars as his head snapped back.

The man followed his punch with another to Daniel's gut and he doubled over.

The combined forces of rage, pain, and fear propelled him to straighten up. He landed another punch before the man barreled into him and they flew to the ground.

One eye was swelling shut and the pain from his knife wound near blinding, Daniel never saw the punch to his jaw.

It landed just before Robbie dove over and yanked the man off of him.

Groaning, Daniel ignored their scuffle, his hand going to his stomach, blood soaking his fingers. "Christ."

There was a ruckus of feet stomping, and Robbie was back at his side. His thick mop of hair stood straight up as if someone had yanked it in different directions, but otherwise, he looked as he always looked. Large as a bear and just as formidable.

A welcome sight for sore eyes.

"You all right?"

No, he was not all right. Every bone in his body ached, his head throbbed, and he was bleeding like a leaking barrel of ale. But he nodded. "Brett?"

Brett staggered over and seeing Daniel's state, he shrugged off his redingote, knelt and pressed it to Daniel's side. "Christ, he had a blade?"

Brett had a bloody lip, and one of his eyes was half closed, but he was still another good sight. "Did they get away?" Daniel managed to ask.

"They wouldn't have." Robbie grunted. "But they ran like the cowards they were, rather than stay and fight it out. Should I have followed them?"

"No time. We need to get him to a doctor," Brett answered.

"Right. Where?" Robbie said.

"Are you asking me?" Brett snarled. "The ones I know are in Boston. A bit too far to carry him."

"It's not deep, just a scratch," Daniel murmured as Brett doubled in his vision. "Just get me back to my room."

Both of Robbie's heads swam in Daniel's blurry eyesight, their expressions looking dubious. "I don't think that's a good idea."

"Because it's a bad one," Brett said. "He needs a doctor. Where is the nearest hospital? Get a hackney coach."

"No, no hospitals. I don't trust them," Daniel panted.

"The earl is in residence. Let's take him there," Robbie suggested. "He'll get him seen faster than anyone. Our peerage comes with benefits."

"Glad to know they are good for something," Brett muttered. "Hail a hackney."

"No. Absolutely not . . . no," Daniel protested feebly, blinking to clear his sight. Black spots danced before his eyes. He thought he recognized the constellation Orion, his large belt dazzling.

"Quiet," Brett snapped. "You are outvoted. What's his address?"

Daniel blinked at Brett, seeing his mouth move, but not understanding.

"Fortunately for you, I am sure your hackney drivers know the residences of your exalted peers. Cheer up, for there will not be any balcony scaling to reach your Juliet. We are delivering you right to her doorstep. No woman can resist a weak, wounded man. She'll have to say yes to you. That is if you don't bleed to death."

"I heard that." His response was barely a whisper. "Keaton House, Mayfair."

"Your Juliet will thank you," Brett said. "And you can thank me later."

Juliet. Daniel smiled. *Wherefore art thou.* Something nagged him about the name . . . Robbie hefted him into his arms and he groaned, searing pain gripping him, erasing all other thoughts. He searched for Orion's belt, but his world went black.

Chapter Sixteen

❧❧

JULIA was settled in the library, curled up with a book, when the loud clanking of their brass doorknocker followed by a thunderous pounding shattered the silence. She jumped, and then wondered at the late hour. When the noise came again, the raps in rapid succession, she tossed down her book. She had given up on sleep a long time ago, plagued with memories of Edmund overlapping with those of Daniel. She welcomed the distraction from the Bryant twins. Her book was failing her.

She belted her robe securely and scooped up her candle. Emerging from the library and heading along the front foyer, she caught up with Emily and her father descending the stairs. The noise must have wakened her father, and Emily had always been a light sleeper.

"What in God's name? What is the time? It's the wee hours of the morning. Doesn't this cursed city ever sleep?" Taunton grumbled.

They converged in the front foyer, just as Burke, their butler, arrived from the servant quarters, carrying his own light.

"My lord, shall I see who it is and send them packing?" Burke arched a brow.

Despite the hour, her father looked amused. "Ah, why don't you carry out the former, and depending on that, we will execute the latter."

"Very good, sir." The pounding came again.

Burke opened the door, and Julia crowded with Emily behind her father, careful to not be seen as she peered onto the front stoop. Her hand flew to her mouth, her eyes locked on the prostrate form of Daniel in Robbie Tanner's arms. His face was bruised and bloody, one eye sealed shut, a large coat draped around his waist.

She brushed her father aside and gestured the men in, barely registering the tall, blond man who accompanied them. Her heart thundered, and it was all she could do to stop herself from snatching Daniel from Robbie and carrying him into a room to see what was wrong with him herself. He was too still. Terror, a heaving wave of it, sent her pulse racing.

"Lord Taunton," Robbie said. "My apologies for the intrusion, and the late hour. We ran into some trouble over by the docks."

"That is usually where one finds it. Is he all right?"

"He will be." The blond man spoke with firm conviction, his accent identifying him as an American. "He looks worse than he is, but he has lost a bit of blood. We were hoping you could assist us with procuring a doctor at this late hour."

Julia took charge of matters, seeing as her father stood stone still. "Please then, hurry. Let us get him settled in a room. This way." Her fear was assuaged somewhat at the American's calm assurance. "Burke, can you collect Doctor Malley? Also, have Petie boil some water and bring up towels. Gentlemen, if you would follow me."

"So this is Lady Juliet. Despite the circumstance, I am honored," the blond man said as he hurried after her.

"Straight ahead, down this foyer," Julia directed Robbie, her eyes glued to Daniel's pale features. At the man's words, she tore her gaze away, noting his bloodied lip and swelling right eye. Daniel wasn't the only one in need of a doctor. "I am Lady *Julia*, and you are?"

"Oh, my apologies, Brett Curtis at your service." He gave a short brow.

"His business partner." Her father beamed. "That explains your being by the docks. Most shipping firms are located down there."

"Yes. Docks tend to be a necessity for large ships to displace cargo," Brett said, his irony lost on her father.

Julia ignored their conversation as she opened the door to the guest room, and hurried inside to yank down the bedcovers. She moved aside for Robbie to deposit Daniel, then returned to his side. She gasped when the redingote draped around Daniel fell away, revealing his torn and bloodstained jacket.

"Good lord, what happened?" her father exclaimed. "That's more than trouble. Gunshot?"

"Knife wound," Robbie clarified.

Julia's eyes shot to his, and seeing his worried expression, she sprang into action. "Grab me that towel from the commode, let us keep the wound covered." *It will be all right. He will be all right.* She wouldn't let anything happen to him. *Because he is mine and . . .* She blinked. He was not hers. He was . . . her friend.

Tears blurred her vision, and she fought them back. He was her arrogant, irritating, lovely Sancho Panza who had vowed to take care of her. Well, it was her turn to care for him even as her heart twisted at his stillness. Daniel was a coiled bundle of energy, and she could not bear to see him so calm, so quiet. Silenced.

She bit her lip as Emily handed her the towel. "Let us remove his waistcoat and shirt. Assess how bad it is."

Brett was already removing Daniel's Hessian boots.

"Be careful," she cried as he gave a hard yank, jerking Daniel's figure.

"I am, but short of cutting them off, it is the best I can do," Brett said. Seeing Julia's expression, his voice softened. "He will be fine. He said it was just a scratch. I think he is right, because it didn't look too deep. He turned to his side at the last minute. He always was quick on his feet." Pride laced his words.

"Why did he have to be?" she muttered, desperate to know what in the world had transpired at the docks. After Robbie had slipped his redingote from Daniel, she set the towel aside and quickly unbuttoned his jacket and his waistcoat, stepping back for Robbie to remove those as well.

"Ah, Julia . . . Julia, perhaps we should get Petie . . ." her father began.

"Yes, where is she with the extra towels and the water? I told Burke to . . . What is it?" She blinked distractedly when her father grasped her elbow, tugging gently on it.

"It is time to leave Lord Bryant to Petie and the doctor's care when he arrives—"

"But they aren't here yet." She tugged her elbow free to continue her ministrations.

She untied Daniel's muslin cravat and slipped it off, unbuttoning his shirt and sweeping it from his shoulders. Heat climbed her cheeks as her gaze feasted on the broad expanse of naked chest, his skin hot against her fingertips. Like a scattering of black and blue blossoms, the bruises bloomed over his taut, ridged stomach. But even bruised and bloodied, he was a beautiful specimen of a man. Drawing a ragged breath, she stepped back to let Robbie tug Daniel's shirt from him.

"Julia," her father cried. "You need to—".

"Do what I am doing," she argued. At her father's stunned expression, she gentled her tone. "I no longer have a reputation to safeguard, so if I am ruined, I might as well take advantage of the benefits of being so." Seeing her father's worry, she gave his arm a reassuring squeeze. "Please, he needs my help. Let me do what I can while you see if the doctor is here. It will be all right. We are among friends here."

"Well . . . I . . ." Taunton stammered.

"Daniel never stood a chance." Brett spoke to the room at large, shaking his head. When Julia gave him a questioning look, his eyes were bright with admiration.

"Yes, well, you remain with me. I would like to know what

happened." She turned back to the bed and eased beside Daniel.

Petie bustled in, a maid with her, both carrying pitchers of water and clean towels. The buxom housekeeper pinched her lips and surveyed the scene. "Who needs to be in here and who doesn't?" Her sharp gaze narrowed on Emily and Julia before piercing Robbie, her father, and lastly, Brett.

"Lady Julia and Mr. Curtis will be assisting you." Her father kept his voice level and met her look with one of his own. She huffed out a breath, knowing when she was out-ranked. "Emily, why don't you and Robbie come with me so I can be updated on matters."

"Are you sure *he* should stay?" Emily said, giving Brett a suspicious look. "After all, he got him into trouble in the first place."

Surprised, Brett protested. "I did not get him into trouble. It was three thugs who did, one wielding a knife. I extricated him from it."

"Mmh," Emily said, turning on her heel to leave with Robbie and her father.

"The blond beauty bites," Brett murmured.

"That be Lady Emily Chandler to you, sir," Petie said, giving Brett another of her looks.

"Lady Emily Chandler," Brett mused. "Daniel neglected to mention her."

Julia ignored Brett as Petie handed her a cloth soaked in hot water. Gingerly, she lifted the towel from Daniel's waist and lay the cloth onto the bloodied wound, grateful that the bleeding appeared to have eased. Daniel's body arched, and he twisted away from her. "Shh, it's all right. You are all right," she soothed gently, laying her palm flat against his chest, the feel of his strong heartbeat settling her nerves.

Brett leaned over the bed and grabbed Daniel's shoulders, easing him back into the pillows.

Julia delicately washed his bloodstained skin, her heart in her throat as a groan escaped Daniel. She drew her first steady breath as she assessed for herself that while the cut was long and mean, it was not deep. More importantly, it looked pink and clean. "He will be all right," she said. Mortified, her voice hitched, and she had to blink back tears. "He had so many layers on, it protected him."

"Yes, and he has a thick skin," Brett said.

Julia's eyes lifted to his, and seeing his shrewd blue gaze regarding her as if he could read her thoughts, she looked away. For he could not. She didn't know them herself. Was not ready to study them. "Yes, well, let us be grateful for that."

"And also for the good doctor's arrival," Petie proclaimed loudly.

At her words, Julia swept to her feet and turned to see Doctor Malley bustle in.

"What have we here? So late at night." He frowned, pushing his spectacles up his nose, his bushy eyebrows furrowed beneath his shock of ginger-colored hair. "Looks like I am redundant. Fine job, Lady Julia. Why don't I take a closer look, while you see to that gash on his face."

"Yes, of course." Julia took Brett's place, accepting the clean towel from Petie, and ignoring her censorious look. The woman was worse than her mother. Julia was too old to care. Another benefit she fully enjoyed at the housekeeper's prudish expense. Julia cursed her unsteady hand as she pressed the cloth to Daniel's cheek.

The cut was small and she quickly dabbed it clean, her eyes roving over his face. He had incredibly sharp, high cheekbones, she noted, studying the unbruised cheek. And long lashes. There was that dent in his chin. His lips were parted, and she knew from experience how soft they were and just what they tasted like . . . he . . . Her head snapped around. "What was that?"

"I was saying it does not look like he needs to be stitched. I am going to bandage the wound. Young man, if you could switch places with Lady Julia again and assist me by propping him up, we can wrap this around him."

Flushing, Julia skittered from the bed, making room for Brett, but she was unable to retreat too far—in case Daniel needed her.

Brett slid his hands beneath Daniel's shoulders and hefted

him to a sitting position. An involuntary cry escaped Julia, causing Brett to set him back down. "What? What is it?" He looked at her. "Is he bleeding again?"

"No, no, it is not that." She valiantly struggled to recompose herself. Brett's expression was alarmed, and Julia realized he was strung as tight as she, despite his calm façade. "It is just . . . that is, he has . . ."

Baffled, Brett stared at her and then understanding dawned, and he relaxed. "That is a decade-old injury. Scar tissue," he explained to the doctor. He leaned over and propped Daniel up while the doctor wrapped a bandage around his waist.

Julia stared, the questions coming fast and furious, for she recognized the signs of healed burns all too well. Cook's right leg from thigh to heel was a mean mass of burned skin, her skirts having caught in a fire that Julia would never forget. Like her leg, Daniel's right shoulder halfway down his back and along the back of his right arm was red, knotted, angry scar tissue. She swallowed.

He had been badly burned in a fire. *A decade-old injury.* She feared she knew where.

"There," the doctor was saying. He tugged up the covers and lay them over Daniel as he spoke. "Not much to do for that eye or cheek but ice or a cold piece of meat on it to reduce the swelling. He needs to rest and to apply a fresh bandage to this wound each day. There is a slight chance of infection, so let me know if he spikes a fever. The icing goes for you, too, young man. You are a matched pair. Dare I hope your opponents look worse?" He chuckled. "Now then, my work is done. Petie, can you see me out?"

The housekeeper warily eyed Brett and Julia, but seeing as neither gave her deliberate looks any heed, she tightened her lips and escorted Doctor Malley from the room.

"Mr. Curtis, it's time you told me what transpired this evening." Her voice was steady, her gaze locked on his. She had other questions, but she would save those for Daniel.

He lifted a brow, and after a silent study of her, he sighed and crossed to the water pitcher by the commode. He poured himself a glass and drank it. "We were leaving a tavern a few doors down from the offices of Curtis Shipping, when we were jumped by three men." He paused and added. "One had a knife and he appeared to be targeting Daniel."

Julia staggered back and sank onto the bed, the blood draining from her face. She had to moisten her lips before she could speak. "It was not a robbery gone awry? You cannot possibly be sure—"

"I can be," Brett cut her off. "I can be because this is not the first time someone tried to murder him." His eyes were hard, his expression implacable.

"The fire? You think it was deliberately set? They said it was a candle that caught on curtains, an accident. They said—"

"I know what they said. And Daniel let them say it." He set his glass down and swept a hand through his hair. "Look, this isn't my story to tell. If Daniel wants to share it with you, he needs to do so, not me. He is my business partner, but more important, he's my friend, and I have to honor his wishes.

"However, I can share one confidence. I did not want him to return. I tried to talk him out of it. But he had questions that needed to be answered that ten years later still plagued him. I agree he has a right to get those answers, but at what price? I helped him to leave after the fire, once he had healed, to build a new life in America. If you care for him, whether you accept his hand or not, you need to see that he returns to that life. He cannot stay. Someone wants him dead here, and if he remains, he is jeopardizing his life."

Brett strode to the door.

"Wait," she cried. He paused and faced her. Julia stood, her heart pounding. "Do you . . ." She hesitated, not wanting to ask it, but it needed to be asked. "Do you think Bedford could be involved? He and his brother did not care for each other. He told me that his brother had never been kind to him."

Surprise crossed his features. "I didn't think he ever spoke of Bedford or his childhood," he murmured. "Feared he was ashamed of it."

"Ashamed?" Julia said, a chill suffusing her.

"Well, explaining all the bruises. Daniel was such a small boy . . ." His voice trailed off. "But he had eyes in the back of his head because he was always one step ahead of every prank at Dunbar Academy. Being the sole American in the school, I quickly bet on his hidden talents to save my much-bruised body. We joined forces and extricated ourselves from our share of troubles over the years." His eyes strayed to the bed and Daniel's still figure. "We still are. And he's still quick footed." He grinned, but it faded and his eyes saddened.

"You asked me if I thought Bedford is behind these attacks? I honestly don't know. As Daniel says, Bedford has nothing to gain through Daniel's murder, and everything to lose. But if a boy is capable of beating and maiming another, nearly severing his finger, then perhaps that boy is capable of murder as a man." He paused and gave Julia a deliberate look. "You aren't ruined, Lady Julia. Far from it, Daniel saved you." He bowed, turned on his heel, and left.

Stunned, Julia stared at the closed door, swiping at the tears she realized streamed down her cheeks. She was an embarrassing water pot. Thank goodness, the room had cleared. She lifted Daniel's hand, and grabbing a discarded washcloth, she washed his bloodied and battered knuckles, the mindless task soothing her.

Daniel had said his reasons for leaving for America were unimportant. He had lied. Murder. *Why?* Why would someone want to kill him? To what purpose? He was the second son of a duke. His lands comprised a mere four hundred acres of Lakeview Manor. She did not understand it. Too many pieces of the puzzle eluded her. Her eyes strayed to Daniel, and her breath hitched.

Someone had tried to murder him.

It was the only piece she did have. Brett had confided so much more than Daniel. Good lord, his childhood must have been a living nightmare. She shuddered, seeing a slim, almost delicate boy, head bent, hands thrust in his pockets as he strolled the banks of Lakeview Manor. So very alone. And bruised. She had seen it herself. A blackened eye or cheek, his innocuous explanations were often accompanied with a dismissive shrug.

Her thumb rubbed over his bruised knuckles, and she found

another white scar on his middle finger. Nearly severed, Brett had said.

While she had realized her mistake in accepting Edmund's hand, she had never fathomed how close her escape had been.

I think I was meant to come home for you.

Daniel saved you.

"Thank you," she murmured. She lifted Daniel's hand and pressed her lips to his scarred finger, her vision swimming again.

"My pleasure."

The words were barely audible, but they had her jerking back as if they were shouted. She stared into Daniel's eyes, or rather, one open heavy-lidded eye. It met hers for a few heartbeats before it slid closed, and his breathing evened out. Her heart fluttered. When she was sure he slept, she expelled her breath.

Sometimes it takes the scare of losing something precious for someone to realize its true value.

Daniel's words about her father and Emily returning from grief echoed in the quiet room. Through a moist sheen of tears, she brushed Daniel's hair from his forehead, her smile wavering. He was precious to her, but Brett was right. He needed to return to America before it was too late. She vowed to make sure he did so. Short of finding his murderer, it was all she could do for him.

He had saved her.

It was her turn to save him.

Chapter Seventeen

❧❦

D ANIEL awoke when he rolled to his side and a stabbing
pain shot through him. His eyes flew open and he blinked,
disoriented. He didn't recognize the brass bed, the emerald
green and gold brocade curtains and drapes, or the marble-
topped nightstand. When his befuddled gaze located a young
woman, curled up in a padded armchair and fast asleep, he
relaxed. The room may be unfamiliar, but the beautiful woman
was not.

Julia.

Once again, he approved of her streak of bluestocking independence, for a young woman did not enter a gentleman's
bedroom alone, let alone fall asleep in said chamber, in bed
or out. His lips curved as he savored this rare chance to study
her at his leisure, without her blue gaze staring him down or
her delicate brow arched in question.

She wore a rose-colored silk dressing gown, her legs drawn
up on the chair and tucked beside her. For the first time since
his return, her hair was down. Loosely tied back, the long
strands fell in a riotous mass of curling waves over her shoulder

and to her waist. The pain in his side paled in comparison to his aching need to reach out and wrap his hand in the thick locks and pull her close.

He would then kiss those full, parted lips, long-lashed eyelids, the curve of her cheek, and . . . he groaned. This would not do. Same throbbing pain, new location, and there were no bandages to alleviate matters. He eased onto his back and glowered at the painted swirls in the ceiling.

"Are you all right?"

He turned his head and found Julia wide-awake. He swallowed. Good lord, if she would accept his bloody proposal, he could awaken to her looking at him like that every morning, though hopefully, minus the furrowed brow of concern.

She unfurled her legs and stood. Leaning over, she brushed his hair from his temple, and placed her hand on his forehead. "No fever. That's good." She straightened and smiled. "How are you feeling?"

It surprised him that he didn't have a fever, for his body was burning, and her touch elevated his temperature another degree. He cleared his throat. "Like an apple tossed into the cider mill's crusher." He paused, wonder filling him at the moisture pooling in her eyes before she blinked it back. He hastened to allay her worry. "I look worse than I feel. Really. Bruises heal. The footpads picked the wrong group to rob." When she still looked unconvinced, he pressed on. "They didn't see Robbie. With his size, he only had to growl and they fled like the cowards they were."

Julia quickly turned away and strode over to the commode. He frowned as she lifted her hand to swipe at her eye.

Something in his chest constricted. No one had ever shed tears over him before, had ever offered him compassion, and he was not sure how to respond. He swallowed down the lump in his throat and with it the compulsion to babble like an idiot. "Julia, I promise you, I am fine, been battered worse. I—"

She swung back around and fisted her hands at her sides. "It was not a robbery gone wrong, so don't placate me with a lie. Someone tried to plunge a knife in you, and you could have been killed. And not for the first time. I know they tried to burn Lakeview Manor with you in it." Unshed tears glistened in her eyes.

Stunned, his mouth dropped open, and then slammed shut. *Brett.* He cursed him and his big mouth. When Daniel got through with him, he would wish he had been the one cut last evening. He struggled to a sitting position, cursed the pain piercing his side, and fell back with a groan.

Julia's anger vanished, and she was at his side, her hand on his shoulder. "Stay still. Do you want to open the wound again? For goodness' sake, you need to lie down and let yourself heal."

Daniel glowered and propped himself more slowly on his elbows, resisting her efforts to push him back.

"Daniel, stop it," she cried. "Stop it or I'll get my father in here to hold you down."

Amused, he paused to consider her words. "Not a good idea with you dressed like that and me like this and us having spent the night together—"

She yanked her hand back as if his skin burned and hissed at him. "We did no such thing," she gasped.

"We did. I woke up and you were sound asleep on the chair. It's official now. We have spent the night together, so you have to marry me. I have now compromised you twice." He groaned and collapsed back on the bed, the strain of propping himself up having taken its toll. "But don't send for the vicar just yet. Give me a few days . . ."

"Don't be ridiculous. You cannot compromise someone twice. Once they are ruined, the matter is finished. There is no . . ." Her voice trailed off and she pressed her hand to her forehead. "This conversation is not relevant. You are deliberately trying to distract me. It will not succeed, and we are not marrying in a few days, because you are leaving. You are returning to America as soon as possible. You cannot stay. Last night proved it. It is too dangerous. Brett Curtis told me—"

"Too much, that is what he told you," he muttered. He attempted to sit up again, but Julia was beside him, pressing back on his shoulders.

"Wait, stop! If you insist on sitting up, let me help you

before you open your wound and bleed all over the bed linens."

"Fine." He started to sit up, but when her hand moved to slip behind him, he stopped and sank back into the pillows. "I . . . I ah . . . I can manage on my own. I am fine, really."

She stared at him and straightening, she spoke softly. "I have seen the scars. It is a small sacrifice to pay for your life. You could have been killed and you survived. Those scars are a reminder of that and carry no shame."

Stunned, his lips parted, and his heart beat off rhythm. Many women had turned away at the sight, appalled. Not his Julia. Nothing scared her. Except marriage. To him.

"Stop scowling, and let me help you," she said.

He eased himself up enough for her to slip her arm beneath his shoulders.

She yanked his pillows up to cushion his back. "There. Now ease back slowly."

He glanced over his shoulder and grinned. "Can you leave your arm around me and sit beside me? It reduces the pain."

Their gazes met, and a thrum of awareness filled the air before she snatched her arm free, letting him sink back onto the pillows with a groan.

"You deserved that. For goodness' sake, I am trying to help you and you cannot be serious for one minute. This is a dangerous situation. You need to treat it as such."

"I am," he protested, his humor gone. "You can be sure I will watch my back from now on. But what I will not do, and what you are asking me to do, is to run away. I did that once. I am done running."

"What do you think you are going to accomplish by staying? Provide them with a target to practice on until they perfect their aim?" She folded her arms across her chest and awaited his response.

He did not have any answers to that.

The silence stretched, but Julia was formidable.

Sighing, he lifted his hands and swiped them through his hair. "I am going to kill Brett."

"Yelling at friends who care about you will not change the

situation. Besides, he did not tell me anything, just warned me that it was dangerous for you to remain here. He told me I had to get the full story from you, which will be difficult because you only give half of the story, like you did about Edmund."

"He told you about Edmund, too? He is going to die. Right now!" Daniel flipped his covers back and made to get up, but Julia rushed over to him.

"No! No, he is not here. For goodness' sake, you can kill him when you heal. You have enough bruises on your body. Please, no more." She yanked the covers out of his hands and bent over him to tuck them back in around him.

When her eyes lifted to his, her anguish dispelled his anger. He cupped her cheek, turning her face toward his. "I am sorry, Julia. So very sorry that I scared you."

"Then don't do it again! Go home. Go to America," she begged.

His hand dropped and he sighed. "I cannot. I did that once. I left everything behind, buried myself in work and tried to forget. But over the years, the questions were like this wound, only they would not close and they festered. A decade ago, I lost everything precious to me, nearly including my life. I will not leave until I get answers. I do not know what Edmund is looking for, and I have no idea why someone wants me dead, but I will find out."

Julia dropped like a stone onto his bed. Her gaze studied him with a sharp scrutiny, and she must have read the conviction in his expression, for she nodded, looking resigned. "Fine. Then I will help you."

"What? No! Absolutely not. It is too dangerous. I will not allow it."

"You are too weak to stop me. We are also not betrothed, so you cannot tell me what I can or cannot do. But you did make me an offer, and you are responsible for ruining me as you like to remind me, so I have a vested interest in your survival. Saving you saves me."

He stared at her. "That is the most ridiculous piece of logic I have ever heard."

She shrugged. "I *am* involved. I have spent a long, uncomfortable night caring for your worthless, ungrateful hide, even if it is so thick that knives cannot pierce it. I have earned the right to make sure it remains in one piece. Just in case I decide to marry you."

He blinked at her and then he couldn't help it, he laughed. He stopped immediately, for it irritated his side. "So if I let you assist me, and I survive, does this mean you will marry me?"

"I will give it serious consideration."

She looked so earnest, he had to stifle his laugh again.

He could not resist. He grasped the long rope of curls that tumbled over her shoulder. His knuckles brushed her breast, and he heard her ragged intake of breath. He did what he had yearned to do since he had opened his eyes to a lovely angel sitting bedside vigil. He wrapped the thick strands around his hand and reeled her in. "Maybe I can help expedite your decision." His voice was husky as his eyes dropped to her lips.

"You can," she whispered back, her gaze meeting his, inches away. She was so close he could see tiny white streaks like starbursts flaring out in the blue of her eyes.

Mesmerized, it took him a moment before her words registered. He leaned forward, but her hand, firm and warm on his shoulder stopped him. Damned if his temperature didn't ratchet up another notch.

"By telling me what you mean about Edmund looking for something. By telling me all you have not told me. By trusting in me."

Surprised, he paused. So she was telling the truth. Brett hadn't told her everything after all. He considered her plea. He was a good negotiator; it was time he employed those skills in order to practice other more pleasurable skills. "I will tell you everything and let you assist me—at a safe distance and with my supervision—if you give me something in return." He kept his voice to a low murmur.

"Isn't my assistance in keeping you alive enough?" she whispered back.

He smiled. "Well, Robbie's bigger than you. As I said, he growls and people scatter. But you have something else that I want, that only you can provide."

"What is it?" she breathed, her own lips curving.

"One kiss, freely given."

She paused as if to consider the matter. "And then you will tell me everything? No more secrets?"

He looked offended. "I never kept secrets. I just did not tell . . . Never mind. Yes, I will tell you everything." Why not? There was not much to tell because he did not know a damn thing—yet.

Her eyes met his, and she lifted her hand to gently finger the swelling surrounding his left eye, nearly closing it, and then featherlight, she swept it over his bruised cheek. The gentle touch combined with her look of tenderness nearly undid him. He did not dare to move, not even to breathe, for she was like a bird, poised for flight. The clicking of a distant clock filled in the hushed, expectant silence.

Her eyes dipped to his lips. "One kiss." And then she lowered her head.

Her lips were full, and so incredibly soft. She kissed him tentatively, a light pressure against his lips. She teased and tempted, in small nibbles, filling him with a longing so strong, he nearly begged.

His fist tightened in her hair, his other hand cradling the nape of her neck, his thumb resting on the beating pulse in her throat. With gentle pressure, he lured her closer. And then he opened his mouth and drank her in. She tasted of innocence and sweet promises. His tongue delved deeply and desire pounded through him.

He wanted her. More of her. All of her.

She groaned against his lips, igniting his passion to a fevered pitch.

He released her hair to thread his fingers down the split V of her silk robe, his fingers touching warm, silken skin.

She drew away and stared at him through passion-glazed eyes.

"Good lord, I want you," he breathed.

Her eyes widened, her pink tongue darting out to moisten her lips. "Yes, well, the bargain was for one kiss." Her voice was hoarse, as if she hadn't used it in a while because her mouth was busy with other matters. She started to pull away, but his hand around her nape held her in place.

"I want more than one kiss. I want to touch you and have you touch me. I want to make love to you." He lifted his head and captured her lips again, which had parted in surprise. His fingers slid lower, curving over a full breast, his thumb slid over an aroused peak. "Give in to me, Julia. Be mine, and let me be yours."

Her eyes flew open and she drew back with a gasp. "We must stop. This is not right. You are wounded . . . and . . . need to regain your strength." She struggled to her feet, cinching her robe tightly together, her hands not quite steady.

"All the parts that need to work are perfectly healthy," he muttered.

"You are trying to seduce me to make me forget our bargain. You need—"

"Of course I am," he growled, lifting his hands to drag them down his face, grimacing at the swelling on his eye. Perhaps she was right. He was a bit of a mess. But he wouldn't be for long. He spoke more calmly. "Fine. I will slow down, give us both more time. Just not too much of it."

She frowned at the echo of his earlier warning. "I will return after I dress. I will have something brought to you to break your fast. Are you hungry?"

"I was, but not necessarily for food." He couldn't resist the trite quip.

She grinned. "Yes, well, knowing you, I am confident that you will not pass up hot scones, or anything else edible as long as I have the cook douse it in sugar or syrup."

"Too true. It is my favorite dream of you." Delighted, he admired the pink flush suffusing her cheeks, like rose wine filling a delicate glass.

"I have to go." She whirled and practically ran to the door.

She stopped, her hand on the knob, the other pressed flat on the doorframe, and spoke with her back to him. "I am glad you are all right."

And then she was gone.

His smile was smug as he settled himself more comfortably into the pillows. Brett was right. Wooing a woman was much easier when you were safely ensconced in their house, and they were worried for you. He was not keen on Julia assisting him with his agenda, but recalling her clever mind and keen eye for detail, the idea held merit. He would let her help—as long as he could keep her safe. If not, all bargains were off.

Because she was his destiny and he had every intention of claiming her.

Chapter Eighteen

❧

Daniel lasted one day bedridden and housebound. Julia was not surprised, for a man with such a thick hide, she had little expectation that something as trifling as a knife wound and savage beating would keep him down.

The one day he did rest, he was visited by Brett, Robbie, her father, Emily, and a fascinated Jonathan. The endless parade of guests provided buffers between Daniel and her, giving him no time to fulfill his agreement to her. But she was not deterred.

After their kiss, he owed her explanations. Not that the kiss was a hardship. In fact, for a man adept at negotiations, she wondered why he did not ask for something more . . .

She paused as she headed to the dining room. What more was she willing to give him?

Everything.

Shocked, she gave her head a sharp shake to clear it. They were not ready for *everything* quite yet. Far from it.

Things could go no further until she knew what Daniel was confronting. Until she had decided whether to heed Brett

Curtis's advice and encourage Daniel to go home, or to honor Daniel's wishes and assist him in resolving this mystery. *Until he trusted in her. Until he confided in her. Until he said he loved her.*

More important than her need to hear those words was the gnawing, inexorable fear, like a tide she could not push back, that Daniel's life was at stake. Whatever her feelings, his life was not something she was willing to risk losing.

She was coming to value it more than her own.

Drawing herself up, she continued to the dining room with renewed purpose. She would simply have to determine the best manner in which to save his arrogant, thick hide. For she had plans for it.

Considering Daniel's restlessness, it did not surprise her to find him seated at the dining room table breaking his fast. What surprised her was that in addition to the usual serving of bacon, eggs, ham, and assorted scones and rolls, there was a large china platter of treacle tarts. Their mouthwatering aroma of warm breadcrumbs, treacle, and lemon filling drifted to her.

She could just imagine how Daniel had wheedled Cook into serving dessert so early in the morning. Who could resist the man? Brett had brought over his belongings yesterday, and Daniel had shaved and bathed, and was impeccably groomed in a gray waistcoat and navy blue jacket. His white cravat was in sharp contrast to his skin, sun-bronzed from days spent outdoors. The swelling in his eye and cheek had receded, and the purple-and-blue-colored bruises highlighted those sharp green eyes.

Julia was not unaffected by his appearance, and she had to recompose herself. It was not every morning a woman awoke to a stunning specimen of masculine beauty greeting her.

"Julia, are you going to stand poised like a statue or do you plan to dine?"

Only then did she realize Daniel was not alone. Joining him at the table were her father and Jonathan. Three pairs of eyes were focused on her, but she only noticed the green set brimming with amusement.

Daniel rose to his feet, and inclined his head in greeting. "I think she makes a rather fetching statue, reminds me of Botticelli's Venus."

"Hmph." Her father gave that opinion on the matter as he rose to his feet. His attention snapped to Jonathan, who was climbing to his knees and reaching for the tray of tarts, his face smeared with lemon juice. Her father deftly lifted the tray out of reach. "Why don't we leave some for your sisters?"

Jonathan scowled. "Cor, Emily is having a lying in, and Julia always shares her treats with me."

"She can do so later in the morning, for you have had your share."

"Bryant said one can never have enough treats, and why should they be reserved for after dinner?" Jonathan protested, a pout on his face.

"So he did. Your belly might voice another opinion if you continue in this vein. Please excuse yourself, clean up the food you have chosen to wear rather than eat, and then meet me in my study."

"But Lord Bryant promised to teach me sword fighting. So I can skewer the good-for-nothing, dirty-rotten, green-eyed Cyclops who pounced on him at the docks."

"Another time. Lord Bryant has an appointment this morning. And we have plans to visit the British Museum today."

"Don't worry, Jonathan. If we cannot skewer the Cyclops, I'll have Robbie sit on him." Daniel winked at her brother.

Jonathan snorted his delight, but at his father's look, he scampered off.

"Cyclops? Venus?" Her father arched a brow as he returned the platter of tarts to the table. "You appear to be a veritable font of mythology this morning."

"A Cyclops makes a far more interesting villain than everyday dock ruffians."

"Point taken," her father mused. "Mr. Curtis and Robbie have been speaking to the authorities about these Cyclopes who waylaid you. Do you think they will be able to learn anything?"

Daniel's smile faded. "I don't know. The city is teeming

with such miscreants, but also for a price, there is a wealth of informers, willing to squeal on their brethren in crime. While I am offering to pay that price, it might take a while before we learn anything."

Her father nodded. "I suppose until then, there is little we can do but avoid the docks and watch your back. I do hope you will do so." He gave Daniel a deliberate look. "If you will excuse me, I have some work to complete in my office, and I will leave you to your dessert to break the fast."

Julia, who had followed Jonathan's exodus to assist him with cleaning his face, waited for her father to leave the room before she ventured forward, wary when Daniel circled the table to draw her chair out for her. After he returned to his seat, she spoke. "Speaking of bribery, dessert to break the fast is unprecedented. What did you promise Cook?" She leaned forward to help herself to some coddled eggs, toast, and a slice of ham.

Daniel took umbrage. "No bribery. However, I might have taken advantage of Cook and Petie's battle for supremacy." A teasing light entered his eyes. "Once Petie declared oats porridge best for my recovery, Cook was delighted to thwart her. I might have mentioned that the Prince Regent himself broke the fast with them. And as he is now King of England, clearly no harm was done."

"So Cook determines if it is good enough for royalty, it is good enough for Keaton House." She laughed.

"Exactly. So here I am, breaking the fast with treacle tarts and my very own Venus."

"If you have not noticed, I am fully clothed, while Botticelli's Venus is not," she pointed out, compelled to bring that pertinent detail to his attention.

"Sadly true, but I have no doubt that if you emerged naked from a shell with your hair blowing untamed in the wind, you would be absolutely stunning. I would be begging for brush and canvas. In fact, next to you coated in sugar and icing, it is my new fondest dream."

Julia paused in lifting her napkin to wipe her mouth, Daniel's perusal stripping her as naked as Botticelli's Venus. His words stole her voice, but she quickly recovered and shot him a quelling look. "Please, stop. Someone might overhear you."

"You are not a morning person? Prefer being seduced at early evening? Dusk more your preference?" At her blank look, he simply laughed, picked up a treacle tart, and leaned across the table to speak more intimately. "The dessert reminds me of you—tart, but sweet." He flashed her a devilish grin, lifted the slice to his mouth, and bit into it.

There was something about a handsome man with a smudge of treacle on his mouth. It was boyishly endearing. When his tongue darted out, she stilled. She couldn't tear her gaze away as he slowly and deliberately licked his lips clean. At the sinfully erotic display, desire shot through her. Her body tilted forward, like a leaning mast, and she yearned to lick the sticky remnants from those sensuous lips, to run her tongue over them and taste the sweet flavor of the golden treacle filling. And Daniel.

Appalled, she straightened.

Her breathing quickened, her heart skipped erratically, for his eyes were heavy-lidded and fixed on her mouth. Suddenly aware hers gaped open like a gutted fish, she snapped it closed and dropped her eyes to her plate, her mortification complete.

This would not do. Daniel was like a strong current, sweeping her off her feet and carrying her to places she was not ready to go. He was strong, forceful, and incredibly hard to resist.

The clanking of the front knocker rescued her. She jumped as the noise shattered the awareness that pulsed between them, brimming with unfilled desire and unspoken yearnings.

She was grateful for the distraction when Burke escorted Robbie and Brett into the dining room.

After the initial greetings were made, Robbie settled into the chair beside Daniel and leaned forward. "Is that treacle tart?"

"It is and you are welcome to a few as long you leave a portion for the rest of us," Daniel said, warily eyeing Robbie's mammoth frame.

Robbie huffed out a breath and helped himself to a plate and a generous serving.

Brett shuddered. "How can you eat that so early in the morning?"

"With little difficulty. Watch closely," Robbie said, and half the tart disappeared into his mouth.

Brett shook his head. "I fear an early demise for you both."

Julia inhaled sharply and noticed Daniel's foot connecting with Brett's shin beneath the table.

"Ow, what?" Brett sputtered, but at Daniel's warning glance, he hastened to amend his words. "My apologies, poor choice of expression. With your quick feet and hard skin, you will live to a ripe old age. Fat, happy, with a waddle for a walk. An elephant with a top hat."

"As long as I am not alone, like you undoubtedly will be due to your pathetic wit, I look forward to it." He narrowed his eyes at Brett, but as he finished his sentence, his gaze homed in on Julia, and she shifted in her seat.

"Speaking of longevity, I think it is time we discussed yours more seriously," Julia interceded.

Robbie paused, his hand halfway to his mouth.

"Lady Julia is going to assist us with our investigation. We made a deal. I promised to update her on everything and include her on events moving forward." His gaze met hers, and she braced herself when a devilish glint lit his eyes. "In return, if I survive, she promises to accept my hand in marriage."

"I made no such promise," Julia gasped, appalled that he would air their private discussion before Brett and Robbie. "I said I would *consider* your proposal."

Daniel grinned, unrepentant. "Fine. She promised to *consider* it. So, gentlemen, I have a vested interest in surviving."

"I suggest you cut back on desserts for breakfast, then," Brett said dryly.

Daniel appeared to give serious consideration to the suggestion, and then shook his head. "No. In fact, I should consume more to provide additional padding that—"

"Better yet, if you had stayed in Boston, where—"

"Gentlemen, please, this is not productive," Julia again intervened, wondering how the two managed a company together. With their matching black eyes, they looked more like wayward pirates than successful men of trade. "Let's start at the beginning, and tell me what you know. Then let us proceed from there."

She sat back and waited as all three men scowled. After a prolonged silence, Daniel blew out a breath and began to tell her a story with seeds planted over a decade ago.

When he had finished, she marveled that Daniel had survived. She kept her voice steady, despite her racing pulse. "You definitely heard men yelling before the fire? But you did not see anyone?"

"I did. It is what saved me. And no, they were gone by the time I escaped."

"I talked with the Bow Street Runners to see if they could find out anything about the attack at the docks. An agent is going to come by to get a statement from you," Brett said, nodding toward Daniel. "While I was doing that, Robbie visited a few of the gambling hells in the city, looking for Weasel, who hopefully has information about the fire."

"Right," Robbie added, laying his napkin on the table and leaning back in his chair, settling his large frame in more comfortably. "I also hired a few thief-takers, who might be able to glean more information than the Runners." Robbie shrugged. "Worth a few quid if they turn up something."

"We cannot make any connections between the searches and these attempts on your life?" Julia said.

The men exchanged glances, and it was Brett who responded. "Not yet, but I think—"

"Bedford has nothing to gain by my death." Daniel cut him off again, his eyes hard.

"Why the devil do you defend him? He would love to see you six feet under. He abused you for years and—"

Daniel slammed his hand on the table, silencing Brett. "Enough. Until we have cause, we have nothing."

Brett snapped his mouth closed and leaned back in his chair, seething. "Fine, but my bet is on Bedford."

"Why don't we consider who does have something to gain from your death, if as you say, Edmund doesn't. Who inherits if something happens to you, Daniel?" Julia asked, changing the topic.

Daniel's eyes widened at Julia, and his smile broke out again. "Isn't she magnificent? Didn't I tell you? Beautiful *and* brilliant. You have to marry me. You are—"

"Daniel, please," Julia cried, her embarrassment competing with the familiar rush of pleasure at his praise, but they were in company. He might be able to dismiss that, but she could not. "Please stop." She gave pointed looks to Brett and Robbie.

Daniel frowned. "You are right, absolutely. We have company. Maybe you two should leave?"

"Daniel," she gasped.

Robbie's hand shot up to cover his laugh, while Brett appeared to be intently studying his plate.

"Fine. Fine. But they have not been much help and—"

"For goodness' sake, they saved your life and do not make them regret it," she snapped.

"Do not marry him. As I told my three sisters when they pined for him, you can do better," Brett said, while Robbie snorted.

"Who inherits if you were no longer in the line of succession?" Julia pressed, ignoring the men's banter.

"My father's younger brother's son. Theodore Bryant," Daniel offered, a curious expression crossing his features.

"What is it?" Robbie said.

Daniel shrugged. "He is a decent bloke. Quite bright actually. He is an ornithologist."

"Come again?" Brett said, his interest perking up.

"Birds, he studies birds," Daniel supplied. "I haven't seen him since I was a boy, but I spent a weekend with him once. Bird-watching," he admitted, avoiding Brett's eyes.

"I see, or rather, I would have liked to have seen that." Brett smiled. "But you say he is bright? Bright enough to manage six properties and a couple hundred thousand acres, not to mention employees, and kill you in order to do so?"

"I do not know," Daniel said. "I wrote to him before I came. My uncle lived in Hertfordshire, and Theo lives there now. I had plans to ride over for a visit, but I have been tied up of late."

"You sound doubtful. You do not think he is capable of murder?" Julia found herself tripping over the word, her hands fisting in her skirts.

Daniel rubbed his temple. "Yes and no. He has no compunction in killing. But birds, not humans. In fact, his bird skins are showcased at the British Museum."

"Skins?" Brett frowned. "What the devil are skins?"

"Well, as he has explained to me in his letters, the difference between mounted exhibits and skins, is that skins consist of the soft parts of the bird being removed while the shape is left intact so the skin specimens accurately resemble the dead bird." As he delivered the information, he avoided eye contact.

Julia's lips parted, not quite knowing what to make of this information.

"Good lord," Robbie breathed. "He not only kills, but he guts his prey as well." He shook his head. "Not looking good for you. Have another tart." He shoved the tray at Daniel.

"Look, I will meet with him. I knew the boy, not the man. As Lady Julia has reminded me, a man can change." He lifted his eyes to hers as they both recalled that long-ago day.

But she had been wrong, hadn't she? What a naïve, besotted fool she had been. "And you are going to visit your father's solicitor's office? See where his papers went. As my father uses the same firm, I will accompany you and Brett to their offices while Robbie continues his search for this poacher. Now then, whom else might your father or Abel Shaw have confided in?"

Robbie frowned. "The vicar? They hear deathbed confessions."

"I doubt they would share any confidences. That would probably break a confessional vow," Brett said.

"What about his doctor? During your father's last days, his doctor might have been privy to your father's sickbed rambles or heard his confidences," Julia suggested.

"See?" Daniel beamed. "I told you she is brilliant. You have to marry me."

"Oh no, here we go again," Robbie muttered, shaking his head.

Brett laughed. "I have to agree with you, though. As I said, he never stood a chance." He grinned at Julia and with all the men's eyes upon her, her cheeks warmed.

"So who was your father's doctor during those last days?" Robbie asked.

"Doctor Reilly, and he retired after my father's death. He might be difficult to find."

Julia smiled in memory. "I remember the good doctor Reilly. He covered for Doctor West a few times when West could not answer our calls. We can ask my father. He might have information. So it sounds like we have some plans." Always a planner, she felt better having a few leads to pursue.

"You sound like Daniel," Brett commented. "Always making lists and agendas."

Surprised, she glanced at Daniel. "Yes, well, much is at stake."

"We will find who is behind these attacks on Daniel," Brett said, conviction in his tone. "And learn what Bedford wants. How can we fail now that you are assisting us?"

"Damn right we, ah . . . I mean, right, we will find him," Robbie echoed, abashed.

"Then you will have to marry me because why bother saving me if I have decided I cannot live without you." Daniel beamed.

"I will consider it," she said, unable to resist a smile at his expression of boyish hope. *But I need you to love me.* She dropped her gaze.

"You better accept him," Robbie grumbled. "Because if I have to listen to him go on about—"

"Don't you have more gambling hells to visit? And take Brett with you. We will meet with Shaw's partners tomorrow."

With a sigh, Brett uncrossed his arms and rose to his feet. "My presence is no longer needed. Lady Julia, it has been a pleasure. If you marry Daniel, you can help us run Curtis Shipping."

"Daniel has already offered me a job." She grinned.

"Of course he did. He has good business sense, nor can I argue with his choice of a wife, if you will have him." Brett dipped his head. "I was hoping to see your lovely sister before I leave, but alas, I shall have to wait until tomorrow."

"She usually is up, but today she is having a lying in," Julia said, intrigued by his query. Was he interested in Emily?

She followed Robbie and Brett to the door, seeing them both out, the awareness of Daniel behind her almost tangible.

When Burke closed the door, Daniel grabbed her by the hand and tugged her into the drawing room. "I thought they'd never leave."

She freed herself and stepped away. "They are devoted to you, you are fortunate to have such wonderful friends."

"I am. But I am far more fortunate now that I have you to myself."

She shook her head regretfully. "I promised Jonathan I would take him to the British Museum. I was hoping to see the Elgin Marbles."

"From the Parthenon? News about those reached Boston. Elgin first pilfered them, then our government recently purchased them, and now they are displayed at Montagu House. Now that is very clever negotiating. I would love to see them."

She frowned. "It is my understanding that Elgin was exonerated. And . . ." She paused. "You want to go to the museum with my family?"

He dipped his head, his eyes warm. "It is my desire to go where you are going."

The pleasure of his words was abruptly drowned out by a gnawing, pulsating fear. "What about . . . I don't know if . . ."

"I will not hide," he cut her off, his eyes hard. Seeing her stricken expression, he gentled his tone. "I will be fine. You do not need to worry. They will not attack me in broad daylight in Bloomsbury. And I will watch my back, even though I much prefer watching yours."

She tossed him a chastising look and managed a nod. "I suppose you are right. I have never seen any green-eyed Cyclopes in Bloomsbury."

"No, they much prefer to skulk about the docks."

His teasing smile was so sweet, it nearly broke her heart. "All right. Jonathan will be delighted to have your company, as will I."

"Thank you."

She wanted to keep him here. To lock him in Keaton House and never let him out. To keep him safe. But she had to let him go.

He was not hers to keep. Yet.

Chapter Nineteen

※

O N his way to the front foyer the following morning, Daniel overheard Brett's voice. Did the man have to be so bloody punctual? Fine for business meetings, but it put a damper on his seducing Julia. There were far too many people around as it was. Family, friends, servants. It was a problem. With Julia so devoted to her family, it was difficult to separate her from them during their visit to the museum, but damned if the Chandlers weren't growing on him.

Planted in the middle of their tight-knit group, it was inevitable that like vines, he would become entangled with them. More surprising was that they were filling in places he had never realized were empty.

How could one resist a five-year-old warmonger, the brusque, "hmphing" Taunton, and Emily with her clandestine assistance in his pursuit of Julia?

He had believed his freedom from family bonds a gift. The Chandlers had taught him otherwise. What his family had given him, with the exception of a love of the land, was a gaping hole of loneliness that he had filled with makeshift families. First with Robbie's, then Brett's, and now Julia's. That is, if she would have him.

She had to marry him. His mind was made up. He refused to sit by and watch a wave of scandal wash over her family, not when he had come to think of them of his own. He could not stem the full flood, but he could prevent it from drowning them. There could be no ruination if Julia was protected under the bonds of wedlock.

Why wouldn't she say yes?

It did not matter. He would simply have to change her mind. To be more persistent in convincing her. Perhaps court her more gently, rather than insisting she marry him. He had learned from Brett, who with three sisters was more familiar with the minds of women, that women did not like to be told to do anything. It ruffled their feathers. After meeting with Shaw's partners, he would dispense with Brett, figure out a way to get Julia alone, and court the stubborn woman.

Looking forward to this plan, he continued into the foyer, where he found Brett conversing with Emily.

Seeing Daniel, Brett grinned. "Lady Emily is wondering when I will be returning to America. I assured her that I would not overstay my welcome, but I have a few more matters to take care of before she will see the last of me."

"I did not mean it in quite that manner." Emily looked abashed.

"Then I have not overstayed my welcome and can stay longer?"

She flushed at Brett's obvious pleasure. "You are welcome to stay as long as you like. It is none of my concern. I just wondered how your company can manage with both of its owners here."

"While I am indispensible, and Daniel is somewhat of a necessity," he said, ignoring Daniel's snort, "we do have capable managers in Boston. I trust they can handle most matters until my return."

"As I said, it is not my concern. In fact, I understand your business is with Daniel and Julia, so if you will excuse me, I will see if my sister is ready." She nodded to Daniel, and then left them alone.

"What was that all about?" Daniel asked.

"I am not sure." Brett sounded bemused. "For some reason, I believe Lady Emily has taken a dislike to me. Very strange. Women like me. They adore me. I should know. I have three sisters who tell me so."

"Please, spare me your sisters. It just confirms what I thought about Emily."

"What is that?"

"She is an astute judge of character. Very perceptive. She did not like Edmund either."

"Mmh," Brett mused. Then he shook his head. "No, that is not it. Can't be. Everybody loves me. Must be something else." He furrowed his brow.

"You are in England now. The women here are more refined. Not all of them are going to fall simpering at your feet, like . . ." His words trailed off at Brett's black expression.

"You have been back just over a fortnight, and you are already sounding like a useless aristocrat. It is the titles. Give a man a title, start calling him lord, and suddenly everyone else is beneath him. If you keep your head tilted at that haughty angle, you will get a crick in your neck."

He pricked wounds that still festered, so he was quick to concede the point. "I will keep that in mind."

"You do that, Bryant," Brett said, deliberately dropping the title. "How are things progressing with Julia? She say *yes* yet?" At Daniel's glum expression, Brett relaxed. "Looks like Emily is not the only Chandler who is an astute judge of character."

"I have only had the one night since you left," he protested.

"One night to do what?"

Daniel turned to see Julia walking toward them. The empire gown was like a lovely green cloud, the material some soft gauzy thing, with lace crisscrossing the bodice and cinching her waist. Her hair was neatly tucked up in a chignon, emerald ribbons snaking through the curling mass. He dismissed Brett, having eyes only for Julia. "To do nothing but pine for you, of course."

"Clever." She turned to greet Brett. "Mr. Curtis, it is a pleasure to see you again."

He dipped his head. "Lady Julia. You are a lovely sight to brighten a man's day."

"Thank you." Julia smiled.

"Time to go," Daniel interceded, stepping between them, grasping Julia's hand and looping it through his.

"Daniel, stop. I need to get my frock and bonnet." She withdrew her arm and met Burke, who stepped forward, items in hand.

Daniel snatched Julia's coat from Burke, whose eyebrows arched at his uncouth manners. He held it up for Julia, who gave him a chastising look before slipping her arms into the jacket. As she closed it securely around her, buttoning it up, he wondered if one could be jealous of a garment, but then seeing Brett's silent laughter, he turned away and accepted his redingote from Burke.

"Shall we go?" Julia said, tying the ribbons to her bonnet, her gloves clasped in hand.

"Yes, after you," Brett said. As Burke opened the door for Julia and she stepped outside, Brett wryly addressed Daniel. "It is no wonder she has yet to accept your hand. You are behaving like an idiot. Jealousy doesn't become you." He followed Julia outside.

"Jealous?" He snorted. "Of *Curtis*? That's absurd."

"Quite right, sir," Burke intoned, but Daniel caught the flicker of amusement in his eyes before he schooled his expression.

Burke's reaction confirmed Daniel's earlier opinion—there were too many damn people around for a man to conduct a proper courtship. Frowning, he hurried outside to catch up to Julia before she further eluded him.

The offices of Messrs. Shaw, Dodges, and Fuller, located in the vicinity of Gray's Inn, occupied the second and third floor of Harcourt House. It was an imposing structure with Corinthian pillars lining the front entrance. Heavy gilded-frame oil portraits of past and present partners loomed over the dark paneled waiting room, as if guarding the legal reverence of the atmosphere.

Daniel was relieved not to be met by the same clerk who had attended Robbie and himself on their first visit to the offices. The young man who greeted them was less distracted and more amicable. Daniel wondered if it had anything to do with the dazzling smile Julia had flashed him—or he didn't recognize Daniel with his bruised face, which he eyed warily.

"My apologies, but my father, the Earl of Taunton, had asked if I might assist his secretary in picking up some papers for him while I was in town," Julia glibly lied, her expression both apologetic and embarrassed.

She waved a hand in Brett's direction, who gave a low bow. "He is new to my father's employ, and as my father did not have time to send word around that Mr. Curtis would be coming, he thought it best I accompany him to make the introductions. Once I do so, I will of course leave the business matters to you gentlemen. I do apologize if this is an inconvenience. However, he insisted Mr. Curtis speak to Dodges or Fuller himself, if that is at all possible. And of course, I have his card." She withdrew it from her reticule and handed it to the clerk.

Daniel recalled Julia had handled all her father's business for a short period; possession of her father's card was trivial in comparison.

"No, no problem at all. Delighted to be of service to the earl." The clerk bowed, his ginger head bobbing up and down like a pecking bird.

"Oh, lovely. Again, my father, the earl, would be so appreciative." Julia lifted her hands and pressed them together, as if she would applaud his assistance.

Down the head bobbed, and he pushed his spectacles up his nose as they threatened to slide off.

"Why don't you see if Dodges or Fuller are available?" Daniel interceded, having enough of the man's obsequious behavior. He stifled his grunt when Julia's elbow jabbed into his gut.

"No, rush, Mr. . . . ?" Julia flashed her blinding smile again.

"Tait, Mr. Tait." The man nodded. "If you would care to have a seat," he gestured to the waiting room. "I shall see what I can do."

"Thank you," Julia said. When they were alone, she turned on Daniel. "You cannot rush these things. We want his assistance, do we not?"

"I did not want him to get a crick in his neck from all his head bobbing," Daniel said, unable to resist exchanging an amused look with Brett.

"It will be worth the pain, if he can be of assistance to the *Earl of Taunton's* daughter," Brett intoned. "How many times did you mention *my father, the earl*? Cleverly done."

Julia cringed. "I know I sounded like a haughty aristocrat, but I feared a repeat of Daniel's last visit. The clerk might dismiss the request of a mere lord, but he wouldn't dare to do so with those of an earl."

Brett laughed. "Understood."

Julia settled on the settee, and Brett into one of the chairs, but Daniel found himself, as usual, unable to sit. His penchant was to pace, and he did so now as they waited. In a surprisingly short time, another man came forward to greet them. From his carriage, Daniel surmised this to be one of the partners, Fuller or Dodge.

He stood in the upright stance common among short men when they want to appear taller than they are. His thick head of hair was snow white. He started toward them, but paused, his bushy eyebrows arching as his gaze settled not on Julia, but on Daniel. After the hesitation, he continued and stopped before Daniel, bowing deeply. "Your Grace," he said. "I was not informed that you were here. I was told my business was with Taunton's new secretary. However, I hope I can be of more assistance to you than I was able to provide on your prior visit."

Daniel opened his mouth to correct the man, but Brett shot to his feet and intervened before Daniel could reply, positioning himself between Daniel and the partner.

"Excuse me, but I work with His Grace. Brett Curtis, at your service." He bowed low. "It was the Earl of Taunton who encouraged us to return. He was hoping you could review what you told His Grace on his prior visit, as he was not clear on everything discussed." Brett leaned toward the man, his tone rueful. "My apologies, but details tend to elude him. Is that not right, *Your Grace*?" Brett raised his voice and faced Daniel, his back to the partner, his sharp blue eyes narrowed in warning.

His Grace? Not clear on matters discussed? Details eluded him? Daniel struggled with his smile. He did not know the repercussions for impersonating his brother, if indeed there were any, but he figured it was suitable revenge. After all, Edmund had impersonated him not once, but twice, and had tossed his rooms with impunity. "Yes, that is correct. If you could repeat to my man what you said to me, it would be most helpful."

"Yes, yes, of course." He gave Daniel a curious look, eyeing his bruised face as if that explained the memory loss, before he veiled his features into polite understanding. "I explained to His Grace that we no longer have charge of the late Mr. Shaw's papers. Shaw has not been in practice for nearly a decade, and most of his effects were cleared out long ago. His retirement coincided with the late duke's passing.

"I further explained that Shaw never mentioned any important papers or outstanding items in regard to the late duke's estate. I know His Grace was agitated by this, so I regret that we could not be of more assistance." He looked regretful. "However, I believe if there was anything outstanding of import, it would have come to light in these ten years past.

"The only thing I can add is that when Shaw died three months ago, we did execute his last will and testament. It settled everything on his eldest son, with sundry trinkets and monies going to the two younger sons. So as you can understand," he spread his hands in a helpless gesture, "I fear we were of little help to His Grace."

"And when—" he began.

"And when was it that His Grace stopped by?" Brett cut

him off once more. "Again, he has difficulty with dates as well."

Difficulties with dates? He was making him out to be an obtuse halfwit. Daniel bristled, then froze. Bedford was the idiot, not him. Well, then, Brett only spoke the truth. "Yes, I am afraid, my memory is not what it used to be. Dates, details, days," he waved his hand airily. "Hard to keep everything straight. That is why I have my man here." He clasped Brett's shoulder. "Cannot get along without him. He is brilliant with pesky details."

Brett gave him a brittle smile.

"Of course, of course." The man's eyes widened, his eyelashes almost meeting his eyebrows. "It was shortly following Shaw's death."

"Thank you, Mr. . . . ?" Brett said.

The man eyed him warily, before bowing. "Fuller, sir, Marcus Fuller of Shaw, Dodges, and Fuller."

"Thank you, Mr. Fuller. On another matter, do you think you can give us the address of Mr. Shaw's surviving sons? We might follow up on this matter with them. On the off chance this outstanding item that is of concern to His Grace is simply buried somewhere in Mr. Shaw's possessions."

"Well . . . I . . . I am not certain that addresses . . ."

"Please," Julia glided forward and curled her arm through Daniel's. "I hope it is not too much trouble. My father, the Earl of Taunton, would be much obliged as well for any assistance you can provide. He knows how important this is to my fiancé, and he does hope we can resolve this matter."

"My fiancée, Lady Julia Chandler," Daniel made the introduction. That was one detail he refused to trip over. His hand curled around Julia's, holding her in place.

"Ah, yes, Lady Julia, it is a pleasure." He dipped into a shallow bow. "I understand. I am sure we can locate that information for you. If you excuse me, why don't I do so."

"Thank you." Julia graced him with one of her smiles, and he was off to do her bidding.

Brett expelled a breath. "I used to think titles were for

flaunting and snubbing. Seeing how quickly they can get things done, I might have to purchase one."

Daniel laughed.

Julia withdrew her hand and faced him, her expression somber. "Bedford was here. Whatever it is that your father left or Abel Shaw had, he wants it. Badly. He visited here right after Shaw died. What on earth can it be?"

"I don't know, but it appears we're both now in a race to acquire it. Could it be a deposit box? Stocks, bonds, or unclaimed annuities?" Daniel asked. "The man is desperate for money, bleeding Bedford Hall dry to get it. And willing to hold off on making his broken betrothal public in order to be relieved of his debts to Taunton and receive Julia's dowry."

"And whatever it is, he thinks you might have been given it. Perhaps you were meant to inherit it. No one told you that you were owed monies when your father's estate was settled?" Julia asked.

"No." Daniel shook his head. "I am unaware of anything left outstanding. And Edmund never mentioned my inheritance those last weeks. Then again, he was more drunk than sober."

Julia's eyes widened.

"Then we'll just have to find it before he does. Do you think he will visit Shaw's sons as well?" Brett said.

Daniel shrugged. "If he is, he is not a man for details, cannot keep dates and days straight, so we might have an advantage over him."

Brett grinned. "There is that. Pity that word of his affliction might spread."

A small revenge, considering the gossip that would trail him and Julia once their transgression became public.

Mr. Fuller returned, a piece of paper in hand. He passed it to Brett. "The addresses, as requested, sir. I am afraid his elder son's address is not up to date. He does not remain in one place long, as he has a need to remain a step ahead of his creditors," he added, looking pained. "I fear he has inherited his father's penchant for cards. Shaw was never himself after leaving our offices. Always worried someone was after him, creditors catching up to him, no doubt. He had left papers we were to read if he came to an early demise, so it was a good thing he died of a ripe old age. At his passing, those papers were left with his family to determine their importance, or lack thereof."

He always carried a deck of cards. Taught me to play vingt-et-un. The man was a cardsharp, probably marked the deck or hid cards up his sleeve, for while he had taught Daniel to play the game, Daniel had never won tuppence. Lost his allowance to the man every time. Were the papers to be read in the case of Shaw's early demise related to his gambling habits? Or did Shaw's last words provide their answers as to what Edmund sought?

"Thank you so much for this information. His Grace appreciates it." Brett pulled Daniel from his reverie with a gentle nudge of his elbow.

"Yes, yes." He waved his hand again. "So have you everything you need, then?"

Brett struggled to keep a straight face as Daniel looked at him with an expression of distracted boredom. "Yes, my lord," he inclined his head. "Thanks to Mr. Fuller here."

"Good, good, then we shall be off. Coming, love?" He smiled down at Julia, pleased to see she had kept her arm curled through his. As they made their exit, he admired the pink roses blooming on her cheeks. She had heard his endearment.

Good. It was time she got used to them.

Chapter Twenty

><

JULIA rolled over in her bed and punched her pillow. They were no further in their investigation. They had a series of addresses for Mr. Shaw's three sons, all of which could lead nowhere. Mr. Shaw hadn't practiced law in over a decade, thus the papers he had transferred to his sons could very well have been tossed. The man had had a gambling habit, so he could not be trusted. Once again, they could be chasing after windmills in a race against Edmund.

However, she now believed Edmund's quest and Daniel's attempted murder were related. On that matter, she sided with Brett. There was a desperation to the searches that rattled her.

More important, Edmund frightened her.

She recalled the look of venom that flashed in his eyes when he had pulled her to him, his fingers leaving bruises on her upper arms. And how quickly he had veiled it with an icy calm, like a curtain dropping over a revealing act.

Edmund had taken risks by tossing Daniel's rooms himself rather than hiring someone. It was either ducal hubris, or that he wanted what he searched for to be kept a secret.

What could Daniel's father have given Abel Shaw that Edmund wanted no one else to see and Daniel not to receive?

Something incriminating to Edmund?

Her clock struck the midnight hour. *The witching time.* She huffed out a breath and tossed her covers aside. There would be no sleep tonight. Even were she to set aside this maddening mystery, Daniel's laughing green eyes, smiling, teasing, or seducing her would steal into her dreams. His haunting could rival any witch's, for under his spell, she burned.

There must be a book on gardening or some such dry topic in the library. Something to bore her senseless and lull her to sleep. She slid on her robe and slippers, grabbed a light, and fled her room.

While she hoped to get her mind off of Daniel, she could not help but wonder where he had disappeared to after their midday repast. He and Brett had planned to meet up with Robbie and search for the elusive Weasel.

She did not like to think of Daniel visiting London's infamous gambling hells. Despite his assurances that some were housed in respectable clubs around St. James and the Pall Mall area, it was not safe. Daniel had Robbie, but a menacing growl couldn't deflect a knife, or God forbid a bullet.

And Daniel had not returned for supper.

The candle's flame cast ominous shadows that did not alleviate her worries. She quickened her steps to the library, her favored sanctuary. Lost in a book, she had temporarily escaped her mother's death, her father's despair, or her sister's vacant look. She needed an escape now.

The remnants of a fire smoldered in the hearth. She set her light on the mantel, lifting the poker to jab at the dying embers. The October days could be balmy, but a chill settled into the evenings. The fire sputtered to life, and she tossed a log on it to chase away the bite in the room. Admiring the dance of orange flames, she replaced the poker in its stand.

She turned to lose herself in the shelves of books, but stopped short at the sight greeting her. No staid, boring tome was this, but rather a living, vibrant specimen of a man.

She froze, her gaze riveted to the sight. Daniel reclined,

fast asleep, on the large settee. He wore only his trousers and an untucked linen shirt. He must have blithely waltzed through the foyer in his stocking feet. So typical of the man. On the table beside him were the remnants of a half-eaten treacle tart. He had undoubtedly raided the kitchen. The man had no regard for proper decorum.

That inexorable pull toward him tugged at her, like a fishing line hooked and reeled in. A book lay across his chest, one hand resting on it, the other draped across his taut waist. She crept closer to study him at her leisure. The fire bathed him in a golden glow, highlighting the hollows of his cheekbones, the waning purplish bruises circling his eye and his cheek. A lock of hair curled over his forehead. That dent in his chin tempted her. She wanted to press her finger into it, her lips to it . . .

She feared if she exhaled, he would awake, and she wanted to savor this moment. To study him without being under the scrutiny of those sharp green eyes that made her feel things that frightened *and* excited her. That moved her to feel desire and other feelings she did not understand but secretly wanted to explore.

She edged closer. He was beautiful. All sleek, well-toned muscle, like a cat at rest, a lion, usually poised to pounce.

Taking advantage of his rare stillness, she leaned down, smelling sandalwood soap and another elusive masculine scent that was all his own. She breathed him in. If she were blind-folded and he stood in a roomful of men, she could locate him from his scent alone. It had the power to send her pulse leaping.

She recalled his plea, teasing, coaxing, pleading.

Marry me, Julia. Just say yes.

She wanted to. He was brave. He had survived a wretched childhood. He was bright and inventive, growing Curtis Shipping into a successful enterprise. He was compassionate. She remembered his concern for the tenants. He was kind. She pictured him with her brother and Emily . . . and with her. He touched her. Moved her. Weakened all her resistance.

She wanted to say yes. And give him everything.

And she would. *If only.*

Holding her breath, she gently slid the book from his grasp. She froze when he shifted, settling himself more comfortably into the plush cushions of the settee. Releasing her breath, she set the book on the table. Then, unable to resist, she pressed her finger to the cleft in his chin, swallowing as she did so. His skin was surprisingly soft and warm.

Daring further, she ran her finger in a whisper-light caress along the bruised contour of his cheek. When he still did not awake, she edged closer and whispered the words of her heart. "Love me."

She cried out as her hand was caught in a steel grip, and sharp green eyes speared her.

"I will."

Daniel yanked her forward and she landed sprawled on top of him, his arm clamped around her waist, holding her in place. Her legs tangled with his, her breasts crushed against his chest, her belly flush to his. The scalding heat emanating from him burned. And then he kissed her.

It was passionate, exhilarating, wonderful. His kiss deepened, his tongue tangling with hers. A niggling voice reminded her about this not being part of her plans. There was a reason she was not ready for this. She dismissed it, had no interest in recollecting it at this particular moment. She was busy. Delightfully so.

Emboldened, she let her tongue dart out over his full lips, tasting him, savoring him. The softness, the warmth.

Emitting a guttural groan, Daniel tightened his grip and twisted around so that she lay beneath him.

She wondered if this was proper. Then stopped wondering anything at all, as the hard, delicious length of his body pressed into hers. It felt glorious. Decadent. He was heavy, strong, his back a long, sweeping curve to his waist.

She would soon be a ruined woman. There were advantages to her loss in status; she might as well enjoy one of them.

He tilted her head to the side to better align her mouth with his.

Good lord, he tasted good. The words her father had used to describe a good Bordeaux came to her, *fresh*, *bold*, and *rich*.

More so, he reminded her of a sip of brandy she had sneaked once with Emily, for he was an explosion of burning heat careening through her in a scorching wave.

Feelings she had long suppressed sprang to life. Unfulfilled desire. Dormant longings. Flashing needs. She clasped him closer, opening her mouth as his tongue ran along her lips and he tasted her in small, delightful nibbles.

He unpinned her hair, sighing as his hands dove into her curls, his fingers combing through the strands. He emitted a groan, her sleek cat purring, as he played with the curls.

His hair was surprisingly soft and thick. She grasped a fistful of it, fingering the dark locks. Her hands dropped to his shoulders, her fingers digging in hard, feeling the heat of his skin through his linen shirt.

She nearly cried out in protest when he lifted his weight from her and sat up.

"This will not do."

"Excuse me?" Was she doing something wrong?

He laughed. "Too many clothes." Straddling her, he whipped off his shirt. The light danced over his broad shoulders and smooth skin, his white bandage bright in the dim light. Her eyes fell to it, worried. "Maybe we shouldn't, Daniel. You are wounded."

"Oh no, if you leave me now, I will be in far more pain than the healing wound in my side."

Her eyes widened, blatantly aware of his arousal. "Oh," she murmured, mortified.

"Oh, indeed." He laughed. "But one thing at a time. We still have too many clothes."

He untied the belt of her robe, slipped it open and pushed it from her shoulders. She waited for her denial to come, but it never did. After all, she was already a ruined woman. It fleetingly occurred to her that all women should be so fortunate.

His eyes met hers as his fingers dispensed with the pearl buttons of her nightgown. One by one, they slid free under his persistent fingers, and he spread her nightgown open and sucked in a sharp breath.

Warm air caressed her bare breasts. She struggled to summon the modesty to cover herself, but Daniel's smoldering look held her still, her heart pounding in her chest.

"Botticelli's goddess," he said, awe in his voice.

His admiring stare moved her, his green eyes heavy-lidded as they drank her in, his lips parted, his breathing shallow.

"Jonathan says you always share your treats with him. Share with me, Julia. Let me love you. Give yourself to me."

The husky timbre of his voice seduced her as thoroughly as his touch. Her head lolled back, her eyes closing, as a trail of those delicious kisses made their way along the hollows of her collarbones, down over the curving slopes of her breasts, until his mouth closed over a pliant peak. His tongue flicked around it, suckling and doing such forbidden, erotic things, creating a pool of moisture between her thighs.

"Much, much better than treacle tart. So very sweet." He murmured. "But I have another dream." Too languid to open her eyes, she felt him shift and lean over.

"Daniel!" She jumped and her eyes flew open, when he smeared the sticky, sugary tart filling over her breasts. "What . . . ? What are you doing?"

"Enjoying dessert. You know how I love my sweets." His eyes flared as they roved over her and he swallowed. "Better than I ever dreamed."

His head lowered and she sank back into the cushions as his tongue worked its magic, licking up every inch of the filling, and much too quickly to her mind. Another thought struck her. "Just . . . just don't count on my emerging naked from a shell," she managed to gasp.

His head lifted and his eyes flared, a drop of lemon on his lips. "No? Will you let me immortalize you naked on canvas?"

"Do . . . do you paint?" She lifted her head and did as she had yearned to do the other morning, licking the lemon filling from his lips.

He groaned. "Not a stroke, but if you promise to pose for me, I promise to learn," he vowed before devouring her mouth, as if he could not get enough of her.

She pulled his head back, smiling as he frowned at her. "I

don't think painting can be learned. I think you have to have a talent for it."

His frown vanished, replaced by a slow, wicked smile that teased his lips. "Lots of things can be taught. But until then, it is a good thing I have a talent for other things."

His head lowered, and his hands and mouth tormented her. He was indeed very talented. He had strong hands and long, tapered fingers.

"Daniel." She liked the sound of his name, whispered on her lips. "Daniel, perhaps we should slow down. This might not be a good idea." The husky tone of her voice sounded strange to her ears.

"It is, Julia. You feel good, taste better, and I cannot get enough of you." He pressed his lips to the sensitive patch of skin under her ear, the pulse throbbing in her neck, and the valley between her breasts.

Desire coursed through her in a liquid wave and she rode it. He was right. It felt so very good, and she wanted more.

His words echoed. Sometimes it took the scare of losing something precious for someone to realize its true value.

Groaning, she arched. She clutched his bare, sweat-slicked shoulders. Her fingers moved over the puckered, roped scars on one shoulder, a stark reminder of how close she had come to never experiencing such passion. Such beauty. Her breath hitched, and she tightened her hold as if she could keep him safe.

His hand moved almost reverently over her skin, caressing her waist, her belly, slipping her gown up her legs. She shivered as his body eased down hers, his mouth moving from her breasts, to her belly, and then still lower. He pressed wet, sultry kisses along the line of her thigh, the ticklish feel of his soft lips on her sensitive skin incredibly arousing.

She closed her eyes, her body a piece of clay that Daniel was molding to his will, coming alive under his touch. He had a bit of the artist in him after all.

Her eyes snapped open when he ventured to places she was not ready for him to explore. "No, no, stop," she gasped, her fingers yanking his hair.

Grunting, he blinked at her, his eyes dilated. "What is it? What is wrong?" His voice was gravelly.

"We need to slow down. I need to slow down." She bit her lip. "Please."

When he registered her plea, he cupped her cheek in his hand. "It's all right, Julia." He kissed her, gently, a small taste. "Let me pleasure you." He kissed the side of her mouth. "I will not take things too far, I promise." He slid lower to assault her neck with those tender, light butterfly kisses that had her limbs turning to jelly.

His hand had returned to slide between her thighs, his fingers finding the most sensitive part of her.

"I will not hurt you. I will never hurt you," he murmured, and his mouth returned to capture hers.

His tongue parried with hers as his fingers slid inside her and moved with the same erotic skill as his tongue. Good lord, it was indecent. Sinful. And so exhilarating. She writhed against his hand, needing him to stop. Needing him to continue. An explosive need grew in her, climbing to a fevered pitch.

"Are you all right?" Daniel panted against her lips.

Her eyes flew open. He asked her now?

His laugh was guttural. "I think you've answered. Let go, Julia."

Her lips parted. His fingers became more persistent, and something built inside of her. The pressure grew until she arched against him, her fingers curling around his upper arms, her nails digging into hard muscle, needing to hold on to something as her body came unmoored. The heat climbed to a feverish pitch, and she moaned.

Daniel's breathing was hoarse and ragged, his desire rising to match hers.

His hard arousal pressed against her leg and the sounds of his own passionate response, his heavy breaths, ignited the fire growing within her. A cry escaped her with the sudden burst of her release. Stunned, she collapsed, lay still and dazed, blinking up at Daniel, her body a puddle of satisfaction. She had never experienced anything like it before. Wondered if that was what she had been yearning for all her life?

Daniel gathered her into his arms, his hand brushing back strands of hair stuck to her temple. His lips pressed there. "Ladies go first. It is proper etiquette."

His breath was warm against her temple, and she closed her eyes, mortified at how outrageously she had behaved. They lay that way, intimate and entwined until her world righted itself.

Daniel had brought her to places she had never been, but had secretly wished to go. He had ruined her, thoroughly now, or at least for any other man.

Let me love you, Julia.

And she had. But he did not love her. She pushed against his chest.

"I have to go."

"Julia, it is all right, we are going to be married. This is natural between a husband and a wife. What goes on between us, what we feel, it is not wrong."

But he did not feel what she felt. She had asked him to love her, and he had said, *I will*, not *I do*. He wanted her. He desired her. But he did not love her.

She stared at his face, the candlelight highlighting the perfect symmetry of his features, those incredible green eyes entreating. She wondered if that could be enough. If this passion they shared was enough to sustain a marriage. It was more than she had felt for Edmund.

She did not know. Could not think with him staring at her so, the heat of him still warming her. She tugged feebly at her gown, drawing it closed. "Please, I must go."

He stared at her in silence and then with a sigh, rose to his feet. He combed his hand through his tousled hair. He stood, bare chested but for his bandage, his breathing deep and fast, as if he had run a small race.

With shaking fingers, she drew her robe together and belted it. Her legs trembled when she rose to her feet. She shoved her curtain of hair from her face.

"Julia, it's all right."

"Please. Don't say anything more." She collected her candle, and glanced back at him. "Did . . . did you determine Weasel's whereabouts today?"

He nodded. "We did. We have made arrangements to meet with him tomorrow."

"You . . . you will be careful?"

He stared at her, then gave her a heart-wrenching smile. "I will. I have much to live for. Painting lessons." His humor fled, and his eyes roved over her features. "I promise, I will never let anyone take me away from you or you from me."

She bit her lip, the familiar flush of pleasure burning her cheeks.

If a woman could not hear words of love, those were close.

It should be enough for most women, but Julia was not most women. She was older and wiser, and she craved what she was willing to give to him. Love.

Everything.

That is, unless she had to send him to America to keep him safe.

She shuddered at the thought, could only trust in him to keep his word and never, ever leave her.

Chapter Twenty-one

❧❧

THE worst areas of London were located in the rookeries of St. Giles and Seven Dials, but it was wise to avoid venturing east into the territory along the docks that bypassed the Tower of London. It crossed into another slum area housing nothing but poverty and misery. As they walked in that direction, Daniel could only hope that Robbie hadn't agreed to meet the elusive Weasel any farther east.

His senses alert, he forbade his thoughts to detour to far more pleasurable sights of Julia. Good lord, she was passionate. When he did not fear his neck being slashed and his body dumped into the Thames, he planned to relish the prior evening at his leisure, when he had time to savor her every touch, taste, and response.

He sidestepped another pile of refuse, nearly gagging on the rank stench of raw sewage from the Thames. His eyes sought out Brett, who strode ahead, and then behind him to Robbie, tight-lipped and grim faced. All three of them carried canes, which could be wielded as a weapon. Robbie had a revolver and had vowed to use it if they were waylaid again, not wasting time with fists when a bullet settled the matter more quickly.

The Devil's Lair was an apt name for the pub, for only those destined for hell would willingly set foot in the dark, dank tavern. The stench of unwashed men, sweat, and stale gin assailed him. With the end of two wars, the new congregating place for returning veterans was the taverns. Too many drank their days away as the population in the city exploded with their return, the surplus of labor leading to a scarcity of jobs. This then led to the competition with workers outside of London, which Mabry had lamented.

Daniel surmised that it wouldn't be too long before the empire found another conflict to rid itself of its surfeit of able-bodied men and ease the strain on the economy. Shaking his head at the sad state of affairs, he followed Robbie down the length of the tavern. His mammoth frame, like the prow of a ship, cleaved a path through the press of men. Daniel and Brett followed in his wake before the opening closed behind him.

Robbie must have arranged a designated meeting spot, for he ignored the seedy occupants and kept on a straight course to the rear of the bar.

They stopped before a brass-studded oak door, and Robbie gave it three hard taps. The door cracked open a mere slit.

"Ye be late. Will cost ye."

"And you're wasting my time and that will cost you," Robbie snarled. "You have him?"

The door opened without further comment, and a rail-thin man ushered them in with a flick of his wrist and then disappeared.

The room was lit by a cheap rushlight and held a battered desk and two spindle-legged chairs. Daniel's gaze immediately locked on the man behind the desk. *Weasel.*

His wiry frame was hunched over, a sullen expression pinching gaunt features. Straggly yellow hair drooped over his brow and into his eyes. Daniel followed the three-fingered hand that brushed the hairs aside. He swallowed at the sight of the scarred-over stubs.

Weasel's eyes flared as they drank in his features, obviously recognizing the resemblance to his brother. Weasel slunk lower in his seat. "Don't know why I'm here." He jerked his head toward Robbie. "A bloke can't be dragged 'gainst his bloody will. I's got me rights," he whined.

"You will be free to go momentarily," Robbie sighed. "As I have promised you. You will also be compensated for your time, which you did agree to give."

"I mighten 'ave, but I mighten 'ave changed me mind." A cagey look entered his eyes, and he tipped his head to the side, as if sizing Daniel up. "Perhaps a bit more blunt mighten change it back."

Wordlessly, Daniel extracted a sovereign from his jacket pocket and slapped it into Weasel's hand. "I am not my brother, you will not be mistreated here. I just need to ask a few questions." The thought did occur to him that if Weasel could be so easily bought, he was not to be trusted.

Weasel shoved the coin into the pocket of the rumpled garrick redingote that swallowed his scarecrow frame.

"I have been investigating the fire at Lakeview Manor. Someone said you were in the vicinity, talked about witnessing the start of the blaze and seeing some men on the grounds."

Weasel swiped at his hair again, eyeing Daniel, and the speculative gleam in his eyes belied his denial. "That's bollocks. I don't knows wot you is natterin' on bouts. I ain't seen nothin'. I ain't no squealer."

Daniel sighed and produced another coin. He tossed it to Weasel, who was quick to snap it from the air, clearly well practiced at his game.

Weasel furrowed his brow. "I mighten' remember now. I was settin' me traps, when I saw a few blokes ridin' away from the blaze. An' why wouldn't they be, for it be a right inferno they set."

"Are you certain that these men deliberately set the fire?" Daniel edged closer.

Weasel pressed his three-fingered hand to his temple, fingering the greasy strands flopping over his forehead.

Brett swore and rummaged in his pocket for a crown, which he tossed to Weasel and which vanished as quickly as the others.

"Spect that be wot their bleedin' torches be for. Saw 'em toss 'em away as they scurried off. Tried to get 'em, for could 'ave used 'em against 'em to fleece 'em proper. Money lost there," he murmured the last regretfully.

Daniel snorted. Weasel would forage for eyes to sell to a blind man.

"Fire was too hot, couldn't get near 'em."

"Final question, Weasel," he pressed another coin into his hand. "Did you recognize any of these men?"

Weasel hesitated, and then gave a curt nod.

Daniel's eyes shot to Brett's, hardly daring to breathe.

"Ain't no use to you now." Weasel shrugged. "Long dead and gone. Not from natural causes, if you knows wot I means. Should 'ave come 'ome sooner."

Daniel exhaled, the words a punch to the gut. Robbie came to his side, clamping a hand on his shoulder. Daniel only had one more question. "If you knew them, do you know who they worked for?"

When Weasel opened his mouth for his requisite fee, he paused. Robbie had withdrawn his gun, a beautiful Manton revolver, much coveted by the ton for dueling, and on loan from Taunton. He pulled out his handkerchief and leisurely ran it over the piece, polishing its silver finish so it gleamed in the candlelight.

Weasel swallowed, his face going a shade of gray. His eyes snapped to Daniel's and he spat his response. "Cor, they be workin' for yon bastard the duke, who else? Why'd ye think no one listened when I said so all them years ago? Thot's why he done this to me and planned to do more, 'ad I not escaped." He brandished his maimed hand. "But Weasel's too smart to be trapped. Unlike the sad gits who set the blaze and were found hanged dead." He snapped his mouth closed, his expression truculent.

Silence followed. Had anyone spoken, the roaring in Daniel's ears would have swallowed it up. One word cut through it, shoving at him like a battering ram that nearly dropped him to his knees.

Fratricide.

His brother had attempted to kill him.

Daniel had fought the truth. Repeatedly. Because he could not believe it? Or because he could, but couldn't grasp the magnitude of it? He had always known Edmund hated him. Now he understood just how much.

But why?

The question remained unanswered.

Edmund had the title, the estates, the money, even Julia at one point. What the devil did he care about him for? Before the night of the fire, his only interest in Daniel had been for vicious sport, and as they had grown, even that waned.

What had changed his mind? Turned him toward murder?

"You've earned your blunt." Robbie nodded toward Weasel, his tone weary. "That will be all."

Weasel's fist swallowed another coin. Like his namesake, he darted to the door as fast as his short legs could carry him, and was gone.

Daniel could locate him again if needed—for a price—but there was no point. A duke would be tried before a jury of his peers. The word of a sordid village poacher who could be bought with a few coins would not stand up in the House of Lords against one of their own. No, Weasel had done all he could for them. And it was enough.

"Now do you see the danger you are in?" Brett cried. "We should make arrangements to leave on our next ship returning to Boston."

Daniel raked an unsteady hand through his hair. "It makes no sense. To what end does my death help Edmund? For God's sake, I have been gone ten years. As far as he is aware, I will be gone again soon."

"*Soon?* How about *now*? What are you staying for?" Brett looked stunned.

"Julia," he snapped back. "I will not leave her. Besides, I have to know—"

"Take her with you. Have you not learned enough? What more do you need to know? To see if the next attack succeeds? Your goddamn dukes do what they want with impunity. Killing his twin shouldn't be a problem for Bedford, not with the resources he commands." Brett swiped a hand down his face and lowered his voice, his words quieter. "Come home, Daniel. It isn't safe for you to stay here."

"I cannot," his words were curt, but final. He met Brett's eyes, wishing he could make his friend understand. But there were questions yet to be answered. Abel Shaw's words about a destiny to be claimed still haunted. And Julia. He doubted she would leave her family and her home. Not even for him. Yet.

Brett read his resolve and sighed. "You are determined to see this through, despite its deadly stakes. I do not like it, hope to change your mind, but it is your decision."

"At least, he doesn't have to worry about being gutted by the bird skinner."

Daniel turned with Brett to stare blankly at Robbie.

"Your cousin, the bird man," Robbie clarified.

"The ornithologist," Brett corrected. "He doesn't skin them, only guts them." He faced Daniel and his lips twitched. "There is a spot of good news."

Daniel shook his head. "Good, because the rest of it looks bleak."

"Well, Defoe did warn that meeting a weasel is a bad omen," Brett muttered.

"Who?" Robbie said.

"Unlike you, Robbie, Curtis reads. Defoe was a British journalist. He wrote *Robinson Crusoe*."

"He said that about weasels? Damned if he was not right. It's one thing for Bedford to toss your room, but murder of your own brother? As much as I'd like to kill a few of my own, I settle for knocking their heads together. Duke or not, Bedford will hang."

"No, he will not because we cannot prove anything. It is Weasel's word against Bedford's," Daniel explained. "No one listened to me when he beat me bloody time and again. You think they will listen to a village poacher spouting murder against a peer of the realm?"

Daniel began pacing. "We need to think this through. Whatever Edmund wants, he is willing to kill for it. We suspect it must have been in Shaw's possession because Edmund visited Shaw's offices to acquire it immediately following the solicitor's death. We assume it has to do with my father because of Shaw, and we believe Edmund does not want me to possess whatever it is because he tried to kill me shortly after my father's death." He paused. "It must be something incriminating about Edmund or my father."

"Maybe your father knew of someone else Edmund murdered?" Robbie suggested.

"I wouldn't put it past the bastard," Brett agreed.

Daniel shook his head. "Perhaps, but Edmund never gave enough of a damn about anyone to want them dead. The only candidate he held that level of enmity toward was me."

"I have a plan," Robbie said, brandishing the Manton revolver. "Shoot the bastard before he shoots you. We can bury his body in one of our back pastures. It's where Tanners for generations have put all their inferior stock."

"I like it." Brett nodded. "If you shoot him in London, we can toss the body in the Thames."

"I will keep your suggestions in mind," Daniel said dryly. "Let us first discover what he is after. I would like to determine his motive. Depending on that, I will shoot him."

"Then you should carry this. You need it more than I." Robbie handed Daniel the revolver.

"And watch your arse," Brett added. "Lady Julia might miss it."

Damn. Julia. He did not mind her assisting him when it was a simple matter of tracking down some solicitor's papers, but it was a different matter altogether now that he had learned his half-crazed twin was trying to murder him. It was too close to home.

Thank God, she had not married him. The thought congealed his blood. Now that he had saved her from Edmund, he refused to put her in danger again. His gaze shot to Robbie and Brett, and his eyes narrowed.

They were in a heated argument over the best manner in which to dispose of Bedford's body.

Pair of idiots, but he would trust both with his life. He was beginning to appreciate the binds of both friendship and family. He would need all of them to keep Julia and himself safe.

Chapter Twenty-two

✦

J ULIA's knees went weak and she sank onto the drawing room settee, too stunned to comprehend the full import of Daniel's words. "Edmund," she breathed aloud. She curled her arms around her waist, feeling violently ill.

Daniel held up his hands in a helpless gesture, and then let them drop. "I did not know if I should tell you, but I thought . . . I believed you had a right to know."

"Of course you should have told me," she insisted, his words snapping her back to the moment. "For goodness' sake, I was engaged to the man for five years. I almost married him," she said, a shudder seizing her.

"Good thing I ruined you." At her chastising look, he became defensive. "Well, it is the only bit of good news."

She sighed. "It *is* a novelty. Few women should feel gratitude for being ruined, but I am grateful."

"It was my pleasure," he said and grinned.

Her eyes met his and the warmth in his expression was her undoing. Particularly after their evening in the library. She tore her gaze away and swept to her feet. She couldn't think about that now. Not after what he had told her. "But why?"

Daniel shoved his hands in his pockets and shrugged. "I do not know. I have racked my brains trying to understand. But I cannot."

"To hate with such passion," she murmured, remembering the vitriol in Edmund's expression, but also remembering his charm. The two faces of Janus. Beautiful Bedford and the Damn Duke. She shuddered. Another thought struck her. "You have known since yesterday. You have known and you did not tell me. You were not planning to." She voiced the most damning accusation of all. "You do not trust me."

He tossed her an impatient look, but seeing her pained expression, relented. "This isn't about trust. Look, I wrestled with this all night. For God's sake, Julia, he is my brother, but he is also a duke, one of the highest-ranking peers of the realm. I have nothing but the word of a petty, two-bit poacher who can be bribed with twopence. But I know he speaks true. I know my brother," he said emphatically.

"And I believe you," she said, calmly. "Or rather, Weasel." Her words appeared to strip the wind from his anger. "You do?"

"I do. In the future, you have to trust in me to do so, or . . ."

"Or you will not marry me?" He looked rueful.

"Well, it wouldn't bode well for our marriage if you intend to keep things from me. If you think I cannot be trusted—"

"I told you, this isn't about trust—"

"Then what is it about?"

"Fear," he exclaimed, tossing his hands up, his expression incredulous, as if he could not believe she didn't understand. "I am afraid. For you. For me. Some might call that cowardly to admit it, but I think it is smart because it makes me cautious. As a duke, Edmund has unlimited resources at his disposal. They allow him to carry out whatever nefarious schemes he damn well pleases. And it pleases him or it would please him to see me dead and buried. I should be afraid and so should you. You need to return to Taunton Court. To get as far away from me as possible. It is not safe here with me."

"Me?" she cried, her voice rising to match his. "No one wants me dead. You are the one gallivanting about town, a hair's breadth away from getting killed." Her voice choked and she spun away, mortified at her loss of composure.

Silence fell.

"Julia." His tone was soft, apologetic. He curled his hands over her shoulders, gently turning her to face him.

She tried to resist, tears blurring her eyes. He persisted until she was enfolded in his arms. Undone, she hugged his waist. She needed the touch, the warmth, and the comfort. She needed him. Her cheek rested against his heart, and the steady beat calmed her.

"My fearless warrior."

She could hear the smile in his voice. "Not so fearless."

"Well, this is another novel situation. You and I seem to be making a habit of tangling ourselves in them."

"Yes," she sniffed, half laughing, half choking. "Perhaps we should stop."

"I agree. Why don't you go home with your father until I—"

She stumbled back. "No, absolutely not." If he was staying, so was she. Someone had to look after him. She crossed her arms. "You forget, we are not married—yet—so you cannot dictate my actions. I have not said yes, and at this rate, I will not be doing so if you think that I am going to run away and hide in the country while you stay here, risking your worthless hide."

"Julia, this is not some business venture." He frowned, his expression one of strained patience. "Worthless?"

"It will be if you are tossed into the Thames, or riddled with bullets or—" She cursed her voice for cracking again.

He swore and raked his hands through his hair. "I cannot risk your life. I cannot do it, and I will not."

"You are not. You are making the choice to risk yours, just as I am making the choice to risk mine. Besides, father said you borrowed his Manton revolver to show a friend who was interested in purchasing one. I know why you borrowed the gun, so it is good that I accompany you on your next trip."

He looked at her as if she were speaking French, his tone

a mixture of frustration and perplexity. "I would think most women would avoid a man with a gun. But what the devil does the Manton have to do with your accompanying me anywhere?"

"I happen to be a crack shot with those guns."

Daniel looked surprised, and then he began to laugh.

She bristled. "I don't see what is so funny."

"No, of course not. There is nothing remotely funny about this situation." He sobered, and before she knew what he was about, he had caught her hands and threaded his fingers through hers. He dipped to press their foreheads together. "You have to marry me. I cannot live without you."

She smiled into his eyes. "I am considering it."

"Still?"

"More seriously," she conceded. "For the time being, I will pretend to be your fiancée while you visit Mr. Shaw's sons."

He groaned. "You have no mercy."

"You need a lesson in trust."

"I have told you everything. You got the better half of the bargain. I only got one kiss. Maybe we should make another bargain. For another kiss, I will let you accompany me to Mr. Shaw's sons, with the cavalry following for protection—the cavalry being Brett and Robbie."

"You've had more than enough kisses, but I can be generous." She stood on tiptoes, and gave him a quick kiss.

He frowned. "I taught you better than that."

"Yes, well, it is equal to your pathetic invitation to Shaw's. To the fact that you do not want me with you. That you do not trust me—"

Daniel yanked her back into his arms, crushing her body to his, his mouth swooping down in a kiss that stole the rest of her sentence and all memory of whatever point she was trying to make. She could not find the will to resist or mind. After all, he kissed so very well. She kissed him back, using all he had taught her.

After a breathless span of time, he lifted his head, looking dazed. "That is much better. I do want you with me, all the time. Just alive, Julia, and out of danger."

Me, too, her heart cried. She opened her mouth to voice the words, when a throat clearing had her trying to move away, but Daniel's arm was like a steel cable encircling her waist.

"Hmph."

Daniel barely glanced her father's way, his eyes on her. "Lord Taunton, you are now my witness. I have ruined your daughter. Again. I think you should intercede and demand she marry me."

She gasped and slapped her hands against Daniel's chest, struggling to gain her release.

"Hmph. She doesn't look too pleased about it. You haven't gotten her to say yes yet?"

Daniel sighed and released her. "Well, you did mention her stubbornness. It is formidable. I'll need a hatchet to chip away at it."

"It looks to me that you have enough weapons at your disposal. I suggest you use them sparingly until you get your acceptance." He gave Daniel a meaningful look.

"Father," she gasped. "I cannot accept Daniel yet, for if you have forgotten, Edmund has yet to sever our betrothal. That is not for another week, so I have time before I must give my answer."

Her father grinned affectionately. "Always one to remember the details. But Julia, after what I witnessed here, see that your answer is yes."

She flushed. "I am . . . I am leaning toward it. He is persuasive."

Daniel beamed. "I have moved up in her esteem. I am beginning to think courting is like a tide, if I keep battering away, the barriers will erode."

"There will be no further battering under my roof. None. Persuading is fine, battering is not fine. Do I make myself clear?" Her father skewered Daniel with a narrow-eyed warning.

Daniel's smile vanished and he straightened, but at Julia's snort of laughter he winked.

"I saw that," her father warned.

Daniel coughed, and struggled to adopt a more serious

mien. "Right, no more battering. Absolutely. My apologies, sir."

Her father cast Daniel another stern look, but the twitch to his lips undermined his glower. "Now then, Julia tells me that you were inquiring about the good doctor Reilly."

Daniel exchanged a look with Julia. "Yes, sir, I was. He was my father's physician for years, and cared for my brother and me until I moved away. I had formed a bond of sorts with him."

Her father nodded. "I am not surprised. He was always treating you for your share of scrapes and bruises. Your father said you boys knocked heads worse than two spitting bulls. My Meg spoke to your father about it after you showed up with a broken arm. She suggested your father separate you two, but he disagreed. Believed you needed to work it out yourselves, that it built character. With your smaller size, he worried that you needed to be toughened up or he feared you would always be beaten down." Her father fell silent, his look regretful. "I wondered if I should have said something, but then it resolved when you enrolled in a different school. You boys were no longer together as much."

Julia's heart twisted at the thought of that small, bruised boy, and the knowledge that her mother had noticed the abuse and had tried to intercede. *It built character. He needed to be toughened up or be beaten down.* She shuddered at the late duke's callous parenting.

She tamped down her sadness when she saw that Daniel was battling his own emotions. The memories her father had dredged up cast a shadow across his handsome features and darkened those vibrant green eyes.

She ached to wrap him in her arms. To offer the comfort no one had given to that lonely, bruised boy. But she could not. Not yet. Or rather, not with her father standing a few feet away and curtailing any form of battering. She wished he would leave.

"Yes, well, Doctor Reilly patched me up sufficiently, for I did survive as much as I think Edmund wished it otherwise, *wishes* it otherwise," Daniel amended.

"Yes, but that is often typical of brothers," her father offered.

"Edmund is an atypical case," Daniel said dryly, his eyes hard.

"Yes, I suppose being a duke makes that so."

"Among other things," Daniel murmured and briskly changed the topic back to the good doctor. "What did you learn of Reilly? Where is he settled these days? I would like to pay him a visit. Thank him for his kindness."

"I am sorry, Daniel. I hate to be the bearer of bad news. However, I was at White's yesterday and I ran into a Bedford-shire neighbor, Viscount Randall. His estate abuts Bedford Hall."

"Yes, I remember the viscount." The viscount was a book-ish man who liked to drone on about philosophy and religion, wearing Daniel's father's patience thin.

"He shared Doctor Reilly's services with Bedford, and I recalled Julia's recent query about the doctor, so I asked if the viscount had any knowledge of him. I regret to tell you, Daniel, but the good doctor is no longer with us. What's worse is that his demise was rather recent and I am afraid it was not of natural causes." His gaze flicked briefly to her.

Thankfully her father was aware that she was not a woman prone to swoons or flutters, so he continued before she could beg him to do so.

"He had retired to a small cottage on the coast of Kent. Apparently, he upset a burglar in the act of robbing his home and paid too dear a price for it."

She covered her mouth. She recalled Doctor Reilly's boom-ing laugh and the toffees he used to dispense to Emily and her when he was called to treat whatever ailments they had at the time. With a twinkle in his eye, he would tout their medicinal benefits.

She knew as surely as she knew her own name that his death was not a coincidence. On unsteady limbs, she walked over to the settee and sank down.

"I am sorry, Daniel."

Daniel appeared to be grappling with his own shock. He

swiped a hand down his face, shaking his head as if he could shake off the truth. "Yes, well, as am I. He was a good man."

"Yes, he was. But he did have a grand retirement, and no thieving blackguard can steal that from him. Randall said his cottage was set on a plum piece of property along the coastline. The doctor had traveled widely over the past decade, going to the continent and even doing missionary work in India. In fact, he had only recently returned to England and purchased the acreage in Kent. Your father was a generous benefactor."

"I am glad he finished his life in comfort. I would have dearly liked the chance to speak with him. I had a few questions in regard to my father's last days that only he could have answered."

Her father nodded. "I understand. There are always unanswered questions when one loses a loved one." He walked forward and clasped a hand on Daniel's shoulder, giving it a reassuring squeeze. "If there is anything else I can assist you with, let me know, besides convincing my daughter to marry you. I am afraid you are on your own there."

Daniel summoned a grin for her father, who, after a few moments, nodded and left the room.

When he had disappeared, Daniel broke the silence. "Reilly knew. He knew what Edmund was after. My father must have confided in him. He survived by staying out of the country, as I unwittingly did. Shaw survived by . . . blackmail." His eyes widened, and he fell silent, turning to pace, as if he needed the movement to get his thoughts going.

She could almost see the wheels spinning in his head, moving him to his next thought. He was the businessman riffling through all the information to complete the full picture.

He stopped and swung toward her. "There is blackmail here. Shaw and Reilly were blackmailing my brother."

She gasped. "How did you conclude that?"

"It explains Edmund's debts. Where his profits went, why he needs more money. You heard what your father said. Reilly retired grandly, traveled the continent, bought a plum piece of property. My father was generous, and I am sure he left him a stipend on which to retire, but to purchase acres on the coast?

To travel extensively? He was a doctor, not an aristocrat with deep pockets."

"What about Shaw? He did not live extravagantly."

"No, but he was a gambler, a cardsharp. He bled Edmund to feed his habit and pay off his creditors. But he was afraid, scared of something that had him drafting a safeguard for his life. What did Fuller say? He had a letter to be made public should Shaw meet with an untimely demise? Fuller thought he feared creditors. He feared Edmund. But Edmund's fear of Shaw's revelations being publicized was greater. Thus Edmund did not touch him, and Shaw lived to a ripe old age."

"Yes, but afraid and guilt ridden, so he wrote to you. He wanted you to hear his confession, but you were too late," she added.

"Too little, too late," he murmured softly, his expression sad. "The epitaph on my grave."

She gasped and stood up. "Do not speak of such things. There will be no epitaphs on any graves. Least of all yours. As I said, I am a crack shot, and I will shoot anyone who tries to get near you."

The look Daniel gave her had her holding up her hands and backing away.

"Do not come any closer! Stay back! Remember my father's words. No battering permitted." He ignored her words and stalked her, his eyes hot. She kept talking. "Reilly's death changes nothing. We still do not know Edmund's motive for trying to kill you. We need to speak to Shaw's sons. Time is . . ." her words trailed off, for Daniel had caught up to her and was drawing her to him. "We need to . . ." It was no use. She could no longer remember what she was nattering on about. "Daniel," she breathed.

"Julia," he whispered back, his eyes roving over her face. "My fierce warrior. You have looked after your father, your brother, your sister. I appreciate that you are a crack shot, but I hope to never have that put to the test. Now I think it is time someone looked after you. And that is what I intend to do." His head lowered and his lips played over hers in teasing, light nibbles that had her legs weakening.

"We will look after each other," she whispered, tilting her head back to give him better access to the column of her neck. His lips curved against her skin.

"Of course we will. Together. Don Quixote and Sancho Panza."

"Yes . . . but . . . it is time we changed literary references. I was thinking Robin Hood and Maid Marian."

He lifted his head, his eyes bright as he appeared to ponder it. "Fine, but even if you are a crack shot, I still get to be Robin Hood." He nodded. "It is apt in this situation. A displaced aristocrat—that is me—saving the poor people—the tenants—from a penny-pinching king—Edmund. And in the end, he wins the hand of the fair Maid Marian."

She smiled. "And they live happily ever after if Robin Hood doesn't get shot, or do anything foolish, or . . ."

He kissed her to silence, which was fine, because she did not really like that ending. She had a far better one in mind.

Chapter Twenty-three

❧❦

"So how should we proceed?" Daniel asked as he settled back into the upholstered seat of Taunton's elegant town coach.

"I think you should impersonate Edmund again," Julia suggested as she neatened the skirts to her carriage dress. "Ducal power humbles everyone. Once they finish bowing and scraping, they scramble to do his bidding before they consider whether they want to or not. And toss in a level of charm. Edmund is haughty, but he could be so very charming and quite dashing, he wasn't all—What is it? What are you scowling about?"

"For God's sake, Julia, the man's a cold-blooded murderer and you are talking about him as if he is a prince."

Julia drew herself up. "Well, the best villains aren't just black and white. They are multilayered."

"Right. Like an onion, and no matter how many of those layers you peel back, all of them still stink." Daniel snarled, crossing his arms over his chest. Charming and dashing, his arse. How about cruel, duplicitous, and murderous.

"I do not disagree, but how do you intend to extract any information from Martin Shaw if you arrive scowling? We will be tossed off his stoop before his butler can make the introductions."

He shifted in his seat, refusing to answer. Refusing to let her know she was right again. More often than not, he admired her astute mind, the way she thought dazzling him, but now was not one of those times.

"Stop scowling. You can do charming. For goodness' sake, when you are not pacing a hole in my carpets, demanding I marry you, or sparring with Brett and Robbie, you charm me. And you charm Jonathan. He follows you around like you can single-handedly win all the wars."

He shifted again, bristling as he caught the flash of a teasing light in her eyes. She was reeling him in like a fat fish. He frowned, not quite ready to concede. "Very well. What about dashing?"

"Dashing, too. You dash very well. Just like Robin Hood."

He considered her words. "He has the advantage on me in dashing, for he does lead a group of merry men."

"And you have Robbie and Brett playing sentry," she pointed out.

He frowned at the reminder of his friend's curricle, which followed them. He could not afford to take any chances, not with Maid Marian refusing to stay safely at home. "So they play the guards, I play the blackguard, and you play my lovely fiancée. Maybe we should practice our roles. As I have charming and dashing down, perhaps you should practice."

"Oh? What should I practice?" She eyed him warily.

"Fawning and batting your eyelashes, looking suitably besotted, like you cannot wait to get your hands on me and—"

"Are you quite finished? Very amusing. Another one of your dreams?" She batted her eyelashes.

He snorted out a laugh. "It was one of my fondest ones, but I am revising it. Damned if your stare, direct and forthright, has undone me. That's the look for me."

"I think that is one of the kindest things you've said to me." She beamed.

"Oh, come now, I have said some rather lovely things about your skin, your eyes, your . . ."

Laughing, she held up her hand to stop him. "We are slowing down. Save your charm for Mr. Shaw's son or his wife, if she appears. Pity Shaw did not have a daughter. I have little doubt she would deliver the papers and whatever else you want after you flashed your smile at her," she muttered.

"One smile?" Delighted, he cocked a brow.

Unfortunately, the door was opened and the step lowered before he could tempt her with his smile. Julia edged forward to be assisted down. He'd have to pursue the matter later, see if a few well-aimed smiles worked on getting his Julia to say yes. It sounded as if she gave them some heed if she believed they had the power to get women to do his bidding.

He stepped outside, meeting Brett and Robbie, who had drawn up behind them.

Martin Shaw, Abel Shaw's middle son, resided in Russell Square, and while it was not the West End, it was a respectable address. Daniel could not fathom anyone following them here. Then again, he hadn't believed his brother capable of fratricide.

"Robbie says the hairs on the back of his neck are crawling. He thinks you should turn around." Brett lifted a brow, which conveyed his opinion on the matter.

"I did not say that," Robbie snapped. "I said I have seen the same tilbury following us for a bit and driving to the inch to keep up with us. The horses don't like it, feel crowded."

Daniel nodded. "If it appears again, see if you can catch them. They might have useful information."

"Right," Brett said. "And if they have guns? I think we should be more concerned if they have those."

"He has a point," Julia said, warily eyeing the passing traffic.

Daniel frowned. "Just be aware of anything untoward. They're not going to fire on us in the middle of Russell Square. This is not your Wild West."

"True," Brett agreed. "We're in refined London, which

happens to boast a history replete with plagues, decapitations, torture, dukes murdering their own brothers—"

"Just be alert." Daniel cut him off. "We will leave the carriage at Shaw's and have a footman pick it up. We can exit through the servant's entrance and take a circuitous route home. Does that meet with your approval?"

"Fine," Brett sighed.

As Brett returned to their curricle with Robbie, Daniel overheard Brett ask Robbie why the horses who felt crowded didn't share their concerns with Brett. Robbie's answer was a cuff to Brett's head, knocking his top hat askew.

Julia slipped her arm through Daniel's, gripping his forearm tighter than necessary. Cursing the situation, he led her up the front stoop to the entrance to Martin Shaw's residence.

⬧⬧

THEY WERE LED to a drawing room that was decorated with understated elegance, floral wallpaper, pastoral paintings, and a grand piano filling one corner. Sundry pictures and bric-a-brac competed for space on available surfaces.

Julia settled on the settee, while Daniel admired the painting of some nautical scene, yearning to escape into it with Julia.

They did not have long to wait. Abel Shaw's son strode into the room, a tall, dark-haired man, whose brown eyes behind silver spectacles were sharp and narrowed on Daniel. He dipped his head in greeting. "I am Martin Shaw, Your Grace. To what do I owe the honor of your visit?"

Something in the man's reserve, an infinitesimal edge of hostility that emanated from him, and made Daniel cautious in his approach. No winsome smiles were going to win this man over. "Mr. Shaw. My apologies for calling without notice, and I will not take up too much of your time. Before I begin our business, allow me to introduce my fiancée, Lady Julia Chandler."

Julia rose at his introduction and came to stand beside Daniel. She dipped into a curtsy, her smile bright. "You have a lovely home, Mr. Shaw. I do hope we are not causing too much of an interruption in your schedule, but I encouraged Bedford to make this visit, as it is a matter of some delicacy that has been festering for a few years."

Shaw raised a brow, but held his silence. No bowing and scraping or scrambling to do their bidding. He bent enough to incline his head toward Julia. "Lady Chandler, it is a pleasure." As the silence stretched, he felt compelled to offer them a seat.

Daniel waited until they were all settled before he leaned forward, choosing his words carefully. "Mr. Shaw, I understand that after all these years, my visit is untoward. However, your late father was my father's solicitor for decades, and I wanted to offer my condolences to you for your loss. I have fond memories of him, for he always had a kind word for a boy and the unending patience to teach me vingt-et-un."

Shaw's smile was brittle, stopping short of his eyes. "Yes, well, my father had a fine hand at cards. But a decade has passed since his employ with your father, so I should be honored that you deigned to take the time to remember him, considering you have not all these years past."

Daniel heard Julia's intake of breath as Shaw's words held a wealth of condemnation, clearly not honored by Edmund's visit or condolences. This would take more than charm. He edged forward. "Yes, well, let me begin by saying that I was not myself after my own father's death. Over the years and with Julia's encouragement, I have come to regret some of my hasty actions in dismissing so many of those loyal to my father. Please accept my sincere apologies if it caused undue grief to your father during his retirement."

Mr. Shaw straightened, apparently nonplussed at the belated apology. Sighing, his tension appeared to ease. "Yes, well, I should offer my apologies as well. While the last years were difficult for my father, and I'd like to place the blame elsewhere, my father shouldered most of it. As you know, he had a love of cards, and therein lies the true root of his difficulties. I don't doubt he would have landed on the same unfortunate path regardless of whether or not he remained in your employ."

Daniel heard the sadness underlying Shaw's words and

cursed his need to press into unhealed wounds. "I did not realize his habit was so consuming. I now understand why I never won a hand from him," Daniel ruefully conceded.

"Few could. He had an uncanny ability."

"Edmund, why don't you share with Mr. Shaw the letter you received? We don't want to make this visit more difficult than it has to be."

Daniel tamped down his revulsion at her use of his brother's name. "Mr. Shaw, my brother received a curious letter from your father. It was mailed to his Boston residence a few months ago. It was rather cryptic. He wrote that it was time for him to return home and claim his destiny, and that your father would explain more when ah . . . when Lord Bryant arrived home." He cursed the trip over his own bloody name.

Shaw furrowed his brow and nodded. "Yes. It is similar to what he kept murmuring those last days. I am afraid I gave it little heed, for you must understand my father was never the same after he left your father's employ. And not just due to his gambling or his fight to keep creditors at bay and stay out of gaol."

"How so? That is, if you don't mind my asking." Daniel found himself edging forward on his seat.

"He kept rambling on about a betrayal, and how it would be the death of him. That he would pay the price for it, had a corner in Hades reserved for him and some doctor." He shrugged. "My apologies, but I always assumed he was referring to you, the betrayal being your dismissal of his services."

"A betrayal? Was my name, ah my brother's name, that is, ever mentioned?"

"No. Not until the last. He mentioned a need to speak to Lord Bryant. He was quite insistent upon it, but he never mentioned a letter or anything about a destiny to be claimed. That is all I know. I regret that I can not be of more help."

So am I. "You have been of great help. Did your father leave any papers or anything else from his days working for my father?"

Shaw was already shaking his head and looking pained. "My eldest brother inherited most of my father's effects, which in the end was not much. Anything of value went to pay off my father's creditors. You are welcome to speak to my brother, that is if you can locate him. I regret to say, Charlie inherited my father's proclivities toward gambling. It nigh on broke my mother's heart before her passing. Charlie periodically returns, but more often than not, he is lost to the gambling hells and a world from which I keep a safe distance."

Daniel frowned. "And your younger brother would not be of any assistance?"

"George? Oh no. Like your brother, he has found his fortunes in America, been there these eight or nine years past. It is unlikely he would be of any help to you."

It helped only in that it was one less visit they had to make. He wondered if when they located the elusive Charlie he'd still possess his late father's papers. Daniel feared that what they sought was long lost and their search futile. However, if Edmund was still intent on pursuing this search, Daniel refused to give up the chase. Not yet.

"I appreciate your taking the time to answer my questions. I will not keep you further." He stood.

Julia came to her feet and smiled at Mr. Shaw. "Thank you for your time."

Daniel paused and attempted a sheepish look. "I was hoping we could slip out your garden gate. There were a few cronies that recognized my coach and were hoping to have a word." He smiled at Julia. "I promised my fiancée my undivided attention for the remainder of the day, and I would like to keep my word."

"Of course; I understand." Mr. Shaw grinned. "If you will follow me."

They made their way outside, Julia's hand on Daniel's arm, where it was a perfect fit. He warily eyed the back alley before venturing forward.

"Not the most informative of visits. I doubt we will get much more from the gambler, but it's still worth pursuing, for it is our last lead." He could not keep the glum tone from his voice. Julia remained silent. "I will ask Robbie to keep searching the gambling hells to see if he can locate Charlie Shaw."

He stopped and grinned at Julia. "Actually, I have a better idea, it might cost a pretty coin, but it might be faster."

Julia was casting furtive glances around, her hand tightening on his arm. "What is it? If it gets answers more quickly, it is money well spent."

"I was thinking of hiring our infamous village poacher. Weasel could catch a rabbit in the desert. I am sure he could trap one cardsharp in a gambling hell. And he deserves the money after what my brother did to him."

Julia squeezed his arm. "He does. Another brilliant business investment. Hire him, Daniel, so we can get answers and end this. This talk of betrayals frightens me."

"Yes, *something is rotten in the state of Denmark,*" he murmured, recalling having uttered the prophetic words when he had visited the grounds of Bedford Hall. Whatever the betrayal was, he worried that his father had planted the seeds that had grown into an "*unweeded garden*" with Edmund. He commiserated with Hamlet, hoping his father's ghost would not return to haunt him.

"True. '*Things rank and gross in nature,*' " Julia rejoined.

He clamped his jaw at the despair in her voice, cursing himself for allowing her to be drawn into this quagmire. Seeing her fierce resolve, he knew he never had a choice. Warriors did not stay home, nor did his Maid Marian—as much as he wished it otherwise.

He hoped this last venture proved lucrative. Because Shaw's bloody letter had been right. *It was time.*

Chapter Twenty-four

❧❦

JULIA's steps were as heavy as her heart as they climbed the stairs to Keaton House. She ought to be worried about her ruination and the ensuing scandal, or her decision to accept Daniel's proposal. Minus the ruination and scandal bit, that was what occupied the minds of most young women. Instead, she sought proof a duke was indeed a murderer and the motives behind his reasoning.

Daniel did this to her. From the moment he had stormed into her life, he was like a gust of wind that scattered her thoughts and swept her feet out from under her. She used to be a calm, responsible young woman. Now she was Maid Marian chasing after windmills. She pressed a hand to her temple, for she was mixing up her literary allusions. She needed time to herself to sort out all that Shaw had imparted, for something about it nagged at her.

However, the time was not now, for the minute the front door opened, she knew something was amiss. Burke, a butler known for being as unflappable as stone, was gray-tinged and wide-eyed. "Thank the lord," he blurted, shocking Julia so much that she stood dumbfounded.

Daniel grasped her elbow and practically dragged her inside, letting Burke slam the door behind them. "What is it? What has happened?"

Burke recovered his composure, but his expression was still grim. "Everyone is well. You need to speak to Taunton."

"Bryant. Come with me. Now." Her father was storming out from the foyer leading to the guest quarters, Emily on his heels. His hair stood up straight as if he had attempted to pull it out.

Without a word, Daniel followed her father from the room.

"Oh, thank goodness." Emily's arms were around Julia, squeezing her tight.

Julia assured her sister she was all right and gently drew away, her heart nearly at a standstill as she took in Emily's pallor. "What is it? What has happened?"

"It is Brett. He is all right, just a broken arm." She hitched a breath. "Doctor Malley is in with him now. Robbie brought him here. We have been keeping Doctor Malley busy. What is going on, Julia?"

"Please, I will explain everything later. I promise. Tell me what happened?"

"Apparently someone shot at them. In Russell Square, no less." She shook her head, her expression incredulous. "Robbie saw something, for he dove on Brett, pulling him down, but the horses shied from the noise. Robbie got them under control, but the curricle tipped over. Brett's arm broke in his landing. Apparently, he's not as hardy as Robbie."

"No one is," Julia commented ruefully, noting Emily's use of Brett's given name. It was something to file away for later when she had time to ponder it.

"Robbie is checking on the horses again, but father is fit to be tied, for Brett was tight-lipped about what happened. You need to intercede." Emily gave her a worried look.

She nodded, her mind already down the hall. Thank the lord for Robbie or the horses or whoever deserved the credit for suspecting they were followed. She swallowed, not willing to contemplate what might have happened otherwise.

A maid directed her to the room where they had settled Brett, and she lifted her hand to knock, but the door opened and Doctor Malley emerged.

"Ah, Lady Julia. A pleasure, despite the circumstances. Once again, my work is done here. The young man shall be fine with a little rest. Send for me if the pain gets worse, or if he starts asking for his mother or his horse, and not necessarily in that order." With a wink, he made to turn away. "Is Lady Emily around? She was distraught; I would like to assure her that her young man is well. Jason, is it?"

"Excuse me?" Julia whispered, feeling the blood drain from her face.

"My apologies, is that not his name? That is what Lady Emily called him."

Julia dumbly shook her head. "She was mistaken. It is Brett. Brett Curtis."

"Ah . . ." He looked puzzled. "Well, she was upset. I shall speak to her."

He turned away, leaving Julia staring after him. Emily had been doing so well. *Was* doing so well. She refused to believe that had changed, but she could not fathom why she would confuse Brett with Jason. They shared similar coloring, blue eyes and fair hair, but therein the similarities ended. Brett was a head taller than Jason. *And* American. She frowned, forcing herself to put the matter aside for now.

She opened the door to Brett's room and stepped out of the calm and into the wrath of Taunton. Her father was on a tirade. She knew from past experience, it was best to wait until the brunt of his anger had passed.

"What the devil were you thinking? Attempted murder? Twice? You think you can resolve matters better than the authorities? Were you planning to use the Manton? And what would happen then? Bedford is dead without incriminating evidence implicating him in anything, and you are standing there with the smoking gun."

He had a point. Her father was pacing and when his back

was to her, she wiggled her eyebrows at Daniel, who stood with hands clenched, looking annoyed. At her look, he loosened his stance, a rueful grin curving his lips.

"I don't know what to believe. All of these accusations based on the word of some Weasel? Who is he? What is he? A poacher, you say?"

She ignored her father, who rambled on, and crossed to the bed to assess Brett's condition. His expression assuaged her worries. He was sitting up, his hair tousled, a dazed grin on his features, and appearing highly entertained by her father's monologue. She surmised Doctor Malley had given him something to dull the pain, for his pupils were like pinpricks and lacked their usual vibrancy. His splintered and bandaged arm rested on the covers. A new bruise bloomed on the cheek opposite his bruised eye.

He caught her hand. "Where did Emily go? I think I will heal quicker with her by my side."

His words eradicated any lingering worry over his health; the handsome rake would be fine. It was her sister she needed to worry about. She brushed his hair back from his forehead. "I will see that she returns," she whispered, but her father heard her.

"And *you*, Julia. How long have you known about this? And when were you planning to tell me? Were you to marry the man one day and bury him the next?"

At her gasp, her father closed his eyes and pressed a hand against his temple. "My apologies. That was uncalled for."

Only Brett appeared unperturbed. He waved his good arm dismissively. "Do not worry yourself. I have been saying the same thing. Tell him to go home every day. But you go on, your lordship, just keep talking. Scare some sense into him. He will not listen to me, but I am finding you need a fancy toff's title to get things done around here. Good thing Daniel looks like Bedford and can borrow his." Brett's eyes were heavy-lidded, and a loopy smile split his face.

Julia blanched, her gaze shooting to Daniel, who groaned and swiped his hands down his face.

"Please tell me that is the laudanum talking," her father warned.

This was why she hadn't confided in her father or gone to the authorities. Their story was based on trust and instinct. She trusted Daniel, and instinct had her distrusting Edmund.

"Perhaps we should talk in your office," Daniel hastily intervened. "He should get some sleep."

"Brilliant idea, s'tired." Brett murmured. "Have Emily come read me to sleep. She looks like an angel." He closed his eyes and his breathing leveled, but the smile remained.

Daniel could not get her father out of the room fast enough, obviously fearing what else Brett would ask of Emily. "Sir?"

"Fine. I could use a drink. It's the only way for this story to go down."

>=<

TWO HOURS AND half a bottle of good brandy later, Taunton's anger had been drowned out enough for him to hear the conviction in their words.

He slumped behind his desk and sighed, looking aged. "Christ. My Meg was right about you two as boys, but I was right about Edmund the man. She thought Julia would be a good influence over him, peel away his haughty veneer and find the man beneath the duke. My Meg said she had to do the same with me." His words were soft, and his smile wistful. "I trusted her opinion more than my own, but I guess none of us can be right all the time or we'd be intolerable bores." He lifted his drink and took another sip as if to ease the sting of his sainted wife being mistaken.

"My apologies, sir. I would have told you when I asked for Julia's hand, but I was not certain then. Given your reaction to the news, you can understand my reservations. There is no evidence to bring to the authorities. We reported the attack at the docks, but that can be dismissed as a robbery gone awry, particularly in that area."

Taunton nodded. "Yes, I understand." He leaned forward. "We cannot bring charges against a duke of the realm lightly. What you have is a leaking boat. Too many holes and your story sinks. We need to stopper up the holes."

Daniel swallowed at Taunton's use of the word *we*, stunned at how deeply the man's trust touched him. Next to Robbie, Brett, and now Julia, there were few people in his life who had trusted him on his word alone. There were benefits to being a member of a family, particularly the Chandler family, and each day he was learning to not only appreciate them, but to lean on them.

Julia circled her father's desk and kissed his forehead. "Thank you."

"Pray tell, for what? Not killing him or turning you over my knee as I should have?"

"For believing us."

Daniel quickly dropped his gaze to his drink. He had never been an *us* before either. He hoped this meant that Julia would finally agree to marry him.

"It's the damnedest thing, but I do." Taunton sighed. "So let us get to the bottom of this. Stopper up the holes. What would he be willing to kill for?"

Julia frowned. "We have been going on the assumption that your father left you something in his will that Edmund wants. But Shaw's son spoke of his father worrying over a betrayal. What if it isn't something your father left you, but something he did. A betrayal he committed."

"It makes sense," Daniel agreed. "My father could have had Shaw draw up documents in an attempt to right the wrong done. Doctor Reilly might have learned of the betrayal through being present at my father's conversations with Shaw or through my father's sickbed rambles. But when my father died, Edmund likely refused to honor whatever wishes my father had put forward. Instead, he bought Shaw and Doctor Reilly's silence and they bled him dry, thus Edmund's debts and the bleeding of his own estates.

"Shaw must have kept the damning document, blackmailed Edmund with it, and threatened Edmund that if anything were to happen to him, it would be made public." Daniel had started to pace, but he stopped. "It is little wonder Edmund spent a fortnight drinking himself sick over my father's death."

"Hmph," Taunton emitted his usual eloquent opinion. "That still circles us back to the same question. What the devil can it be?"

"It is something Abel Shaw planned to give you, making you privy to the betrayal." Julia added to Daniel's words. "Edmund must be afraid you would make it public rather than collude with him to bury the scandal. Because you have integrity and he does not," Julia said, her chin jutted out firmly and her eyes shining as they met his.

He beamed back at her. Murder, mayhem, and betrayals forgotten. For the moment, there was just Julia and how magnificent she was.

"Hmph."

Taunton's grunt snapped him out of his reverie. Damned if his cheeks didn't burn.

Julia covered her mouth, barely stifling her laughter.

Grinning, he yanked his eyes from hers, needing to focus. "It has to be something that irrevocably tarnishes the illustrious title, for God knows, that is all Edmund gives a whit about." Weariness settled over him, as they kept traveling over the same well-trodden path.

"What if you and Edmund aren't the rightful heirs," Taunton suggested.

He blinked. "Pardon?"

"Your parents were in despair over getting an heir to the dukedom. Your mother had lost so many children, Daniel, a full dozen. What if when she died, the child she birthed died with her?" He waved his brandy glass as if to direct them to fill in the rest.

"What and two changelings were placed in our stead?" he said, unable to hide his amusement.

"Daniel," Julia chastised, but her own eyes were alight with laughter.

"My apologies, sir," he said.

Taunton shrugged, unperturbed. "Considering I haven't noticed any fairy wings on you, I suppose it is farfetched."

"No. No wings, but I have a birthmark that every other

generation of the Bedford lineage has inherited, and we have my grandmère's unusual eye color.

"A birthmark?" Julia perked up. "I did not see any . . ." She snapped her mouth closed, and her cheeks bloomed a bright rose.

Taunton simply gave her a long look, but returned to the subject at hand. "It was a thought. Do you have any better?"

He shook his head, unable to summon a single idea.

Julia frowned, her ideas apparently depleted as well.

After a prolonged silence, Taunton gave him a curt nod. "Right. So then, we need to find that document before Edmund does. I approve of your idea of hiring this Weasel fellow, but I suggest we broaden the net and employ some private investigators. I also think we should return to Taunton Court. You make an easy target here, this city bursting with too many people, few of them honest. I like my odds on my own land, with my own people, where strangers would be noticed. Also, Edmund will be in London for a while, tied up with the little matter of severing a betrothal contract. Let us go home, build our defenses, strategize some more, and form our line of attack."

"Yes, let's," Julia agreed.

Daniel sought Julia's gaze, and his heart warmed at her look of determination.

He was not alone. He had friends and family who believed in him.

He had Julia.

Chapter Twenty-five

≫⬦≪

JULIA paced a well-worn path in her room, wringing her hands. The other night in the library, she had wondered if the passion she and Daniel had shared was enough to sustain a marriage? It had been the wrong question to ask. She had another, far more pressing concern. What she needed to know was if one person's love for another was enough to bolster a marriage?

She had no answer for that question either. And it frightened her, for she desperately needed one because she had fallen completely, madly, irrevocably in love with Daniel.

He was intelligent, caring, amusing, and kind. He loved her business sense and her forthright stare. He thought her clever and brilliant. Most important, he filled the empty chambers in her heart.

She thought she knew what debilitating grief was, having witnessed her father's and sister's, but to truly understand grief, she had to find someone whose loss she would mourn deeply. Someone whose disappearance from her life would carve a hole deep inside of her. She had never grieved over Edmund.

Theirs was a contractual arrangement based on duty, not love. Never love, she knew now.

It was different with Daniel.

She loved him.

She wanted a marriage like her parents', and what Emily had with Jason. But more than any of that, she wanted Daniel. She wanted him whole and alive and to be hers. She was beginning to think he was all she had ever wanted, and that she had been waiting for him for her entire life. He was the *something more* for which she had yearned. And if he sailed home to Boston, then she would go with him. But as he was rebuilding Lakeview Manor, she had hopes to get him to stay here . . . with her.

She stopped her pacing and lifted her chin, recalling the letter sent to Daniel. *It is time. Come home and claim your destiny.*

Tonight was hers. Time to say yes . . . to everything.

Before her courage failed her, she snatched the oil lamp from her bedside table, fled her room, and never looked back.

She hurried down the dimly lit stairs to the guest quarters. Reaching Daniel's door, she paused, nerves stealing over her. It was nigh on midnight, and she was standing poised to knock on a man's bedroom door. The pounding of her heart renewed her courage. Brett's accident reminded her again that she could have lost everything she held dear. Tonight she planned to claim it so that she would never harbor any regrets.

She knocked. Her heart jumped in rhythm with her rapping knuckles. Just as her courage wavered, the door opened, and there stood Daniel.

He was so handsome, he stole her breath. His shirttails hung loose and the top buttons at his throat were undone, revealing a tantalizing strip of bare skin.

"What? What is it?" Daniel said, worry clouding those vibrant green eyes.

"I . . . ah . . . I . . ." It was one thing to be ready to surrender everything, it was another thing altogether to initiate it. She had brought her family back from the brink of despair, kept Taunton Court afloat, and was helping to solve a decades-old mystery. But she had never seduced a man before.

Excitement gripped her.

Daniel gave her a curious look, then peered into the corridor. Once he assessed no one else was afoot, he caught her hand and drew her inside, closing the door behind her.

The click of the lock echoed in the silence.

His hands on her shoulders, his eyes roved over her in concern. "You are pale as a ghost, Julia. It was a lot to learn today, and I understand if you need time to consider how involved you want—"

"You cannot rid yourself of me. Do stop trying."

Surprised, Daniel blinked, then his eyes softened and he smiled. "Good, because I do not intend to."

She nodded, her body warming under his touch. She released a breath, struggling to formulate a plan of how to proceed. She was good at planning.

But not at seduction . . .

"What is it? Shall I get Emily?"

"No!" Good lord, that was all she needed. A witness to her transgression—or her bungling attempt at it.

"All right." He nodded. "Why don't you sit." He guided her over to an emerald brocade chair that engulfed her. Lifting the decanter on the table beside it, he poured a sip into a crystal tumbler. Her lantern was exchanged for the drink as Daniel folded her fingers around the glass.

She glanced at it blankly. "What is it?"

"Ah, no idea."

He bent, and his head dipped close to hers as he assessed the contents. His thick, wavy brown hair was inches from hers. His familiar masculine scent teased her, sandalwood soap and Daniel, and she shamelessly inhaled.

"Smells like port." He straightened, and brushed aside a tousled strand tumbling over his forehead. "Probably well aged, a tad sweet, and too expensive to drink."

She lifted the glass and sniffed. Like a waft of smelling salts, the sweet odor snapped her back to her purpose. Wrinkling her nose, she placed the glass onto the table and stood. "I am all right now."

"That is good," he nodded, his hands on his hips.

He stood wearing a bemused expression, clearly awaiting an explanation. Her eyes strayed to the tumbler, and she wondered if she should have fortified herself with the liquid courage after all, then dismissed the idea. She was no coward.

She cleared her throat, lifted her chin, and delivered her words without preamble. "I have come to give you my answer."

"Your answer?" His lips twitched.

"But first you . . . You have to ask the question properly." She cursed her stuttering. She never stuttered.

Baffled, Daniel rubbed his neck. "All right. Remind me what the question is?"

Incredulous, Julia simply gaped at him, then started for the door. She had changed her mind. He was an obtuse idiot and she was done with him.

"Wait, wait." He caught her arm and spun her around. "I am beginning to understand. Forgive me."

He was laughing at her. He stood dangerously close to her hand, which was itching to slap him.

"So will you—"

"If you want an answer," she cut him off, her eyes narrowed in warning, "I would think very carefully before you continue."

Aware of her indignation, which must have been emanating from her in waves, Daniel dropped his hands and stepped back. "I understand. You are quite right. We should do this properly." He bobbed his head, but then looked hesitant. "So you want me on bended knee?"

She did not deign to respond but folded her arms across her chest and watched him squirm. She enjoyed his discomfiture, for it put them on equal footing.

"Right." He nodded. "And do not dare try to leave or I'll come after you," he muttered. He raised his hands as if to hold her in place, slowly backing away as he searched the room. Seeming to locate what he was looking for, he hastened over to his bedside table where there sat a fresh vase of flowers. Scooping up the lot, he shook the water droplets free and returned to her side.

"Close your eyes."

"Why?"

"You want this done right, I should get dressed," he suggested with amusement.

She bit down on her lower lip to stifle her own sudden spurt of hysterical laughter. She nodded. "Perhaps tuck in your shirt." She closed her eyes. A grunt and some rustling movements came from him.

"You can open them now. I give you fair warning, if you say no, I will toss you over my shoulder and carry you off to Gretna Green."

"I understand." She tried to look solemn, but her lips twitched at the low grumble. He had neatened his hair, which she regretted, for she found she rather liked him disheveled. He had tucked in his shirt and neatly buttoned it, but the sight of his bare feet was strangely comforting.

His eyes met hers, warm and his expression appropriately serious, all humor gone. He dropped onto one knee and clutched the flowers. "Lady Julia Chandler, would you do me the honor of becoming my wife?"

She let her eyes rove over his handsome features, breathing in the moment. He looked nervous, a bit expectant, and so very dear. She had waited too long.

"So will you? Marry me, that is." He had waited long enough.

"Yes, yes, I will." Exhaling, she was surprised at the lightness in her chest, as if a constricting band had released and something exploded inside of her.

He stood and grinned. Realizing he still held the makeshift bouquet, he thrust the flowers at her.

She frowned. Well, what had she expected from a loveless proposal? An *Ode to Julia*? Annoyed at herself, she reached for the bouquet, but Daniel snatched it away and tossed it onto the chair.

She wanted those flowers. They weren't a declaration of undying love, but they were a sweet touch. She leaned over to reclaim them, but cried out as she was abruptly whisked off her feet.

He hoisted her into his arms and twirled her around and around, his laughter ringing in her ears.

She did not need the port, for her head spun without it.

He set her on her feet and his mouth captured hers in a deep, plundering kiss.

Heart hammering, pulse racing, she gasped as desire pulsed through her. His kiss was as powerful as all the others, stealing her breath, all thoughts in her head, and leaving her gasping for breath.

She gulped for air as his head lifted. Moments later, her eyes fluttered closed as his lips traveled down her neck, his hands lifting to fist in her hair.

"Good lord, I want you." He pressed his face into the column of her neck and inhaled deeply. "What are you wearing?"

"Excuse me?" she breathed.

"Beneath your robe?" he whispered.

She hesitated and then, flushing a bright pink, she murmured. "It's something Emily bought."

"Can I see it?" His hand shot up. "Do not answer that. Not yet." His eyes met hers and slowly, almost as if he waited for her to protest, he lifted a strand of her hair and watched it curl around his finger.

"You have beautiful hair. All these enticing curls with a life of their own. I have been dying to take it down and see it thus, ever since that day in the library. I thought of locking your father, Emily, Brett, Burke, and Petie in a closet, and stealing you away."

She snorted at the ridiculous notion, masking her nerves. She was not prepared for Daniel's heat, or the warmth seeping through her limbs as he continued in that husky voice.

"You do not believe me? I am serious."

"It might be crowded."

"I believe they would fit, provided I secure the good Mr. Tanner in his own closet. With them locked away, I would pull out each pin, run my fingers through every curl." He drew the strand straight, released it, and watched in fascination as it sprang back into a tight curl. His voice dropped to a growl that had gooseflesh rising across her body.

"Let me love you, Julia. I want to touch you as I have longed to do. We are engaged now, Julia, and as your betrothed, I would like to pleasure my fiancée."

Dazed, she had to swallow as she tipped her cheek into his palm. His words enflamed, weaving a seductive spell around her.

He slid his arms around her waist and drew her to him. Her eyes widened at the press of his hard chest. "I want to touch you and have you touch me."

His tender words whispered through her, a warm, tickling breath against her cheek. His lips moved to the sensitive underside of her chin, trailing a scattering of small kisses down her throat. She tipped her head for him to gain better access, struggling to drink in his words.

He kissed her, and she curved her arms around his broad shoulders and clasped him closer, kissing him back. Tentative at first, and then with more confidence when she heard his guttural groan. She let her tongue explore the warmth of his mouth, the fullness of his top lip, tasting him as she yearned to do. Brandy sweetened his mouth.

His hands moved to the shoulders of her robe and slipped it down her arms. Light-headed, she swayed on her feet, his supportive arm no longer bracing her. He stepped back, and his eyes roved over her body, from the top of her head to the tips of her toes. He missed nothing.

Her dressing gown was a diaphanous cloud of green, its décolletage loosely draped over her breasts, and a slit strategically cut down one side to bare a tantalizing glimpse of naked leg. It was part of Emily's trousseau, and Julia had discovered it on her bed when she had retired. Emily had always been perceptive.

Daniel's eyes flared, his lips parted, and a swath of red climbed his neck. He unbuttoned a few buttons on his shirt and slipped it over his head, letting it pool over her discarded robe. He yanked her to him.

"Remind me to thank your sister." His voice was hoarse.

His mouth captured hers, and she moaned as his hand cupped her bottom.

Her fingers moved over the taut muscles of his back, feeling the warmth of his burning skin, hearing his sharp indrawn breath as her fingers danced over him, careful to avoid the bandage circling his waist.

His arm slid under her legs, and he swung her off her feet. Startled, her heart pounded as he carried her to the bed. He tumbled backward, still clutching her, and she cried out as they landed with a bouncing thump. She struggled to lift herself, but his arm around her waist rolled so she lay beneath him.

"Daniel—" she gasped.

"Say yes, Julia."

What was the question? The shock of his hand, bold upon her breast, had her thoughts scrambled. Her eyes closed and she sighed. Good lord.

"Say yes, Julia."

She opened her eyes to see Daniel looming above her, his eyes dark and passion-glazed, imploring her. She slid her arms around his neck, lifting her head up to meet his lips. "Yes. Yes to everything."

His smile was slow and wicked and wrapped around her heart as he leaned down to kiss her, his tongue gliding over her lips. "I promise to take care of you, to go gently. To ensure you enjoy it. Wait here." He sat up and slowly shed his trousers.

She sat up, too, fascinated. Her eyes widened and she swallowed at the sight of his erection. Her lips parted, and her heart stuttered. "Perhaps . . . perhaps we should slow down," she managed, after she cleared her throat.

He laughed and gave her a gentle push back onto the bed, following her down. "You are so right. Slow is better." He breathed her in, burying his face in the valley between her breasts as he eased her gown from her body.

His mouth closed over her nipple, teasing it into response.

"Better than treacle tart," he murmured against the sensitive skin, his lips moving to the underside of her breast. His hands dug into the soft flesh of her waist, holding her still as she squirmed.

"Daniel." His name was a mere whisper on her lips. He was

firm against her, and his arousal emboldened her. Her hand slid between them and closed over his warm shaft.

He sucked in a breath, his breathing ragged. She opened her eyes and watched his pupils dilate, the green of them dark and slumberous.

Eventually, he grasped her hand and pressed it to his chest, kissing her. "That," he kissed her again, "is not helping to," another kiss, "slow things down."

She smiled against his lips. "Perhaps it's time to move a little faster."

His laughter was low and almost pained. "I do adore that you are a brave woman. My fearless warrior."

She gasped as his hand moved lower to slip between her legs, his lips curving against hers. She knew she was moist, and she flushed, though she was unashamed. Her passion stunned her, for she wanted him. Now.

He moved his hand beneath her knee, bending it. "It will take a few minutes for your body to become accustomed to me, Julia."

He shifted and slowly eased into her entrance, pausing at her sharp intake of breath. "Are you all right?"

Her eyes tightly closed, she bit her lip against the unfamiliar pressure inside her, opening her to him. It felt hot and tight, and so deliciously erotic. She nodded jerkily. He cupped her cheek, lifting her face to his, bathing her face in sweet kisses. He pressed them to her closed lids, her nose, her cheeks, then claimed her mouth as his hips lifted and he began to gently move.

His movements were slow, setting his pace by her response. Seeking something more, something elusive, she arched her hips against his, gasping as he increased his rhythm. A sheen of sweat rose on their skin.

"Still all right?" he gasped, sounding as if the question pained him.

"Battering. Battering is good."

He sputtered out a half laugh, half groan, and thrust deeply into her, fully embedding himself.

She dug her fingers into his back, holding his body to hers

as her desire and the sting of pain had her crying out. He clutched her close and kissed her deeply, his tongue darting in as he thrust his hips against hers.

Good lord, she was whimpering, and the sounds appeared to inflame him further. It was like riding a tumultuous wave of desire. Over and over. Her passion overwhelmed her, sensations warring. And then the wave curled, peaked, and the warm tide of her release flooded her. She cried out Daniel's name and clutched him tighter.

Her cheek pressed to his chest, she listened to the pounding beat of his heart. He moaned low and deep, his movements now faster and less graceful. He gave a few more deep thrusts, and her name exploded from his lips, his climax pouring from him.

He collapsed on top of her, his cheek against her breast, their bodies sweat-slicked and spent. It was wonderfully delicious, decadent . . . She inhaled and realized she could not draw air into her lungs. She pinched his side. "You are heavy. Slide over."

He grunted, his lips curving against her breast. "My forthright fiancée." He shifted to her side, and gathered her into his arms. Her back was to his chest, and he cradled her close.

"I have a question," she said softly, her voice sleep-slurred.

"Of course you do."

"How soon can we do that again?"

"You might be sore. But not too long." He leaned over her to meet her eyes, a smile warming his.

"Good." She closed her eyes and snuggled against him, pressed to his heart, right where she wished to be. "I have another question."

Love me. Say you love me, she silently implored.

"What is it?" His hand was playing with her hair, and she had to summon up her last vestige of energy to speak, tamping down the fervent cry of her heart. "Does Lakeview Manor have a nursery?"

His hand stilled and she felt the pounding of his heart. It took him a while to respond and he sounded as if he had to clear his throat to do so. "I believe we can make room for one."

"See that you do."

She smiled at his soft laugh, closing her eyes as he held her close. She had always yearned for something more, and Daniel had given it to her. She never could have fathomed there were such blissful advantages to being a ruined woman. Had she known, she might have become one much sooner.

After all, it had brought Daniel to her.

Now she just needed him to tell her that he loved her back. That he could not live without her.

She was planning on it.

Chapter Twenty-six

❦

THEY had been in Bedfordshire for over a week when the news of Julia's broken engagement became public. As bets were settled at White's, Daniel and Julia remained buffered from the worst of the accounts, sequestered within the fortress-like walls of Taunton Court. The earl had insisted Daniel move into the guest wing, resolving to demonstrate his support of Julia and Daniel's relationship in the hopes of stemming some of the tide of gossip. Brett had joined them as well, his arm still splinted and healing.

Daniel was quite content to move into Taunton Court. It certainly made his evenings far more pleasurable. Or, at least some of them.

Julia was circumspect in their illicit trysts. He often had to peel back her prim-and-proper layers in order to uncover his daring and improper Julia. He had no complaints, other than being desperate to solve this damnable mystery so he could get married and toss out the last of Julia's reservations as well as his own. He had feared proposing to her, but he feared letting her go more.

However, a trip to the parish church would have to wait. He had yet to obtain a special license, and Taunton advised waiting until the furor of Julia's broken betrothal died down before stirring up more excitement with the announcement of their engagement. Underlying all of this was Daniel's fear of wedding Julia one day, only to widow her the next, proving Taunton's words prophetic.

Edmund was a dark shadow haunting him. Daniel found himself starting at sharp sounds and restless at night. Once he had awoken struggling to breathe, gripped in the nightmare of the fire and his near suffocation. Julia's soothing words had brought him back. She anchored him. He had been a foundering ship without a homeport until Julia.

Edmund be damned.

In addition to waiting out the gossip, they hoped for news from London as to the whereabouts of Charlie Shaw. In the interim, Daniel rarely left Taunton Court, with the exception of visiting Lakeview Manor where the grounds had been cleared and construction on the frame of the new house begun. There he had found Mabry toiling alongside other of Edmund's tenants, all grateful for the additional work this project provided. Parishioners had begun the process of delivering baskets to address the tenants' pressing needs for food. Mabry had also promised to alert Daniel should he hear word of Edmund's return.

Getting the men to work, the families fed, and forging these trusting relationships was a start in alleviating the tenants' suffering. Until Daniel resolved matters with Edmund, he could do no more for these men or the families who so desperately needed his assistance. It gave him added incentive to achieve his goal.

Daniel returned to Lakeview Manor with Brett, riding over that morning to answer questions from the foreman in charge of the construction. To provide the needed work as well as to expedite the project, Daniel had increased the number of men he employed. He had also added a nursery to the plans.

"It looks like it is progressing smoothly."

Brett's voice cut through Daniel's thoughts, and he glanced up to see the framed structure of Lakeview Manor rising before him. The wood was mostly oak, Lakeview Manor having maintained a small forest of the trees. His absence had saved the wood during a period when so much of the county's timber had been sold off for shipbuilding.

The framing would be fronted with bricks to provide protection against fire. The skeletal frame was sparse. He did not mind. He was quite content with his present lodgings, particularly during the evening hours. Perhaps he shouldn't have doubled the work force.

"It is a good location." Brett walked over, his gaze drifting over the grounds.

He followed Brett's gaze. The fall colors had darkened into the deeper browns, umbers, and burgundies that heralded November. They carpeted more of the forest floor than the trees.

"It's good that you are rebuilding this, Daniel. I know how much it meant to you. You shouldn't have let Edmund take this away from you."

Brett's right arm was in a sling, but like Daniel's own, his bruises were fading. Daniel thanked God for it. Considering Brett had thought his return trip was idiocy, if his friend had died, Daniel had little doubt that Brett would have found a means to haunt him for the rest of his life. He nodded toward the house. "I thought this was all he could take. Besides my childhood," he added under his breath.

Brett did not respond, for there was nothing to say to that.

Daniel breathed in the scent of pine and the fresh earth, letting it roll over him. They were boyhood smells, and they reminded him that Edmund hadn't stolen everything.

Together they strode down to the lake, a gentle breeze brushing over him. The background murmurs of the builders, an occasional bird cry, and the rhythmic pounding of a hammer drifted their way.

Brett turned to him, his gaze assessing. "You are determined to see this through, aren't you? I cannot talk you into coming home?"

This is my home. He stiffened, stunned. The retort had been on the tip of his tongue, ready to explode from him like a fish leaping out of the lake. As if they had been forcibly submerged far too long, and had been desperate for release.

"I am beginning to understand." Brett held up his hand as if he had spoken out loud. "I do not like it, but I suspected this day might come." His smile was rueful, his eyes sad. "America cannot compete with lofty titles, ancient castles, and heroic knights. Despite your history of witches burned at the stake, drawing and quarterings, kings beheading their wives, and—"

"I understand," he interceded before Brett launched into the age-old argument. "Didn't Salem have witches as well?"

"They were hanged," Brett muttered. "One pressed to death with a stone."

"Ah, much more civil," he nodded, trying to look solemn, but his lips twitched and he caught the amusement dancing in Brett's eyes.

"The scales were tipped when you found Julia. Competition over." He shrugged.

"Julia changes everything," he agreed. "When I left, I had no intention of ever returning. I think I needed time to heal, from the fire, from my childhood. The problem was that I left a part of me here. In this land. This ground. It means something to me. It's my home, too." His gaze swept over the grounds, and his voice lowered. "I lost something here, and not by choice. I need to rebuild it to be whole. Do you understand?"

"I do." Brett sighed.

The silence that fell was companionable, as his friend finally understood. It gave Daniel an element of peace, something that had eluded him since his return.

"To be honest, you were getting tedious buried in your ledgers. Not to mention, it was becoming difficult to tear you away from your desk. I knew then that you were not really living, but burying yourself in work or perhaps biding your time."

Daniel looked at Brett with surprise.

"I suppose that is another reason I wished to persuade you from this trip." Brett said ruefully. "However, your absence means that Isabelle Hardy will finally look my way."

Daniel snorted.

"She is the toast of Boston. Now that your lordship is out of reach, I have a chance."

"You are right. After all, it was just my *title* that was of interest to her."

"Of course. Why else would she look to you when I am around?" Brett dismissed the idea as ludicrous.

"No idea," he agreed wryly. "Cannot think of a thing."

"However, there are lovely sights here as well." He eyed Daniel askance. "I am good with sisters, you know. Have three of them myself."

He shook his head. "I trust Emily to take care of herself." He nodded to Brett's right arm in the sling. "When do you intend to tell her you are left-handed? She will not be pleased to hear you have cajoled her into drafting your correspondence when you are perfectly capable of doing it yourself."

Brett grinned. "It was the only way I could get her near me."

Daniel gave him a level look. "Tread softly there. It is my neck that would be on the block if you hurt her again."

"Again?" Brett said, his amusement fading.

"Her fiancé died in India, and she's still raw, so I beg you, do not push her, Brett. She had a bad time of it after his death."

Brett frowned. "She is a wisp of a thing, like one of those delicate English roses. But she has thorns, as she has pricked me a time or two. Cannot understand it. Women love me. I should know, my sisters tell—"

"Spare me your sisters." Daniel held up his hands.

He would miss Brett when he returned to Boston. Perhaps he shouldn't be cautioning him against Emily. Brett's poetic comment on English roses was not like his friend. It was worth considering.

❧

IT WAS NEARING dawn when someone pounded on Daniel's door, streaks of dim light just beginning to sliver through the curtains. They coincided with the chimes of the mantel clock, and he sprang up before the first knock had finished. Years under Edmund's roof had made him a light sleeper. He had his breeches on and the door opened within seconds.

The footman looked as if he had tumbled out of bed and haphazardly tossed on whatever clothes were at hand. He tripped over his words in his haste to spit them out. "Sir, you need to come quick. It's Lakeview Manor. It's on fire!"

Edmund was home.

He clamped down his blind fury and snapped out orders. "Roust Taunton and Mr. Curtis. Have them meet me there. Wake the stables. Have them saddle the horses."

Slamming his door, he finished dressing, his heart thumping.

Bloody hell. *Not again.* It was like a nightmare repeating itself. He forced air into his lungs as his throat tightened. He was all right. More importantly, Julia was asleep in her bedroom, and for once, he thanked God he was in his. He hoped she stayed there, cursed under his breath when he knew without an iota of doubt that his Maid Marian most certainly would not.

Gritting his teeth, he whipped open the door and raced out. He did not give a damn about salvaging the beginnings of the timber frame, knowing how quickly fire consumed, but he could protect his headstrong fiancée. Or at least try.

≫❦≪

THE ORANGE GLOW lit up the sky. Flames, like dancing ribbons, engulfed the structure, consuming all they entangled. Crackles of popping lights splashed into the night. Oak timbers succumbed under the scorching heat, crashing down in a roar of spitting sparks. An inferno of heat forced everyone back from the burning mass.

A horse-drawn cart had been loaded up with barrels of water. Men had formed a human chain, passing buckets to douse the perimeter around the blaze. It was too late to save the frame, but there were thickets, brambles, and the lines of trees that created a border between Taunton Court and the manor, which threatened to carry the blaze farther.

As the heat engulfed Daniel, he stood in impotent fury. Moments later, he became aware of Julia's presence and found her beside him. Having her there eased him. Edmund had taken nothing away from him that he couldn't rebuild. It was just loss of work, time, and wood.

Julia was everything.

His throat tightened and he grasped her elbow. "Stand back. Burning embers can spit free and catch on anything."

She nodded, curling her arms around her waist. The firelight danced over her bleak expression.

Unable to resist, he cradled the back of her head with one hand, and planted a kiss on her lips. He did not care that they had an audience. He needed to touch her. In the midst of this destruction, he needed to feel life. Her lips on his were a reassuring balm to his soul.

"We will rebuild." He straightened and skimmed a finger down her cheek.

"We will. But that is the last of the oaks," Julia said, her eyes sad.

"Next time we will hire guards."

Daniel turned to see Taunton and Brett approach.

"Bedford is sending a warning," Taunton said, his eyes hard.

Daniel clamped his jaw. His eyes strayed to Julia, and he cursed himself for ever having involved her.

"It is a warning to Daniel *and* vengeance," Julia said.

Taunton and Brett exchanged looks with him, and after a brief hesitation, Daniel gestured them ahead. When they had left to assist the men, he rested his hands on Julia's shoulders. They were warm from the heat emanating from the fire, and he tipped his temple to her forehead. "This is just wood. The only thing that matters is that you are no longer his. You are mine, and I thank God for it every day." He cupped her cheek. "And I am yours."

He released her shoulders to catch her hands and give them a reassuring squeeze. He needed to keep her safe. Feared his ability to do so.

She nodded, her eyes moist. "Go. I will be all right." Her voice broke, and she covered her mouth, blinking back tears.

He kissed her temple, not wanting to leave her alone.

"Go. You will feel better if you do something," she insisted, swiping at her eyes, and retreating farther from the heat of the fire.

With grave reluctance, he joined the line next to his foreman. He struggled to keep his mind on the task at hand, to tamp down his fear. He drew steady breaths, and ignored the burning heat that irritated his scarred shoulder. They worked in tandem, methodically passing buckets hand to hand.

Eventually, Brett caught his attention, and he stepped away to join him and Robbie. Their faces were streaked with dirt and sweat, their hair plastered to their brows, and both reeked of soot and smoke. Brett would need a new sling, his dirt-stained and damp. He surmised he looked no better.

"I agree with Taunton. Edmund is warning you to return to America. The bastard." Brett's tone was punched with anger. He took a handkerchief and swiped his brow, his gaze fastened on the fire.

"I suggest you build with brick next time," Robbie said, a fit of coughing seizing him.

"I think we need to revise our strategy," Daniel said.

"We're finally going to shoot the bastard and bury him in the back paddock?"

Daniel shook his head at Robbie's eager look. "No, but we are going to reverse roles. Edmund has been watching us, as attested to the attack at the docks and on your curricle. It is time we lined up some men and monitor his movements more closely. I had asked Mabry to inform me of Edmund's return, but my brother must have slipped home quietly. We are better protected if we know where Edmund is or with whom he is meeting. And I need to protect the Chandler family. This was too close to home. I need to make sure Edmund doesn't get any closer."

"Clever, but you always were," Brett said.

Daniel feared it was not enough. Was desperate to do more. He was not good at standing still.

The line of men had broken up, the perimeter soaked with water. They all stood back to watch the last of the feeble structure tumble to its ignominious demise.

The foreman caught Daniel's eye. "My lord, the earl asked me to tell you he is taking Lady Julia home."

Daniel thanked the man, locating Taunton, who was assisting Julia to mount Constance. She turned to him, and their eyes met across the distance. Curling strands of hair tumbled free from her chignon, and she lifted a hand to tuck an errant strand behind her ear. Something shifted in Daniel's chest, as if an empty hole had been filled. She raised her hand to him, a ghost of a bittersweet smile tipping her lips before she nudged Constance with her heel.

His home was another smoldering pile of rubble, but Daniel did not feel the same sense of loss that he had felt the first time it had been reduced to ashes. Admittedly, that first blaze had stolen all he had owned or cared for in the world, and almost taken his life. He rolled his shoulder, loosening the scarred skin.

Sometimes you had to lose something to realize its value.

He was a far richer man than when he had left ten years ago, and he'd be damned if Edmund took anything away from him again.

He would best Edmund. He did not know his brother's motive, he only knew his own to succeed was bigger.

❧

HOURS LATER, DANIEL left the waterlogged, smoldering remains and wended his exhausted way home.

He eyed the empty corridor before he slipped into Julia's bedroom and softly locked the door behind him. He felt like the proverbial fox in a henhouse with the rose-colored wallpaper, the assault of pink and white offending his masculine sensibilities.

He leaned against the door, folded his arms across his chest, and admired the view.

Julia sat submerged in a large tub before a glowing fire. A pitcher of water sat on a table within arm's reach. One slim, soap-lathered leg lifted in the air as she sponged it off. Her movements were quick and practical, and he cursed her efficiency as she dispensed with one leg and then the other.

Pulling the ribbon from her hair, she shook out the cascade

of curls, and slid low into the tub, drenching her hair. She reached for a block of soap on the chair.

"No, wait," he cried.

Julia shrieked, dropping the soap and whipping around, one arm curled protectively over her breasts. Eyes wild, she gaped at him. "What are you doing here?" she cried when she had recovered her voice. "You need to leave before someone sees you. Good lord, it is morning and—"

"No one saw me, and I have locked the door so no one *will* see me." He laughed away her protests, yanked off his Hessian boots, shucked his jacket and waistcoat and dispensed with his shirt.

He walked to the commode and vigorously scrubbed his hands and face, shedding the layer of soot and grime caking him like a second skin. Shaking the water droplets from his hair, he crossed to Julia's side and retrieved the soap that had fallen to the floor.

"What are you doing? Daniel you are filthy."

"Whatever do you mean? I washed." He lathered soap into his hands, and knelt beside the tub.

He planted his hands on her head, turned her wary expression away from him and proceeded to soap her hair. She was resistant at first, stiff-necked and annoyed, but as his fingers massaged into her scalp, she relaxed. Her shoulders eased, and she sank back against the tub. Her hair was so thick. A lovely lustrous brown, with streaks of gold. And so many curls, even damp as he pulled one straight, it snapped back into a ringlet when released.

"It is a hopeless cause. Don't even try to straighten it."

"Why in God's name would I ever want to do that?" He was aghast at the thought.

Julia peered at him over her shoulder. "You like it?"

"I do. If anyone said anything negative about it, they were an idiot." At her expression, he paused, sensing he had touched a vulnerable nerve. "I have always loved your hair, Julia. It is like you, vibrant and beautiful." She stared at him silently, and then turned away. He cleared his throat. "It is the perfect compliment to what you are wearing."

"Mmh." Her response was half moan as his hands massaged her head and soaped her hair, moving down to her shoulders. "I wonder if my family would agree."

"Let us not push matters. Your father still has his pistols loaded."

She laughed, but her laughter trailed off. "I am sorry about Lakeview Manor, Daniel. To lose it once must have been devastating, but a second time must have—"

"Shh. I lost nothing that cannot be replaced."

"But—"

"Shh, Julia. It was a wood structure, nothing more, nothing less." Eyes closed, he leaned down to press his lips to the slim column of her neck. "As long as you are safe, we will be fine. I—" His eyes snapped open and he lifted his head, swallowing back his words.

I love you.

They had been on the tip of his tongue. Almost casually unleashed, like any loving husband would say to a wife.

"Daniel?" She peered back at him, her expression one of concern. "You look ghostly white. Daniel, speak to me. I understand loss. Am an expert on grief."

The concern in her eyes was nearly his undoing. How could he not fall in love with this woman? Who saw the hurt in others and needed to help. Who had experienced so much loss and yet fought to hold her family and an earldom together. She was kind, loyal, and courageous. And he was deeply, irrevocably in love with her.

He swallowed again, choking on the myriad of emotions coursing through him. "I am all right, Julia. Just sad for you. It would have been your home, too. Complete with a nursery."

"We will hire guards." She echoed his earlier promise and lifted her chin in a determined thrust.

"Yes, we will." He swept soapsuds over the curve of her cheek and her nose.

She huffed out a breath, blew it off, and turned away. "Finish my hair."

He grinned. "As you command, my lady." He let the long soapy strands slide through his fingers. "Dunk," he muttered, after clearing his throat. He pushed lightly on her shoulders and she dipped her head under. He leaned over and lifted the pitcher of clean water, tipping her head back and pouring it over her head.

He rinsed the soap from her hair. As he squeezed the water from the damp strands, the mindless task soothed him. This was her gift to him. She settled him.

He could make no more promises regarding their future until he dealt with his past. Not until they were safe. When he shared all that was in his heart, he wanted his words to launch their own happily ever after without the menacing specter of Edmund darkening their days.

But there were other ways in which to convey his feelings.

Daniel stood up, stripped off his breeches, and laughed as Julia cried out when he stepped into the tub. He ignored the water sloshing over the rim, pooling on the floor, and Julia's protests as he pulled his beautiful water nymph into his arms and loved her.

Chapter Twenty-seven

❧

After days of unrelenting rain, the sun had finally deigned to make an appearance. It graced them with a vast blue sky with the added boon of unseasonably warm November temperatures.

Daniel rode to the southeastern acreage of Taunton's property. Oblivious to the beauty of the day, he dismounted and tied Chase to a tree. He had eyes only for the figure in the green carriage dress, the sight returning his heart rate to a normal rhythm.

Admitting his love for Julia added a new desperation to his standoff with Edmund. He now had someone he valued more than his own life, and he vowed to protect her. He hoped the letter burning a hole in his jacket pocket was a step in that direction. He just feared informing Julia that he intended to respond to it without his Maid Marian at his side. For that he would not allow.

"Your bleak expression matches the look Mr. Curtis wore when I left him."

He found Emily had come upon him, her eyes amused. "Is Brett in trouble again?" He arched a brow at her.

She lifted her chin in a gesture reminiscent of her older sister. "He makes his own trouble. If he did not appreciate the addendums I added to his letters, he shouldn't have deceived me."

He stared, and his bark of laughter had Julia glancing their way. Seeing them, she smiled and walked over to join them.

"Don't tell Julia. She doesn't appreciate subterfuge," Emily hissed beneath her breath.

Her words were prophetic. His forthright fiancée would expect nothing but the truth. It went to the issue of trust. He did trust her. He just did not see why wanting to protect her put that in question.

"What is so amusing?" Julia asked, as she retied the ribbons to her bonnet.

"I was telling Daniel about a letter I drafted for Mr. Curtis. Mr. Curtis was lamenting his recent weight gain and horrible case of gout." She shrugged ruefully.

"Weight gain?" Julia furrowed her brow. "I didn't know he suffered from gout."

"He does now," Emily said, scrunching her features in distaste. "Most unbecoming an affliction. I must return, for I promised to go riding with Jonathan. Are you staying, Julia?"

"She is," Daniel answered for her, looping her arm through his while admiring Emily's handling of Brett's trickery. Poor Mr. Curtis indeed. Daniel did not dare contemplate what other afflictions he suffered from.

"I guess I am." Julia smiled. "After being sequestered inside for so long, I am going to savor the day. You go ahead."

Forget the day, he planned to savor far more lovely sights. Like the way the breeze molded Julia's skirts to her long legs, or brushed her cheeks a satin pink, or how her eyes rivaled the deepest blue of the sky.

Julia stepped away from him and spread her arms to indicate the area in which they stood. "Look what I have found."

"What is it?" He smiled at the excitement in her voice, but did not shift his eyes from her. He doubted there could be anything more interesting than the way her riding habit fit over feminine curves.

"We have an apple orchard."

He paused, forced to take in their surroundings. "Are you considering building a cider mill?" He gave her a questioning look.

"A wise businessman once pointed out that it was a lucrative venture."

"Mmh, very wise indeed."

"Perhaps we could embark on another venture together." She tilted her head to the side and mock batted her eyelashes.

He laughed, but then his laughter faded. "That sounds marvelous. We'll start on it as soon as I return from a short trip I have to undertake."

She straightened, her humor fleeing. "Return? Short trip?"

He withdrew the letter he had received from the courier and handed it to Julia. While he waited for her to read it, he recalled that it had been delivered with responses to Brett's letters. He now understood why he had left Brett cursing up a storm and vowing to have Emily's beautiful, lying, deceitful head on a platter.

"So they have located Charlie Shaw," she said, handing the note back to him.

"Yes. He was found in one of the seedier gambling hells. Robbie, Brett, and I are going to leave for the city tomorrow." He folded the note and returned it to his pocket.

As predicted, storm clouds moved in to shadow Julia's eyes and she fisted her hands at her side, braced for battle. "I am coming. You cannot leave me here, Daniel. That is not your decision to make."

"No. It is not, but I am making it mine." He struggled to keep his voice level, knowing Julia responded more to reason than anger. "Look, I am going with both Brett and Robbie, and a few other men. I am not stupid."

"And neither am I."

Forget reason, exasperation filled him and he tossed his hands up. "For God's sake, Julia. This is not like the time Edmund locked you in the root cellar all those years ago. This is attempted murder. I cannot save you if you are dead, and I refuse to risk that."

"What did you say?" Julia breathed.

He paused and wondered at the odd expression crossing her features. "This is not a children's game. The consequences of this are dire, and—"

"No, about the root cellar. I thought *you* locked me in. Edmund said it was a game of hide-and-seek, and you were to be the seeker. I hid there and heard the click of the latch. I was locked in for over an hour, and it was dark, cold, and damp. It was awful. I hated you for doing that."

His anger depleted, he shook his head, a sadness settling over him. "No. I tried to explain when I found you, but you were too upset to listen. I would have located you sooner had Edmund ever told me I was to search for you. I found you because your father asked me to look. He said you had disappeared with Edmund, and he had lost you both. So I searched and heard you crying." At the sheen of tears glistening in her eyes, he drew her into her arms. "My apologies, Julia. Edmund liked his games."

"So you saved me from Edmund's cruelty then, and a second time when you kissed me, ending my betrothal to him."

He leaned back and stared into her blurry eyes. "It was my pleasure."

"Yes, you do enjoy telling me so," she sniffed. "But Daniel, you like to tell me that it is your turn to take care of me, but you already have. Twice. So it is my turn to keep you safe. I cannot do it if I am here in Bedfordshire and you are in a London gambling hell getting stabbed or . . ." Her voice hitched.

"Shh . . ." He pressed her face to his chest, resting his chin on the cap of her bonnet. "Nothing is going to happen to me. They would have to employ their own army to get through mine. If it was not a gambling hell that I was going into, which no respectable woman could ever enter—even a brave warrior who is a crack shot with a Manton revolver—I promise you, I would take you with me." That would be when horses flew, but he kept that detail to himself. Self-preservation and all that.

"Liar," she murmured.

She knew him too well. He'd have to remember that in their marriage. He smiled.

"It is just, I love you so much that I don't think I could bear it if anything were to happen to you. I never understood what my father or Emily felt, but now I do, and I saw what they experienced when they lost—"

She stopped speaking when he forced her away from him. He held her at arm's length, his heart sputtering to a dead stop. "What? What did you just say?" He dared not breathe as he waited for her response.

Her face was mottled and tear streaked, and she sniffled as she stared at him balefully. She had never looked more beautiful.

She swiped at her eyes. "I am not saying it again. You do not deserve it."

Good lord, she was perfect. Absolutely perfect. He swung her off her feet, lifting her high, and twirling her around. "Too late. I heard you. You cannot deny it."

She rolled her eyes and tried to kick out at him, but she could not suppress her smile either. He set her on her feet and kissed her hard as he enfolded her in his arms.

He had not planned to say the words. Had vowed to wait, but they poured from him. "I love you, too. I have never said those words to another living person. Ever. You are the first. The only one for me, Julia. I never thought I would find some-one like you, someone I would want to say that to," he declared.

"Oh, Daniel," she breathed, stepping back as she accepted the handkerchief he proffered and dabbed at her face. "Why didn't you tell me? I might have said yes sooner."

"Well, as I always say, ladies should go first."

She hit him playfully.

He sobered. "I planned to, but maybe I am not as brave as you." He shook his head. She deserved the truth. "I wanted to wait until matters with Edmund were resolved. Until our happily ever after did not come with a caveat, that being my surviving—"

"Stop, please, I cannot bear it. We will resolve this."

"You are right, forgive me. You ask me to trust you, Julia. I need for you to trust me to go to London and finish this. I will be careful. I give you my word. I have much to live for." He drew her back into his arms, liking the feel of her there, for it was where she belonged.

"I have no choice. Silly rules forbidding respectable women," she muttered.

"They had not met you when they made them."

"True," she sniffed. "And you will stay in England? Can we live in Lakeview Manor?"

"I will live where you are. It is the advantage of having a partner, and a transatlantic company. We have offices in both Boston *and* London. Besides, I added a nursery to the plans. We do need to fill it, which will be difficult if I am an ocean away from you."

She snuggled closer. "Good," she whispered. "I would hate for you to abandon Jonathan after promising him to ride Black Angel once he gains a few more stone. He has decided Black Angel will make a good cavalry horse."

"Heaven help us." He laughed. He held her, silent for a long moment, savoring her comfort. The distant bird cries and occasional squawks drifted their way.

"I refuse to leave you mottle faced and sad—"

She pulled back and slapped at him. "Mottle faced. How you flatter."

"Much better, the colors are already evening out in your cheeks." He lowered his voice and untied her bonnet, pulling it out of her reach and tossing it to the ground.

"What are you doing?"

"We are going to make a happier memory for me to leave with. We have our own songbirds serenading us, which my cousin Theo, the birdman—"

"The ornithologist," Julia corrected with mock severity.

"Right. Well, Theo says songbirds bring good fortune." He unbuttoned his jacket and shrugged it off.

"And what else did your cousin tell you?" she pressed, her lips twitching.

"Well, he did natter on a lot about spottings of goldcrests, stonechats, and yellow-winged wagtails."

"You are making that up." She laughed, then gave him a chastising look. "You have no appreciation for the ornithological field."

He caught her hand and yanked her close. "Maybe not, but I understand an all-consuming passion." He dipped his head and kissed her.

Smiling against his lips, she leaned into him, slipping her arms around his waist.

He paused, looking up. "Wait, I think I heard something."

"What is it?" She followed his gaze.

"Here, it's over here." He towed her over to a patch of grass a short distance away. He knelt and spread his jacket over the ground, grabbing her hand to tug her down beside him. "It's a better vantage point from down here."

Grinning, she started to reply, but he pressed his finger to her lips.

"Shh, I think it's a rare gray-winged wagtail wormer." He whispered, unbuttoning his waistcoat and discarding it as well.

"I believe it is a simple grey wagtail."

"Exactly. The point is, you thought I made it up." He shook his head as if in disappointment. At her snort, he raised a brow. "You dare to doubt me? I will show you." Putting his hand on her shoulder, he pushed her back onto his jacket. "Flat on your back is the best vantage point to appreciate this."

He pressed his body to hers, loving her soft warmth, the intimacy as her breath quickened. "Look into the trees, he must be up there somewhere."

She tipped her head back and as if given a succulent treat, his lips fastened on her neck and he quickly dispensed with her jacket's buttons.

"Daniel, I do not think this is a good idea," she whispered against his mouth. "We ought to go inside."

"Oh no, then we might miss this rare opportunity." He stripped her jacket from her.

"Daniel," she gasped as his hand sneaked beneath the neckline of her gown, and cupped her breast.

"Julia," he returned in a husky murmur. He knew he had triumphed when she tugged his shirt free from his trousers and her hands slid up his back. He groaned at the feel of her soft fingers stroking his bare skin, shivered as her nails raked over his back, her touch a healing balm against old scars.

He inched her gown above her knee, caressing the long length of leg, the smooth skin. An avid rider, Julia's legs were slim and muscular. He wanted to savor and love every inch of her, but she did have a point about being outside.

Slow was better, but fast had its merits. When she arched against him, he slid his hand between them and fumbled with the placket of his trousers. Freeing himself, he settled his hips against hers. He moved his hand between them, and gently pleasured her until he had elicited her responding whimpers. He continued with a few deft strokes until he could bear it no more, and he slid inside her with a groan.

When he started to thrust, hard and deep, her nails dug into his back. Forget songbirds, the sounds she made were a serenade to his heart. His arousal grew as he increased his pace, his breath ragged against her temple.

Her body arched as she began her climb toward climax. He tried to slow himself down, but she molded her hips to his and arched against him, matching her movements to his rhythm. Her eager response heightened his arousal, and he deepened his thrust, holding her close. He felt her heart pound against his. Eventually, she cried out, clutching him tighter, her damp cheek buried in his chest.

He groaned, his hands gripping her hips as he thrust a few more times, feeling something wild and primitive building within him. Slow was better, but good lord, fast and hard was a close second. He poured himself into her, breathing in deep pants as his passion climbed. He was surprised to hear his own cry of release ripped from him as his body arched and jerked. With a final grunt, he collapsed on top of her. He lay there, waiting for his heart rate to return to normal and his passion-dazed senses to settle.

After a few minutes, she tapped his back. "Please, move. You are quite heavy, and the ground is hard."

"Well, then it is a good thing I am no longer," he smiled, having no complaints about falling in love with a forthright woman. He summoned the energy to roll to her side. He slid a hand beneath her shoulders and tenderly drew her close, cradling her against him. "Will you look at that? It was not a gray-winged wagtail wormer, after all."

"Oh, what was it?" She rolled her eyes as she drew her gown down, and settled herself more comfortably against his chest.

"It was a Peeping Tom." His eyes laughed into hers. "Ogling my Lady Godiva."

She punched him playfully on the arm, her laughter joining his.

A much better memory than tears. He would carry it with him tomorrow when he left. Hold it in his heart forever, which he hoped would be a long, long time.

Chapter Twenty-eight

❦

Daniel had been gone for over a week, and Julia regretted her decision not to join him. She had never been a woman to sit home. That is the wife Edmund would have preferred. Once again, she shuddered at the thought of the disastrous marriage she had narrowly escaped. She would have failed Edmund miserably, but her failure would have been well met by his being a duplicitous, murderous bastard. Their marriage would have been like trying to keep a rock afloat. It was best it sank before ever being launched.

She shook her head free of Edmund. For the hundredth time, she wished for Daniel's safe return. To distract her. To love her as he had promised. She smiled wistfully, her body warming at the memory of his declaration and the look in his eyes when he had spoken.

She needed to get her mind off of her aching need for Daniel or she would go mad, but that was like trying to forget a missing limb. In a doubtless futile attempt to do so, she had planned an excursion into town.

She took the coach, as it was another dreary fall day, gray and spitting rain. Huffing out a breath, she drew the lap blanket over her legs and settled deeper into the velvet cushions, wishing Emily had accompanied her. Then again, these days Emily was in a rather foul mood herself. A separation would be good for them both.

When the coach rolled to a stop, she frowned, for the ride had been far too short to reach the village proper.

Curious, she drew aside the curtain and peered outside. Through the foggy mist, she noticed that they were at the crossroads to Adgate Road, which would take them onto High Street. She saw no reason for the stop and worried something was wrong with either the horses or the carriage.

The door opened and she glanced over, expecting a footman with an explanation. Her eyes widened and she straightened in her seat, her hand going protectively to the collar of her woolen cloak.

"Hello, Julia."

Edmund.

Her damn discarded duke. The two-faced Janus. Her pulse raced, and she struggled to calm racing nerves. She refused to cower. "I have nothing to say to you. Please tell my driver that I would like to be on my way."

He simply laughed, and she could only watch astounded as he bounded into the carriage and brazenly settled himself into the seat across from her. "We will be on our way shortly, but there is a change of destination."

Ignoring him, she straightened and rapped her knuckles against the back panel.

"No one will answer. I gave them leave to take a short break, for I required a moment of your time."

Everyone rushed to do the bidding of a damn duke, she silently seethed. "Well, I do not want a moment of yours," she snapped, cringing at the peevish tone in her voice. She drew a deep breath, and spoke in a calm manner, the antithesis of what she was feeling. "Please, we have nothing to say to each other. I must ask you to leave." She refused to spar with the man. Had forgotten her sabre and gloves. Perhaps more importantly, the Manton revolver.

Edmund snorted. "Don't you sound properly aggrieved. Like

a maligned innocent, but we both know otherwise, don't we?"
He slipped off his leather gloves and lay them across his lap,
crossing his legs as if settling in for a leisurely chat. "I doubt
my brother would approve either. All the more reason to remain.
As I am sure you have been apprised by now, we never did see
eye to eye on things. Never will, but that is all to end soon."

"If you are not inclined to leave, Your Grace, then allow
me to do so." She slid forward but froze when he leaned over
and slapped a large hand against the door, his ducal ring mock-
ing her. His eyes were hard, mere slits.

"You always did have a mutinous streak. It is time you
learned your place." He arched an imperious brow.

She paled and slid her shaking hands beneath her blanket,
hoping the tremors in her legs didn't convey her terror. She
moistened dry lips. "What do you want, Edmund?"

He leaned back, his calf with its elegant silk stocking
swinging casually. He straightened his cuff and flicked a piece
of lint from his nut-brown jacket. "I want you to listen very
carefully to everything I have to say because if you do not, I
promise you, you will rue the day."

She swallowed. "I am listening."

"Good. Shortly, we will leave this coach, and you will accept
my escort into mine. I will make the explanations and you will
go along quietly. Should there be a scene, it will not go well for
you. My men will carry out my orders and it will be your men
who will suffer the consequences. Do you understand?"

She nodded. It was as if his words had sucked all the air
out of the carriage, and she needed to concentrate on taking
small breaths.

He appeared to become aware of her pallor, and his eyes
narrowed in warning. "You are not one to swoon, so please do
not adopt the odious habit now."

If she had felt faint, his condescension snapped her out of
it. Bristling, she found the voice she had lost. "Where are we
going? What do you want?"

"You know damn well what I want, and you are going to
help me get it."

He was wrong. She didn't know what the devil Edmund

sought other than some possibly incriminating papers that once belonged to his late father's solicitor. But she did know enough to be petrified. Perhaps if she helped Edmund to retrieve what he was so desperate to acquire, she might just survive this nightmare. If he wanted her to beg, she would do so. "Please, Edmund, let us discuss this in a rational manner. I am sure we—"

"We cannot." His eyes, the compelling moss green, were a perverted mirror of Daniel's. "It is time to go." He slid on his gloves, uncrossed his legs, and eased forward.

"Why do you hate him so?" she breathed.

He paused and his smile was slow and insidious, never reaching his eyes or warming his expression. "Let us just say he has something I want. But now we are even. Because now I have something he wants."

"But why—"

"Enough!" His hand shot up, and she recognized the rage in his eyes, a flame that lit and died when she eased back into the cushions of the seat, cowering.

"Behave and no one gets hurt. Of course, it is your decision, Julia, but I doubt you will be so foolish as to jeopardize your servants." He smiled triumphantly.

In her fear, she was oblivious to the explanations Edmund gave to her driver and footman. She could not resist a small cry when his gloved hand vised around her elbow, but one sharp look had her biting her lip so hard she drew blood.

She stumbled going up the steps to his coach, and his arms were there, lifting and pushing her inside. She scrambled onto the seat and buried her unsteady hands in her cloak.

Edmund climbed in behind her and the click of the lock echoed in the cabin.

She lifted her chin and ventured to speak above the pounding of her heart. "Where are we going?"

"To meet my brother. Where else?"

When he flashed Daniel's smile, she closed her eyes, unable to look at the perversion.

She marveled at the strange irony that the one person whom her heart had been yearning for every hour of every day over the past week was now the last person on earth she hoped to see.

Chapter Twenty-nine

＞◁

TRAVEL weary and covered in a layer of road dust, Daniel barreled up the stairs to Taunton Court. He anticipated sweeping Julia into his arms and kissing her senseless. His plans changed at the sight of Taunton pacing the front foyer. His smile faded, and the hairs on the back of his neck stood up.

Something was wrong.

"Bedford has Julia. He waylaid her coach on the way into town this morning. Told the driver he would escort her the rest of the way. They never reached town."

"I will find her." Daniel turned on his heel, but Taunton caught his elbow, holding firm.

"Wait, damn it," Taunton's voice thundered. "This is my daughter we're talking about. I am going with you."

"I am going, too," Brett declared, having followed Daniel inside.

There was a sharp intake of breath, and Daniel turned to find Emily, her face pale and her hands twisting her handkerchief into a roped coil.

"Fine. We will all go," Daniel said, not wishing to waste precious minutes with an argument.

Robbie entered on those words and surveyed the scene. "Where are we going?"

"To Bedford Hall," Daniel gritted out.

"Now? I thought we were going to Hertfordshire. I can't believe Shaw's son mailed your father's papers to your cousin. It would have saved us saddle sores and a bleeding fortune if your cousin had pulled his head out of bird guts long enough to post a letter on to you."

Daniel was deaf to Robbie's grousing. "Bedford has Julia. We have to go now. We're wasting time."

Robbie straightened to his full, imposing height, his humor gone. "We'll need new horses."

"Already saddled. I was waiting for the cavalry to arrive. I am taking a few extra men as well," Taunton said, his eyes on Daniel.

"Fine." He wouldn't need them. The rage propelling him gave him the strength of a one-man army.

⇝⇜

IT WAS A short stop at Bedford Hall, and they were on the road again. Edmund's pompous butler had informed them that His Grace was visiting their cousin in Hertfordshire. His Grace had left word for Daniel to join him as soon as possible, for they had matters to discuss. As if he were a pawn on a bloody chessboard.

Edmund liked his games. He was forcing Daniel to move to protect his queen. He had an hour-long ride to seethe over it. He sought comfort in the fact that he had retained more players than his brother. He also hoped to meet up with the men whom he had hired to follow Edmund. The more players on his side of the board, the better his position for attack and to save his queen.

Julia. His heart thudded her name. He would refrain from killing Edmund only if she was untouched. Otherwise, they would indeed be digging a hole in the Tanners' back pasture, the one reserved for inferior stock.

It felt like an eternity had passed before they crossed the border into Hertfordshire and the perimeter of his cousin's property. He signaled the others to rein in their horses, not wanting his cavalry to charge in with pistols drawn. Living with Edmund, he had learned there was something to be said for stealth.

"Is this your cousin's?" Robbie asked.

"His property is down this rutted lane. An iron-gated entrance should be on the right, and woods and bushes border the perimeters. Tie the horses to the gate, and let's assess the scene before moving in."

"Aye, aye, Captain," Brett said. He had discarded the sling, but his right arm was still splinted and wrapped in a heavy bandage. Daniel warily eyed the arm, but made no comment. Brett had heeded Daniel's advice about staying home as well as Daniel had heeded his.

God knew how they ran a successful business together when neither listened to the other. Their success must lie in their blind, single-minded optimism. Or simply a string of good fortune. Right now, he hoped for a dose of both.

After tying the horses, they eased the iron gates open and proceeded inside. A distant noise brought them to an abrupt halt. Heart in his throat, damn near choking him, his hand closed over the Manton revolver in his jacket pocket. Unlike Julia, he had only fired hunting rifles and was a poor shot at that.

A man stepped into the clearing, hands raised. "It's Riker. Hold your fire."

He recognized one of the men he had hired to follow Bedford. "It's all right." He frowned when Riker jerked his head to indicate movement behind him. Following Riker's gaze, he found Brett, Taunton, and Robbie with pistols aimed with deadly intent at Riker's head. "Put those things down before you kill someone," he hissed.

"How the hell do we know friend from foe?" Robbie muttered.

Riker shoved his tweed cap back from his ample forehead. "Come this way. There are things afoot. I sent a man back to Taunton Court, did you cross paths?"

"No, I received a more personal invite," Daniel muttered as he followed Ricker into the thicket.

Riker led them to a group of a half a dozen men, two with their hands tied behind their backs, sporting bruised faces and truculent looks.

"What's going on?" Taunton said, his sharp gaze raking over the bound men and the detritus surrounding them. Long coiled ropes were curled up beside a wooden crate with the lid cracked open.

"Somebody was planning to have a celebration. That's gunpowder." Riker indicated the crate.

"Bloody hell," Daniel breathed. "He was going to incinerate the place." He strode over to one of the men, caught him by the lapels of his jacket and jerked him close. The man stank of body odor. "So you like fires, do you? Did you ignite the last one at Lakeview Manor?"

The wiry man did not respond, just looked mulish, white lips pressed tight. With a snarl, Daniel shoved him toward Robbie. "See that he talks."

"My pleasure."

The sheer size of Robbie had the man babbling. "I didn't do nothin' here. Nothin'."

Robbie grasped him by his upper arms and lifted him so the man's toes barely brushed ground. "Lord Bryant asked you a question. I suggest you answer it."

"I did. I set it. 'Twere just timbers. A frame. No harm done."

His cohort cursed. "Shut your trap, Monie."

Robbie snarled at the speaker, who heeded his own advice, snapping his mouth closed and retreating. "So you were going to take this manor to the ground as well? No harm there?"

"The toff said t'would be empty. No harm done. He'd come tell us when all was clear."

"So why are you lighting it up?" Brett asked, curious.

The man's eyes scanned the group, then cast a longing look toward the crate of powder. "I like . . . I like watching it explode and then burn. It's grand."

"Bloody hell." Robbie abruptly released him, stumbling back as if he had the pox.

"Bedford was going to light the whole place up. How many of us does he plan to kill? The man is mad," Brett said, uttering a curse beneath his breath.

"Be careful when you go inside. Curtis is right, he is deranged. We will surround the perimeter and slowly move in behind you," Taunton said. "But you need to go. He has Julia." His usually vibrant blue eyes were shadowed, and he looked years older.

"He's right, Daniel," Brett said. "Distract him or keep him talking until we can find a way in."

Robbie snorted. "Shouldn't have any problems with that. You talk circles around me, getting me to do your bidding whether I want to or not."

Daniel clenched his jaw, appreciating Robbie's stroke to his confidence. His friend was right. He was a good negotiator. He had convinced the most taciturn of New Englanders to trust in him. He hadn't had success with Bedford in the past, but the stakes had never been this high. He would succeed or die trying.

The men divided into groups. Some walked farther down the thicket, others going in the opposite direction.

Robbie, Brett, and Taunton followed Daniel. A vast expanse of green lawn swept uphill to the front entrance. The imposing sandstone house capped the incline with peaked roofs and a balcony lining the length of the second story. To gain entry, it required walking across the lawn or down the lane, in full view of the house. Daniel needed to go in alone and distract Edmund long enough to keep his attention away from the windows so that the others could follow without being seen.

He gave Robbie and Brett a deliberate look, and then turned to Taunton.

"I am trusting you to bring my daughter home, son." Taunton clasped his shoulder.

"I will, sir," he said. Taunton's confidence in him, and the conviction in his own tone helped to ease the vise of fear squeezing his chest.

He closed his hand over the Manton and strode into enemy territory, fervently praying that he was not the sacrificial pawn in a final game of Edmund's as he moved across the lawn, exposed.

Daniel lifted the heavy brass ring looped through the mouth of a feral lion, and slammed the doorknocker again and again. Its noise reverberated in the silence that followed. When no one answered, he tried the doorknob and found it unlocked. It was a trap, but he had no choice.

He stepped inside and a guttural growl of rage greeted him.

He froze, his heart stopping until a feminine shriek and the racket of pounding feet severed his immobility.

Julia.

He barreled into the front drawing room. Empty. He careened through a cavernous dining room and then the library, cursing each room and the time wasted until he stepped into the dark-paneled study and located his cousin. Glasses askew, a cut cheek, Theo was bound and gagged in a corner chair. Despite his binds, he frantically jerked his head toward a door standing ajar at the back of the room.

Daniel raced over to his cousin and loosened the ropes binding his hands. Leaving Theo to deal with his gag, he bolted through the door indicated and bounded up a back staircase.

"He has a knife. No guns, a knife," Theo panted from below. "She stabbed a hairpin into his hand to get free."

Daniel did not break stride. He took the stairs two at a time, heart in his throat. Knives, no guns. Edmund couldn't shoot him. It bought him time to negotiate. As to his brave warrior, of course Julia would find a means of escape. He should never have doubted it.

He barreled through too many empty rooms. For God's sake, his cousin was a bachelor, why the devil did he have such a grand home?

Another scream rent the air and his heart stumbled. Other cries followed. A struggle. He entered what appeared to be the master bedroom, and French doors gaped open, leading out to a balcony.

He sprinted through them, stopping short at the sight before him. *Julia.*

Alive, and straining against Edmund's grip. One of his arms

cinched her waist, the other circled her neck, a mean, serrated knife pressed against her throat.

Julia's fingers scored his forearm. Half of her hair tumbled loose in long, curling strands. Her eyes widened with fear, and she breathed his name as Daniel released his grip from the revolver and held up his hands in a nonthreatening gesture.

"I am here, Edmund. I got your message. It is me you want. Let us make that exchange. Let her go. Me for Julia."

Edmund emitted a mad, scoffing laugh. "Do you think me that big a fool? She's not going anywhere, and neither are you. Not yet. Do you have it?"

"The papers Abel Shaw wanted me to have? No, but they were sent to Theo. He did not give them to you?"

"That little bird-beaked bastard, he lied. He said he mailed them to you."

"Well, then he did." Daniel kept his voice calm. "I am sure we can get a hold of them in Boston. But if you kill me and the papers are addressed to me, you will never acquire them, Edmund. You would be wise to think on that."

"Enough! Just be quiet."

He swallowed when Edmund tightened his grip, and Julia cried out. Edmund frantically glanced around the balcony as if seeking an escape.

Daniel edged closer.

"Stop," Edmund barked. "Do not move any closer. Why the hell did you come back? I thought I got rid of you the first time. Why didn't you stay away?"

"Edmund, what the devil is this about? You are jeopardizing all you have and for what? What did I do to provoke this? I have been gone for the last decade."

Edmund's face was thunderous. "What *did* you do? What *didn't* you do? You have been the bane of my existence my whole life. Father nattered on about you until I was damn near mad from hearing about how brilliant you are. God, how I hate you. It is inconceivable to believe that I would ever stand by and let you strip everything away from me, not when I was groomed to have it all."

"I have not taken a bloody thing from you except Julia. I

would say I am sorry for that, but I am not. But I give you my word of honor that if you let her live, I will do the same for you. I have a life in America, we can go there." He kept his voice level, his eyes steady on Edmund's, not daring to glance Julia's way.

"You don't get it. You have no idea," Edmund sounded incredulous.

"Why don't you tell me?" He fought to maintain the calm façade that Edmund was losing.

"It was your life or mine," Edmund said. "For the title is my life, and it belongs to you."

Daniel stared at him blankly. "Excuse me?" he managed, not certain he had heard him correctly.

"He thought you were going to die, and you did not. You did not! You never do." Edmund emitted a hysterical laugh. "You were delivered first, but were so damn thin and sickly. And all the others had died."

He fell silent as if waiting for Daniel to catch up, to fit the last piece into the puzzle. And suddenly, he did.

Destined to die like all the others.

His mother had suffered a full dozen heart-wrenching miscarriages. Twelve babies in ten years. He had heard of his father's joy at the birth of two healthy boys. But he had not been as robust, nor as strong as his twin. Edmund had stolen the nutrients from him as he had continued to do throughout his life. Edmund had been born larger, thriving, while he had been delivered sickly, half the size.

So a betrayal was born. His father had not bothered to wait for his death certificate, but had convinced the doctor to change the order of their birth, declaring Edmund his heir.

"He was so sure," Edmund spat. "But you survived, like you always bloody do. And father finally had an attack of conscience. Said he was morally obligated to correct past mistakes. For the sake of the estate. He kept droning on about your understanding the land better, more attuned to it and the tenants. Said I lacked patience. As if I was going to run the estates myself, like a bailiff or worse, a farmer." He sounded appalled at the thought.

Daniel shook his head as the full picture became clear. "Shaw drew up the petition to the Prince Regent. That is what Shaw held over you? What you have been searching for and what Shaw's son mailed to me care of Theo?"

"Yes," Edmund snapped. "Father kept talking those last days. Would not keep quiet. Nattering on about moral obligations, protecting the estate, purging his soul, and making amends to you for his wrongs. I was his son, too. But he never saw me anymore. Just you."

Daniel cringed at the bitterness etched into Edmund's words, born of a hatred that had festered for years, driving him to madness.

His father had more than one betrayal for which he needed to make amends. He had wronged them both. They were his sons, but he only saw his heirs, conduits to the estate and the next generation, who was best to ensure that longevity.

"Shaw drafted the petitions, confessing everything. I would have lost it all," Edmund cried. "Everything I had been groomed to own. Did you honestly think I would let that happen? I knew Shaw and Reilly could be bought. Everybody has a price, but theirs kept going up. Reilly charging me for trips, land, and whatever his latest venture was. And Shaw. Christ, the man was like a sieve with money; could not stay away from the cards or ahead of the bloody creditors. They were bleeding me dry," he bellowed.

"So you started doing the same to the estate."

Edmund snorted. "You never understood. You still do not. I am not paying the tenants to feast off my land when I can get the same work at cheaper wages." Edmund shook his head as if to clear it. "I am not explaining myself to you. This is over."

It is time. Come home and claim your destiny.

He had never been too late, but Shaw's cryptic missive may have been.

Good lord. His whole life a lie. It did not matter. It never had. The land was in his soul, but Julia . . . Julia was his heart.

He looked Edmund dead in the eye. "You can have it. You can have it all. You asked for an exchange and I am giving you a damn fair one. Our lives for a dukedom. Release her and it is yours. You get your life back, and I . . ." His eyes met Julia's and he smiled gamely at her. "I save mine."

Julia's lips parted, her eyes widening, tears streaking her cheeks. "Daniel."

She did not speak, but mouthed the words. He heard them and so much more.

Edmund scoffed. "You have been in America too long. This is England. You cannot give up a dukedom. It is not done. Do not take me for a fool."

"Let her go, Edmund. Let her go and you live, harm one hair on her head and you die."

Edmund stiffened, Julia crying out as he instinctively tightened his grip. "Be silent! It is too late. Too damn late," he scowled.

Daniel paled at hearing the ominous epitaph he had once sworn would grace his gravestone. He held up his hands in a placating gesture, seeing the cornered look in Edmund's eyes.

"The whole place is set to explode. And that will be the end of it."

"You do not want to do that, Edmund. There are too many people who know. I am not alone. Robbie is here and Brett Curtis and—"

"Robbie has no title, and Curtis is an American," he sneered the word derisively. "Their word against mine will not stand."

"What about Taunton? People take notice of the word of an earl."

"You brought Taunton with you?" Edmund breathed. He cast another frantic look around the balcony. "No matter. He is the aggrieved father of a ruined, dead daughter."

Julia cried out.

"Enough," Edmund bellowed. "Enough of this." He dragged Julia farther backward, closer to the balustrade as Daniel advanced upon him.

"Edmund, please, listen to me. It is not over." Daniel kept moving toward him.

Edmund dragged Julia back until his legs hit the balustrade. As he glanced behind him to gauge the distance to the ground, a shot rang out.

Edmund's bellow rent the air as the bullet ripped through his jacket, piercing the arm holding the knife to Julia's throat. The wounded appendage dropped and dangled uselessly to his side, the knife clattering to the ground. Stunned, Edmund glanced down, as if not fully comprehending the red stream leaking from the hole in his jacket.

He had only seconds to contemplate it, for with a cry Julia shoved free.

Daniel lunged toward Edmund, who staggered back, his knees hitting the cement wall behind him. His good arm flailed like a windmill to right his balance, and then he was gone, tumbling backward, green eyes wide with horror.

Daniel raced to the ledge to see Edmund sprawled on the slate patio, his sightless eyes open, blood pooling around his arm.

Daniel swallowed hard. Then Julia was in his arms, and he crushed her close, against his heart, where she belonged.

There was a pounding of boots, and he lifted his head to see Taunton and then Brett barrel onto the balcony. He gave them a brief nod, which Taunton returned, his eyes on his daughter. Julia looked up, and seeing her father, she ran into his open arms.

Taunton held his daughter. "I thank you."

"No, I thank you," Daniel said, grinning.

"It was your cousin," Brett said, wonder in his voice. "Lord Bryant shot him. The man's a crack shot. Probably years of watching birds. Has a keen eye."

"I owe him my life."

"I would say you are even," Brett said. "Had he mailed you Shaw's package, this might have been avoided. Lord Bryant said he had received a letter from you saying you were returning home, so he was holding Shaw's papers until you visited. Thought to turn them over to you in person. What the devil was in them?"

"Confessions and a change in my inheritance. Later, I will explain it all later," Daniel said, a weariness sweeping over him.

Julia stepped away from her father and returned to his side.

"I am sorry about Edmund, Daniel. So very sorry. I had no idea he was . . ." She shuddered. "Thank God you ruined me."

"It was my greatest pleasure." He tucked a loose curl around her ear. "I am sorry, too. But I have friends who stand beside me, a new family, a wife whom I love dearly, and a nursery to fill. All things considered, that is pretty good for a scrawny runt."

Julia smiled, her eyes shining with love. "Let us go home."

He hesitated, and then cleared his throat. "About that. It seems we will be residing at Bedford Hall. You will make a magnificent duchess."

"As long as you are there, Your Grace."

"Just try to rid yourself of me," Daniel murmured, pulling her into his arms.

He had claimed his destiny.

Epilogue

❧❧

"Sᴉᴛ down for God's sake, you're going to carve a hole in the carpet," Brett barked. "And you are giving my neck a cramp watching you. Everything will be fine, Your Grace."

Taunton laughed.

Daniel glowered at them. "You do not know everything will be fine. You forget, your sisters are unmarried and thus never had a baby before. This was a mistake. Whose idea was this? And stop calling me Your Grace."

Taunton squeezed his shoulder. "She is young and strong. She will be fine. I have been through this." Despite the conviction in his voice, he tugged at his tie and swallowed. "Three times."

Daniel noticed his father-in-law's pallor and guilt stabbed him. He was not the only one suffering. This had to be difficult for Taunton, who had lost his wife in childbed. Daniel's legs went slack and he dropped into the chair behind him.

"He sits. It's a miracle."

He snarled at Brett, who held up his hands.

This was a bad idea. He had taken on too much. He was

still adjusting to having inherited a dukedom, being a member of a close-knit family, and marriage.

As godfather to the baby, Brett had announced his decision to stay until the baby's birth. Daniel knew his friend was not ready to concede defeat with Emily, but his sister-in-law was clever. Daniel trusted her to lead him on a merry chase.

Remarkably, he was getting accustomed to being at home at Bedford Hall. Julia's presence helped to chase away the lingering shadows. She brought love and laughter to the house. There was still much healing to be done, but things were progressing and Taunton's tutelage had proved invaluable.

A private funeral had been held for Edmund. News of his accidental death while hunting on his cousin's estate was keeping the gossip mill well oiled.

Daniel's life had settled into a comfortable rhythm, so why had he disrupted it? He should have kept his hands off of her. He was still stinging from the slash of Julia's temper earlier. Between clenched teeth, she had warned him he would never sleep in her bed again, and that she planned to build a room for him in the stables. She had said some other rather harsh things until Emily had whisked him from their room.

What did he know of being a father?

He stood up. He had changed his mind. He sat down again. He had provided Brett with enough amusement for the night. Brett still kept chuckling over his vow of celibacy. He dropped his face into his hands and exhaled.

"Congratulations, Your Grace."

He lifted his head. Emily stood framed in their bedroom door and she was smiling. He shot to his feet and staggered over to her. "Is she . . . ?"

"She is. Come and see."

He charged into the room. Julia lay in the center of the bed, a tired smile on her face.

He gingerly lowered himself onto the bed beside her, taking her hands into his. "Are you all right?"

"I am wonderful. And so are the babies."

The tension gripping him poured out in a wave of relief. She did look wonderful, albeit a bit weary. Her cheeks were mottled, and loose tendrils of hair curled over a damp cheek and her forehead. He brushed them back from her temple and froze.

Babies?

"You mean baby."

"Congratulations." Julia removed her hand from his to lift the cover of the swaddling she held. He exhaled, for there lay the tiniest baby he had ever seen. "Meet your son." *One baby.* One thing at a time, for he had too many responsibilities as is.

"And your daughter." She smiled and Daniel froze as Emily thrust a warm bundle into his arms.

He stared at the sleeping face of a pink angel. He couldn't breathe.

"Daniel, are you all right? Aren't they beautiful?"

His eyes shot to hers, and he relaxed again. She was beautiful and strong and his anchor. She wouldn't let him falter. His gaze drifted between his son and his daughter. They were . . . small. Runts like him. Fear gripped him. "They are terribly small."

"Thank goodness. Any larger and you really would be sleeping in the stables," she said dryly. She must have read his panicked expression, for she squeezed his hand. "They have you to protect them until they grow."

For her sake, he managed to summon a smile. But she was right. He would protect them with his life. He knew all about surviving against a hostile world, not that their world would be hostile . . . his smile faded. "What if they hate each other?"

Julia laughed softly. Her hand cupped his cheek, and she turned his face from his daughter toward her. "Then we will teach them that love is stronger than hate. They will learn it from watching their father because he has so much love to give and does so generously." She squeezed his hand. "You will save them just as you saved me."

He kissed her gently and felt his throat clog. He had to blink furiously, for his eyes were suspiciously moist.

"Thank God I ruined you."

A tale of love, deception, and redemption
in the face of mortal danger…

from
VICTORIA MORGAN

For the Love of a Soldier

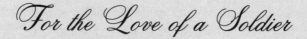

Captain Garrett Sinclair, the Earl of Kendall, has returned
to England a changed man. As a survivor of the legend-
ary Charge of the Light Brigade, he has spent months as a
remorseless rake and dissolute inebriate in order to forget
it. But Garrett has also made powerful enemies who want
him dead…

Desperate and down to her last pound, Lady Alexandra
Langdon has disguised herself as a man for a place at the
gaming tables. But when a hard-eyed, handsome man wins
the pot, he surprises her by refusing her money. Indebted,
she divulges an overheard plot against his life, and promises to help him find his foes—for a price…

PRAISE FOR *FOR THE LOVE OF A SOLDIER*

"This book is an absolute gem…a remarkable debut novel."
—PennyRomance.com

"Morgan deftly handles returning soldiers' trauma within
the context of a love story and adds spice with a bit
of mystery and unexpected secrets."
—*RT Reviews* (4 Stars)

victoriamorgan.com
penguin.com

M1346T0713